D1407777

ANGELBOUND
CHRISTINA BAUER

WITHDRAWN

BAY COUNTY LIBRARY SYSTEM
ALICE & JACK WIRT PUBLIC LIBRARY
500 CENTER AVENUE
BAY CITY MI 48708
989-893-9566

Copyright © 2013 by Monster House Books LLC

All rights reserved. This book or any portion thereof may not be reproduced or used in any manner whatsoever without the express written permission of the publisher except for the use of brief quotations in a book review.

ISBN 9780989405027

Monster House Books, LLC. 34 Chandler Place Newton, MA 02464

Dedicated to my husband.
Je t'aime.

CHAPTER ONE

A.

It's been one month, three days, and six hours since I last 'got my gladiator on' and battled in the Arena. Not that I'm obsessing or anything. Sure, I can sneak in and watch someone else fight, but that's a snore.

I roll over on my dingy bed, scooch under the drab covers, and watch the gray drizzle outside my window. Mondays are the pits.

Mom's voice echoes into my bedroom. "Time to get up! You don't want to be late for school, do you, honey?"

I roll my eyes. *Of course*, I want to be late for school.

Raising my head, I open my mouth to say just that, and then decide against it. Instead, I bite my lower lip, yank the pillow over my head and groan. Loudly.

"Don't make noises at me, young lady." Mom rustles papers in the kitchen. "I've a letter right here. You're on something called the Official Watch List for Unreasonable Tardiness." Her footsteps echo down the hall and pause outside my room. "You'll be suspended from high school at this rate. What do you think about *that?*"

I peep out from under my pillow. Mom looms in my doorway, her fist set on her hip. She's a quasi-demon like me, so she resembles a lovely human with a curvy figure, amber skin, chocolate-brown eyes, and chestnut hair that falls in waves over her shoulders. All quasis have a tail; Mom and I both sport the long and pointed variety. The big differences between us are laugh lines, some grey hair and our opinion of what's 'dangerous' for eighteen-year-olds.

I fluff the pillow and slide it under my noggin. Being suspended means no school. Maybe even catching a few Arena matches on the sly. I wag my eyebrows. "And suspension would be bad because?"

"I'd make it that way."

Ugh. She would, too.

Off go my covers. "This is me getting up."

"Good." Mom stomps away.

I shower, pull on some sweats, and sleepwalk into the kitchen, seeing the familiar lime-green appliances, mismatched furniture, and peeling linoleum tile. Everything looks peaceful, quiet, and empty. Another typical Monday morning before another average day at school. *BO-ring.* I'll have to charm Walker into taking me to the Arena later. Until I'm called to fight again, it's better than nothing.

A thick white envelope sits at the center of the kitchen table. I scoop up and read: "To the Quasi-Demon, Miss Myla Lewis, 666 Dante Row, Purgatory." I lick my thumb and run it over the loopy calligraphy. *Real ink.* My long black tail flicks in a nervous rhythm.

Frowning, I tap the unopened letter against my palm. No one sends me fancy stuff like this. In a blur of motion, my tail darts across my torso, grips the envelope with its arrowhead-shaped end, and tries pulling it from my fingers.

"Hey now!" My tail's always had a mind of its own. For some reason, it's decided this letter is dangerous. I jerk the envelope out of reach, but not before one corner gets totally shredded. "Now, look what you did." My tail slinks behind me to curl guiltily about my ankle.

I reread the outside of the letter. Nothing here to worry about. I *am* a quasi-demon (mostly human with a little demon DNA). I've spent all eighteen years of my life in Purgatory (where human souls get judged for Heaven or Hell, aka the most boring place in the history of ever). This letter's like dozens of others that hit our doorstep each week. Why's my tail on a mission to trash this thing?

I stare at the words again, feeling like they should read: "Open this to turn your life upside-down and your heart into mush."

Clearly, I'm having an off-morning.

I slip the envelope-slash-time-bomb into my mangy backpack. I'll read it later at school.

Mom steps into the kitchen. "How's my sweet baby, Myla-la?" Yes, I'm eighteen years old and Mom still uses pet names from when I was three.

"I'm good." I open a cabinet and pull down a box of Frankenberry cereal.

Mom eyes my every movement, her forehead creasing with worry.

"Did you sleep well last night, Myla?"

Oh, no. Here it comes. I square my shoulders and mentally prepare my 'I'm so very-very caaaaaaalm' voice. "Absolutely." *Nailed it.*

"Any bad dreams?"

"Nope." The 'calm voice' isn't working so well this time.

"Hmm." She taps her cheek. "Met anyone lately? Made any new friends?"

I grit my teeth. All my mornings start off with maternal interrogations like this one. I find it's best to give soothing, one-word answers. "Negative."

"No friends at all?"

"Only the same one since first grade." I raise my spoon for emphasis. "Cissy."

"That's good." She offers me a shaky grin. "You're safe."

I shoot her a hearty thumbs-up. Today's cross-examination ended relatively quickly; maybe Mom's getting less overprotective. A grin tugs at the corner of my mouth.

"More than safe." I speed-chop the air, karate-style. "I'm a lean, mean, Arena-fighting machine." Wincing, I freeze mid-chop. *How could I be so dumb?* Mom loses her freaking mind whenever I say the word 'Arena.'

There's a pause that lasts a million years while Mom stares at me, her face unreadable. Finally, she moves. But, instead of jumping around in hysterics, she flips about and rifles through cabinets in search of a coffee mug.

Wait a second.

This morning Mom cut her interrogation short *and* she didn't panic when I said the word 'Arena.' I wind my lips into an even-wider grin. Sweeeet. Things *could* be changing, after all.

Leaning back in my chair, I watch Mom pour coffee. I know she goes overboard because it's just me, her, and this nasty gray ranch house. I have no brothers, sisters, or straight answers about who my father is, except that he's some kind of diplomat. Add it all up and Mom's a wee bit clingy.

Or, at least, she *used* to be. I drum my fingers on the Formica. A less overprotective Mom opens up all sorts of possibilities. I could watch more matches. I could fight in more matches. I could develop interests in things other than the Arena.

Eh, maybe it's a 'no' on that last thing.

Mom slides into the chair across from mine, her large brown eyes watching me through the wisps of steam curling from her mug. "Want a ride to school today? I don't mind waiting outside the door." A muscle twitches at the corner of her eye. "You know, in case anything happens."

My heart sinks to my toes. Then again, maybe Mom's worse than ever.

"Uhhhh." My mouth falls so far open, some Frankenberry rolls off my tongue and onto the tabletop. Did she *really* offer to stand outside school all day long 'in case anything happens?' Cissy told me how parents get extra-twitchy during senior year. A shiver rattles my spine. My Mom *plus* 'extra-twitchy' *equals* a huge nightmare.

I force a few deep breaths. "Thanks for the offer." It's getting really hard to keep my 'calm voice' handy. "I'll pass this time."

Suddenly, the air crackles with energy. A black hole seven feet high and four feet wide appears in the center of the kitchen.

Out of the void steps a ghoul.

My fingers twiddle in his direction. "Hey, Walker." Technically, he's named WKR-7, but I've called him Walker for as long as I can remember.

"Good morning." Walker nods his skull-like head. If he were a few inches taller, the movement would knock his cranium through ceiling, and he's on the short side for a ghoul. It's a mystery how Walker and the rest of the undeadlies handle an eternity of being so crazy-tall.

Walker pulls back his low-hanging hood, showing pale, almost colorless skin and a strong bone structure. He sports the same hairstyle from the day he died: a brush cut with sideburns and no beard. Great black eyes peep at me from deep sockets.

I grin. It's nice to have Walker around. Most ghouls are obsessed with rules and act irritating as Hell. But Walker? He pushes boundaries like a pro, especially when it comes to sneaking me into the Arena. Having him around is like having a cute and somewhat sneaky older brother, only one without a pulse.

"Be careful, Myla." Walker's thin lips droop into a frown. "That's no way to greet your overlords. I don't mind, but other ghouls could send you to a re-education camp."

I roll my eyes. Purgatory is one massive bureaucracy with the charm of suburbia and the fun of a minimum-security prison. All the work's done by unpaid quasis like me (we're not allowed to call ourselves 'prisoners'). Ghouls keep us in line and make sure we're–*cough, cough*–super happy in our service.

I'm ready to complain about all this to Walker for the millionth time when Mom pipes into the conversation.

"Greetings, my beloved overlord." She's laying it on thick to make up for my sloppy hello. "Want some decaf?" She bows.

Walker nods; ghouls love java.

Mom picks up one of Walker's loopy sleeves, rubbing the fabric between her fingertips. "This is a little threadbare. Are you here for a new one?" All quasis must perform a service; Mom sews and mends robes. It could be worse. My friend Cissy's mom is a ghoul proctologist.

"No, thank you." Walker eyes the coffee pot greedily.

Mom hands him a full mug marked 'Afterlife's Greatest Ghoul.' Her chocolate eyes nervously scan his face. "What service do you require then?"

Walker frowns. "Myla must battle in the Arena today."

A huge grin spreads across my face. When human souls reach Purgatory, they're given a choice: trial by jury, or trial by combat. Based on the result, they end up either happily floating around Heaven or having their souls consumed in Hell. If the human selects a trial by jury, then it's someone else's problem. But if they choose combat—and the combatant in question is totally evil—then someone like Walker ends up in the kitchen of someone like me. I'm one of a few dozen quasis who kick butt. Literally.

I jump to my feet and clear off my bowl. "Now, this is what I call a Happy Monday."

Mom steps back. "You're sending Myla off to fight today? You can't." She leans against the countertop for support. "Every time she goes, she risks her life." A muscle twitches by her mouth. "Those battles are *to the death.*"

I stifle a moan. Mom always focuses on the whole 'to the death' thing like it's the first time she's learned how matches work. Hell, I've battled in the Arena since I was twelve and have yet to get a scratch. You'd think the drama would tone down over the years.

Panting, Mom points to a tattered calendar by the door. "My little one fought a month ago. She serves once every *three* months, right?"

I raise my hand. "It's not a problem. I'm up for this. Totally."

Mom flashes me a desperate look. "I know that." She grips the countertop like she'll pull it out of the wall. "Please, Walker, tell me it's a mistake."

Walker's black eyes fill with understanding. "Myla must serve today. There's a spike in Arena matches; all fighters have extra battles."

Mom stares at Walker, her jaw grinding out silent rebuttals. After a few moments, she presses her palms to her face, a low sigh escaping her lips. I frown. She's hitting a new level of drama this morning.

Walker shoots me the barest wink. I fight the urge to smile, knowing it means one thing: there's no across-the-boards spike in Arena matches. Purgatory must have an uber-evil soul on their hands, the worst of the absolute worst, and they need their best fighter on it.

That would be me.

Mom shakes her head from side to side. "All those demons and angels. Promise me, you'll keep her away from 'danger.'" She puts special emphasis on the word 'danger.'

"I always do, Camilla."

Mom releases her death-grip from the counter. "Of course."

My back teeth lock. Mom's always going on about protecting me from angels and demons. The demons I understand, but *angels?* Come on.

I zip up my gray hoodie. "Time to trash some evildoers." Stepping to Walker's side, I wait for transport to the Arena.

Mom's hand lightly touches her throat. "Be safe!"

"I'll be super-safe, don't you worry."

"And don't be late for school."

I slap on a smile. "On it, Mom."

Walker bows his head. "Stand back, I'll summon a portal." A new black hole appears in the center of the kitchen. I glance into the darkness, feeling the Frankenberry in my belly come up for a repeat performance. Using a portal feels like tumbling through empty space with a killer case of the stomach flu. Helpful safety tip: hold a ghoul's hand or you'll fall forever.

Taking a deep breath, I grab Walker's chilly fingers so tightly, I'd cut off his blood flow, if he had any. Together, we step into the portal, topple through nothingness, and walk out again onto the sandy earth of the Arena floor. I try my best to look ready-for-battle instead of ready-to-puke.

Walker offers me a sympathetic glance. "Shall we find a place to sit?"

"Nah, I'm fine, thanks." I scan the open-air stadium around me. The Arena's a nasty old ruin, all chipped gray rock and busted sandstone columns. How the place stays upright is a total mystery. The fighting floor is one huge uneven clod of dirt, the bleachers are basically rubble, and the entire top level looks ready to collapse.

I freaking love it here.

The stands lie open and empty, except for a few quasis. They're all fighters like me, trying to catch someone else's match. Mom used to attend too, but all the moaning and gasping got so out of hand, she was banned ages ago. I can't say I was bummed. Nothing like having your Mom yell 'Baby, don't diiiiiiiiiiiiiiiie' when you're twelve and fighting a demon for the first time.

A gravelly voice echoes through the air. "Greetings, *slave*." The word 'slave' is said with particular venom.

Every muscle in my body goes on alert. I'd know that voice anywhere, and I absolutely loathe its owner. I scrape lint from under my fingernails and pretend not to notice the seven-foot tall ghoul looming behind me.

Walker steps between us. "Greetings, SKE-12."

My mouth winds into a mischievous grin. "Hey, Sharkie.'" SKE-12 hates his nickname, so I work it into every encounter.

Sharkie frowns. "My name is SKE-12, *slave*."

Walker sets his hand on my shoulder, gently guiding me so I stand face-to-navel with Sharkie, master of Arena ceremonies and all-around dickhead. He hasn't changed a bit since my last match, not that ghouls often do. He's gray-skinned with large coal-black eyes, a skull-like hole for a nose, and teeth that have been filed to tiny points. His long silver robes hang in tatters; a tall black staff is gripped in his bony hand.

Walker gives my shoulder a squeeze. "Myla was just about to greet her ghoul overlord properly, weren't you, Myla?" Standing next to Sharkie, even Walker looks vertically challenged.

"My bad." I bow extra-low. "Greetings, SKE-12."

His buggy black eyes narrow into slits. Sharkie always knows when I'm making fun of him, and it drives him crazy. "I'll have no mischief from you today."

I bow again, even lower this time. "Yes, I'm fresh out."

Sharkie turns to Walker, his black eyes flaring bright red. "Control her." His gaze swings back to me. "We've an especially evil human soul fighting today. I hope to watch you die at last."

I pick something off my molar with my pinky. "I'm sure you do."

Sharkie steps closer, his pointy teeth click-clacking as he speaks. "The soul you fight today is so evil, the angels have begged the Great Scala to stand by, ready to transport him to Hell the moment he's defeated. Which will never happen." He leans in closer. "You. Are. Doomed."

My brows pop up. Normally, the Scala migrates tons of souls at once in what's called an iconigration. For this guy to get solo treatment, he must be a SUPER nasty. *Fun.* "Bring it on, Shar–."

Walker grabs my elbow. "Look, Myla! Your friends are here!" He points across the stadium floor. "We must depart." He bows once more to Sharkie. "Excuse us." As we speed-walk away, Walker whispers in my ear. "If I weren't already dead, I'd have had a heart attack just now."

"Eh, Sharkie's harmless."

"Because I placate him for you." He shoots me a sly look. "Why must you always taunt him?"

"Not sure." I shrug. "It's a hobby." A few yards ahead stands a ghoul named XP-22, and a hovering green blob that's Sheila, the Limus demon.

I shoot Sheila a friendly wave. "Hey Shiel, how are the kids?" Sheila's nice, so long as you don't stand close enough for her to swallow you whole. XP-22, on the other hand, is a total drip. I don't even glance in his direction.

"The kids are good, Myla, getting bigger every day…Just like you." Sheila's entire body shivers, which is a little scary since she's six feet tall, three feet wide, and has fourteen red eyes the size of tennis balls. "It seems like yesterday you were twelve and about to fight your first demon." Her huge gaping mouth twists into a grin. "How old are you now, honey?"

"Eighteen."

A blob-like arm stretches out from Sheila's side, lengthening into a gooey hand with eighteen long fingers. "Almost grown up! Have you been assigned your service yet?" 'Assigning your service' is ghoul-speak for locking a quasi into a life-long job after high school. We're not allowed to call it 'prison labor.' I shiver. There are some mighty foul careers out there too, like the infamous anal probe development lab.

Before I can reply to Sheila's question, Sharkie thumps his staff against the ground.

"Attention!" Sharkie raises his arms, his ragged gray robes swaying in slow, ghostly motions. Beneath his huge hood, his eyes shine as two points of red light.

Sheila waves her eighteen-fingered hand in my direction. "Well, what'll your service be? Port-a-Potty Squad? Greeter at Ghoul-Mart?"

Pointing to Sharkie, I make a 'sh' face to Sheila. It's rude to talk once the ceremony starts, plus I hate answering the whole 'what'll your service be' question. Sheila nods and oozes away. Bonus.

THUD. THUD. THUD. THUD. Sharkie thumps his staff four more times. "I bring you the Oligarchy!"

Four ghouls in scarlet robes appear along the top tier of the stadium, one at each point of the compass. Called the Oligarchy, they rule Purgatory as one collective mind, and a not-so-creative mind too, based on how they name ghouls.

In one motion, the Oligarchy close their eyes, bow their gray heads, and open a series of massive portals around the lip of the stadium. Angels and demons appear in the dark openings, and then stream down the uneven stone steps in one great wave.

The angels take their seats in an orderly line, their bodies coming in many shapes, sizes and colors. All have massive white wings, floor-length linen robes, little open-toed sandals, and eyes that glow with an unearthly blue light. They can hide their wings if they want to, but they keep them out for important occasions, like watching Arena fights.

In other words, angels are cool.

On the other side of the stadium, the demons move in a frenzied pack, roaring in a mad rush for the best seats. Large, furry creatures stomp along next to small and slimy monsters. Tiny, spiked demons zoom above their heads. Eye color is all they share in common: black stands for 'neutral' while red means 'run for the hills.'

As I watch them scramble over each other, my head shakes from side to side. Demons are cool too, but only when I get to kill them.

The lively hum of stadium chatter collapses into anxious silence.

She is coming.

I scan the top level of the Arena. The four great portals stand empty and dark. Acting in unison, the Oligarchy ghouls lower their heads. A low hum fills the air. Pale yellow light glimmers in the eastern portal; all eyes turn in that direction. A figure in white appears in the darkened entryway. My breath catches.

This is Verus, Queen of the Angels.

She stands willowy and tall with long black hair, high cheekbones, and exotic, almond-shaped eyes. She's timeless, beautiful, and more than a little bit frightening. Sometimes she watches me so carefully during matches, it gives me the creeps.

Beside her stands a short-ish ghoul with a handsome face, square jaw, and large black eyes.

I elbow Walker in the ribs. "That guy could be your brother."

He looks up, smiles. "You don't say."

"I did say." I glance at him out of my right eye. "So, is he?"

"You know your mother doesn't allow me to share personal information." He shoots me a sympathetic smile. "Take it up with her later." He clears his throat and rocks a bit on his heels. "When I'm not around, if you don't mind."

My 'why don't you tell me anything' fights with Mom are nothing short of legend. I stick out my tongue at Walker. "Fine. I will."

Verus steps onto her balcony, a small entourage behind her. As she slips into a white stone throne, the stadium's silence is ripped apart by howls and screeches. A new outline appears in the western portal: Armageddon, the King of Hell. He's tall and lanky with black onyx skin that's smooth as polished stone. A blade-like nose divides his long face, ending in a pointed chin. He scans the stadium, his eyes blazing as two searing points of scarlet light. A shiny black tuxedo hugs his wiry frame.

Unholy Hell. Every nerve ending in my body goes on alert. While Verus is a wee bit scary, Armageddon gives off a 'greater demon' aura. If you get too close (which has happened to me more than once), every cell in your body shudders with terror. But that's not what *really* gets me about the King of Hell. Most demons are short-term thinkers. They want to kill your body and eat your soul, end of story. Not Armageddon. He planned for years to take over both Hell and Purgatory. That kind of craftiness brings evil to a new level.

Armageddon saunters away from the portal, a large entourage of gorilla-like Manus demons behind him. The Oligarchy collapse onto their knees as he passes by, their movements reminding me of marionettes whose strings are cut. Their deep voices echo through the stadium. "We praise thee, Great King." The ghouls may rule us in name, but everyone knows who *really* runs the show.

Without so much as a glance toward the Oligarchy, Armageddon speeds onto the balcony across from Verus, his entourage close behind him. The King of Hell slips into his own black stone throne.

Sharkie thumps his staff again. "Ghouls, demons, and angels!" The stadium falls silent.

I glance at my watch and grin. Right now, I should be in homeroom.

With a flourish of his bony arm, Sharkie gestures to the four scarlet-robed ghouls standing along the stadium's top level. "Today, the Oligarchy bring you a spectacle of governing efficiency: an Arena battle to the death witnessed by the magnificent leader of our joint troops in the Ghoul Wars…The acclaimed liberator of all Purgatory…Armageddon!"

The demons positively lose their freaking minds in a deafening cheer. My upper lip twists. *Screw Armageddon and his fake liberation of Purgatory. He handed us over to ghouls so we'd send more souls to Hell, pure and simple.* It's only when demon DNA mixes with a human that you get different powers. On their own, demons are mindless soul-munchers. My eyes flare red. I start to make a lewd hand gesture in Armageddon's direction, but Walker snags my wrist before I get too far. He shoots me a stern look, mouthing the words 'put a lid on it, Lewis.'

Nodding, I grip my hands behind my back. I'm enough of a warrior to know he's right: taunting Armageddon is a B-A-D idea. I focus on the ground, force myself to breathe slowly, and try to keep my cool. My inner demon has a mind of its own with more than my tail. When my eyes flare red, it's my demonic side getting rowdy. Sometimes, it's a struggle to keep it in check.

From his great stone throne, Armageddon watches the frenzied demon crowd, his thin red lips curling upwards. He scans every face, soaking in each expression and nuance, weaving them all into some complex and dark plan.

I shiver. He's being crafty again, and damn, that makes my skin crawl.

Raising his hand, Armageddon quiets the crowd. "Today's soul was a favorite of mine on earth. Unbelievable strength. No capacity for conscience. Pure untainted evil. When he wins this battle—which he will, make no mistake—then we'll finally have one of our own inside the gates of Heaven." The dark seats howl with glee while the angels collectively shiver. Grinning, Armageddon retakes his seat.

All faces turn to the Angel Verus. She slowly rises to her feet, her white wings spreading regally behind her. She shouts one word: "NEVER!" The force of her yell sets columns rattling and rubble tumbling to the ground. Her gaze turns to me, eyes flashing bright. Armageddon follows suit, his irises glowing red as he scans me from head to toe. A satisfied smirk winds the corner of his mouth. I've seen that look on other faces; it's the one that says '*that* little girl? Maybe she's won before, but against *this* opponent? Are you serious?'

Which pisses me off, big time.

Sharkie thumps his staff again; a human soul appears nearby. In life, this ghost was a man about six feet tall with broad shoulders and two-hundred fifty pounds of solid muscle beneath them. Now he appears as a spectral version of his mortal self: a ghostly hulk whose pale body looks ready to burst from his faded jeans and dirty white t-shirt.

Sharkie addresses the spirit. "Vincent Francis Morris, you've chosen trial by combat, is this true?"

"The Choker. My name's…The Choker." Squinting his piggish eyes, the ghost flicks a fat tongue over his full lips.

"I will ask again." Sharkie's irises flare bright red. "Have you chosen trial by combat?"

The ghost curls his hands into fists. "Yes, combat."

"Select your opponent." Sharkie grins, his knife-like teeth glimmer in the pale light. "First, we offer XP-22."

The Choker eyes our 'fighting ghoul.' With barely-there skin and the muscle tone of toilet paper, anyone could crush XP-22. In fact, the Choker would probably snap him in three seconds or less, but I don't think he'll choose to. Ghouls look mighty terrifying, even the weak ones. Most humans avoid them.

The Choker is no different. "I'll pass."

Sharkie moves his thin arm to the next figure in line. "Second, we offer Sheila, the Limus demon."

Sheila's fourteen red eyes whip about her upper body, finally stopping to glare at the ghostly human. She stretches wide the black hole that serves as her mouth, letting out a gurgling roar. When that girl puts her game on, she's terrifying.

"Hmm." The Choker's beady eyes give Sheila a long stare; the entire Arena seems to hold its breath.

I glance at Sheila and shake my head. Limus demons are almost as easy to kill as XP-22. The trick is, they're super-flammable. One match and you turn a six-foot monster into a puddle of harmless goo. But like XP-22, they look worse than they actually fight.

The Choker frowns. "Nope."

"And third, we offer the quasi-demon, Myla."

The Choker's eyes slowly scan me from head to toe, his creepy gaze lingering on the curves under my t-shirt and sweats. Rage shoots up my spine. What a scumbag. If he stopped thinking with his pants for two seconds, he'd notice my demon tail instead of my boobs and butt. Some quasis get stuck with pig- or bunny-bottoms, but I hit the jackpot: the long and thin variety with an arrowhead end. Even better, it's coated in dragon scales, so the thing's nearly impossible to block or cut.

But the Choker isn't being smart. He stares into my big watery brown eyes and long lashes; I shamelessly blink in fake-terror. For trial by combat to be valid, the soul must have a chance at winning. They get three options, two of which are relatively easy to defeat. Then, there's me, the one nobody should pick. Except they always do.

"I choose her." His thick mouth stretches into a vicious smile. "I'll fight Myla." In a low voice, he adds: "You'll find out why they call me the Choker."

I jam my hands in my pockets and fake-shiver. *And you'll find out why they called me to fight you, dickhead.*

Sharkie thumps his staff on the ground again, and the ghostly Choker turns into two-hundred fifty pounds of real human. "So be it."

"Here are the rules," announces Sharkie. "Upon the count of three, you shall battle onto the death. If the Choker loses, he goes to Hell." The angels look at me with encouraging glances. "If the Choker wins, he goes to Heaven." The demons let out a deafening roar.

I watch the demons cheer, my hands balling into fists. Those freakies would love for a purely evil soul to enter Heaven. If a spirit has even a smidgeon of good in it, they 'go angel' once they cross the pearly gates. A purely evil soul could cause no end of trouble for the angels, and demons love trouble.

The crowd quiets into a nervous hush. Sharkie waves his hand; Sheila, Walker, and XP-22 make a hasty exit into an obliging archway. I hop from foot to foot and crack my neck. This will be a hoot.

Sharkie raises his arms. "The battle begins in 3, 2, 1!"

If your nickname is 'the Choker,' it doesn't take a genius in battle strategy to predict your first move in a fight.

"I kiiiiiiiiiiiiiill you!" Sure enough, the Choker lunges for me with both hands outstretched, aiming directly for my throat.

That gets my demon up. Anger spikes along my spine as my attacker speeds toward me. Each step goes in what feels like slow motion. I look around helplessly as if I'm cornered instead of surrounded by an empty arena the size of a football field.

The Choker's fingers brush my neck. My rage boils over. Jumping super-high, I haul up my knees, then kick my opponent squarely in the chest with both feet. The Choker falls flat on his back with a satisfying thud. Meanwhile, I use the momentum from my chest-kick to flip backwards into a somersault, landing right by his head.

Twisting my hips, I send my tail whipping toward my attacker's boots, careful to loop the length around his ankles. Stepping backwards, I tighten my tail around the Choker's feet and haul them up to his waist-level. The movement makes him curl his body so his hands rest right beside his ankles, which is exactly where I want them.

Shaking my hips again, I loop my tail around the Choker's wrists, cinching together his ankles and hands.

I grin. *This scumbag's now hogtied.*

The Choker's face flushes red as he rocks on his back, trying to wriggle free from my tail's grip. Not going to happen, buddy.

Tapping his boot with one finger, I whisper: "I beeeeeeeeeeat you."

The Choker struggles in a losing battle against my tail. Sharkie raises his bony arms. "The human loses!"

The angels cheer while the demons act like someone knocked their collective ice cream cones on the pavement. Boos and hisses erupt from the dark seats. Turning to the angelic side of the stadium, I wave to my cheering fans.

Sharkie glares at me, his eyes flaring red. "How many times do I have to tell you? Don't dawdle."

Sharkie hates it when I get any positive attention, so I always drag my winning cheers out as long as possible. The emcee keeps glaring at me, his eyes glowing ever brighter. Meanwhile, I scratch my neck as the Choker struggles with my tail. I'm not ending this for another minute, minimum. Sharkie can kiss my butt.

Raising his staff, Sharkie brings the long handle down on the Choker's chest, spiking it straight through his heart. The human twitches, then falls slack. A ghostly version of the Choker appears above his lifeless body.

Sharkie turns to me, his beady black eyes flaring bright red. "Next time, my staff skewers *your* heart, too."

I open my yap, ready to tell Sharkie exactly what he can do with his staff, when the hairs on my neck prickle. Raising my head, I scan the stadium. Every face is focused on me. Verus's eyes glow bright turquoise while a satisfied smile tugs at the corner of her mouth. Armageddon watches me with a curious interest, his right eyebrow cocked.

Time to vamoose. I don't need any attention from those two.

"Excuse me. It's time to call the Great Scala." I bow low, turn on my heel, and jog into a nearby archway.

Walker waits there for me in the shadows. "Nice work." He winks. "Hogtied is new."

I bow slightly. "I'm trying to mix it up a bit."

"On behalf of your audience, I appreciate the creativity." He rubs his hands together. "Shall we depart?"

"Hmm." Right now, I fall into the category of 'incredibly late for school.' I might as well make it count. "Nah." I peep around the edge of the stone archway. "I want to see the Scala move a soul." We don't get monster truck rallies or boy band tours in Purgatory, so this is the closest to a spectacle that I ever get. No way am I missing it.

A muscle twitches along Walker's jaw. "I promised to keep you out of danger."

I roll my eyes. "Every time I finish a fight, you pull out the old 'I promised your Mom I'd keep you safe' speech, and try to talk me into going home. And every freaking time I talk *you* into letting me stay." I elbow him in the arm. "You need some new shtick, my friend."

Walker chuckles. "I'll take it under advisement."

Sharkie's staff thuds on the ground, the noise echoing through the stadium. I peek toward the Arena floor. Sharkie stands alone on the grounds, his gray-skinned head bowed. "Bring him out." In this case, 'him' is the Scala, the only creature that can permanently move a soul to Heaven or Hell. Otherwise, they can (and mostly do) escape.

The Arena falls silent, the air thickening with anticipation. My heart rate quickens. We've had the same Scala for hundreds of years now. He's like the human's Easter Bunny, Santa Claus, and Tooth Fairy all rolled into one. Seeing him is a *huge* deal. Picture the oldest, most wrinkly guy possible, then add a hundred years, a white robe and mind-boggling levels of power. That's the Scala.

The sandy floor trembles beneath my feet. In the center of the Arena, a group of eight ghouls appear through a large portal, carrying an old man on what's basically a fancy stretcher. The dude is ancient, crinkly, and only five feet tall. His white beard winds around his entire body.

Armageddon leans back into his dark throne, his eyes narrowing. Pure hatred rolls off him in waves. The King of Hell fathered the Scala, but the child chose to embrace his mother's heritage as a thrax demon fighter. Armageddon never got over it.

Bit by bit, the Scala opens his eyes. Angels and demons alike fall silent. In a reedy voice that somehow carries throughout the stadium, the Scala asks in Latin: "Qui turbat Scala?"

A ghoul beside the Scala translates: "Who disturbs the Scala?"

The ghostly Choker looks still and disinterested, although beads of sweat glisten on his spectral cheek.

Sharkie bows low. "This soul has been defeated in a fair fight." He gestures to the Choker. "We ask he be sentenced to Hell."

The handler translates the response. The Scala nods feebly, raising his hand. Small bolts of lightning dance about his three-knuckled fingers.

"Parare ad ad infernum," whispers the Scala.

"Prepare for Hell," comes the translation.

Dozens of tiny lightning bolts whirl about the Scala's withered hand. *Igni*. Miniscule elements of power that only he can summon.

So. Badass.

I lean against the stonewall and hug my elbows. "I love this bit."

A smile sounds in Walker's voice. "Me too."

More igni appear, whirling about into a shaft of light about two feet high. A soul column. The pillar of brightness slides off the Scala's stretcher, growing wider as it spins across the Arena floor.

The soul column surrounds the Choker's ghostly legs. The spirit stands stunned as igni slowly climb up his body, each tiny lightning bolt swirling and diving around its neighbors like so many silver fish. For a moment the igni flare bright about the Choker's body, then they all disappear. The damned soul vanishes to Hell.

I brush-slap my hands together in a gesture that says 'my work here is done.'

Walker taps my shoulder. I turn my attention away from the Arena floor.

"Time to get you home, Myla."

"Not so fast, mister."

Walker grins. "Is this the part where you won't leave until I agree to sneak you in to see some matches?"

He's got me there. "Why, yes it is." I purse my lips. My encyclopedic knowledge of demons and the Arena comes in super-handy during conversations like this one. "Some Cellula demons are being brought to the Arena next week. Suuuuuper-rare. They're supposed to be semi-transparent and lit from within." I twiddle my fingers on my belly as a visual aid. Walker's a really good artist. Sometimes, he lets me keep his demon sketches too.

"Cellula, you say?"

Pay dirt. He must never have drawn these before. "Yup."

"Deal." He offers me his hand. "Now, I should get you to school."

"I need to go home, actually. I still have to change and grab my stuff." Which means I have more time-suck to enjoy before I actually have to get to class. Nice.

Walker lets out a dramatic sigh. "I'll get an earful about you and the Tardy List."

"You and me both." I take his hand. "Let's hit it."

Walker bows his head, creating a portal nearby. My stomach turns queasy just looking at it. Together, we leave the Arena's dirt floor, tumble through the portal's darkness and then land on the ratty carpet in my living room. I stifle my puke reflex. Stupid portals.

Walker leans over, examining my face. "Are you alright, Myla?"

"Yeah, I'm fine." I take a few deep breaths and clear my head. "Thanks."

"Until next time." He turns toward the open portal; I grab his sleeve.

"What?" My mouth winds with a crafty smile. "You won't hang out with me and Mom while we discuss my awesome morning in the Arena?"

He shoots me a level stare. "Ah, no."

"Chicken."

"And proud." He steps back through the opened portal and disappears.

I wish I could escape so easily. Straightening my shoulders, I prepare myself for the maternal inquisition, part deux. Usually, this flavor of interrogation starts with rapid-fire questions followed by slow hugs, sloppy tears, and loud exclamations of 'I almost lost you, baby.' If I'm lucky, I get homemade brownies out of it, too.

I grin. I'm feeling lucky.

CHAPTER TWO

A.

Rocking on my heels, I scan the empty living room. "Mom?" No reply.

That's weird. Mom rarely leaves the house. Especially rare if she knows I'm going to an Arena match. Those days she stays glued by the front door.

I look around. Our one-story ranch is a long rectangle with a kitchen on the far left and a living room in the center. Two bedrooms and one bathroom make up the far right. There's a creepy basement too, but I only go there to shove clothes into the washer and run like Hell. Everything's empty and open, except for Mom's bedroom.

I knock on her closed door. "Hello?"

Still no reply.

Bit by bit, I swing the door open. Mom sits at the foot of her bed, holding a purple robe. Her amber face glistens with tears. I sit by her side and wrap one arm around her slender shoulders.

"What's wrong, Mom?"

Her voice comes out low and quiet. "I was looking for sewing supplies and found this." She twists the robe into a ball on her lap. Tears drip from her nose onto the delicate fabric.

The over-worrying Mom I can handle. Hysterical, nagging, dramatic? No problem. But this incredible, bone-crushing sadness? It makes me want to wrap her up in a blanket, then go out and kill whoever made her this miserable.

I gently squeeze her shoulders. "So, what's that robe?"

Mom turns to me, her chocolate eyes bloodshot. "You don't know?"

There's a hidden knife in this question. If I answer incorrectly, I plunge it directly through her heart. My thumb moves in soothing circles on her shoulder. "No, Mom, I don't." I hold my breath, hoping that answer will comfort her.

It doesn't.

Mom freezes. "I see." All the color drains from her face.

My chest tightens. Somehow, I made her feel worse, and that makes me feel like the foulest daughter ever. *If she'd only tell me what happened to her.*

Mom rises to her feet, hugging the robe tightly against her belly. "I need some time alone."

"No problem. If you ever want to talk about it, I'm here." She's got to open up sometime.

Mom jams the robe into the bottom drawer of her dresser. "I won't talk about it." Her voice breaks. "Ever."

The reality of her words slam into me like a fist. My bottom lip quivers. I never seriously considered that Mom wouldn't eventually tell me everything about her past. But now, seeing the desperation in her bloodshot eyes, I know she never will. Whoever my father is, whatever happened to her in Armageddon's war, those secrets will die with her.

I nod slowly, my eyes stinging. "Okay."

She collapses on the edge of the bed. "I'm so sorry, Myla."

"It's fine." It's not really, but I don't want to say the wrong thing twice today. Closing the door behind me, I step into the living room and plunk onto the tattered couch. Knots of emotion tighten my throat. Whatever her secrets are, they're choking the life out of us both.

I straighten my spine. The same Myla Lewis who fights incredibly evil souls can't give up on finding out who I really am. Bit by bit, I rise to my feet, steel my shoulders and march toward my bedroom. Time to get ready for school.

After taking a quick shower, I hunt through my closet of black t-shirts and gray sweatpants. The Department of Avoiding Quasi Nakedness assigns everyone clothing; for teenagers, it's sweats and t-shirts. My upper lip twists. What classic ghoul nonsense—like we'd all run around naked if they didn't tell us what to wear. I throw on my least mangy sweats and t-shirt, then glance at my wristwatch. I can still catch a class before lunch with Cissy. Cool.

Swinging my backpack onto my shoulder, I head off to the nastiest, loudest and least reliable car in the universe: Betsy, our green station wagon.

Betsy's a massive gas-guzzling masterpiece of awesomeness. She's huge, green and filled with frayed upholstery accented by the smell of wet sneakers. Her radio doesn't work, her engine's unreliable, and someone glued orange pom-poms all around her windows. I love her.

I slip into the ragged front seat and rev the engine. Betsy bucks and thumps as her innards come to life. A heavy column of toxic black smoke rises behind us.

As we putter along the roads to school, I quickly give up on getting Betsy's radio to work and scope out the landscape instead. Rows of gray tract houses stretch off in every direction. Gravel driveways divide weed-choked squares of yellow grass. Gray clouds fill the sky, as always.

Ahead, there appears a red brick building three stories high with an arched roof. The wooden sign on the yellowing lawn reads 'DL-19 School for Quasi Servitude.' I park Betsy in a remote corner of the parking lot. This is it, school. *Yuck.* It's always an extra letdown to hit class after the adrenaline rush of the Arena.

Eh, no point delaying the inevitable any longer.

I tiptoe across the yellowing lawns. The rules state that students show up on time, and ghouls follow rules to the letter. Fighting evil souls in the Arena? Cuts me zero slack when it comes to the infamous Tardy List.

With maximum stealth, I step up to a small steel door on the side of the school. If I can sneak in here, I won't get nailed for being late. Crossing my fingers, I jimmy the door open with my tail. *Please let there be no one around.* Grabbing the handle, I grit my teeth and slowly swing the rusted door open a crack. Time to peep inside.

Empty. Yeah!

I punch the air with my fist, slip through a few more doors and step onto the school's main hallway. Students rush by. Everyone's wearing the same standard-issue gray sweats and dark t-shirts.

Excellent, I caught the break between classes.

I scan the monochromatic crowd for Cissy. After this morning with my Mom, I really need to see her smile.

My best friend stands by her locker. While we're both tall, I'm more on the curvy side with long auburn hair. Cissy is willowy, her blond hair hanging in shoulder-length ringlets. She has a golden retriever tail, which isn't good in a fight but sure looks cute on her. Seeing me, her face brightens and her arms open wide. I melt into her hug.

"Good morning, Cis."

"Hello, sweetie." She air-kisses my cheek, then flips about to fuss with a mangy old shoebox on the top shelf of her locker.

I nod toward the strange box. "What's that?"

Cissy closes her locker door with suspicious speed. "Nothing."

I set my fist on my hip and smile. "What did you rescue this time?"

"Some little cocoons." She shivers. "Dad's redecorating our basement again and he was going to kill them all." Cissy's father runs our black market. Sure, the ghouls let quasis manufacture a few things, but mostly they foist earth cast-offs on us: huge black-and-white TV sets with wire bunny-ears on top, answering machines as large as a Buick, that kind of thing. Everyone goes nuts for new stuff, which is how Cissy's family makes their money. It's also why Cissy's dad goes bat-shit crazy that his daughter's more interested in saving strays than shopping. As an Arena-fighting anomaly, I definitely fall into the 'stray' category, in her parent's minds anyway. We mostly hang out at my house.

Cissy pats the top of her locker door and beams. "I think one of the cocoons will open today."

I stare at her closed locker, my mouth screwing onto one side of my face. We don't get butterflies in Purgatory so those are... "Moths?" I wince. This is unbelievable, even for Cissy. "You saved moth larvae?"

"False! I saved cute little cocoon thingies." She puffs out her lower lip. "They need me." She sniffles.

Ugh, now I made her feel bad. "No worries." I pat her shoulder with what I hope is a comforting grin. "I think it's pretty cool." Maybe. I yawn and scratch my neck. What a day and it's not even noon yet. "Did I ever tell you about the time I fought the Mothma demon?"

Cissy rolls her eyes. "Only about four hundred times." She steps back, scanning me from head to toe. "You look like Hell... In a bad way. Were you home sick all morning?"

"Nah, they sent me into the Arena." I wink. "Took the guy down in less than a minute." I get into battle stance. "Let me show you what happened." I reach toward Cissy's neck. "This guy came at me with a classic choker hold."

My best friend raises her arms, palms forward. "Whoa, there!" She takes a giant step away. "Haven't we talked about this?"

I stare at my toes and play dumb. "I don't know. What do you mean?"

"I'm glad you enjoy killing things, but–"

"They're not things. They're super-evil souls." Cissy's not a fan of the Arena. Normally, that's fine with me, but today? For some reason, it stings. Frowning, I stare at the floor. "We should get to class."

Cissy tilts her head to one side. "Hey, honey. I didn't mean to shut you down." She points to her cheek. "But you did chip my tooth in fourth grade, remember? You just *had* to show me your screw driver."

"Pile driver. It's a wrestling move."

"And *that's* what I'm talking about." She chucks my chin with her knuckle. "Why not join the rest of us in Teenager-land and talk about something *other* than the Arena?" Her tawny eyes twinkle as she smiles. "It would be good for you."

Memories of this morning with my Mom flip through my mind's eye: her trembling hands, red-rimmed eyes, and tear-stained robe. "I get that I'm different, Cissy." My voice catches a bit. "I wish I knew why."

My best friend lets out a long breath. "Did we have a close encounter of the Camilla-kind this morning?"

"Yup." I frown.

"Well, then." She sets her hand on my shoulder. "I know someone who gets to eat my brownie at lunch." She gives my shoulder a squeeze; warmth fills my chest. Cissy knows just what to say to make everything right.

A grin tugs at the corner of my mouth. "Really?" Cissy makes kick-ass brownies.

"Absolutely."

Paulette Richards walks by, ruining the moment. "Hello there, lovelies!" She slowly waves her hand, careful to show off her glittering new watch.

Oh no.

"Hey, P." I give her a limp wave in reply.

Brown-haired and cocoa-skinned, Paulette has a funky lizard tail and a talent for driving Cissy crazy. "Did you see my new watch?"

Cissy scans it with an expert glance. "Dad's running a special on these this month." She shrugs. "Who gave it to you?"

"Zeke! Can you believe it? He's like the best boyfriend in the universe." Her eyes twinkle with a red glow.

I fold my arms across my chest. "Really?" Everyone knows Zeke's notorious for random hook-ups with gifts. Cissy's even *more* notorious for being obsessed with Zeke. What a bitchy move from Paulette. My eyes narrow. "So, P. Have you met Zeke's friends yet?"

Paulette's lizard tail cracks behind her like a whip. "No, but I'm sure I will soon." Turning on her heel, she almost skips down the hall.

I grit my teeth, knowing the shit-storm that'll hit once Paulette's out of earshot.

Cissy grabs my arm. "Zeke gave her that?" Her eyes flare red. "My. Zeke. Ryder."

Here it comes. Every quasi has a bit of demon DNA aligned to one of the seven deadly sins: lust, gluttony, greed, sloth, wrath, envy, and pride. In my case, my deadly sin is wrath, which is why I'm such a good fighter. For Cissy, it's envy, which is why she's about to launch into an hour-long monologue on why Zeke should be giving *her* Rolexes, not Paulette. Over the years, I've learned to half-listen.

"...and if he hasn't introduced her to his friends, then she's just a fling." Cissy sets her fists on her hips. "Plus, that boy gives pricey presents to anyone who shows him their tits." Her gaze swings toward me, her eyes glowing red. "Myla, have you been listening to me?"

"Um, yeah." I glance at my own watch. "Hells bells! We'll have to catch up at lunch; class is about to start." Unfortunately, this class might as well be on the other side of the planet. With a quick wave goodbye, I take off at a run for History.

I'm a sweaty mess when I reach the door. Inside, our teacher paces the room. She's the hated MT-12, Miss Thing to her students. Like all ghouls, she's tall and bony with chalky gray skin and a bald head. She's always decked out in cherry red lipstick and matching high heels, which only make her look creepier in her long black robes. At least, she always wears her hood up.

From what I've seen on the human channel of our crappy public access TV, quasi classrooms are like their earthly counterparts. A teacher stands before rows of students; a single door is the only way in or out. The big differences are the Oligarchy glamour shots covering the walls and the modified desk-chairs with back-holes for our tails. Taking a deep breath, I open the door.

"Class, open to page 136 in *Quasi Servitude Through the Ages*."

I tiptoe into the room. Miss Thing freezes. Her coal-black eyes bore into my back.

"Myla Lewis, you're late."

"Sorry. I was at the Arena for—"

"I don't want excuses." Miss Thing pounds the tabletop; I'm pretty sure she breaks an overly-long red nail. "Just because you're called for servitude at the Arena does not give you special rights to break the rules."

I race into my favorite seat, which is a corner desk in the last row, aka as far away from the teacher as possible. "Understood."

Miss Thing glares at me for a full minute, then returns her attention to the opened book on her desk. "As we see on page 136, the quasis mis-managed Purgatory for eons, forcing Armageddon to liberate these lands twenty years ago. All of which was inevitable, since quasis are the weakest creatures in all the five realms."

I grit my teeth and grip my desktop like I'll snap it in two. I don't need more 'Armageddon is awesome' talk today. Miss Thing taps her chin with her red pinky nail. "Who can name the five realms and their people?"

Paulette raises her hand, the better to show off her new Rolex. "Paulette?"

"Heaven with angels, Hell with demons, ghouls in the Dark Lands, quasis in Purgatory and—" Paulette frowns.

Miss Things rolls her eyes. "Thrax in Antrum."

Paulette's face reddens.

Our teacher lets out a high-pitched giggle. "Don't worry, you silly little fool. You just illustrated my point about your people being a lower form of life." Miss Thing launches into a 'lecture' that's basically a quasi-hating version of Armageddon's war. The way she teaches history, the class should be entitled 'Why Quasis Suck Through the Ages.'

Sighing, I pull out my textbook and try to focus. I've been reading the same sentence six times when someone clears his throat. *Barf*. I know the sound of that particular someone anywhere. Bit by bit, I turn my head and glance across the row.

That's when I realize the awful truth: I've made the worst seating decision in the history of the universe. I'm parked right beside Zeke Ryder, Cissy's mega-crush and my personal stalker.

Zeke's power is all lust. He's tall, pale, and handsome, every inch packed with muscles and pheromones. His caramel eyes, chiseled features, and messy blonde hair are perfectly matched with a monkey tail. Every girl's knees turn to Jell-O before him, except for me, making me a challenge-slash-target since the third grade.

"Hello, kitten." Zeke waves in my direction. He's wearing standard issue sweats, a black t-shirt, and his trademark come-hither stare.

Pointing to the teacher, I make my 'shh' face.

Zeke arches his eyebrow. "You coming to my party Friday night?"

"No." His last 'party' consisted of two cans of beer and the back seat of his limo. The black eye I gave him lasted for weeks. What a bust for my first attempted kiss. At least, I had fun punching him.

My back teeth lock as I glance around the room. Every girl within pheromone-smelling distance aims goo-goo eyes at Zeke. Why am I the only one who thinks his Mister Romance routine is annoying? I'm probably the only senior at school who's never had a crush, never been kissed. What's up with that?

I straighten my shoulders and angle my body away from Zeke. *I've got more important things to worry about than boys, THAT'S what's up with that.* I pretend to be very interested in my textbook. Hopefully, he'll get the hint.

"Not so fast, babe." He points to the envelope half-hanging out of my backpack. "It's not that kind of party. Take a look."

"This was from *you?*" Pulling out the letter, I turn it over in my fingers. "I was going to read this today anyway." I pause. My tail tries to shred the rest of the envelope. I smack the arrowhead end and reset the letter into my backpack.

Zeke flashes me a white-toothed smile. "Why don't you read it right now?"

Miss Thing stares out the window, monologue-ing on how quasis sent too many souls into Heaven, which was super-unfair to the poor demons. I could samba down the aisle right now and she probably wouldn't notice me.

Zeke has the same idea. "Miss Thing won't see you. Go ahead. Take a look."

I pull the envelope out of my backpack and set it on my lap.

Zeke arches another eyebrow. "I can't believe this. Is the fearless Arena fighter too scared to open one ittle-wittle envelope?"

That did it. I tear open the letter with a vengeance. Inside I find an embossed invitation that reads: *You and a guest are cordially invited to attend a diplomatic gala in honor of our ghoul overlords and their noble allies, the demons. Friday, the 13th, The Ryder Mansion, Upper Purgatory. Formal dress only. Doors open at 8 PM.*

I run one finger over the embossed letters. "Is this for real?"

"Absolutely. You can bring a friend too, if you want." Cissy's crush on Zeke is nothing less than monstrous; she'll never forgive me if I pass this up. Maybe he's not as dumb as he looks.

After the last 'party' Zeke invited me to, I should be skeptical. But there are four good reasons to attend this one. First, Zeke's dad really *is* a wealthy diplomat known for hosting delegations of ghouls and demons. Second, the party's at his parent's mansion where he's less likely to get nasty. Third, I'll bring Cissy (with her crush she's better protection than parents). And fourth, the single fact I know about my own father is that he was a diplomatic something-or-other. I can't miss the chance to learn more.

"I'll think about it."

Zeke's mouth arcs into a satisfied smile. "That's all I ask."

I forget about the invitation until the end of the school day. Cissy and I sit in the back row of Lessons in Servitude class. It's taught by OT-42—we call him the Old Timer—who's known for his huge handlebar moustache, broken teeth, and blazing hatred of talking in class. His receding head of gray hair is tied back into a teensy ponytail at the base of his neck. Other than that, he's pretty standard ghoul material: tall, dark, and gruesome.

"We have an important lesson today." The Old Timer stalks around the classroom, his thin frame setting his long robes swaying. He pulls back his black hood and scans the rows of desks, twiddling his handlebar moustache.

"Today, we'll learn how to prepare appealing meals for your masters." The Old Timer's thin indigo lips round into a demonic smile. "Exciting, eh?" He starts yapping about how happy we'll make our overlords by preparing delicious dinners for them. I start doodling 'Lessons in Stupid-tude' over and over in my notebook.

Cissy's tawny eyes focus on the envelope that half-hangs out of my backpack. "What's that?"

I keep scribbling away. It looks productive and passes the time.

Cissy clears her throat. "I asked you a question, Myla." She points at the envelope again.

I yawn. "Oh, that's our invite for Zeke's party Friday night."

Cissy starts hyperventilating. "That's an invite to *where* Friday night?"

I stop scribbling and realize my huge error. "Uh, I'll tell you later."

The Old Timer finishes his speech on pleasing our overlords. Half the class chit-chat in little groups. One guy snores in the back row.

"Impertinence!" The Old Timer stops twiddling his mustache so quickly, I think he'll rip it off his face. "Pay attention to your master!" The room falls quiet; the sleeping kid raises his head. If the Old Timer were a cartoon, he'd have smoke coming out of his ears right now.

"That settles it." Our teacher strides over to his desk, jotting down a quick note. "To punish your lack of focus, we shall have tests all next week." He slaps his bony fists onto the tabletop. "That means robe-cleaning, foot massage, and groveling etiquette, as well as our lesson for today, meal preparation."

A long groan erupts from the students; everyone sits straighter in their chairs. The dog-tailed kids stop wagging.

"At last, I have your full attention." The Old Timer rubs his gray hands together, explaining how ghouls like things spicy, drink cough syrup like wine, and are allergic to fish. Oh, they eat a ton of worms too. "Everyone follow me to the demonstration area."

The class steps over to a long metal table. Our teacher picks up a huge bowl of wriggling worms in his left hand and a tall bottle of Tabasco sauce in his right. "Who wants to prepare a delicious meal?" He looks like a cross between a black-robed scarecrow and Betty Crocker.

Cissy pokes me in the ribs. "Zeke asked me to go too, didn't he? Please tell me he did." She really needs a hobby.

I hip-check her. "Quiet, Cis. You'll get us in trouble."

"Myla Lewis." The Old Timer snaps his gray head in my direction. "Is there something you'd like to share with the rest of those in servitude?"

"No, sir."

The Old Timer sets the worm-bowl and Tabasco sauce onto the prep table. "Perhaps you believe your special status as Arena fighter means you don't have to follow class rules like everyone else?"

I frown. The one thing that sucks about Arena matches is listening to everyone complain about my 'special treatment' afterwards. In all of Purgatory, there are only a few dozen Quasis across who fight in the Arena, and we're all descended from Furor demons. The Furor are known for not one, but *two* deadly sins: lust and wrath. Clearly, I only inherited the wrath part, which is why I'm an especially good Arena fighter. And yeah, I *do* think I deserve special treatment. Hey, I kept an evil soul out of Heaven this morning. Where's the love?

Opening my mouth, I'm about to say something to that effect when I glance into the Old Timer's oily black eyes. No love for me there, that's for sure. I bite my lower lip. "Whatever you say, sir." *Suck it, loser.*

The Old Timer lets out an indignant puff of air. "What does the rest of the class think? Should Myla have special treatment because she wrestles a few ghosts?"

Thirty sets of eyes turn in my direction, everyone looking at me with a gaze that says 'hey, I forgot about that freaky fighting girl.' This attitude is an improvement, actually. Time was, they all teased me mercilessly. That ended when I put Billy Summers in hospital back in first grade. That's when Cissy took pity on me too, wrapping me up in her little shoebox of friendship. I've cherished her ever since.

The Old Timer taps his foot. "Well, class?"

No one wants to get their ass kicked like Billy Summers, so they all keep their yaps shut.

"I see." The Old Timer eyes the bowl of worms. "Myla, since you seem to deserve special treatment, perhaps you'll demonstrate how to make worm soufflé."

Oh my sweet evil. Not worm soufflé.

I take a deep breath. "Yes, sir." Stepping up to the table, I eye the massive bowl of nasty, writhing, and greasy worms. Even for a quasi-demon, this is gross stuff.

The Old Timer grins, showing a mouthful of cracked and yellow teeth. "First, you must mush the worms into a pulp."

I cringe. *Okay, that's totally repulsive.* Scanning the room, I see every set of eyes still locked on me. I try twisting my disgusted sneer into a cool and casual grin, but I just end up looking constipated.

"Got it." My stomach somersaults. "Is there a spoon or something?"

"Absolutely not," says the Old Timer. "This must be done with your bare hands."

"Ooooooookay." Bit by bit, my trembling fingers inch toward the wriggling mass of gray and brown nasties.

At that moment, Cissy lets out as yelp. "Angels! Angels!" She points to the window; the class runs to look. I follow, thrilled for the diversion.

Sure enough, a pair of angels walk the school grounds below, accompanied by the school's Headmaster and Superintendent. The Old Timer stares through the glass, his black eyes wide as saucers. His voice comes out in a nervous whisper. "Ghouls and angels?"

Angels rarely visit Purgatory outside of Arena matches, let alone go for strolls with ghouls. My mind spins with the possibilities, returning again and again to the same thought: *this little distraction puts worm soufflé time on hold!* I can't help but grin.

"What in blazes are angels doing here?" The Old Timer twirls his handlebar moustache with bony fingers, his ebony eyes lost in thought.

Cissy half-raises her arm. "Sir, class is almost over." We've got fifteen minutes, but Cissy uses new math.

With his eyes still locked on the window, the Old Timer dreamily waves his hand. "You're all dismissed."

Cissy grips my wrist. "We're going to your house after school." She drags me toward the door. "This is an official emergency. We've *got* to talk."

My upper lip curls. One guess what she wants to chat about.

CHAPTER THREE

The entire ride home, Cissy fiddles with Betsy's radio and grills me about every millisecond of my interaction with Zeke. It's amazing how many details she thinks are important. 'Did he look directly into your eyes when he asked that question?' 'Were his arms crossed over his chest like this?' And, of course, there's the ever-popular 'Did he ask you about me?' When I run out of answers, I start making stuff up. It's easier that way.

Cissy's eyes flare with a bit of red. "Did he give you his *smoldering* look?" She's created an elaborate filing system for Zeke's goo-goo eyes. Blech. This boy-crazy crap makes me a little nuts. Not only because it's dumb, repetitive, and a total waste of time, but also because part of me wishes I'd felt that way. Maybe once.

"Smoldering look." I smack my lips. "What do you mean?"

Her eyes blaze red. "You know *exactly* what I mean. He gives you that look all the time. Zeke so likes you and you could care less. It's not fair."

I grip the steering wheel tighter and brainstorm ways to change the subject. There are two Cissys. One is my sweet friend with a big heart who can't help but take care of oddballs like me. The other's an obsessive nut job who goes demon-eyed with envy over whatever's the object of her desire. Like Zeke. "Put the brakes on your inner demon, Cissy girl. Do you want to miss this chance?"

"What chance?" Cissy slumps into the seat, kicking her foot onto the dashboard. "You'll be at the party too. Let's be honest. He won't notice I exist."

"Hey, now." I can't stand to see Cissy so down on herself. "This is like...like..."

Cissy frowns. "Like what?"

"Well, it's like fighting a Cellula demon. Do you let its projectiles wrap around you until it squeezes you to death? NO!" I pound the steering wheel with my fist for emphasis. "You reach inside the membrane and pull out its nucleus!"

The edge of Cissy's mouth quirks upwards; her eyes return to their regular tawny brown. "I'm not *exactly* sure what you just said, but I think it was something like 'don't give up.'"

"Yeah." I whack the steering wheel again; I'm on a roll. "Who lives in the one house in Purgatory that can get any kind of dress, make-up, or hair goop in the five realms? YOU. If Zeke's what you want, sitting in the car and moping isn't going to get him for you. Get your Barbie on and knock his socks off."

Cissy sits up, her mouth rounding into a full grin. "You know what? You're absolutely right."

"Damn straight, I'm right." I pull the car into the driveway and kill the ignition. Betsy's engine kicks with a loud thump. "Now, let's chow down on some Demon bars."

Cissy pumps her fist in the air. "Huzzah!"

I park the car, walk through the front door, and update Mom that Cissy will be here for the rest of the week, talking non-stop about Zeke's party on Friday.

Mom perks up immediately. "A party in the Ryder mansion?" She opens different kitchen cabinets, pulling out ingredients for chocolate chip cookies. Whoa, that's unexpectedly awesome.

"Yup." Cissy twirls one golden lock of hair around her finger. "I don't know *what* I'll wear."

Mom hauls the mixer out from its hiding place above the fridge. "I have an old contact at Versace. I'll write the name down for your parents. They're great at whipping up something special on short notice."

I slide into my favorite seat at our kitchen table (the one with the perfectly-sized back-hole for my tail) and watch Mom putter around the kitchen, a rare smile on her amber face. Since when does she know anyone at Versace?

"Thanks so much, Momma Lewis." Cissy draws circles on the tabletop with her finger. "Want me to get something for Myla, too?" She looks expectantly from me to my mother.

"Nonsense!" Mom juts out her chin. "I attended my share of diplomatic events back in the day; I saved all my dresses. I have the perfect one for you, Myla!"

My face stretches into a sly grin. "All this talk about diplomatic events must remind you of someone." *As in my father.* I shoot her a look that says 'this is me, not giving up.'

Mom gathers up my long auburn hair, piling it at different angles atop my head. "We're not talking about that, Myla." She lightly pinches my cheeks to turn them blush-red. "I know just what we'll do with your hair and make-up too."

I pause, biting my lower lip. Versace, diplomats, parties at the Ryder mansion…Do I push for the millionth time for information about my father?

Cissy sighs. "If you're starting one of those 'who's my dad' fights, I'm going home."

Mom keeps fussing with my hair. "I'm not fighting."

I drum my fingers on the tabletop. "Okay, you don't want to talk about Dad. Maybe you can talk about your diplomatic work? What were the events you attended at the Ryder mansion?"

Mom hums a nonsense tune, twisting my hair in different angles. "I never answered these questions before and I won't start now."

I let out an exasperated gasp. "Come on, Mom! This is so unfair. Can't you tell me one little thing?"

Cissy thunks her forehead onto the tabletop. "No way! This sounds like a 'who's my Dad' fight *plus* a 'what did you do before the war, Mom' battle. Can I please save us all some time?" She sits upright, making her two hands talk to each other like puppets.

Cissy's first hand 'speaks.' "Mom, I really want to know who Dad is." Cissy gives me a very whiny voice. We'll have a chat later about that.

Her second hands 'replies.' "No." Her mom voice is totally grouchy and right on the money.

'My' hand: "What did you do before the war?"

'Mom's' hand: "I can't tell you."

"Not one eensy beensy bit?"

"No."

"But I really, really want to know." Cissy's puppet-Myla jumps up and down.

"No, no, no, no, no. Now, go to your room and ask your friend to go home."

Cissy stands up, taking a bow. "Thank you, thank you! Show's over." She plunks back into her seat. "Now, can we talk about the party?"

I set my hands over my face. "No." She's not charming me off the subject this time.

Cissy gently moves my hand until I peep at her between my fingers. "That's not my Myla." She shoots me a sweet grin.

I try to pout, but I slowly smile instead. Once again, Cissy knows exactly what to say to get everything back on track. No doubt our school will be overrun with moths in a matter of weeks, too. I drop my hands. "Fine, let's talk about the party."

Mom grins as well. "Absolutely. I was saying I could do your hair and make-up."

"I can do my own hair and make-up, Mom. But if you can find a dress for me, that would be awesome."

"And shoes too," adds Cissy.

"Of course!" Mom sashays from the room; I hear the pit-pat of footsteps in our attic crawlspace. The rest of the afternoon, Mom pores through old boxes while humming a tuneless song. Meanwhile, Cissy and I actively avoid homework by watching the *Brady Bunch* marathon on the Human Channel.

All in all, a good day.

♫

A bony finger pokes my bare toe. I peep out from under my comforter, seeing Walker at the foot of my bed.

"You are called to serve."

I glance at my alarm clock. "It's 5 AM, Walker." And tonight is Zeke's party. "This makes it twice in one week."

Walker shrugs, rubbing his sideburns with his bony hand. From the other side of our ranch house, I hear Mom nervously clunking around the kitchen.

I roll over and stare at Walker out of my right eye. I know there's no way out of this (not to mention that there isn't anything else I'd rather do with my morning), but that doesn't stop me from giving him a hard time. "Couldn't find anyone else, eh?"

A smile tugs at his mouth. "No."

"In that case, I *guess* I could go."

Walker steps toward the door. "Don't worry, there's another fighter that I could—"

I jump in front of him, blocking any exit from my room. "Don't you dare!"

Walker smiles. He really is way too handsome for ghoul. "So, you *will* fight?"

I punch him in the upper arm. "You know it, slim." I speed through getting dressed, stuffing my face with cereal, and passing my morning interrogation with the Maternal Grand Inquisitor.

Walker steeples his hands under his chin. "Time to go, Myla."

"Finally!" I clear my throat. "I mean, let's go." I'm totally pumped to have two fights in one week, but I don't want Mom to have an aneurism. I give her a quick peck on the cheek. "See you later."

She grips my shoulders. "Be safe, Myla-la. You're all I have in the world." She sniffles. "If I lost you…"

"No worries. I'll be super incredibly safe. Bye now." I grab Walker's hand and almost run through the portal. It doesn't matter how many times I do this, it always makes me sick to my

39

stomach. When I step out onto the Arena floor, my head feels a little loopy too.

Fighting the fog in my brain, I inspect the grounds around me. Beside me stands Walker, Sharkie, XP-22, and good old Sheila, the Limus demon. As I struggle to focus, my fuzzy mind misses the procession of demons and angels into the stands. By the time my head clears, Sharkie's ready to announce the match.

"Demons and angels!" The emcee's deep voice echoes through the massive Arena. "I bring you another spectacle of efficiency in ghoul administration of Purgatory."

At this point, a roar would typically erupt from the Arena's demon population. Instead, there's perfect silence. I scan the stadium; Armageddon sits unmoving on his ebony throne. His red eyes glow brightly; his thin mouth is set into a frown.

Sharkie eyes the stands carefully, then gestures to the dark balcony. "I would ask the greatest general in history to say a few words before the match. Armageddon, if you please!"

The demon lord swings his leg over the arm of his black throne, his scarlet eyes scanning the crowd with pure malice. "I have nothing to say to you."

Okay, that's weird. Normally, these matches start with a mutual love-fest between Armageddon and the ghoul hierarchy. Things seem oddly icy today. I rub my neck and yawn. Or maybe my brain hasn't woken up yet.

Verus rises to her feet. "I'd like to say a few words."

Sharkie stares at Armageddon for a long moment, his jaw hanging open. Verus never speaks at these events. Sharkie bows to her. "Uh, yes. Please." He snaps back into emcee mode. "Ghouls, demons, and angels! You all know Verus as the Oracle, the only angel with the gift for seeing the future. What would you like to share with us today? A prediction for the match?"

Verus takes to her feet, her great wings extending. "We angels can't help but notice that the Scala is getting on in years." Her gaze rounds on Armageddon, a sly look twinkling in her eyes. "It is time the Scala Heir was announced and brought to these matches."

I gasp. There hasn't been a Scala Heir for ages. I've heard the stories, of course: at any point in time, there's one Scala and one Scala Heir. Of all the creatures across the five realms, only these two mortals have the blood of a human, demon, and angel. My tail arcs over my shoulder, ready to strike. Somehow, Verus bringing up the Scala Heir sets my warrior instinct on alert. Bad mojo.

Around the top lip of the stadium, the Oligarchy turn their heads in unison toward Verus. They speak in one voice, the sound a mix of low rumble and hiss. "We have no need of a Scala Heir."

Verus slowly wags her head from side to side. "The Scala is powerful, but he is mortal. That's why there's always been a Scala and a Scala Heir. We haven't seen an Heir since Armageddon's War." She folds her arms into her long white sleeves. "The angels appreciate these matches as a demonstration of efficiency, but how effective is your administration without an Heir?"

Armageddon snaps his long black fingers. A red-skinned demon with horns and a pitchfork steps up to the greater demon's side. "Where's the Scala Heir? The thrax we caught at the border to Hell?"

The red demon swallows. "Dead, my lord."

Armageddon's eyes flare red. "Why?"

"You thought him insolent, my lord."

The King of Hell scratches his cheek. "Ah yes, I remember now." His mouth curls into a sickening grin. "He died very well indeed."

I shiver. 'Very well indeed' means he came up with something especially creative and painful. Oy.

Armageddon gestures to Verus. "There's been no Scala Heir for nearly twenty years. Why question it now?"

Verus bows her dark head. "We deem the time ripe."

"Whatever are you up to?" He drums his long fingers on the armrest of his throne. "Is there a *prophecy* involved?"

"To an Oracle, there's always a prophecy." Her eyes flare bright blue. "Answer my question. The Scala Heir."

"We'll find the poor sod." He leans forward, setting his bony elbows on his knees. His eyes narrow as his stare locks with Verus's steady gaze. The air becomes charged with strange, oppressive energy. My chest tightens.

Armageddon's eyes flare bright red. "It's about time I made another Scala Heir suffer."

The word 'suffer' echoes strangely about my head. In my mind's eye, I see a man with mismatched eyes and jet-black hair. He's a burly powerhouse of muscle, covered in blood and screaming. I don't know why, but I feel certain he's the last Scala Heir. My knees turn watery beneath me. A heavy patch of clouds roll past the always-gray sky, darkening the Arena.

Somehow, Walker is at my side, his hand set about my shoulder. His arm is lean and roped with muscle, stronger than I would have expected. "What's wrong Myla?"

The man's screaming face fills my mind. "You don't see it?"

"No, Myla. You're catching energy from Verus and Armageddon. Sometimes, it causes hallucinations." He scans the skies. "Just a few seconds more."

Verus inspects the crowd with ice-blue eyes. "Let the games begin." She wears a satisfied smile as she slowly resettles into her white stone throne.

"So be it." Sharkie thumps his staff onto the ground. The sky lightens, my legs become solid beneath me again. What the Hell is going on?

Walker releases his hold on my shoulder. "Alright now?"

"Yeah, thanks." I suck in a few deep breaths. "What was all that? I felt like I'd pass out."

"Battle of wills between Verus and Armageddon. I felt it too, but not to the point of seeing any visions." Walker wraps his hand in mine. His skin is warm and comforting. "You need to prepare yourself to fight, Myla. They're about to summon the soul. Can you do that for me?"

I give his hand a squeeze and crack my neck from side to side. "Hells, yeah." With each passing second, more strength pours back through me. "Bring it on."

Walker grins. "That's my girl."

Sharkie thumps his scythe again. "We summon the soul for battle." A ghostly woman materializes beside him. Wiry and thin, she has slightly hunched shoulders and frizzy gray hair down to her waist. A constellation of scars covers her swollen face.

The human woman quickly raises one arm, pointing to Sheila. "I choose her."

Sharkie pauses. "So, you choose trial by combat?"

"Yes," the woman says quickly. "And I choose the green demon."

The emcee gestures toward me, Walker and the other ghoul. "You three must depart." Turning to the woman, Sharkie adds: "And you must prepare for battle." The human nods, bows slightly to the Limus demon, and crumples onto her knees. From the way her shoulders shake, I'm pretty sure she's crying.

I follow Walker into one of the Arena's archways, anxiety curling its way across my shoulders. That scene back there is just plain wrong in so many ways. Once inside the shadows, I stare at the ground, only vaguely aware of Sharkie reading the rules of combat.

I turn to Walker. "This has got to be my weirdest day in the Arena. First, there's all that stuff about the Scala Heir and a weird power struggle between Verus and Armageddon. Second, I'm yanked out of bed to fight some old human who's sitting there crying? I only go up against the worst of the worst."

"There's nothing I can say." Walker's gaze meets mine, his black eyes glistening in the pale light. "You're precious to me, Myla." He raises his hand and presses it to my cheek. His skin is warmer than I expected.

Realization slams into me. "You know what this is all about, don't you?" I wrap my fingers around his hand. "Tell me."

"I've watched Verus for years. I know how she thinks."

"And how's that?"

Walker frowns. I know Mom bullied him into telling me zero about himself. But he does more with his life than ferry me back and forth to matches. He must know something about what *really* happened today.

He drops his hand. "I've said too much already." Turning on his heel, he starts to walk away.

I block his path. "Tell me what you were going to say. I promise I won't press you for more. I know you made some kind of promise to my mother." I stare into his liquid black eyes and hope with everything in me: *please, tell me something.*

Relief washes over Walker's face. "I can say this. I believe you impressed Verus with your defeat of the Choker. She's taken an interest in you now. She specifically requested you come to the Arena today, but I don't think it was to fight."

"Why then?"

"To hear about their search for the Scala Heir, perhaps. But definitely to see this." He gestures to the open archway to the Arena floor. The human still crouches on her knees, sobbing quietly. Sheila closes the distance between them, green saliva dripping from her gaping mouth.

Waves of red-hot anger rip through my body. Every fiber of my being says that woman should not be killed and sent to Hell. I just *know* it. "That's wrong, Walker." My eyes flash demon red. "Why isn't that woman going to Heaven?"

"Some souls believe they deserve Hell, even if a trial would send them to Heaven." He shakes his head from side to side. "Under the old regime, quasis would never have allowed this human to choose trial by combat."

And she'd be going to Heaven right now. A hollow feeling creeps into my bones. She's purposefully losing the battle so her soul can be consumed in Hell.

On instinct, my back arches. My toes dig deep into the dirt, preparing to run. I scope out the distance from my spot to the woman's. I could reach her in seconds. She doesn't belong in Hell. I won't let it happen.

I'm halfway out the archway when Walker yanks me back. "What are you doing, Myla?"

I shake him off. "It doesn't seem right. Maybe I can grab her—"

"And get torn apart by a thousand demons." He wags his head from side to side. "That would help no one."

My voice catches in my throat. "Isn't there anything I can do?"

"Not at this time, I'm afraid." He scans the Arena, his gaze resting on Verus. "But soon, maybe. I believe our angel allies have a plan to give Purgatory back to your people."

My heart kicks into overdrive. Purgatory free? Armageddon and his cronies gone? Count me in. "What will they want me to do?" I slap my palm onto my forehead. "Of course, that's more than obvious. Fight."

"Most likely." He sighs. "But with angels, you never know for certain until it's too late."

CHAPTER FOUR

A.

I try to focus in history class, but it's no use. The human's sobs haunt my mind. I draw her scarred face in my notebook, but the lines blur. My hand keeps shaking.

Across the room, Zeke stares in my direction, his blonde eyebrows wagging suggestively. He mouths four words: "You. Me. Party. Tonight." *And this actually works on other girls?* Shifting in my chair, I angle my back toward him and keep scribbling.

Miss Thing's voice breaks through my internal haze. "Class, today we'll learn about the Scala." I drop my pen and look up.

For once, school is getting interesting.

I've only seen the Scala a handful of times. With so many souls to move, he basically specializes in mass migrations, thousands of souls at once. You have to be pretty nasty badass to get a solo transfer. I picture the mysterious old dude on his stretcher, moving souls to Heaven or Hell with a wave of his hand. Coooooooool.

"Turn to page 402 in *Purgatory Through the Ages.*"

I open my book and stare at the page. Then, I close my eyes, blink three times to clear my head, and stare again. On the sheet before me is a picture of a young man, burly and strong. An ebony beard covers much of his smiling face. His arm is wrapped about a slender woman with mismatched eyes and long blonde hair. The caption under the image reads Maxon and Esme Bane.

"This is our current Scala when he was a youth." Miss Thing smacks her cherry-red lips together. "Maxon Bane was born in 1157 on the realm of Earth in a place called England. Who can tell me what type of creature he is?"

Zeke raises his hand. "He's thrax. They're demon hunters."

"Excellent, Zeke; you'll make a fine servant one day. And how do we know he's thrax?"

"The eyes." Zeke points to the picture on the page. "One's blue and one's brown. Thrax are part human and part angel. The blue eye's the angel part; the brown's human."

"Very good." Miss Thing waves her hand dismissively. "None of you will leave Purgatory, but if you do, remember Zeke's words. Anyone with different colored eyes are thrax, and thrax hunt demons. It doesn't matter if you're a quasi or greater demon. Anyone with demon blood will be murdered by these criminals." She claps her hands. "Now turn to page 457."

I fiddle with my book until a familiar face fills the sheet before me: one with shining black skin, a blade-like nose and glowing red eyes.

"Class, can anyone tell me who this is?"

My mouth answers on its own. "Armageddon."

"That's right. Who said that?"

I half-raise my hand. "I did."

"Myla." Miss Thing's upper lip curls. "I see you've learned at least one useful fact in the Arena. Yes, that's Armageddon, the King of Hell and the father of Maxon; his mother's a thrax woman named Sara. Together, the blood of angel, demon, and human run in the veins of Maxon, turning a useless thrax into the one and only Scala." With a flick of her fingers, she snaps shut the book on her desk.

I raise my hand.

"Yes, Myla?"

"Has the Scala ever decided not to process a soul?" I picture the woman with the scarred face. Maybe the Scala would refuse to move her.

Miss Thing's huge eyes stretch even wider. "No, never. Every Scala does exactly as they're told. Always, always, always. In fact, no Scala would never dream of doing anything other than what a ghoul tells them."

The way she's overdoing it, I'm guessing the Scala could be a real pain the neck if he wanted to be. Although, considering how old the current Scala is, he probably does exactly as ordered, as long as they take care of him. My heart sinks. That's not good news for the woman at the Arena.

I stare at the picture of Maxon Bane again. I hadn't thought about it before, but if the Scala stops processing souls, Purgatory grinds to a halt. I suppose it's a good thing for the ghouls that the current Scala only cares about sleeping, eating mushy foods, and getting carried around on a stretcher.

Paulette lifts her hand, careful to flash her beloved Rolex in the process. "So, the only time a thrax and a demon got, um, together was in 1157?"

"Hardly." Miss Thing rolls her buggy eyes. "But while a Scala lives, no other being can be born with the blood of an angel, demon, and human. The Scala is literally one of a kind, which is why Armageddon rescued him in the first place." She grins, showing a smear of red lipstick on her yellowing front teeth.

Rescued or kidnapped? Miss Thing is the Mistress of Spin.

I raise my hand. "What about the Scala Heir?"

"An interesting point." She narrows her eyes. "At one time, it was believed there was both a Scala and a Scala Heir. Both mortals had the blood of an angel, demon, and human in them. Many years ago, a thrax man claimed to be the Scala Heir. He was killed, and no one else has come forward to replace him. It's been so long, many of us question if the Scala Heir ever really existed."

Miss Thing folds her arms over her chest. "But whether or not it exists, the Scala Heir is nothing." When she speaks again, her words echo strangely around the room: "Whoever controls the Scala, controls everything."

The rest of the day zooms by. I drive Betsy back home, grab a snack and dive into my new issue of *Quasi Life* magazine. I plunk onto my bed, pick up the glossy journal and start skimming the pages. One story catches my eye: *Ten Ways to Make Your Ghoul Love You.* I scan the article. *Number ten: try our new worms and jalapeno recipe.*

Ack.

Gagging, I toss the magazine onto my bedroom floor.

Mom waddles into my room, a huge cardboard box balanced in her arms. "Hello, my little Myla-la!" She plunks the container onto my dresser and bounces on the balls of her feet. "Let's get ready for the party!"

I slide off the bed and stand on my tiptoes, trying to peep into the box. "What did you pick out? I can't wait to see it."

"You're going to love it. But close your eyes…I want this to be a surprise." Her face looks so joyful I can't say no.

"Okay." I shut my eyes.

As the dress slips over my head, Mom asks the question all seniors dread: "How are your assessments going?" This is a grueling year-long process that ends with being assigned a life-long service.

"The tests haven't started yet."

"Have you thought about becoming a seamstress?" Mom gives my arm a gentle pinch. "We could work at home and be together all the time. Would be much safer than the Arena."

Stop fighting in the Arena? No freaking way! I'm about to tell her that, but the hope glistening in her brown eyes stops me cold. I can't burst her bubble yet. "Wow, that's a really great offer." I shift my weight from foot to foot. "But, you know, senior year started a few weeks ago. I've still got time."

Mom zips up the back of my dress. "Don't take too long. Graduation will be here before you know it, and Arena fights aren't enough of a service on their own."

"Uh, they aren't?" My mouth falls open. "Are you sure?"

"What do you think?" She winks. She probably researched this years ago.

My body feels cold. "Uh, let's not talk about that now."

"Fine with me. But if you don't start to advocate to be a seamstress, you could be assigned something awful like latrine duty."

She may have a point.

"Okay, Mom. I promise I'll think about it soon." I fidget in my gown, dying to open my eyes a crack. The skirt feels a little weird, but then again I don't wear dresses very often. "Can I look now?"

Mom claps her hands. "Yes!"

Glancing in my mirror, I see myself wearing an ankle-length gown with a massive hoop skirt. The entire monstrosity is covered in flounces, bows, and the color orange.

Hells bells, orange. I so want to puke, die, or both.

At that moment, the doorbell rings. "Cissy must be here." Mom clasps her hands beneath her chin. "I'll go get her. I can't wait for her to see you!"

Um, I can.

Mom walks to the front door, letting a giddy Cissy inside. There's a lot of cooing and hugging, then footsteps pad toward my bedroom. Cissy pauses in my doorway, her hand covering her bow-shaped mouth. She's wearing a slinky black dress that's floor length and sliced half-way up her thigh.

I let out a low whistle. "Cissy, you look gorgeous." All quasis are beautiful by human standards, but Cissy's dress takes it to a new level. Why couldn't Mom have called Versace, too?

"Thanks, Myla. You look…" Cissy smacks her lips, searching for the right word.

"She looks amazing, doesn't she?" Mom weaves her arm through Cissy's. "Hard to believe I wore this gown twenty years ago."

"I believe it," says Cissy quietly.

Suddenly, I'd like nothing better than for the earth to open up and swallow me whole. I kill things; I don't wear dresses.

"Just one second!" Mom rushes back to the box, pulling out a floppy orange hat with an enormous bow. "This goes with it."

I picture Captain Hook's hat, then realize Mom's hat could eat that one and still have room for dessert.

"No, thanks," say Cissy and I unison.

A knot of tension crawls up my spine; I can't wait to get this dress off. "I'm not feeling too well, Cissy." I fiddle with the zipper on my back. "You'll have to catch the party without me."

"You're fine. It's nerves." Cissy turns to my mother, blinking her tawny eyes madly. "You wouldn't mind if we made a few little alterations, would you? To bring the dress up to date a wee bit?"

"Of course. There are scissors in the box. Do you need anything else?"

Cissy smiles sweetly. "A little girl-time." She stares pointedly at the door. "Do you mind?"

"Not at all." Still beaming, Mom almost glides out of my room. Cissy closes the door firmly behind her, then grabs the scissors and goes to work. Within minutes, the flounces and bows lay on the floor, alongside the hoop. In the end, I'm wearing a very simple, very electric orange gown. I stare at my image in the mirror.

"I look like a nuclear carrot."

Cissy grabs my hand. "No, you don't, you look fine. Please let's go to the party please, please, pleeeeeeeeeeease?"

I'm going to regret this. "Okay, let's go."

Cissy and I race toward the front door, but my mother's too quick for an uneventful escape. "No, wait!" Mom holds up her hands. "I have an instamatic camera somewhere in the attic crawlspace. I want to capture this moment!"

Cissy pauses by the threshold, fluffing her blonde ringlets. "Sure." Mom runs off, the sound of footsteps echo through the house.

I glare at my best friend. "No pictures, please. Besides, we're running super-late."

"Oh, yeah," Cissy cups her hand by her mouth. "Gotta go, Momma Lewis!"

Mom's muffled voice sounds from the attic. "Are you sure you can't wait?"

I grab Cissy's hand and lunge for the front door. "Absolutely positive."

Cissy and I rush to the driveway and slide into Betsy. After Betsy coughs up a few clouds of toxic smoke, we putter along the route to the Ryder mansion, our gowns carefully folded around us. As I drive along, I watch Upper Purgatory slide by my windows.

What a bummer this place is. When I was a kid, this used to be the fanciest spot around, filled with rows of overly-large houses on overly-small plots of land. The lawns were always green and fancy black sedans lined all the driveways.

That was before the ghouls took over.

Like all conquerors, the ghouls decided they deserved the best real estate. The same houses I remember slide by my window again, only now they're filled with the undead. The lawns have been turned into open earth, the better for worm farming. Every window has been boarded up; each fancy sedan sits rusting in its driveway.

All the houses, that is, except the Ryder mansion. It slides into view, a white citadel of quasi-ness sitting atop a lush green hill. It's a little patch of the old republic that survived, lovely and alive. We park Betsy and march up to the mansion's front door. Cissy presses the bell, her face positively beaming. "We're on!"

I suppress the urge to grab her hand and run for it.

Seconds later, the door swings open to reveal Zeke, who looks extra smarmy with his slick-backed hair, black tuxedo, and red plaid vest. His eyes me slowly from head to toe before saying: "Helloooo, Elmo!"

"Ha, ha, very funny." I step inside. "And it's orange, not red."

Zeke rubs his chiseled chin. "Yes, Elmo's not the right Muppet for you. Beaker maybe? Ernie?"

Cissy steps directly in front of me. "Hi, Zeke! Wanna dance?" She hitches one leg out to show the high slit in her dress. Damn, that girl looks like a million dollars.

I cross my fingers behind my back. Please, please, please let him notice her. Just once.

Zeke's caramel eyes twinkle with a reddish glow. "I'd love to, uh…" He snaps his fingers. "It's on the tip of my tongue."

"Cissy." She steps closer to Zeke. "My name's Cissy."

"Wow. Are you new in school?"

"No, we've been in the same class since Kindergarten. You broke my nose playing dodge ball in third grade, remember?"

"Oh, yeah." Zeke nods slowly. "Sorry about that." He brushes one finger down the bridge of her nose. "You look fine now, though."

Cissy's face turns about eight shades of red. "Thanks."

I pull down my fist and whisper 'yeah!' Neither of them notice, which shows how far gone they both are. *Finally.*

"Follow me." Zeke grabs Cissy's hand and they disappear into the crowd.

I watch them go, wondering what it's like to feel all blushy for a guy. I suppose that's step one, while step two is actually kissing. Not that I know anything about either.

Ah, well. Back to the party.

I step around the ballroom floor. This must be the prettiest spot in all Purgatory. Great glass chandeliers hang from the ceiling. A line of balconies arch over the long wooden dance floor. A specially-designed stage perfectly fits the jazz band.

The floor is packed with ghouls and demons, but angels and thrax walk around too. I even spy the Oligarchy and Verus. Staring at the different faces, I smile from ear to ear. Maybe this is the angelic plan Walker was talking about. We may be nearing a new age of cooperation between angels, ghouls, thrax, quasis, and demons.

Then again, maybe not.

In one scrambling and biting mass, all the demons cluster into a corner, staring around the room with a look that says 'yum, dinner.' At the center of their group stands Armageddon, his long arms folded across his narrow chest. The human from today's match flashes through my mind's eye, and I have a mad desire to race across the room and give the King of Hell a piece of my mind. I take a deep breath and ball my hands into fists. Tonight's probably not the night to lecture Armageddon.

The guests within twenty feet of Armageddon all whimper and sulk away. That's his greater demon aura knocking into them, overwhelming them with terror. Combine that aura with my neon orange dress and heels, and tonight's *definitely* not the night to take on the King of Hell.

I force myself to look away. My gaze finds Cissy and Zeke dancing up a storm. Cissy's eyes glow with a bit of demon-red (which means half the room envies her and she knows it). Meanwhile, there are ruby sparkles in Zeke's irises too (which means I *cannot* let him drive Cissy home, and I know it).

Considering how they're dirty-dancing, I'm not driving Cissy home any time soon. I'm spending the next hour or so alone, but it's worth it to see Cissy's dream come true, such as it is. I decide to circulate through the crowd, sizing up the different faces. Which ones could tell me something about my father?

I spy an older quasi woman with oodles of silver hair and diamonds. Her long peacock tail perfectly matches her green gown. She's eating a shrimp so slowly, I know her demon power is sloth.

Taking a deep breath, I square my shoulders. You have to start somewhere.

I step up to the stranger. "Hello, I know we don't know each other, but I was wondering if you went to any diplomatic events, say, eighteen years ago?"

Bit by bit, the woman sets the shrimp in her mouth and starts to chew. I take that to mean 'yes.'

"Well, I was wondering if you knew any of the diplomats from those days. The quasi guys in particular?"

The woman swallows, then slowly turns to face me. She eyes me carefully. "Are you...Are you?" My heart beats so quickly, I think it will explode.

I grab her wrist. "Do I look like someone? Who? A diplomat?"

"Are you the floor show?" She points to my dress. "What's that Muppet's name again? Fozzie Bear?"

"No, I'm not the floor show." I bite my lips together. "Excuse me."

Clearly, it's time for a new party survival plan.

Setting aside the quest to find my father, I discover that if I stand under a balcony, the shadows hide my orange-ness. An extra bonus is that no one can see me and/or make Muppet comments. I've hoarded a pile of canned soda and sugary snacks on a nearby table. My night is full.

In fact, I'm having a sweet time when two figures step into the darkness beside me.

Squinting in the dim light, I size up the pair of strangers. The first man is older, tall and burly with long white hair past his chin. He wears a classic tuxedo that matches the one on the figure beside him. The second stranger is a boy with broad shoulders and a rigid military stance. His hair is shorter, earthy brown and loose. Since it's super quiet under the balcony, I can't help but listen in.

Okay, maybe I could help it, but I'm a little curious and a lot bored.

"I don't understand why we're here, father." It's the boy.

"More orders from the angels, son." The older man has a deep and rolling voice. "They want closer relations between the realms."

My heart thumps in my chest. Angels? Closer relationships between the realms? Maybe we really are on the edge of a new era. I smile, thinking about a ghoul-free life where I choose my own job, clothes, anything. The boy speaks, interrupting my thoughts.

"I understand. What should I do?"

"Try to socialize; meet some quasis in particular." The father's eyes glimmer in the shadows. His irises are mis-matched: one blue and one brown.

They're thrax. High-fives to Miss Thing for actually teaching something useful.

"Quasis aren't people," snaps the boy. "They're demons."

What?! My hands clench into fists. Actually, we're mostly human, thank you very much.

"Angels say they're different. Try to keep an open mind." The father points to the dance floor where Cissy shimmies up and down Zeke's thigh. "Take that girl, for example. Why don't you ask her to dance? She seems quite, uh, *friendly.*"

I roll my eyes. *What an old-guy thing to say.* Sure, Cissy's a little over the top right now, but she's been dreaming of this night since she was nine. I glance at my friend and smile. Cissy looks absolutely blissed out. Maybe a wee bit slutty as she paws Zeke's abs during the mambo, but who cares? She's eighteen; it's her job to be stupid.

The boy folds his arms over his chest. "That quasi has a dog's tail and acts like one in heat."

My blood simmers with anger. *What an* ASSHOLE-GUY *thing to say!*

The boy grips his fist behind his back. "Besides father, you know I'm no diplomat."

You think?!

"Where's my best soldier?" The older man punches his son's upper arm. "I know I can rely on you for this mission."

The boy nods briskly. "Of course."

"That's my boy." Grinning broadly, the father marches off into the crowd and starts glad-handing a pack of ghoul diplomats.

I sip the rest of my soda, glaring at the boy's silhouette. My inner demon begins to stir. I imagine wagging my finger in his face, screaming the differences between demons and quasis. Or even better, I could leap beside him and land one good kick behind his kneecaps. I'm so distracted that instead of setting my empty soda can back on the table, I drop it to the floor with a crash.

Turning on his heel, the boy steps to my side. "Are you alright, Miss?" Up close, I can see that he's my age with mismatched eyes, one wheat-brown and the other slate-gray. His face is square with a strong jaw and scooped-out cheeks. For some reason, I can't stop staring at his full mouth, wondering what it would be like to brush my lips against his. He looks mighty tasty indeed.

Wait a minute. Me thinking about kissing anybody? When does that happen?

Pull yourself together, Myla. You downed too many candy bars, that's all. Clearly, this is some kind of sugar-induced hallucination.

I take a deep breath, refocusing my sugary brain on how this dirt-bag insulted Cissy. "I'm fine." My voice comes out low and sharp. "I dropped an empty can, that's all."

His mismatched eyes lock with mine. Our stare quickly turns intense, enveloping. "You look familiar." He leans in a bit and I inhale his earthy scent, a mixture of forest pine and leather. "You don't visit the Ryder stables, by any chance?"

Oh, you mean the Ryder stables where I break in all the *freaking time* to hunt demons? Little doxy monsters go there to pester the horses; I've appointed myself stable exterminator, on the sly, of course. But there's no way can he know that, though. The question must be a weird coincidence.

I anxiously shift my weight from foot to foot. "Nope."

A ghost of a smile rounds the boy's mouth. "Ah, my error then." He bows slightly. "My name's Lincoln." He scans me from head to toe, his gaze resting on my tail. "You must be a quasi, um, 'demon.'" His voice lowers when he says the word 'demon.'

"I'm 'Myla.'" My voice lowers when I say 'Myla.' *I have a name, creep.*

"Pleasure to meet you." Lincoln rakes his hand through his mop of brown hair. "Would you..." He has the look of someone about to force himself to do something disgusting. "Would you like to dance, Myla?" He glances toward the ballroom floor, locks his gaze on Cissy and Zeke, then sneers. "It seems to be something *your kind* enjoys."

Rage boils through me. "Do you mean 'our kind' as in my friend with the dog tail?" I hitch my thumb to the dance floor, where Cissy and Zeke are mid-cha-cha. "You remember? The one in heat?"

Lincoln folds his arms across his chest. "What I said was true." His upper lip curls with disgust. "I can hardly bear to watch."

"So, you find quasis repulsive."

"What do you expect?" His mismatched eyes open wider. "You're part demon. I'm a demon hunter. Asking you to dance was a kind gesture on behalf of—"

"Kind gesture?!" I'm so itching to kick him. "I've got a gesture for you." I turn on my heel and walk away, my tail waving goodbye to him from my backside.

Marching onto the dance floor, I grab Cissy's arm. "The lust-a-thon ends. Now." At this point, I'm in a full-blown rage tsunami. My eyes glow bright red.

Cissy knows my wrath-mode when she sees it. "No problem, Myla." Frowning, she gives Zeke a quick peck on the cheek. "Later, sweetie."

As we march from the room, I hear Zeke blah-blah-blahing about getting Cissy's phone number. She gives my hand a little squeeze.

"That was the perfect exit." She almost skips to the front door.

I speak through gritted teeth: "Glad I could help."

We drive away from the Ryder mansion in silence. Cissy stares at her hands in what I call her 'guilty mode.'

As we drive home, my fingers tap the steering wheel in a nervous rhythm. I can't stop thinking about that thrax boy. It's mega-irritating. "I've a question for you, Cissy."

Cissy turns to me, her eyes large and watery. "I totally didn't mean to desert you at the party. You had every right to drag me off the dance floor. But Zeke and I were dancing and I lost track of time." She puffs out her bottom lip.

"No, it's not that."

"Really?!" Cissy sets her hand on her rib cage. "Because I totally feel bad about it."

"Don't worry, honestly. I'm happy for you, girlfriend. I've got another question for you."

"Okay, whew." Cissy leans back in the busted front seat, and props one knee onto the dashboard. "Shoot."

"Hypothetical question. Suppose there's a guy–"

Cissy holds up her pointer finger. "Is he hot?"

How I hate admitting this. "Yes."

"Okay. I like this game already. Please continue."

"So, this hottie guy is a total and complete dick. Yet you still think about kissing him and–"

"Stop right there." Cissy raises her hand shoulder height, palm forward. "The answer is kiss him, kiss him, kiss him."

"You didn't hear the question."

Cissy turns to me, her blonde ringlets jiggling. "What *is* the question?"

"Okay, you got me. What would you do in this situation?"

"As I said, kiss him."

"That's not very helpful."

Cissy glances out the window. "I thought this was just a hypothetical."

I grip the steering wheel so tightly, my knuckles could pop out of my skin. "Of course, it is." A hypothetical about that Lincoln guy.

Cissy stares out the window for another moment, then stops. "Hang on there, amiga." Her head snaps toward me, her mouth pursed. "What's this *really* about?"

"Nothing. A little girl talk on the drive home from the party." I turn to her and wink. "Zeke looked mighty handsome tonight, by the way."

Please take the bait and change the subject. Please, please, pleeeeeeease.

Cissy drums her manicured nails on the dashboard. "If you weren't mad at me for ignoring you, why drag me off in a huff?"

"I didn't huff."

"Myla, your eyes were blazing bright red."

"Okay, maybe I huffed a little bit." In a lovely bit of kindness from the universe, Cissy's house appears to my right. I pull over the car. "I'm fine, totally. I just wanted to ask a hypothetical question and say how handsome Zeke looked. That's all."

Cissy's eyes narrow. "If you say so."

I make a great show of checking my watch. "Oh, wow, look at the time. I gotta go or my Mom will freak!"

Cissy slowly exits the car. I can almost hear the rusty gears of her brain working overtime. I'm going to get a call later, you can bet on it. The moment she's clear of the curb, I rev the engine and speed home (as much as anyone can speed in Betsy). I stomp through the front door.

Hopefully, the drama for the evening is over.

CHAPTER FIVE

I chuck my keys onto the kitchen table and march straight through the living room on the way to bed. I hardly register that Mom sits front-and-center on the living room couch, a pile of ghoul robe patterns beside her.

"You're back early." She pats the empty spot beside her on the couch, but I'm in no mood for a mother-daughter bonding session.

I stop and pretend that it's really important to smooth out the folds of my neon orange dress. "It was time to go."

"Was everyone wearing hoop skirts?" Mom eyes the hem of my gown. "In five minutes, I can sew that hoop back in for you."

"No one was wearing hoop skirts, Mom."

She leans forward on the couch. "What happened, Myla-la?"

I launch into a rare sharing session with my mother. This thing with Lincoln was just too strange. I really need some advice. "Well, there was this thrax boy at the party who–"

"Thrax at the party?" All blood drains from Mom's face. "There can't be any thrax at the party." She races to a nearby table, picking up Zeke's invitation. "It says right here; the event was for ghouls and demons. Even if they were invited, thrax wouldn't be within a mile of that place."

Great. I've set off her hair-trigger for worrying. Maybe I can give her some additional information and move onto my question. "I'm telling you, they were at the party. Angels were there too."

"Angels were there too?!" Mom drops the invite, her hands visibly shaking.

This is not going well. "You *do* realize you're repeating everything I say?"

"Angels and thrax." Mom stumbles backwards until she half-falls onto the couch. "That can't be right."

"It's all good. There's some kind of alliance going on, I think. Thrax, angels, demons, and ghouls...Everybody's one big happy family." I give her a look that says 'now, can we get on to my question?'

"Those four all in the same room." Mom slowly shakes her head from side to side. "Did they fight? Did any of them touch you? Hurt you?"

"The thrax boy asked me to dance and–"

Whipping up from the couch, Mom races over. Her hands cup either side of my face. "Do you feel alright?" She stares into my eyes like my head will explode.

"Enough, Mom." I step back, breaking contact with her. Anger and disappointment churn in my belly. I have so had it with her over-protectiveness about nothing. "Look, I get that I'm all you have. I get that you're worried about me. But I'd appreciate some female advice on what happened with this boy and you're not listening."

"This boy?" Her chocolate eyes narrow. "Or, this thrax?"

Unholy moley.

"Forget it, Mom." I take a few steps toward the front door, pause, and turn back. "You know, maybe I'd rather have latrine duty if it means I can be on my own. Because this–" I motion back and forth between us "–isn't working."

Mom's eyes brim with tears. "Be safe, Myla. That's all I ask."

"I know, Mom. That's the problem." I storm outside, slamming the front door behind me. Tracking my orange gown through the mud, I pace around our backyard. Why does Mom always have to freak out about every little thing? Sighing, I slump against the back outer wall and stare up at the gray sky. For some reason, it really bothers me tonight that we never see the moon in Purgatory.

Voices echo in from the opened window above my head. It's Walker and Mom.

"Camilla, we need to talk." I crouch lower.

"Not if Myla's here." I hear rustling noises as she checks the house. "Okay, we're fine. What's going on?"

"You can't hide her forever. Verus knows; she saw it in a vision ages ago. We need to figure out how to introduce Myla to her true heritage."

I pop my hands over my mouth. *True heritage?* I may actually get some useful intel about who I am tonight. My heart kicks in my chest; excitement pours through me. Yes, yes, YES!

Mom's voice quivers as she speaks. "It's not the angels I'm worried about, it's the ghouls. You know them. If they knew who her father really was, they'd try to own her."

Whoa, there. *The ghouls would own me because of my father.* My stomach turns sour. That must mean my dad's a ghoul. A nasty, rule-loving, worm-eating loser of a ghoul. I grip my elbows. That's not something I'd ever considered before.

"We can't change how ghouls react to what they see as theirs," says Walker. "But we *can* control how the truth comes out."

Hold the phone. 'We' can control? As in Mom and Walker? I knew Mom was always holding out on me, but *Walker knows?* My jaw falls open, my fists plant onto my hips. Okay, he hinted around that he had *some* intel during my last match, but the bloodless bastard knows exactly who I am and he's never given me a clue.

Mom sucks in a gasp of air. I listen so intently, my head hurts. "What do you mean? Do you think Verus will tell Myla on her own?"

"Yes, I do."

So, Verus knows too? Is there *anyone* in Purgatory who doesn't know who I really am? I am so cornering her at my next match, right after I tackle Walker. I want me some answers.

Mom gasps. "I'll reach out to Verus right away. In the meantime, please keep Myla close to her own people: quasis and ghouls."

I slump so low against the house, my bum almost hits the mud. Ghouls are my people? Blech.

"Verus is at the Ryder party right now. Perhaps we can seek her out together?"

"Yes, Walker. I'd like that very much only—"

"Myla can take care of herself for a bit. It won't take long."

Mom sighs. "Alright then." I hear the hiss of a portal being opened, followed by silence.

Leaping to my feet, I pace the muddy backyard for a while, grumbling every expletive I can think of. It's a good twenty minutes of letting off swear words and steam. Freaking Mom! Lying bastard Walker! Not to mention that sneaky Verus and my mystery deadbeat-ghoul-Dad. My hands curl into fists at my side. Wearing my Fozzie Bear dress, yelling at that pompous thrax, finding out my father's a lousy ghoul and discovering how everyone around me are a bunch of lying liars…I so need to kill something right now.

That's when I hear the voice. *Her* voice.

"Hello, Myla."

Verus is standing behind me right now. Hells freaking bells. Bit by bit, I swing about to see her hovering above our muddy lawn, a soft glow surrounding her long linen robes and white wings.

I say the first thing that comes into my head. "Hey. I'm Myla."

Her almond-shaped eyes flare blue. "I know who you are. I've wanted to talk to you for some time. Your mother and I just agreed that I would."

She's standing right there. Verus. Holding all the answers I seek. Every nerve ending in my body goes on alert. *This is it.* "You have to tell me." My mouth opens, searching for the words.

She raises her arm. "No, *you* have to sleep." She gently taps the center of my forehead with her pointer finger. Instantly, the word turns to darkness.

.A.

After that, I dream of white fire.

In my vision, I stand in the Gray Sea of Purgatory, a stretch of charcoal-colored desert that ends in a wall of black stone. Silvery sand dunes ripple and swell around me. Overhead, the sky rolls with storm clouds; silent cracks of yellow lightning strike the horizon. A bitter wind whips through my long brown hair, stinging my cheeks. The scent of sulphur sears my lungs.

Without knowing why, I fall onto my knees and set my palms against the gray sand. A line of white fire erupts on the grains between my hands and then spreads into a giant circle. I stand again, watching the flames crackle by my toes. There is warmth from the fire, but no pain.

Inside the circle of fire, one spot in the sand starts to bubble and churn. A figure rises from that point: a tall woman with great white wings arched behind her shoulders. Her eyes are an exotic almond shape; her hair falls straight and black past her shoulders. All the breath leaves my body.

It's Verus.

She rises until she hovers above the sands. The wind whips her long white robes and straight black hair. Her blue eyes glow softly, two pale points of turquoise in a gray desert landscape. Her eyes glow brighter, turning into two sharp points of searing blue light. I wince, but can't turn away. I want to run, but my body won't budge.

Verus slowly raises her arms, her wings expanding with the movement. The sound of her voice sets the Gray Sea rumbling.

"It is time you knew the identity of your father. I will send you visions of the past."

I want to say 'yes' or 'thank you,' but the words won't come. I guess my agreement to this plan isn't necessary.

Suddenly, the circle of flame swells, transforming into a wall of white fire that towers over my head. Waves of heat sear my cheeks; my body drips with sweat. I want to run, move, duck, but all I can do is stand perfectly still. The fire crackles brighter; the flames grow larger.

Within seconds, fire surrounds my entire body. That last thing I remember is being consumed by white flame as the world dissolves into darkness.

I open my eyes, waking up not in the backyard but in my own bed. It's early morning. My orange gown is gone and I wear standard-issue sweats and a tee. I re-fluff my pillow under my head and stare out of my window, trying to process everything that happened. The sky is calm and gray, unlike the rolling thunderheads in my dream. Verus's words echo through my brain: 'It is time you knew the identity of your father. I will send you visions of the past.'

My tail grips the edge of my threadbare covers. My body burns with righteous wrath. *Enough is enough; I want me some answers now.* Whipping off the covers, I race into the kitchen.

I find Mom at the kitchen table, hand-sewing the hem of a robe. She doesn't look up as I enter. "Good morning, my little Myla-la. How'd you sleep?"

I freeze in place. Chilly realization washes over me, cooling my wrath. These random, annoying morning interrogations may not be so random and annoying. "That question." I set my hands against my rib cage, feeling the cool prickle of gooseflesh under my fingertips. "Is that your way of asking me if an angel has visited me in my dreams?"

Mom looks up from her sewing, her brown eyes glistening with tears. "Yes." Her voice cracks. "Did one visit you last night?" Desperation hangs about her like a dark cloud. "Please, say yes."

At her words, all my frustration and anger melts away. *This may be as hard for her as it is for me.* "Yeah." I plunk down into the chair across from her.

Mom pulls her thread taut. "Was it Verus?"

"Yes."

"I spoke to her last night. We knew each other before the war."

"When you were doing what exactly?" Forcing a smile, I motion my hand in small circles, encouraging her to finish the thought.

Mom sighs. "I know you're frustrated that I don't discuss my past." She stares at the fabric in her hands for a time, then sets it onto her lap. "After we argued last night, I went to speak with Verus. She's seen you in the Arena and wants to help. She has a gift for seeing both the past and future. We agreed that she'll send you dreams of what happened to me."

I lean back in my chair. "The way she described it in my dreams, the whole thing seemed a little more dramatic than that."

"It's called dreamscaping. A handful of angels and demons have the power to show you visions of the past or future while you sleep. Other times they can talk to you, communicate with you while you dream. The morning after a dreamscape from Verus, you can come and ask me questions." She lets out a ragged breath. "That's the best I can do."

I work hard to keep my voice low and calm. I'm so close to the answers I need, why all the drama? "Please, Mom. Why not just tell me?"

"Perhaps after Verus shows you some things, you'll discover the answer to that question on your own." Her lower jaw quivers.

I liked it better when she fought me on this. A guilty weight settles onto my shoulders. Whatever happened to Mom during the war, it must have been pretty awful. I force another smile. "Look, the dream thing is fine. Thanks for reaching out to Verus." I reach across the table, wrap her hand in mine. "When will she send me the dreamscapes?"

"I don't know. Just promise you'll find me right after they happen."

"Sure, I will."

The phone starts to ring. And ring. And ring. Purgatory only gets washed up, ancient technology. In this case, our phone is a heavy brick of a base adorned with a rotary dial and topped by a handset so large, you could use it as a weapon. I watch the contraption vibrate with each deafening ring and grimace. Cissy must have woken up.

Mom dries her eyes with her fingertips. "Are you going to answer that?"

My upper lip curls. "I'd rather not. I have a pretty good idea who it is." The answering machine kicks on. This thing is a contraption as large as shoebox that records our missed calls. I'm not sure humans even use crap like this anymore. I never see answering machines on the Human Channel unless I'm catching reruns of *Golden Girls* or *Murder, She Wrote*.

Beep. The answering machine turns on with a loud click. "Hey Myla, it's Cissy. I want to talk about the party! Wasn't it just so magical? Did you see Zeke and me dancing? Call me. We so have to talk." *Beep.*

The edge of Mom's mouth curls with a grin. "Zeke took an interest at last, eh?"

"Oooooh yeah." I set my chin on my palm. "I didn't realize you knew Cissy had a thing for Zeke."

"Honey, everybody knows Cissy has a thing for Zeke."

The phone rings again.

Beep. "Myla, it's Cissy. Sorry to call again so soon. I know this is my third message–"

Mom picks up her sewing, her smile growing a bit larger. "Actually, Myla, it's her fifth. She left three last night while you were sleeping."

I roll my eyes. Great.

Cissy's voice keeps blaring through the answering machine. "I really-really-really need to talk to you about the party. I have so many questions for you. Love you, sweetie!" *Beep.*

I drum my fingers on the tabletop. "Cissy's a little boy crazy and I can't handle her right now. Mind if I unplug the machine for the rest of the weekend?"

Mom full-on grins. "Nope."

The weekend decays into a blur of bad reruns from human television, good sugar cereals, and dreading seeing Cissy at school. Monday morning arrives way too soon. Before I know it, I'm slogging through the front doors at Purgatory High. I barely set foot inside the main hallway when Cissy skip-walks toward me, a huge smile on her face.

Hells Bells. When you're miserable, there's nothing worse than someone else's happiness.

"Gooooooood morning, Myla!" Her little golden curls bounce by her shoulders. *Even her hair looks chipper.*

"Hey, Cissy."

"Did you get my messages? I tried to get in touch a million times. Then your answering machine was busted or something."

I press my palms into my eyes. "Mom and I had a fight and–" What do I say here? I fought with a thrax, my dad might be a ghoul, and an oracle angel is sending me visions of Mom's past? I sigh. "I've been a little down, that's all."

Frowning, Cissy places her hand on my shoulder. "Oh, that's too bad." I can almost hear her counting to three under her breath, giving my misery a bit of air-time before we move onto the marquee subject. "Okay, then! Let's talk about Zeke."

I debate about feigning illness—a sudden bout of the plague might get me out of this morning's Zeke love fest—but then I remember Cissy's been obsessing about this guy for at least a decade. Let her have her moment. I plaster on a grin. "Can't wait to hear all about it."

I half-listen to her love-babble until she starts demonstrating Zeke's best dance moves down the hallway. The girls stare with a sneer, the guys with open mouths. I'm seriously debating what would happen if I accidentally tripped her when I get the bright idea to check my watch.

"Gosh Cissy, I have to run. Can't be late for History!" Wow, I never thought I'd say *that* out loud.

For once, I arrive early to History, slipping into my favorite back row seat. All the students mill about, chit-chatting about the weekend. Miss Thing puts on lipstick using a small compact. Amazing how she can use a mirror and still not notice the huge red smear across her front teeth.

Miss Thing claps her hands twice. "Everyone, pay attention."

I sit straight in my chair, ready to work. I'm feeling mighty proud of my Cissy management strategy when I realize my massive error: class is starting and Zeke's just now walking through the door. I swing my long hair in front of my face, hoping that will hide my identity (not my best plan.) He heads straight for me anyway.

I almost face-palm myself. What's the first rule of avoiding someone at school? Arrive late to class so you pick the seat farthest away from them.

Miss Thing paces the front of the room, her red stilettos click-clacking with each step. "Class, turn to 542 of *Purgatory Through the Ages.*"

I whip out my book as Zeke slides into the empty seat next to mine.

"Morning, Myla."

Flipping through pages, I pretend not to hear him. Maybe he'll get the message and pay attention to the lecture.

"I said, *good morning, Myla.*"

No such luck. I grind my teeth and low out a low 'grrr.' I'd expected the love-fest from Cissy, but I truly counted on never speaking to Zeke again. Now, I'm trapped next to him in history class and Mister Smarmy wants to talk. This sucks, big time.

Be nice to him for Cissy, Myla. Don't ruin it for her.

I let out one last 'grr' and whisper "Hey, Zeke."

Miss Thing stops pacing. Her black eyes carefully scan the room. "Class, we're about to start a very important lesson. This month marks the twentieth anniversary of Armageddon's liberation of Purgatory. To celebrate, we'll learn all about how clever and merciful your new overlords are. Who wants to begin the reading?" No one raises a hand. "Paulette, why don't you start us off? Page 542."

Paulette carefully repositions her Hermes scarf on one shoulder, then begins to read: "Armageddon's War, Episode One,

Quasis Mismanage Purgatory. For thousands of years, quasi-demons mismanaged—"

As Paulette keeps reading, Zeke whispers across the aisle. "Myla, I know why you were so angry at the party."

My throat tightens. Zeke knows Lincoln?

"You do?" Picking up my pen, I start doodling on my notebook. "It's one thing to be treated that way by a ghoul, but not... You know."

Zeke nods. "I understand."

Setting down my pen, I take a good look at Zeke. Of all the people in my life, I never expected to confide in him, let alone during history class. But here he is, caramel eyes wide with understanding.

I fidget in my seat. "I guess it caught me off guard." Taking a deep breath, I feel my limbs loosen.

"It could happen to anyone." Zeke folds his hands neatly on his desk. "Why did you keep it a secret?"

Why didn't I tell anyone I was insulted by a thrax? "I guess it was embarrassing."

Zeke sighs. "You should have confessed your major crush on me years ago. I would've been cool about it."

My mouth falls open. "My major crush on who?"

"Come on, Myla. You've been crushing on me for ages and now everyone knows it. A bunch of kids saw you lose it when Cis and I were dancing."

Anger zooms through my body. I scan the room; half the class stares at me and Zeke, their eyes filled with pity. Unholy Moley. Zeke's version of Friday night is all over school. Rage smolders up my spine.

"You're wrong, Zeke." My eyes glow red.

"Don't go all demon-iris on me. It's not a bad thing. I was starting to wonder if you were like those single cell thingies we learned about in Biology. You know, the ones that don't need a mate? What are they called again?"

My hands clench into fists. "Amoebas?"

"I was going to say paramecium."

My eyes flare brighter. "Well, now you don't have to say that. Ever. Again."

Leaning across the aisle, Zeke speaks in a low voice: "All I want to know is this: are you okay with Cissy and I dating? I mean, can you actually handle seeing all this–" he gestures across his chest "–with someone else?"

It takes all my strength not to howl and rip the room apart. Three-fourths of the class stares at us now. The scene perfectly matches what Zeke told them: I had a massive obsession with him, not the other way around. I grip the edges of my desk so tightly, I think my knuckles will pop.

Zeke eyes me carefully. "Well?"

"I was never interested in you, Captain Ego."

"That's not what I asked you, Myla." He makes tut-tut noise in his throat, and I have to stifle the urge to punch him. "Look, Cissy and I talked about this over the weekend." He takes a deep breath. "Unless you say you're okay with us, she won't see me anymore." The color drains from his face.

I stare at him out of my right eye. Guys like him don't change overnight. "Why isn't Cissy asking me this?"

"She will." He scrapes at the desktop with his thumbnail. "I didn't want to take a chance, so I brought it up with you first." His voice goes low. "Actually, I promised her I wouldn't bring it up at all."

"So, you lied to my best friend." My inner rage monster lets out a protective roar. "Let's set aside my so-called 'obsession' with you for a moment." I make little quotation marks with my fingers when I say 'obsession.' "You've been nothing but a mindless lust monkey for years. Why should I agree to let you near someone as sweet as Cissy?"

Zeke lets out a long sigh. "My family has power, money." He leans back in his chair, rubbing his neck with his hand. "It makes me a target."

My upper lip curls. Screw him and his fake problems. "Boo hoo."

Zeke chuckles, but there isn't any humor in his laugh. "And *that's* what I'm talking about." He shakes his head from side to side. "Cissy doesn't see me as this privileged dickhead." His shoulders slump. For the first time, I see him as a different person: a warrior, but not someone who battles with rage, like me. More like someone who fights with despair.

"You have to understand, Cissy sees someone else in me." His caramel eyes find mine, and for the first time there's something and real behind them. "I want to be that guy for her, Myla." His jaw sets into a firm line. "Please give us a chance, that's all I ask."

My rage cools. I never thought of Zeke as acting the playboy to hide something else. But all those overly-expensive gifts and one-time hook-ups? The pattern's kinda obvious, come to think of it.

Closing my eyes, I picture the first time I talked to Cissy. It was in first grade, and I was trying to avoid trouble on the playground. It didn't work. Billy Summers was giving me crap for my 'weird tail' for the millionth time. I snapped, flattened him, and then everyone—teachers and kids alike—looked at me like a criminal-slash-freak. That's when Cissy walked up to me and took my hand. She saw something different in me, too. My heart warms at the memory.

I inhale a slow breath. "I'll give you a chance, Zeke. But so help me, if you hurt her…" My eyes flare red. "I'll tear you apart with my bare hands."

Zeke's mouth winds into a relieved smile. "Thank you." He slumps back in his chair, his blonde eyebrows arching. Within seconds, his Mister Smarmy act returns with a vengeance. "That's big of you, kitten." He shoots me with his pointer finger gun. "Really big."

You have no idea.

CHAPTER SIX

A

I stare at my lunch tray: some kind of mystery pasta (green mac and cheese, maybe?) and a diet coke. Man, do I wish I hadn't forgotten to shove some Demon bars in my backpack today. Ah, Demon bars. Eight ounces of candy disguised as granola-based nutrition. Yum. Meanwhile, the school cafeteria's idea of food is nothing less than terrifying.

Cissy slips into the empty chair across from me. Like always, it's just the two of us at our favorite corner table. Her tawny eyes sparkle. "We need to talk."

The room turns strangely quiet. I scan the nearby faces, noting how everyone's actively avoiding looking in my direction. Dread and bile twist my stomach. My conversation with Cissy is today's lunchtime theater, and no one wants to miss a word.

I poke at the greenish pasta with my fork. "Sure."

"I wanted to talk about it over the weekend, but you didn't pick up your phone." Cissy sighs. "We were all a little surprised about the party."

"We?" My back teeth lock with rage.

"You know Zeke, his friends, everyone at school who was at the party." Cissy sips her can of diet soda. Then, she pauses. "It's nothing to be embarrassed about."

"I'm not embarrassed." I force myself to drop my fork; I think I dug a hole through the plastic plate.

"Come on, Myla. I can see you're still upset." Cissy reaches across the table, wrapping her hand around my own. "Listen to me. Say the word and it's over with Zeke. I mean it." Tears bead in her tawny eyes; my anger slowly melts. "Your friendship means so much to me."

Cissy's been my best friend since first grade, and a true one. She taught me how to twist my hair into an envy-worthy braid; I showed her how to trip people with her tail. How could I not be happy for her? I open my mouth, trying to speak through the knot of emotion in my throat. I let out a few garbled words that sound like "Ree roo."

Cissy frowns. "Um, what was that?"

I clear my throat. "Me too. Your friendship means a lot. I'm happy for you and Zeke." Leaning back in my chair, I drum my fingers on the tabletop. "Look, there was another reason I lost it at the party."

Cissy gives my hand a pat. "Sure there was. That's why you asked me your hypothetical question on the car ride home."

"What hypothetical?"

"You know. About wanting to kiss *someone?*" She rolls her eyes.

I inwardly groan. She thought that conversation was about Zeke, not Lincoln. Is there really any point to telling her the truth? I'm not going to get honest advice anyway.

Zeke chooses that moment to sashay up to table. "Hello, lovelies. Are we ready to go?"

Cissy holds up her pointer finger. "Not yet. Myla wants to tell me something."

My gaze shifts between Cissy and her new beau. There is zero point in discussing Lincoln right now. They aren't going to believe it, and I'll never see the creep again anyway. "No, I'm good."

"Are you sure there isn't anything else?" Cissy taps her chin. "Your Mom, maybe?"

Damn, she's good. "What makes you say that?"

"I know my Myla-la."

Hmm. Maybe I should spill my guts about Verus, the dreamscapes, and how Dad's a ghoul. *Hey Cissy, you know how I'm a part-Furor, freaky-tailed, wrath-filled Arena fighter? Now we can add part-ghoul to the list, with an oracle Angel Queen stalker.*

Ah, no. "There's some stuff going on, but I'm just not ready to talk about it yet."

Cissy frowns. "Okay. Whenever you're ready."

Zeke rubs his hands together. "Great, that's all settled." He hitches his thumb over his shoulder. "Want to meet the guys?"

I just about fall out of my chair. Zeke wants to take Cissy to meet his friends? He never takes anyone to meet his boys, at least not during daylight. Zeke hangs with the most notorious hotties in school and everyone knows there's an invisible 'no girls allowed' sign over their lunch table. The fact that he's inviting her to visit is nothing less than monumental.

"We're ready." Cissy grips my arm like she'll rip it out of the socket. "Like I told you, Myla wants to go too."

"I do?" Wow, I have *zero* desire to expose myself to Zeke and his lust-bunny brigade. Plus, I'm not one of those 'I can't eat by myself' types. I can live without Cissy at lunch for one day. "Are you *sure* you want me to go?" Translation: can I stay here, please?

Cissy hauls me to my feet. "Yes, I'm absolutely, positively sure."

My upper lip curls. Clearly, I hadn't thought this whole 'Cissy and Zeke' thing through. Their dating changes me from 'the star of the Cissy show' to a sideline actress who gets hauled around to fill out the stage. My heart fills with a combination of severe depression and a sudden desire to kick Zeke's ass.

This. Sucks.

Cissy shoots me a pleading glance. "Come on, sweetie?" I stare into her tawny, innocent eyes and feel my resistance melt away.

I straighten my shoulders. "Of course, let's go."

"You're the best." Cissy loops her arm around mine. Together, we walk across the lunchroom to a table filled with very hand-some guys who have names like Chip, Tripp, and Bif. All of them have smirky smiles, muscle-bound chests, and no need for demon lust in order to attract the opposite sex. Yet, they can't seem to get a word out without working their *thang*. The conversation's boring stuff, like school and the weather, but these guys say every word with a sultry voice while their eyes flare red. Every other girl within a twenty-foot radius peeps at them and blushes.

Except me.

I shake my head. Maybe I just inherited the wrath side of the Furor 'lust and wrath' combo. Another thought slams into me, this one far, far worse. Since I'm part ghoul, I might only be attracted to *ghoul* guys. That realization is depressing, repulsive, and, unfortunately, all too possible.

Eew, eew, eew.

.A.

"Myla, you've been called to serve."

Yawning, I open my eyes. Two weeks have passed since I last fought in the Arena. Since that day, Cissy and Zeke have become the poster children for public displays of affection, Mom's stepped up her morning interrogations, and I haven't gotten a single new dreamscape from Verus. Life has certainly taken a nosedive.

Man, do I ever need to kill something.

Walker stands at the foot of my bed. I roll over, stretch, and peep at my Darth Vader alarm clock. 5 AM on the nose.

"Hey, Walker." I sit up straight. "How pumped am I that you're here?"

Walker's mouth winds into a grin. "Very pumped, obviously."

"I've been itching for a match for weeks." I throw back the cov-ers and hop to my feet. "Wait. You don't think this'll be another match like the last one, do you? If I see another good human sac-rifice herself to Hell, I swear I won't be able to stop myself from doing something."

"I've been assured you have a suitably awful opponent today."

"Sweet!" I pause, folding my arms over my chest. "Wait a second. I have a bone to pick with you."

"A bone? Oh my." He winks.

"Stop being cute and sarcastic." I waggle my finger in his face. "I have it on good authority that you know exactly who I am. You've been holding out on me, Walker."

"The night of the Ryder party." He tilts his head to one side. "You were listening under the window, weren't you?"

"Damn straight I was." My inner demon starts to stir. Anger pools in my blood. "Now, spill your guts. Exactly what do you know about who I am?"

"I know you're like a sister to me, and I'd never do anything to hurt you." He sighs. "If I don't tell you things, it's because I can't."

I fold my arms across my chest. "I've heard that one before." I stare into his liquid-black eyes and, damn, he does look like he wants to tell me everything. My anger quiets. I really do think he'd spill his guts if he could.

Crap. It would be so much easier if I could just yell at him for a while.

"I do have *some* news I can share with you today." He points to a large box by his feet. "This is for you, from Verus. She's taken quite an interest in your welfare."

I crouch to the floor and tear open the box; smooth black fabric shines inside. "A real combat suit!" I turn the garment over in my hands, it's like a unitard made of flexible steel that's topped with a mesh hood. "This thing is amazing."

Walker rocks on his heels, grinning ear to ear. "Do you want to try it on?"

I grip the suit to my chest. "Are you kidding?" I leap to my feet. "You didn't tell Mom about this thing, right?"

"Nope."

"Then don't say a word. I want to surprise her."

"As you wish."

I rush into the bathroom and slip on my new garment of awesomeness. The mesh hood is especially badass. My heart thumps happily in my chest as I tiptoe down the hallway and peep around the doorway to the kitchen. Mom's back is to me as she rattles around the cabinets. Walker sips java at the table.

Perfect. Neither of them sees me.

Taking a deep breath, I pause outside the kitchen doorway, my back flattened to the wall for optimum stealthy-ness.

"Hey, Mom. Don't move, okay?"

Mom's voice sounds from inside the kitchen. "Why, what's wrong?"

"Nothing, I swear. Can you close your eyes?"

"Sure, honey."

I creep to her side. "You can look now." Her chocolate eyes pop open. "Ta-daaaaa!" I whip the off the mesh hood for extra drama.

Mom's hand leaps to her mouth. "My word!"

"Isn't it awesome?" I twirl around. "It's a gift from the angels." I karate kick the air to demonstrate the suit in action. A bubble of new-garment happiness surrounds me.

Stepping to my side, Mom runs her hands over the fabric on my arm. "This isn't Kevlar, it's something else. Maybe–"

Walker finishes her thought. "Dragon scales."

"Hells bells, what do they think you'll be doing?" A muscle twitches along her jaw. "Is it safe?"

My happy-bubble bursts with a vengeance. Oh no, we're back to the 'what's safe for Myla' conversation. I stop mid-karate kick. "It's totally safe-rrrr, Mom. This suit is the bomb."

Mom rubs her neck with one hand. "Don't you worry *why* they're giving you this thing?"

"No, I don't." Anger lathers up my throat, turning my voice harsh. "I'm sure they have their sneaky reasons, and honestly, I don't care." I step up to her, wrapping my hands around hers. Her fingers tremble beneath mine. "Whatever it is, I can handle it." My anger tightens into desperation. "I need you to have a little faith in me. *Please.*"

Mom sucks in a few deep breaths. "Have a good match, Myla." I can tell it's taking everything she has not to lose it.

I let out a long breath. Not-losing-it is as good a start as any. The knot of emotion in my throat loosens ever so slightly.

"Thanks, Mom." We share an awkward smile. After that, I release her hands and step over to Walker. "Ready?"

His button-eyes twinkle. "Always. You?"

"Battling an evil soul?" My inner demon roars to life inside my belly. Excitement zings through my nervous system. "Bring it on." Reaching out, I wrap my hand around his.

Together, he and I disappear from the kitchen, tumble through empty space, and emerge on the Arena floor.

A

I blink my eyes, adjusting to the stadium's brighter light and my now-woozy stomach. I so hate portal travel. Around me, there stands Walker, Sharkie, and XP-22. A new face skulks nearby as well: a Crini demon, which is basically a seven-foot tall monster octopus. I shrug; I've killed my share of Crini in my time. This one has stumpy tentacles; Cissy could even take it out pretty easily.

Sheila must be out sick.

As the angels and demons enter the Arena, I practice lunges, spins, and kicks in my new suit. The rest of the world melts away. Pulling down the hood, I leap in front of XP-22 and growl. He almost jumps out of his robes. It's beyond awesome.

Sharkie thumps his staff, snapping me out of my garment love-fest. I glance around the Arena; all the angels and demons are in their seats and ready to go.

Our emcee raises his staff. "To begin the match, we ask for a few words from our fearless leader Armageddon—"

Verus rises to her feet. "I shall begin by saying a few words." She turns to the King of Hell. "Have you found the Scala Heir yet, Armageddon?"

Armageddon's upper lip twists into a sneer. "No."

Verus's wings stretch wide. "I see. Such inefficiency in government. We need to—"

Armageddon leaps to his feet, his eyes blazing red. "WE WILL FIND THIS FOOL, I PROMISE YOU!" Bits of spittle fly from his mouth as he speaks. His three-knuckled fingers ball into fists.

Taking a deep breath, he resettles into his chair, eyes still blazing red. He dismissively waves one hand. "Let the games begin."

Smiling, Verus retakes her seat as well.

Long moments of silence, heavy as stones, fall about the Arena. *What in Hell was that all about?* Armageddon almost lost his marbles. Adrenaline pumps through my veins by the gallon; my tail arcs by my shoulder. Something is wrong here, very wrong. These two are in the middle of some kind of power play, and everyone in this Arena is another piece on their game board. A shiver of fear rattles my spine.

Sharkie thunks his staff on the Arena floor, interrupting my thoughts. The emcee's voice echoes through the Arena. "I call forth the soul."

A spirit appears beside Sharkie. This time, the ghost is a powerhouse of a man with a barrel chest over stout arms and legs. Skull tattoos cover his body. I let out a sigh of relief. Finally, an opponent worth the effort.

Sharkie turns to the human soul. "Deacon Lee, have you chosen trial by combat?"

The spirit's misty eyes scan the Arena. "Yes."

"You have three opponents to choose from. First—"

"I choose the girl."

Huh. I've been in matches since I was twelve, and the souls always need to have it explained to them who they can choose and why. Sometimes, twice. It's totally sketchy this guy *not only* knows the rules of the game, but *who* he wants to play with. On instinct, I scan Verus and Armageddon. The lead angel's face is unreadable, but the King of Hell? He looks mighty pleased with himself.

A fissure of unease opens inside me. This is so not good.

Tilting his skeletal head to one side, Sharkie's eyes glow bright red in their sockets. "So be it." He waves to the exit archways. "All others, depart."

The Crini demon is first to slink away, its eight puny legs creeping in an odd rhythm. Walker and XP-22 follow closely behind.

Deacon crosses his heavy arms. "And I want a weapon."

My jaw just about drops off my face. Nobody gets a weapon. Not me, not the evil souls. Never. The sketchy quotient of this match just went through the roof.

Sharkie sniffs from his nose-holes. "No."

Deacon turns to the Arena audience. "This girl is clearly part demon. I'm a man. Don't I deserve the means to defend myself?" The demons screech and howl with delight; the angels sit in anxious silence.

Sharkie slams his staff onto the ground. "The rules of trial by combat are not open to negotiation. The soul may choose their opponent but no weapons. This was decreed by the Spectral Treaty of–"

A slick voice echoes through the arena, silencing Sharkie. "I like him. The man's got sass." It's Armageddon. The demon raises his black hand, snapping his fingers. "Here's your weapon, friend." A long coiled whip appears before Deacon's feet.

Unholy Hell.

I glance at Verus on her white throne; her blue eyes gleam. She quickly rises to her feet. "What say you, SKE-12? Is this how the match should proceed?"

Everyone holds their breath as Sharkie considers his reply. A droplet of black sweat trickles down his gray cheek. There's more at stake here than a weapon, but I can't put my finger on it. My fingers twitch anxiously at my sides.

Sharkie's knobby Adam's apple flicks up and down as he swallows. "The ghouls shall allow a single weapon for this fight only."

Verus quirks her eyebrows. "Such a surprise." Her glance flicks to me with a look that says 'this turn of events is anything but a shock'. I feel like that's meant to comfort me somehow, but it doesn't.

My mind whirls through everything that happened this morning: Deacon choosing me so quickly, Armageddon conjuring a weapon for him, and Verus giving me a fighting suit. It all adds up to one fact.

Verus wasn't the only one who noticed when I killed the Choker.

Clearly, Armageddon's taken an interest in me as well. In his mind, I must be the only thing standing between him and a purely evil soul in Heaven. I pull my suit's protective mask over my face, feeling new waves of adrenaline course through me. Of course, this was no surprise to Verus; she's an Oracle. I grit my teeth in frustration. *Would have been nice to get more of a heads-up than a new suit, lady.*

Sharkie slams his staff on the ground. "Let the match begin!" Deacon turns from misty ghost into solid human. He picks up the whip, shaking out its length before him. My breath catches. Fighting hand-to-hand? No problem. Battling an armed opponent? I am so fucked. For the first time since I was twelve, the thought flashes through my mind that I might actually die here. Terror zings through my nervous system.

Deacon flicks his wrist; the coil unfurls. Red hellfire erupts along the weapon's length. The human's face twists into an evil grin. Fast as a heartbeat, my opponent brings his arm up, snapping the whip down with a loud CRACK.

The next thing I know, I'm choking to death, a fiery whip wrapped about my neck. Terror courses through my nervous system, causing my inner demon to cower with fright.

Pulling up my tail, I try slicing the cord around my throat, but it's no use. I have precious seconds of consciousness left. Turning to my enemy, I jump into the air, crouching my boots beneath me. I slam my feet into Deacon's chest. My body jolts backwards as my heels connect with his ribs. Deacon stumbles, fumbling with the handle of his whip. I land beside him, trying to keep the cord as slack as possible.

This is my chance. Grab that whip before he regains control of it.

The world drips by in slow motion as the whip wobbles in Deacon's hands. Lunging, I try grabbing the weapon from him, but at the last possible millisecond, his fingers grip it firmly again.

Oh, no. I watch helplessly as my last chance to steal away the whip disappears. My lungs burn for air, turning my body numb with fear. Frozen with terror? Not the way to win a battle.

Deacon slams his arm down once more, bringing the whip along with it. The fiery cord around my neck pulls even tighter; my lungs scream for oxygen. At least, my new suit protects my skin from burning. Small comfort amid a huge panic.

The roar of the demon crowd rattles through my head. Somewhere in the back of my mind, I'm aware of Armageddon leaning forward in his dark throne, watching the match with glee, his eyes burning bright red. A horrible thought flashes through my mind: If I die here today, some demon like him could end up consuming my soul. The thought turns my muscles slack with shock.

Deacon runs into me full throttle, ramming his shoulder into my belly. He drags me along a few paces; my body slams against the Arena wall. I'm dimly aware of demons howling ever louder with pleasure. Pinned in place, I heave up my legs for another kick, but this time, my feet miss the mark. My limbs feel oddly heavy, my mind strangely calm as I realize an important fact:

Deacon just made the strategic error of the century.

My inner demon roars to life, my limbs flail with rage. As I writhe under the human's grip, Deacon presses his face closer to mine. My vision turns fuzzy, the tattoos on his skin blur. Deacon's knee makes contact with my stomach as he grunts: "You're not the only one with a kick."

I smile under the layers of my mask. With my last ounce of energy, I move in for the kill. Raising my tail shoulder-high, I stab it straight through my attacker's heart.

And you're not the only one with a weapon.

Deacon's face falls slack. His body slumps to the floor, lifeless. Lurching forward, I unwind his whip from my throat, then yank my tail from his chest. Blood gurgles from his fresh wound. Air floods into my lungs in huge gulps. My vision clears; I give my tail a feeble high-five.

Sharkie rushes to my side. Grabbing my wrist, he pumps my arm into the air. "The winner!"

I tug my hand downwards, but he won't let go. "Thanks." Hunching over at the waist, I gasp for breath. "Want...To... Leave."

Sharkie swivels his skull-like head in my direction, his grip tight as iron. "Not yet. Before you depart, guests from the entourage of Angel Verus wish to praise your valor in battle."

I blink a few times to clear my head, then pant out one word: "Sure." Hell, at this point it's faster to get the thanks and go home.

Finally dropping my hand, Sharkie turns to face the Arena's main archway. "Angels and demons, the Arena fighter will be congratulated on her victory."

An ocean of people pour onto the Arena floor, all of them dressed like they fell out of the Middle Ages. I slow my breathing and inspect the crowd. Who in blazes are these characters? They aren't angels, demons, or ghouls. Why would they be hanging out with Verus?

A line of heralds with silver trumpets step onto the Arena floor, creating a make-shift entryway. Delicate women in brocade gowns step through, followed by sturdy men in long tunics.

Whoever these folks are, they sure take their time to do anything.

I roll my eyes. Enough ceremony. Let's get with the congratulating so I can go home and talk Mom into making me some brownies. That fight was a bitch.

Moving past the line of heralds, two figures step onto the Arena floor, both wearing chain mail covered by formal tunics. First, I see a sturdy older man with white hair to his shoulders, a silver crown glistening on his head. Beside him walks someone younger with wavy brown hair, a muscular frame and square shoulders. Every inch of my body goes on alert.

I know exactly who these two are: *Lincoln and his father.*

Crap. These oddballs in medieval get-ups are all thrax. No wonder I'd never seen them before. Thrax only run around earth fighting demons. I feel like Verus is moving more playing pieces around her game-board with Armageddon, and these thrax are part of some masterstroke. My mind wheels with all the implications, but after such a crazy morning, I can't quite process what it means.

The last herald in line lowers his trumpet, announcing in a booming voice: "King Connor and his son, the High Prince!"

My stomach swaps places with my mouth. Lincoln's the freaking High Prince of the thrax? Thousands of eyes stare as the two men approach; a million years crawl by as the pair march across the floor.

Finally, they stand before me.

Sharkie's voice lowers to a hiss. "Remove your mask, slave."

Pulling the mesh away from my face, I shake my head so my auburn hair flows down my back. My gaze locks with Lincoln's, his eyes widen the slightest fraction. The Prince speaks one word. "You."

I start staring at his mouth again. Maybe I need therapy of some kind. "Yes, me."

The King eyes us both for a moment, and then turns to Sharkie. "What is this girl's name?"

I've never heard Sharkie call me anything but 'slave.' How he'll hate answering *that* question. The emcee's voice comes out a low rumble. "It's Myla Lewis, your Majesty." Yup, he hated that, alright.

"You fought bravely, Myla Lewis." Up close, I can see that the King's face is pale with lightly veined skin and deep laugh-lines around his mismatched eyes. "Part of our mission here is to build better relationships with quasis such as you. Please accept this sword in congratulation." He holds up a long silver sword with a red pummel, then pauses, turning to Lincoln. "Perhaps you should give her this, my son. I believe I saw the two of you talking at the ball."

Hell, no. Don't let that asshat give me the sword. I raise my hand quickly. "We don't know each other."

Lincoln takes the weapon firmly in his hands. "Let me think." His gaze slowly runs over my body. Suddenly, I'm very aware that my dragon-scale cat suit leaves zero to the male imagination. Even worse, it's really-really cold in the Arena today. Great.

The Prince sets the point of the sword onto the Arena floor, his hands rest atop the red pummel. "I believe we had one conversation. About pets, as I recall?" His heavy-lidded eyes lock onto mine, one slate-blue and one wheat-brown. A challenge lurks behind them.

My inner demon sparks to life, not with anger this time, but with something just as powerful. My tail strokes my shoulder, as if warning me to stop. I slap the arrowhead end and lean in closer to Lincoln.

I'm always up for a challenge.

I plaster on a fake smile. "Now, I remember the conversation. You were a *true* Prince." I turn to the King. "I am grateful for the sword, your Highness."

Lincoln swings the weapon until the pummel rests in his right hand, the deadly end against his left palm. The Prince and I start a kind of staring match in the middle of the Arena floor. I pass the time picturing ways to knock him to the ground.

King Connor clears his throat. "Perhaps if you said a few words, son."

Lincoln's upper lip curls. "Sure, father." He takes a deep breath. "This quasi girl—"

"Myla. My name's Myla." Anger hums through every bone in my body.

The Prince's jaw falls open a moment. I don't think he gets corrected very often. I glance at the King; laughter dances in his mismatched eyes.

"Yes, *Myla*." If Lincoln could spit my name out, I think he would have. "You showed some basic ability in the match this morning, certainly enough to warrant an honorary sword. Of course, if you fought a true demon hunter then—"

"Just name the time and place, buddy." My body buzzes with rage.

I pause. My every word has been echoing throughout the Arena. Really, really loudly. I inspect the crowd. The angels sit still, their mouths contracted into an 'o' shape. The demons have actually stopped their ongoing battles for the best seats; they all face the Arena floor. Thousands of eyes fix in our direction. Part of me knows I should be humiliated right now, but the rest of me is too jacked up on rage to care.

My gaze flips between Lincoln and Connor. "Okay, how do we end this?"

The King rubs his chin, hiding a smile. "Perhaps if you set your hands like this?" He raises his arms to chest height, palms extended.

"Oh yeah." I set my hands to match the King's. Lincoln's face is the model of calm as he balances the sword between my open palms. I let out a sigh. This nightmare of a morning is almost over. Then, Prince's fingertips brush the skin between my gloves and sleeves. Where our bare skin touches, I feel an electric pulse of pleasure.

What. The. Hell.

I quickly pull my hands away, curling the sword against my chest. "Thank you." I quickly glance into Lincoln's face, seeing his façade of calm crack for a moment, revealing a look that mixes shock and desire.

So, he felt the connection too, but he still thinks I'm a disgusting demon. Great. My face burns with anger and humiliation.

The King and Prince bow slightly, then walk away. It takes forever for them to stride across the Arena floor. I pass the time picturing ways to kick Lincoln in the back of the head.

The next few minutes are a blur of marching heralds, blaring trumpets, and smiling courtiers. At some point, Walker pulls me into the safety and shadows of a nearby archway. His voice is low and gentle. "Are you ready to portal home, Myla?"

My eyes burn with feelings I don't know how to name. "Walker, I was ready an hour ago." I'm seconds away from bursting into tears. *Some warrior.*

"Don't take it personally, Myla. Most thrax have never met a quasi. They don't understand that you're not a demon."

"That didn't bother me." My voice breaks so much, I sound like I could be yodeling. Crap, I hate it when I do that. "Okay, that totally hurt like Hell."

Walker wraps me into a hug. His body is warm and firm, not at all the chilly undeadly-ness that I expected. "Do you want me to beat him up for you?"

I can't help but chuckle. "Not this time, Walker." My head melts into his shoulder. "Thanks for offering, though."

"Any time."

CHAPTER SEVEN

A

With all the extra ceremonial blah-blah-blah at the match, I don't get to school until lunch is almost over. I quickly fill my tray and scan the cafeteria, looking for my–and Cissy's–favorite table for two. I quickly find it, but now it seats three.

Zeke has moved in. Resentment twists in my belly. Zeke gets all of Cissy's attention after school, and I have to listen to her yammer about him non-stop during the day. Lunch is the last scrap of girl-time left in my life.

Gritting my teeth, I step up to the table and wait for some acknowledgement of my existence from Cissy and Zeke. It doesn't happen.

"Do you want any more, Zekie?" Cissy holds a French fry in one hand. I'm pretty sure she's been hand-feeding him. Gross.

"No thanks, honey bunches." Zeke pats his stomach. "Have to stay in shape." They share an Eskimo kiss (aka rub noses), and then I've had enough.

"Hello, there!" Forcing a smile, I give my lunch tray a little shake. "Any room for a third?"

"Myla!" Cissy twists in her chair. "Where have you been?"

"Another Arena match." I slide into an empty chair, grab a fork and dive into my monster-sized salad.

"That's a lot of fighting lately." Zeke rubs his dimpled chin. "Anything special going on?"

I freeze, my fork half-way to my mouth. How much should I say?

Cissy smiles sweetly. "You know you can tell us anything."

I glance at their eager faces. Maybe Cissy's right. These are my friends; I should trust them. Plus, it's been a long time since the whole 'Myla is obsessed with Zeke' thing happened. They've probably forgotten all about it.

Dropping my fork, I take a deep breath and start babbling. "At Zeke's party I met a thrax guy who insulted quasis and said Cissy looked like a dog in heat, so I'm not gonna dance with that! But today at the match, he turned out to be the crowned Prince of the thrax. He gave me a sword, but then he said I wouldn't last against a *real* demon hunter." I slam the tabletop with both hands. "Hells bells, I want to knock his block off." *And maybe kiss him a little bit, but I'm not telling them that.* I let out a low whistle. "Honestly, what am I worrying about anyway? I'll probably never see him again, right?"

There's a long pause where Cissy and Zeke stare at me; their eyes ready to pop out of their heads. They both burst into peals of laughter.

So much for telling the truth. I set my face into my palms and moan. It's been that depressing of a day.

"Come on, Myla. Be serious." Cissy wipes a tear from her cheek, her tail wagging up a storm behind her.

"If you're not ready to confide in us, it's fine." Zeke hides his smile under one hand. "We get it."

Cissy and Zeke exchange a sympathetic look. Then, with a series of loud squeaks, Cissy scooches her seat closer to mine, while Zeke moves his farther away. "Is that maybe…Better?" She gives me a tentative grin.

Hells bells, they both think I'm still acting weird because of my supposed mega-crush on Zeke. I pause, taking a long sip from my can of diet soda. *Actually, if it stops all the cuddling and pet names, they can think whatever they want.* I give her shoulder a little pat. "That *is* better." I sniffle, loudly. "Thanks so much."

Zeke runs his palms over his blonde head. "By the way, I heard you talked to Aunt Cecily at the party."

Lifting my fork, I spear a new bite of salad. "Aunt who?"

"Cecily. You know: old lady, gray hair, peacock tail?"

"Oh yeah, she was—" I search for the right words "—a good listener."

Zeke kicks his legs onto a nearby chair. "She said you were asking about diplomatic stuff."

I drop my fork again. "Yes, I was." I wanted any information on who my father could be, not that I'm telling Zekie that.

"My house has all the old diplomatic archives from quasi rule. It's in the main library." He taps his plate with one finger, looking at me expectantly. "You could check it out."

Cissy nods, setting her golden curls bobbing. "What a great idea! Doing some research would give you something else to think about besides…"

My lost love for Zeke. Riiiiiight. I swallow down some frustration with another bite of salad.

Zeke puts on his Mr. Smirky grin. "There's more to do than the library, though."

"Oh, yes." Cissy blinks her tawny eyes madly. "The mansion has a hedgerow maze, a fountain, and a huge greenhouse with botanical gardens inside."

Wait a second. I've known Cissy long enough to recognize her eye-blinking routine when I see it.

"This is a great offer and all, but I'm wondering one thing." I fold my hands neatly on the tabletop. "Is there is something in particular you want from me in all this?"

Leaning forward in her chair, Cissy speaks in a hushed tone. "Since you mention it, if you're at the house and all, I should probably be there too."

My eyes narrow. "I see. You'll be at the Ryder mansion to keep *me* company, not just to hang out with Zeke."

Cissy smiles so hard, I'm shocked her face doesn't crack. "Yes, that's absolutely right!"

I smack my lips once. Okay, I can see where this is going.

Cissy gazes at the ceiling, her mouth screwing to one side of her face. "And if my parents ask what happens at Zeke's house, you could say we're together all the time. The *three* of us."

I exhale a long breath. "But the two of you will really be doing *what* exactly?"

Zeke holds up his hands in the universal sign of surrender. "Just watching television and hanging out, I swear. My parents will be around too."

My forehead creases with confusion. "So, what's the problem?"

"My parents heard these awful lies about Zeke." Cissy shivers. "Now I'm supposed to have an official chaperone with me at all times and, well, I know how much Mom and Dad trust you."

"They think I'm a weird-tailed Arena fighter."

"But they know you'd kill anyone who tried to hurt me."

I pop another bite of salad into my mouth. She has a point.

Cissy starts blinking again. "Pleeeeeeeeease, Myla?"

I let out a low groan. The rumors about Zeke aren't wrong, but I've known Mr. Smarmy McSlutster since kindergarten. He's never let a girl meet his friends, let alone his family. I honestly think he's okay around Cissy. Plus, if I can get access to diplomatic records, I may find something out about my father.

"Fine. I'll do it."

.A.

The rest of the day is a blur of boringness, including the long drive home in Betsy. I step through my front door to a very happy mother.

"Welcome home, Myla!"

"Hey, Mom." I give her a kiss on the cheek.

Mom plunks down onto the living room sofa and pats the empty spot next to her. "Guess what, sweetie? I was able to snap a few pictures of you and Cissy in your gowns before you got into the car. I wanted it to be a surprise."

I sit down beside her. She presses the images into my hand. I look and wince. Even with all the flounces cut off the dress, it was still mighty puffy, like a neon pumpkin.

"Cissy looks beautiful." I sigh. "And I look very orange."

"You're *both* lovely. Be sure to show these to Cissy."

I set the photos into the pocket of my hoodie. "I will." *In another lifetime.*

Mom smiles and pats my hand. She's in a good mood. That means now's the perfect time to get the Maternal Inquisitor to approve regular afterschool trips to the Ryder mansion.

"So, Cissy's started dating this guy named Zeke Ryder."

"Oh, I know the Ryder family from before the war."

Wow, another random fact from Mom's mystery past.

It's going so well, I decide to keep things moving. "Now that Cissy's dating Zeke, she goes to the Ryder mansion after school. Her parents want a chaperone, so they asked me along."

Mom bounces in her seat. "Oh, the Ryder mansion's beautiful! I have a map around here somewhere." She takes to her feet and disappears into her room.

Okay, it's totally sketchy that Mom has maps of the Ryder mansion squirreled away. She returns to the living room and plunks down onto the sofa, a pile of folded papers on her lap.

Opening the top map, Mom runs her finger across different points. "The Ryder mansion's shaped like a giant letter 'U.' In the center of the building–the base of the 'U'–is the reception hall. From there, you go to the West Wing–that's where the Ryders live–or the East Wing." Mom sighs. "The East Wing's especially beautiful. It holds the ballroom, diplomatic offices, and library."

"Diplomatic offices, huh?" I let the words hang out there. Mom doesn't take the bait.

Instead, she points to another spot on the map. "Oh, and there's the hedgerow maze right between the two wings. A lovely fountain's at the center. After that, the grounds have tennis courts, botanical gardens, and all sorts of other things to entertain diplomats."

"Whoa. Zeke's house is way huger than I thought." How-oh-how am I going to segue this conversation to get actual answers about Mom's past?

Mom makes a tsk-tsk noise. "The grounds are actually a lot smaller now. You should have seen it before the war."

"I would've liked that." Man, it's taking all my personal control (of which I have very little) not to push her right now for details.

"The library's a marvel, be sure to check it out, Myla-la." She flips to a different map that shows only the East Wing. It's a long and thin rectangle made up of four floors. "The first floor's the ballroom, the second's diplomatic offices. The library covers both the third and fourth floors." She shakes her head from side to side. "That library is unbelievable. The records cover everything from quasi government to demon history to ancient diplomatic archives."

My personal control issues reach the breaking point. "Aren't I doing a great job not asking you about the diplomatic stuff you did before the war?" My mouth starts moving on its own. "I mean, it's pretty clear you worked in the diplomatic offices in the Ryder mansion. Maybe you met my dad there? Researched stuff in the library together or something?" I lean forward, my restraint level at zero. "Am I right?"

Mom opens her mouth as if to speak, but the words choke in her throat. She lets out a long sigh instead. "Has Verus sent you any dreamscapes yet?"

"Not since the first one we talked about."

"Ah, well." She rises to her feet. "Maybe soon."

With that, Mom walks away and hides the maps again.

Damn.

A.

I race up to the front door of the Ryder mansion and slam on the bronze knocker. I am so freaking late meeting Cissy and Zeke, it isn't even funny.

The pristine white door whips open, revealing a blissful Cissy. "Welcome to the Ryder mansion." The way she works the entrance, you'd think she and Zeke had dated for years instead of weeks.

"Hey, Cissy." I step into the reception hall. "I'm so sorry I'm late. Betsy broke down again." Over the years, carburetors, wadget screws, and manifolds have all become my personal bitches. Normally, I appreciate the extra smoke, drama, and grease, but today it was a big hassle. I loathe being late.

"No worries." Cissy makes goo-goo eyes at Zeke. "We were just chatting."

I scan the reception room. It's two stories tall and filled with ornate golden furniture and matching nick-knacks. Normally, it contains Zeke's parents, too. "Where are the Ryders?" To say Zeke's parents took an instant liking to Cissy is the understatement of the millennium. For the last two weeks, Zeke's Dad has been hovering beside the pair of them, glaring at his boy with a look that says 'don't screw this up, literally.' Today's the first day I can actually play chaperone.

"They're playing tennis." Cissy wraps her arm around Zeke's. "Do you want to join us in the West Wing?"

Ah, no. I see enough of the 'Cissy and Zeke Love Show' at school. My goal here is plain and simple: get some intel on my dad. "Thanks, but I thought I'd check out the East Wing today."

Cissy leans her head against Zeke's shoulder. "Are you sure? We'd love to hang with you."

Ah, *sure* you would. I appreciate Cissy trying to be nice, but I couldn't be more of a third wheel if I were a tricycle. "Thanks, but I'm good. I honestly want to check out the East Wing."

Cissy tilts her head to one side and frowns. "What aren't you telling me, sweetie?" She elbows Zeke in the ribs. "I told you, she's hiding things from me lately."

"I'm fine."

"Really?" Cissy's mouth curls into her 'thinking frown.' That means she's debating about making it a group field trip to the library. Searching my ghoul heritage is nasty enough on its own; I'd rather not have an audience.

"Really-really." I shoo them toward the opposite hallway. "You kids run off and have a good time."

Cissy stands frozen, her forehead creased with worry. Zeke sets his hand on her shoulder, guiding her about to face him. Once they're eye-to-eye, he shoots her a come-hither smile. "I'd love to show you our stables today."

Cissy blushes. Oh, yeah. She's coming hither. "That would be great."

I wave good-bye as the pair turn toward the West Wing. They step away, their footsteps clacking down the marble hallway in perfect sync. As they stroll along, Cissy stays snuggled into Zeke's side, his arm wrapped firmly about her shoulders. Something in the movement makes my throat tighten. Will I ever feel that way about someone? At this rate, probably not, unfortunately.

A shiver rattles my shoulders. Maybe my ghoul heritage means I can't love any guy who still has a pulse. Yuck, that's a depressing thought.

Shake it off, Myla. You've work to do.

Turning about on my heel, I face the long hallway to the East Wing. It's all gleaming marble floors, tall gilded mirrors, and anxiety-inducing mysteries. Mom said it held a ballroom, offices, and library. My mouth twists as I consider the options. Nodding to myself, I decide to start my search in the fourth-floor library. From what Cissy's said, that's always open and usually deserted.

Taking a deep breath, I straighten my spine and march up to the fourth floor. The library's a labyrinth of tall wooden bookshelves. The scent of dust and old parchment fills the air. I scan for other visitors, but the place is empty. Good.

I find a section marked 'history' and haul out a particularly large, leather-bound volume. Bay windows with cushioned seats line the library's far wall. I slide into the nearest window seat, open the book in my lap, and gaze through the glass to the mansion's grounds outside. Far below me, figures mill about the hedgerow maze. My tail flips to the title page:

Quasi Diplomacy: A History

A rustling sound echoes from the other side of the library.

"Cissy, is that you?"

Silence.

Shrugging, I return my attention to the book:

Introduction by Sanctus Lewis

I stare at the words again. Sanctus Lewis. I have Mom's last name, and Sanctus Lewis was her mother. *Could be a coincidence.* I read on:

As every quasi citizen knows, the Lewis family has been instrumental in the development of afterlife diplomacy, which is why I'm pleased to write this preface to the tenth edition of…

"We're here!" A strange female voice rings in my ears, but I'm too engrossed to call out to its owner. I pull the pages closer to my nose. The book has a ton of blah-blah-blah about giving people a second chance at a good afterlife, then the author writes:

I'm proud that my dear daughter Camilla has been elected to the traditional Lewis family seat as Senator of Diplomacy, an honor that…

My first real clue! Mom's name is Camilla, so Grandma definitely wrote this before she died in the Wars. I grip the edges of the book tighter. And Mom was a Senator? *My insanely over-protective and weepy mother?* I shake my head and turn the page.

"Lincoln, don't!" A shrill giggle fills the air. "You'll muss my dress."

I freeze.

Did she just say Lincoln? Can't be the same guy.

"Apologies. It's such a lovely dress too." It *is* the same guy. Ugh.

I try to focus on my reading, but I can't help but overhear them. Okay, maybe I could help, but I'm curious what Prince Pompous is up to.

Lincoln speaks again. "The minister said the *Libra Scala* would be over here."

"Oh, I think I see it." She makes little grunting noises. "Oh my, the shelf's soooo high. Could you please pull the book down for me?"

Scrunching up my features, I mime the words 'the shelf's soooo high' and stick out my tongue.

"Of course, Lady Adair." A soft scraping sounds as the book slides down.

"Thank you, your Highness." She giggles again.

My back teeth lock while my tail slices something nearby. Glancing about, I spy a sunny yellow pillow, now lying in two neat halves on the window seat. Anger and shock zing through my body. I just skewered a pillow without knowing it. I don't do stuff like that, even during a Maternal Inquisition. Why does this random guy get my demon up in such a raw way?

A smile sounds in Lincoln's voice. "You're welcome."

Lady Adair lets out a loud sigh. "While we have a moment, I want to say something. I was so honored that you invited me to join Verus at the Arena match."

"My pleasure. I thought you'd enjoy the battle."

"The fighting was fine, I suppose. But I *really* enjoyed seeing you act so graciously afterwards."

There's a long pause, then Lincoln speaks again. "You mean when I gave the demon an award?"

The demon? I'm a quasi with a name. Creep.

"Yes. That demon girl was so lucky you didn't kill her."

"Well, I–"

"Demons don't stand a chance against real thrax warriors." Her voice sounds extra-syrupy when she says 'real thrax warriors.' I'm pretty sure my tail just sliced another pillow into shreds. My hands ball into fists.

Lincoln chuckles. "It's not really fair to compare a thrax and a demon girl, Lady Adair."

"I don't know if you'd think me too forward, but–" I can almost hear her eyelashes frantically batting from here.

"But what?"

"May I feel the muscle of your arm?"

I make a puke-face.

"I'm not sure, Adair."

"Just for one second? Please." A long pause follows. "Oooh! So strong." I picture his arms and, yeah, he's pretty ripped. But I kinda hate myself for knowing that.

She sighs. "How could any girl ask you to 'name the time and place' to fight?"

Lincoln's tone turns cold. "We need to return to the others now, Milady."

"Oh, I didn't mean…That is, I didn't think…" Footsteps sound toward the door. "Wait for me, your Highness!"

I listen to their voices and footsteps fade, rage boiling up my spine. It's official. *Prince Lincoln, I hate you more than anyone else in the universe. Someday I'll show you what a 'real warrior' can do.*

Pacing around the squeaky wooden floor, I imagine how awesome it would have been to trip them both down the stairwell. Hitching the book under my arm, I march straight out of the library, down the stairs, and into the first floor ballroom. As I stomp through across the dance floor, my eyes catch movement through the tall windows around me. Thrax mill about the hedgerow maze outside, all dressed up for some kind of formal shindig.

Grr.

I leave Cissy a goodbye note in the reception hall (including a not-too-believable story of how the two pillows got destroyed) and stomp off to my station wagon. I almost get in six accidents on the drive home, mostly because I'm practicing 'you're a jerk' speeches instead of paying attention to the road. Once in my own driveway, I'm barely aware of parking the car, marching into the house, and slamming the door behind me. I make a beeline for my room.

I'm half-way there when Mom pops her head in from the kitchen. "Hi, Myla. I got us some frozen dinners. Yours is chicken, I think." She shoots me a long stare. My eyes still flash red with rage.

Mom frowns. "Is everything alright?"

No, it's not alright. I hate this thrax Prince guy so much I can't stand it. I take a deep breath. "Everything's fine, Mom. I just have a lot of homework to do."

"Do you want to eat in your room?"

"That would be awesome."

I march into my room and settle onto my bed. Pulling a text-book out of my backpack, I toss it open to a random page.

Mom steps up to my bedside. "Here you go." She sets a tray of greenish-orange goop onto my nightstand. I glance at the 'food' and wince. Even for our house, this is disgusting stuff. Note to self: learn how to cook.

I force a smile. "Thanks, Mom."

"Don't stay up too late doing homework." She gives me a peck on the cheek and walks out the door.

I shovel some frozen dinner into my head and stare at the same random chapter in my textbook. An hour ticks by. None of the words on the page sink into my brain. My eyes flutter shut while the book's still open on my lap.

The moment my lids close, I dream of the Gray Sea. Once again, I stand barefoot on the dark sand, a wall of black stone looming nearby. Dark thunderclouds roll overhead. The stench of sulphur makes me wince. I crouch, setting my hands onto the charcoal-colored earth. A circle of white fire erupts before me. In the center, the sand rises into a familiar form.

My mother.

All breath leaves my body. Verus said she would send me visions of Mom's past. Is it finally starting?

The figure before me takes on more definition. Even though her body is still made of sand, I can tell Mom's wearing toga-style robes, the same kind of garment she held when crying in her room. I suck in a shaky breath. Those must be Senate robes.

My skin prickles with the chilly touch of unexpected under-standing. That's why Mom got upset: she found her old Senate robes while looking for sewing stuff. How awful. One day you're a toga-wearing Senator, the next you're sewing dark robes for a bunch of ghouls. A weight settles into my bones. When she asked me, I didn't even know what the robes were. Her own daughter. That gives the whole interaction a new level of suck.

I return my attention to the desert floor. More sand rises inside the circle of flame. This time the granules form different shapes around Mom. I squint, seeing the sand transform into the Ryder mansion's East Wing staircase.

Okay, that makes sense. I figured Mom worked on the mansion's diplomatic floor. Why else would she have maps hidden away?

A grin curls the edges of my mouth. I'm on the right track.

Before me, the circle of flame flares brighter, and then vanishes. The scene, once made of sand, is now flesh and blood.

I let out a low whistle. *That's pretty cool dreamscaping, Verus.*

A ghoul rushes up the stairs to hike along at Mom's side, his black robes swaying as he moves. "You'll be late, Senator Lewis." He stands less than six feet tall, which is super-short for a ghoul. Pulling back his hood, he reveals a bald head covered with light gray skin. As ghouls go, he's pretty handsome with huge black eyes, a straight nose, and full mouth.

Mom turns to him, her face winding into a dazzling smile. "I won't be late, Tim. And I'm not Senator Lewis *yet*." Her chestnut hair falls in perfect waves over her shoulders; her eyes are brown and bright. An aura of energy and power surrounds her. I can't stop staring at her, questions flooding my mind: How can this woman be the same one who collapses into a puddle when I'm called to the Arena?

Tim pulls an old-fashioned stopwatch from the folds of his robe. "You'll never be a Senator if you miss your swearing-in ceremony." He clicks the metal cover open, glances at the watchface, and then sides the instrument back into his robes. "And that starts in precisely twenty-two minutes." His forehead creases with worry. "Why must you visit the staff at this time?"

"You'll understand once you meet them." Mom pauses at the door to the second floor and turns the handle. Nothing happens. "That's strange."

I take a good hard look at the door. Yup, that's the exact same one I walked by on my way to the fourth floor library at the Walker mansion. Next time I'm there, I am for sure finding a way into *that* room.

"We usually leave this unlocked." Mom pulls a silver chain from around her neck. A tiny key hangs at the end. She slips it into the knob, twists the handle, and slowly pushes the door open.

Mom and Tim step inside. Rows of desks and chairs line the long space, all of them empty. The room is quiet and dark. Mom sets her hands on her hips.

"Where is everybody?" Her chocolate eyes narrow.

I know that look. It's the one that happens right before I'm grounded for forgetting to do something really important. Somebody's in trouble, that's for sure.

The lights flash on. Dozens of bodies appear from behind desks and chairs. "Surprise!"

Mom's face bursts into a wide grin. She scans all the faces, clapping her hands with joy. She knows all these people. More than that, she cares about them.

Whoa, there.

My mother knows actual people, other than me or Walker? I suppose that should've been obvious once I found out she's a Senator, but I never pictured it actually happening. A feeling that's somewhere between joy and shock bounces around my rib cage.

An elder woman with amber skin and white hair steps out from the group. In her arms she carries an enormous cake that reads 'Congratulations Camilla.' She wears a simple blue pantsuit with a purple scarf at her throat. Her wide brown eyes, full mouth, and long black tail all look familiar.

Mom's face lights up with a wide smile. "Thank you, Mother."

Holy guacamole. That's my grandmother, Sanctus Lewis, the one I read about in the Ryder library today. She wrote the introduction to *Quasi Diplomacy*. I scan the room, seeing all the strangely-familiar faces. These aren't just co-workers, they must be the extended Lewis family. I shake my head from side to side. It's one thing to read Grandmother's introduction about the Lewis family legacy in diplomacy, but it's different to see so many semi-familiar faces in the Ryder mansion. And why haven't I met any of these folks before?

Grandmother's mouth curls into a grin. "We're all so proud of you, Camilla. A Lewis has always won the diplomatic seat on the Senate, but never by an eighty percent margin!" The room erupts in applause. "The people of Purgatory agree with me by a landslide. My Senate seat could not be held by a better quasi." She offers the cake to a lanky boy with short brown hair and a boar's tail. "Will you set this in the conference room, Mortimer?"

"Yes, Sanctus." He lifts the cake from her arms and walks toward the back rooms of the office.

Grandmother turns to Tim, her smile melting into an unreadable look. "You brought someone with you."

"Yes, I have." Mom turns to the ghoul beside her. "Tim, meet my family." She gestures around the room. "Family, meet Tim. He's joining the staff as my personal assistant."

Sanctus eyes him carefully. "We've never had a non-Lewis family member work in the diplomacy offices."

"Well, that's something to change. If we're to interact with other realms, we need to start right here, in this office."

"Excellent point." Grandmother nods softly. "Tim, let me give you the grand tour." She gestures across a group of men and women of many ages and sizes, all of them with chestnut hair, amber skin, and great chocolate-brown eyes. "Over here, we have Sophia, Isabel, and Martin. They ran Camilla's election campaign. By the window, you'll find Fortus, Quin, and Felix; they manage office operations. Coco, Seina, Arturo, and Hugo are in the back conference room helping themselves to cake. They take care of correspondence and requests. And finally we have Tanis and Bea in finance."

Tim's jaw falls a little loose. "I'll never remember everyone."

Grandmother frowns. "That's quite unfortunate. There'll be a test later." Her tail whips ominously behind her.

A bead of black sweat trickles down Tim's cheek. "Oh, no. I'm completely unprepared."

Mom sets her hand on Tim's arm. "Don't worry. Sanctus is teasing."

Tim exhales. "Ah, I see."

A girl about four years old steps up to Grandmother and pulls on her pant leg. "You forgot me." She's a little wisp whose chestnut hair hangs in ringlets like Cissy's. Her long black tail reaches upwards, winding gently about Grandmother's hand. She's adorable. I imagine acres of cousins, aunts, and uncles hidden around Purgatory. Cute little moppets that ask me to sing stupid songs. Older relatives who may have some awesome advice on how to land the best service after graduation. Men and women Mom's age who know secret family recipes. My tummy feels warm with Lewis love.

This. Is. Awesome.

Sanctus scoops the girl up into her arms. "How could I ever forget you, Dani? What's your title again?"

"Vice President of Fun."

"That's right. And does our Vice President have any plans for today?"

"Yeah. We all go with Auntie Camilla to the swearing in."

Sanctus raises her white eyebrows. "Now that's a top notch idea, Dani." She turns to Mom. "There's no law against it, as long as you don't mind."

"Mind? I'd *love* it." Mom claps her hands. "Everyone, Sanctus and I have an important announcement to make. You're all joining me at the swearing-in ceremony!" The room erupts in a cheer. Mom turns to Tim. "Can you open a portal for us, please?"

Tim nods. "Of course." A black hole about eight feet high opens in the center of the room.

Mom positively beams. "Now, everyone, grab the hand of the person next to you and don't let go! We'll all portal into the Senate chambers together." There's a murmur and shuffling of feet as everyone forms a long daisy chain. "Are we all ready?"

Another cheer erupts around the room. This time, I let out a happy shout as well. *I can't believe I have this awesome family hiding out somewhere!*

Mom grips Tim's hand firmly. "Alright, then. We're off!"

One by one, every member of my amazing, newfound family steps through the portal. Last in line is Grandmother with little

Dani perched on her hip. As they disappear into the darkness, the image in the Gray Sea changes. The diplomatic offices transform from reality back into sand. The granules slowly collapse into the floor of the Gray Sea.

I wake with a jolt, stretch and smile, smile, smile. Reading about the Senate doesn't compare to seeing Mom in her purple robes, smiling and confident. I press my palms into my eyes and yawn. My mind races through every moment of the dreamscape.

Senator Camilla Lewis, wow.

Resetting my pillow beneath my head, I stare out the window. The sky's still dark; I glance at my alarm clock. 4 AM. Rain streams down the windowpane. My anger with Lincoln feels a million miles away. How'd I let some dope get my demon so riled up? There are more important things to worry about. Like meeting my family.

Speaking of which…

I set my bare feet onto the chilly floor, tiptoe into Mom's room, and stand by the foot of her bed. My body hums with nervous, happy energy.

"Mom, are you awake?"

She yawns. "Having trouble sleeping, Myla?" She pats the space beside her.

"You could say that." I plunk onto the bed with a small bounce, my back resting against the headboard.

Mom's chocolate eyes open wide. "Did you get a dreamscape from Verus?"

I grin. "Oh, yeah."

She takes a deep breath. "Do you have any questions?"

"You were a Senator, Mom. Wow." I slap the mattress in an excited rhythm. "I read something in a book that said you were one, but in the dreamscape I saw it like it was real." I bite my thumbnail. "I guess that wasn't a question, really."

Mom pulls herself upright so she sits beside me. "Was that a book from the Ryder library?"

"Yes." I shoot her a guilty look. "I totally left them a note when I took it."

"I'm sure it's fine that you borrowed it; I'm glad the book exists at all." Mom lets out a long breath. "Zeke's parents are remarkable people. You wouldn't believe what went into keeping their mansion, let alone their library. It's the last bit of our old world left. In many ways, our only connection to the outside realms."

I could dance around the room, I am so pumped about the info I'm getting right now. *Tell me more!* "So, what was it like, being a Senator?"

"Let's see." Mom starts reciting facts like she's leading a tour. "Purgatory once had a Senate with 100 representatives. Our family held the diplomacy seat for generations."

My head wags from side to side. "How am I your daughter and this never came up in conversation with *anyone?*" I shoot her a look that says 'and that means you, too.'

"No one noticed me after the war and I wanted to keep it that way." She picks stray threads from her weathered comforter. "Armageddon took over Purgatory for one reason: to get more souls in Hell. In the Senate, we gave souls every chance to get to Heaven. It's only fair. Demons don't need souls to survive. Consuming souls is just a drug to them, a high." Her eyes flash with a bit of red, something I've never seen before. I knew Mom had wrath powers like me, but I figured she somehow only inherited the tail and not the temper.

"How can we let them get away with this?" My eyes burn with anger. "The ghouls teach us that quasis are basically the biggest losers in history." I point toward my room. "I'll make copies of that book and hand it out to other kids at school. Maybe I'll grab even more books from the library–"

"Myla, no!" Mom grips my hands. "We can't take that risk. You have to understand. Armageddon's war was more than a takeover; it was a massacre. He wanted to wipe out any memories of the old ways, the generosity, the tolerance. Who knows what they'd do if someone started bringing up the republic again?"

"I don't care. People have a right to know." I jut out my chin. "Besides, I've fought evil."

Mom's features sag. "Not this kind of evil." She stares out the window at the rain. "This is the kind of darkness that can't stand even a glimmer of light." She turns to me, her face lined with tears. "During the wars, they hunted down and killed every member of the Lewis family, save for me."

My forehead creases as I wait for this news to seep through my mind. Every relative dead? I picture the happy faces in the diplomacy offices. Shock waves run through my body. *That can't be right.* "I thought there were Lewises in Lower Purgatory. I wanted to meet them." Plus Grandma, Dani, and the million other Lewises from the diplomatic offices.

"Those folks have the name, but they're not part-Furor. None of them have our fight in their veins." Her bloodshot eyes lock with mine. "The ghouls wiped out anyone who could be next in line for our Senate seat. Anyone who could remember or resist." Her eyes glisten. "It wasn't just us; they targeted all Senators." Her voice breaks, and the sound cracks my heart in a way I never thought possible.

"We can talk about this later." I half-rise from the bed.

Mom sets her hand on my arm. "No, you're right. You deserve to know your heritage."

I sit back down beside my mother, my mind spinning. "I don't get it. Why did you and I survive?"

Mom bites her lip. "A friend sacrificed everything so I'd be safe. When you were born, the protection applied to you as well."

My throat tightens. "Who was that person? Was it my father?"

Mom squeezes her eyes shut, fresh tears glide down her cheeks. "That's all I can tell you right now, Myla."

I know my mother well enough to realize one thing: that answer means 'yes.' Yes, your father died to save us both. And more. A web of dark secrets still hangs around this house. Part of me wants to grab her shoulders, force her to tell me more and tear the sadness from our lives. Another part feels super-guilty for having pushed as hard as I have. She looks red-eyed and miserable.

Trembling, Mom sets her hand over her mouth. "I need some time alone." She sucks in a shaky breath. "We'll talk again after Verus's next visit."

I rise to my feet. Rage, empathy, and guilt battle it out inside me. I force myself to step toward the door. Best to end this before we both lose it. "Okay, Mom." I walk away, gently closing the door behind me. Her quiet sobs echo through the house.

Listening to her crying, my internal battle of emotions ends. Empathy wins, big time. I don't want to upset Mom any more for one day, so I'm extra-quiet while getting ready for school. Even Betsy's on her best behavior; she doesn't kick or buck as I drive away. The day zooms by in a blur of classes and chatting with Cissy. I forget all about Mom's sadness.

When I walk through my front door again, I find Mom's still in her room with the door closed, quietly sobbing. My heart sinks. Finding out about Mom's past is sure different than I thought it would be.

CHAPTER EIGHT

_A_

Cissy and I sit in our usual seats in the back row of Biology class, waiting for the other students to settle in. My best friend bobs up and down in her chair. "Did I tell you Zeke's parents are back from their trip?"

Only twelve times. "Yes, you mentioned it, Cissy." The day after I first visited the Ryder library, Zeke's parents went on a week-long diplomatic tour. Before leaving, they called Cissy's house, saying that under no circumstances should she visit the mansion. For a few days, she and Zeke tried hanging at her place, but her parents are still having issues with Zeke's reputation. Long story short, they've been counting the days until the Ryders return.

And if I'm being totally honest with myself, they're not the only ones counting. I can't wait to get back into the library and see what I can find out about my mother's past and father's identity.

Cissy doodles in her notebook. "I'm going over to the Ryder mansion after school. You coming?"

"Hells, yeah." I didn't realize it was a question. "Why wouldn't I?"

Cissy chews her bottom lip. "I wasn't sure if you'd still want to. Last week you left pretty early. I was worried you didn't like hanging out in the library."

Oh that? Only when thrax Princes show up. "No, I'm totally into it. I'll be there after school."

"Good news." Cissy leans across the aisle and taps my desk. "Hey, did you see that?" She nods toward the front of the class.

Craning my neck, I spy a large glass case by the teacher's desk. It's a three-foot cube that's perched on a small silver table. "Cool. The Lady always keeps it interesting."

The Lady is LDY-99, our Biology teacher. With charcoal skin that stretches over her skeletal frame, the Lady looms seven feet tall in her hooded black robes. Her distinguishing marks are her halo-like afro, oversized eyes, and little round glasses. She's definitely the coolest teacher at school.

"Today, I've a surprise for you all." The Lady steps up to the empty glass case. "We're going to learn about Reperio demons."

I do a happy-dance in my chair. Reperio are awesome.

The Lady picks up a garbage can and chucks the contents into the display. Scraps of paper, broken pencils, and paper clips settle to the bottom of the case.

After that, the garbage starts to move.

The scraps of paper form into little men with eraser-eyes. The broken pencils splinter into skirts for tiny ladies with wooden bodies and paper clip heads. They prowl the display floor, pounding on the glass, and swearing up a storm.

"Every demon has a name and classification. Who knows what these are?"

I raise my hand and answer before she calls on me. "They're Reperio Minusculus, classification Possideo."

The Lady adjusts the glasses on her nose. "Yes, they are Reperio Minusculus." She steps over to her desk. "But I'm fairly certain they're classification Insultus." She opens up a thick leather-bound book from her desktop and flips through the pages. "No, you're right. They're Possideo. How about that?"

I roll my eyes. Unbelievable. Even ghoul biology teachers don't know demon basics. Everyone acts like they'll disappear if we ignore them.

Behind the glass, the little demons make lewd body gestures at our teacher. The Lady glances between them and me. "You fight evil souls in the Arena, don't you?"

"Yup. Demons too after I'm done with the souls." I point to the glass case. "Want to know the easiest way to kill Reperio?"

A soft gasp echoes around the room. The Lady's eyes open wide. "No, no, no. We all love our demon allies." She quickly steps back to the display case. "Let's talk about something else, class. Ah, I know. I'll explain how to feed, clothe, and entertain our little friends."

Cissy whispers to me from across the aisle. "Look Myla, I know you used to keep notebooks on how to kill demons, but–"

"Oh, I still take tons of notes. And Walker sneaks me into Arena matches pretty regularly. I've seen other fighters go after Reperio and the easiest way to kill them is–"

"Myla Lewis!" The Lady stares at me, her large black eyes look ready to burst from her head. I scan the room. The other students look at me like I just announced my frozen head collection. "For the last time. Stop sharing kill strategies for our demon allies."

My eyes glow with rage. *Demon allies, my ass.*

Cissy shoots me a desperate stare. "After school, Myla. The library? Remember?"

The library, right. If the Lady sends me to Principal's office, I'll be suspended for sure. Knowing my mother, that'll mean no library trips for months. I need answers more than I need to make a point about demons. I bite my lips together, hard. "I understand, LDY-99."

"Thank you." The Lady spends the next hour explaining how Reperio demons like to eat Cheetos, dress in rotten food, and be entertained with any kid of fart noise.

Unholy moley, what a waste of time.

"Greetings, Myla. You're called to serve."

My eyes pop open. It's early morning and Walker stands at the foot of my bed. *Please let me not be dreaming.* I've been dying for an Arena match for weeks, ever since I downed that Deacon guy. I cross my fingers under the comforter. "Am I dreaming?"

Walker folds his arms across his chest. "No, it's really me."

"An Arena match. Yes!" I jump out of bed and smile my face off.

Walker rubs his sideburns with one hand. "We must depart shortly."

"I'll be ready super-fast." I hunt through my dresser for the least raggedy sweatpants. Glancing over my shoulder, I see Walker still lurking by my bed. I arch my eyebrow. "This is the part where you leave my room."

Walker fidgets in his long robes. "Of course. I'm sorry, Myla."

"No problem." I gesture to door. "Since I'm going to the Arena, I bet Mom's already worrying herself to death in the kitchen. You can keep her company."

Walker patters out of my room, closing the door behind him.

I get ready in record time and sprint to the kitchen. Mom sits at the table, lazily paging through a travel magazine.

"Good morning, Myla sweetie." Her face stretches into a warm smile. "I understand you're going to the Arena today."

Well, that's a little fishy. Normally, Mom's a heartbeat away from a coronary by this point.

"Yup, I'm off to battle the *bad people.*" I karate-kick the air and hear my sweat-pants rrrrrrip. "Okay, maybe not in these pants." I roll my eyes. "What am I thinking? I should wear my fighting suit." I jog back to my room and change.

Mom calls to me from the kitchen. "Set those sweats onto the couch before you go. I'll patch them this morning." She sounds downright chipper.

Hmm. That's *a lot* fishy. Time to ask some questions.

I return to the kitchen and make myself a hearty sugar cereal breakfast. "So, who am I fighting today?"

Walker frowns. "You're not fighting anyone. The angels requested you be present for a ceremony."

My morning instantly deflates. "A ceremony?" I grimace. "There's no chance of fighting, none at all?"

"Knowing you, always." Walker sips his coffee. "Maybe you'll get lucky and really piss off Sharkie."

"Good, because I just ripped my last pair of clean sweats. It's the fighting suit or nothing." I turn to Mom. "And you're totally okay with all this?" I haven't had a Maternal Inquisition yet or anything. It feels downright weird.

Mom loads her coffee cup with cream and sugar. "I've known the angel Verus since before the Wars. She and I discussed this. You can attend."

"Oh, I see." If Mom says I can go, this must be totally boring. I eat my Frankenberry cereal one sugar puff at a time. It's like my last meal before hitting the guillotine.

Walker hovers by my shoulder. "We must depart now, Myla."

Anger burns through my belly. "If you gave me a little notice before these Arena visits, I'd be ready faster."

Walker shares a sly look with my mother. "You never complained before."

"Well, I'm complaining now."

Mom turns another page in her magazine. "Just because you're not fighting evildoers this morning doesn't mean you can be grouchy with Walker."

Ugh. I hate it when she's right. "Sorry, Walker."

"You're forgiven."

I swallow my last bite of cereal. "Okay, let's hit it."

Walker opens a portal in the center of the kitchen.

Mom blows me a kiss. "Have fun, sweetie!"

"I'll try." I give her a halfhearted wave. "See you after school."

Taking Walker's hand in mine, I steel my shoulders and step through the dark door. We tumble through space for what feels like hours. I almost puke at least twice before stepping onto the Arena's dirt floor.

Around me stand a dozen quasis. Men and women, black and white, young and old…This group could not be more different, except for one thing: they all have long pointed tails like mine.

They're all part-furor. Fighters like me. I can't help but size up the other warriors. I could take anyone of these folks down, easily. And although most of them have fighting suits, none are as dragon-scale badass as mine.

Hey, it's not a competition, but I'm winning.

Sharkie does his emcee-thing. The Oligarchy, angels, and demons all take their places in the Arena. An eternity ticks by while I stand near the other fighters. I pass the time playing rock-paper-scissors with my tail. My stomach growls. I must be missing lunch.

THUD. THUD. Sharkie sets his staff against the ground. "Angels, demons, and ghouls! We've a special announcement today from the fearless leader of our troops, Armageddon!"

The demon seats go ballistic. The angels clap politely.

Armageddon stands from his stone throne, his long black face twisting into an especially evil-looking grin. "We have found the Scala Heir." His eyes glow with menace. "As promised."

Verus takes to her feet. "Excellent. If this is indeed the Scala Heir, then we should be able to perform the Scala Initiation ceremony *right now*."

Armageddon slowly reseats himself into his throne. "Of course."

Verus points to our group of fighters. "Please line up along the base of the Arena wall. You're witnesses to the changing."

A Scala changing? That could be cool to watch. To be safe, I pick out a spot by an exit archway, the easier to duck out if things get really boring.

Verus raises her arms. "Let the initiation begin!"

All the angels take to their feet. The air echoes with the rustling of wings and robes. They speak in one voice. "Has the Scala Heir been found?"

Verus lowers her arms. "Yes. Among the thrax nobility."

Thrax nobility? My stomach sinks to my toes. Yuck.

Moving as one group, the angels extend their white wings. Half the arena becomes blindingly bright. They speak again as one: "Let them bring the Scala Heir to us to be awakened and angelbound." They all retake their seats.

"We will bring out the Scala Heir." Verus smiles softly. "But first, the realm that produced the Heir will take the Arena floor. Today, this honor goes to the thrax. The thrax are divided into many Houses, the greatest of these being Horus, Striga, Kamal, Acca, and Rixa. All five will appear before us today. First is the House of Horus, the descendants of the Nubian Pharaohs."

I exhale with relief. Nubian Pharaohs? That means Lincoln isn't likely to take the Arena floor. At least, not yet.

I pick at the lint under my nails with my tail. Not that I care *what* he does, of course.

A trumpet call echoes through the air. The dirt floor shakes as the House of Horus does who-knows-what in the maze of hallways leading to the Arena floor. More trumpets blare as a dozen two-wheeled chariots barrel out of a nearby archway, each one driven by a pair of gray stallions.

The Arena floor rattles beneath my feet as the chariots charge around the stadium. My mouth bursts into a grin. These guys are so badass, it isn't even funny.

As they tool around the Arena floor, I can see that the drivers are tall men with ebony skin, solid frames, and long dreadlocks. They wear brown linen pants topped by black leather tunics. The image of a looping Egyptian eye is sewn onto their chests in bronze thread.

The chariots ride in different formations, their paths creating a complex series of circles and lines. Golden bridles glimmer in the horses' mouths. The chariots crisscross into the most complex pattern yet. Then, they stop in neat rows in one corner of the stadium. Whoa. I can't believe they didn't bump into each other at least once.

I clap wildly, but everyone else is silent. Oops. I pop my hands behind my back.

"Second is the House of Striga," says Verus. "Their skills in sorcery and witchcraft are famous across the five realms."

From the opposite archway, two-dozen men march onto the arena floor, their bodies thin and lanky. All have olive skin and square faces. Purple beads are woven into their long brown hair. They wear the brown leather pants, silver chain mail, and velvet tunics decorated with a purple pentagram. The stick-men march into the middle of the stadium floor, align themselves into a huge circle, and quickly bow their heads. A low chant echoes through the air. A massive ball of red flame appears by the stadium floor.

I gasp. I've never seen magic before.

The scarlet orb zooms up into the sky and bursts like a firework. The Striga men march to another corner of the Arena, taking their place beside the House of Horus.

I bob on the balls of my feet, excited to see what the next House has in store. Sure, it's a bummer I'm not battling anything right now, but this show almost makes up for that. Almost.

"Third is the House of Kamal," says Verus. "These thrax are renowned for their skill with animals."

More thrax march into the stadium, this time their cotton tunics hold the image of three claw scratches in deep blue. The Kamal warriors form a line across the center of the Arena floor, about twenty fighters in all. Their bodies look lean and sinewy; their cocoa faces are set into determined frowns.

Scanning the faces, I look for some girl fighters, but can't find one. Hmm. The other Houses didn't have female warriors either. That is so weird. I wonder if all the thrax women run around batting their eyes and feeling guys muscles like that Adair girl? Hmm. Not sure I want to know the answer to that question.

The Kamal let out a loud whoop. Tigers burst from the Arena archways, racing toward the floor's center. Falcons swoop down from the sky; long blue ribbons hang from their talons. All the creatures settle in place, one animal for each warrior. They roar and shriek so loudly, I think my eardrums will burst. The warriors bow slightly; the animals fall silent. The Kamal march in unison, taking their places beside the other Houses. The falcons perch on their warrior's arm, the tigers stand at their fighter's side. All the animal's bodies remain still as stone.

My mind whirls through all the demons that'd be easier to fight with a Kamal tiger or falcon at my side. I bob my head approvingly. Those would come in mighty handy, indeed.

"Fourth is the House of Acca. These thrax are renowned for their abilities with a crossbow."

I lean against the stonewall, hitching my right foot across my left. This is taking a long time, but the warrior displays are super-interesting. Who knew there were so many ways to fight demons besides hand-to-hand? I work hard to look casual and actively ignore the unwanted images of Lincoln's mouth that keep popping into my mind. An anxious feeling tightens my stomach. *Stop thinking about him, damn it.*

Twenty warriors walk onto the Arena floor, their black velvet tunics sewn with the image of a gloved yellow fist. All have stout bodies, pale skin, and golden hair. Each fighter wears metal-studded gloves and carries a silver crossbow. The Acca warriors march to the floor's center and stand in a long line. Moving as one unit, they all fire a single metal bolt straight into the air.

I purse my lips. That's not so impressive. I know zero about crossbows, and I could do that, easy peasy.

The stadium holds its breath as the bolts fly skywards, then reverse direction and speed back to the ground. The warriors lift their arms, catching the bolts in their gloved hands.

I take it back. That's a pretty neat trick.

"Fifth is the House of Rixa, rulers of the thrax and the only bloodline who can wield the mighty baculum." A hush falls over the stadium as Lincoln, his father, and mother process onto the Arena floor. All three wear silver crowns.

On instinct, my body tenses into battle stance, tail arcing over my shoulder. All my forgotten anger from the library slams back into me, raw and present. 'Real thrax warrior,' my ass.

After the royal family, sixty warriors march onto the Arena floor in neat lines, each step in perfect unison. These men dress in black leather pants topped by silver chain mail and a black velvet tunic. The image of an eagle is sewn onto their chests in silver thread. The bird swoops downward, claws extended.

My tail whips behind me in a slow, predatory rhythm. My inner demon awakens, anger pumps through my veins. I grit my teeth as I take in the scene.

King Connor stands sturdy and tall, a silver sword hanging from a belt about his waist. Beside him, the Queen is arrayed in a black velvet gown with a full skirt and long looping sleeves, all edged in silver ribbon. Her sandy brown hair is wound into a bun at the base of her neck. Lincoln walks beside them with military precision. Shadows shift across his full mouth, brown hair, and strong shoulders.

My eyes flicker red with wrath.

The Rixa march to the Arena's center, forming three columns of twenty soldiers each. The King, Queen, and High Prince stand nearby.

Lincoln steps forward, raising one hand. "On my mark!"

The men in the first column reach behind their backs, pulling what looks like two short silver rods from the folds of their tunics.

I squint, trying to see the weapons in their hands. Are those teensy little sticks the 'mighty baculum?' Not too impressive, Prince Pompous.

Lincoln lowers his arm.

The soldiers place one stick in each hand. A line of fire extends from both ends of the baculum, turning the rods into two short spears made of white flame.

The warriors toss the spears into the air. The lines of white fire whip skyward, then spiral back into the warrior's hands. The Rixa set the two baculum together, creating one longer, heavier spear. Holding it before them with both hands, the warriors thrust the spear into the earth.

Okay, maybe that's a *little bit* impressive.

Lincoln turns to the next group and nods.

The second column brings out their baculum, holding both sticks together in one hand. Fire extends from the baculum, turning the short silver rods into long tridents made of white flame.

The warriors run through a series of synchronized lunges and spins. Like the first group, they end by setting the base of their tridents into the soil.

I hate to admit it, but that was cool, too.

Lincoln faces the last set of soldiers.

The third column raises their arms shoulder-high, one baculum in each hand. A rope of white flame extends between the silver rods. Before each warrior, the fiery baculum cord weaves back and forth until it turns into a small net made of fire. The soldiers toss their baculum-nets high into the air, where they all link together into one huge and fiery web. I can't imagine a demon getting out from under that thing.

The fire-web hovers in the sky for a moment, then wafts slowly downward. When the great net lies just above the warrior's heads, the Rixa raise their arms high, catching their baculum with ease. The fighters lower their hands. The fiery web breaks back into individual nets.

Lincoln pulls out two baculum of his own. He sets them together in his palms. A fiery broadsword appears in his hands. He sets his feet apart in battle stance and raises the fire-sword high above his head.

"In thrax hic sunt!" He speaks Latin, like the Scala. I've no idea what it means, but I guess it's something like 'thrax are in the house.' At the sound of his voice, fresh anger zings through my system. I crack my neck and try to stay cool.

From her white throne, Verus sweeps her arm across the crowd. "The senior maiden of each major House is that house's Great Lady. We're fortunate to have four Great Ladies here with us today: Nita of House Kamal, Keisha of House Horus, Gianna of House Striga, and Adair of House Acca."

Adair? As in 'ooh you have such muscle-y muscles' Adair? I grit my teeth and work hard to slow my breathing. I'm built to show up and kick ass, not stand around while girly dips do their thing.

I inhale a slow breath. Keep it together, Myla. I'm sure she'll just prance out onto the Arena floor and then stand somewhere and look pretty.

Four girls around my age step through a stadium archway, each wearing a gown in their house's color: yellow, purple, bronze, and blue. They saunter across the Arena floor to stand before the King, Queen, and High Prince. Lincoln lowers his baculum; the fiery blade disappears.

I glance at my watch. School's almost over. This bleeding ceremony has to end soon.

"The procession is complete," says Verus. "We will now awaken the Scala Heir."

The angels once again rise to their feet, their great wings extending behind their backs. They speak in unison. "Who is the Scala Heir?"

The Lady Adair raises her hand to shoulder level, palm forward. "I am the Scala Heir."

What?! No freaking way. The Scala is supposed to be part angel, demon, and human. Thrax are only part human and angel. I eye Lady Adair carefully. She's so perfect and cute-sy, she could easily be part-demon. Maybe she's descended from one of those swamp monsters who pretend to be a lovely, drowning lady. You try to rescue the pretty, and you're lured to your death. *Yeah, that's it.*

Lady Adair speaks again, her voice snapping me out of my thoughts. "I look forward to following in the long tradition of a thrax Scala."

I grimace. The old Scala can't last much longer. If she's the Scala Heir, I could spend years of quality time with this loser. Gross.

Adair carefully positions her long blonde hair over one shoulder. She's tall and willowy with porcelain skin, high cheekbones, a thin mouth, and a turned-up nose. One mismatched eye is emerald green, the other's drab brown. All in all, she looks perfectly capable of getting a book down from a shelf without any help.

Verus nods. "We shall now awaken the Scala Heir." All the angels lower their heads. A point of white light appears in the air above the stadium. I wince and shield my eyes with one hand. My body relaxes a bit. Things are getting interesting again.

The Queen of the Angels raises her arms toward the floating white light. "We draw forth igni power to the Scala Heir."

My gaze shifts between the magical light and Adair, who whispers back and forth with Gianna. I raise my brows. I'm bored too, but I'm not chit-chatting from the middle of the Arena floor.

Inch by inch, the tiny star lowers until it rests just above the sandy ground. The Arena grows oddly quiet as the star twinkles away. My tail starts freaking out, trying to drag me out the nearest archway. I smack the arrowhead end and tell it to behave.

With a deafening crack, the point of light bursts, filling the Arena with hazy brilliance. The angels raise their heads, their eyes blazing bright blue in the thick white fog. The demons howl and cough.

I inhale deeply, the air tastes sweet and calming. My tail quiets down.

Once the air clears, Verus gestures to Adair. "Prove you have igni power."

Adair raises her arms above her head. "I am the Scala Heir." Tiny points of light tumble from her fingertips like grains of sand.

Verus nods. "Now that the Heir has been awakened, she must be angelbound. Igni power comes from the angels. Once the Scala Heir displays true love toward someone with angelic blood, it will further activate her abilities with igni. When the current Scala dies, her full powers will appear."

I count off the steps in my mind: awakened, angelbound, and then full Scala when the old one dies. Makes sense that the angels would want to control when and how the Heir is awakened. It's a big job. I look at Adair, my mouth twisting onto one side of my face. Not sure she's really cut out for it.

Verus gestures to the Scala Heir. "To whom do you wish to be angelbound?"

Adair grins. "I choose my true love, the High Prince Lincoln."

My back teeth lock. I think I'm going to be sick.

"Does the High Prince accept this?"

Lincoln's expression is unreadable. "Yes."

Verus gestures to Adair. "Would you like to say a few words before you're angelbound?"

Adair beams. "Yes. Thank you all for this lovely initiation." She glances straight at me. "I'm glad that the lesser creatures could be here too."

Anger spikes up my spine. What did I ever do to her? First, she makes snotty comments about me in the library. Now, she does it again in the Arena. Someone is asking for an ass-whooping.

Adair and Gianna start whispering again.

I roll my eyes. Sheesh, save it for the ride home.

Verus gestures to Lincoln and the Scala Heir. "Please turn and face each other."

Adair quickly steps in front of Lincoln. Their gazes lock. Adair's forehead crinkles. After that, she swoons and tumbles to the ground. Lincoln helps her back to her feet. Adair looks around the stadium, her eyes blinking madly.

The stadium lets out a collective gasp. Adair's eyes, once mismatched, now both glow bright blue. Angel eyes.

"Lady Adair, you are awakened and Angelbound," says Verus. "Our initiation is complete. When the current Scala dies, you will gain your full powers from him. We bow to you, our Scala Heir."

The angels bend at the waist, the demons howl and screech. Armageddon leans back in his black stone throne, eyes gleaming red and missing nothing. The whole scene seems way over-the-top and sketchy to me. But what do I know? I'm used to killing things in the Arena, not watching crap like this.

Lincoln offers his arm to Adair, she wraps her fingers around his bicep. *Of course.* Together, they process off the stadium floor.

Suddenly, I'm totally regretting my decision to stand by an exit archway. They're heading straight for me. My inner rage monster turns positively frantic.

As the Prince and Scala Heir step nearer, Adair eyes me from head to toe. "What do they call these lesser demons again? Partials? Semis?"

Fury twists my stomach. *We're called quasis.*

Lincoln gazes in my direction. His face is stone. "I'm not sure."

Adair sighs. "Whatever they're called, I'm glad they saw 'real warriors' in action today." She grips Lincoln's bicep tighter.

More fury flows through me. I set my feet apart, ready to pounce. My tail arcs over my shoulder. Lincoln watches the movement, the ghost of a smile curling his full lips in a way that says 'how cute; the little demon wants to fight.' My blood pressure skyrockets.

The Prince steps past me through the archway. "Yes, I'm sure it was quite an education for the poor creatures."

That does it.

Mindless rage blasts through my veins. My eyes positively beam with red light. I rush forward, ready to tackle them both behind the kneecaps.

Instead, it's Walker who pounces on me, knocking me straight into a portal. We tumble through space, coming to a landing in the empty parking lot outside my school.

"Walker? What in blazes are you doing?" I ball my hands into fists. My eyes burn bright red.

"You're asking *me?*" Walker shakes his head in disbelief. "You were about to flatten the thrax High Prince. A hundred of his best warriors were standing nearby. Even *you* can't fight that, Myla."

I pace the parking lot. The movement helps the anger seep from my body. My eyes cool a bit. "Okay, you're right." I pause and take three deep breaths. "Thank you."

"You're welcome." Walker rubs his sideburns. "That was some look on your face, Myla. I've never seen your eyes turn that red."

"I guess I lost my temper big time." I shift my weight from foot to foot. This incident has gone from rage-inducing to totally embarrassing.

"I understand. Ghouls are the same way. We're quiet enough and then–KABOOM–we lose our cool."

Maybe that's a genetic trait I got from my father. Barf. A heavy sadness seeps into my bones. I slouch and hug my elbows.

Walker tilts his head to one side. "Is there something wrong, Myla?"

I meet his gaze, seeing his black button eyes fill with concern. I start blabbing everything. "I've been getting these dreamscapes about Mom's past from the angel Verus."

Walker nods. "Your mother told me."

"Well, I think my dad may be a ghoul."

"Have you asked your mother about this?"

"Not yet." I slump a bit lower. "Maybe I don't want the answer to that question so much anymore."

"I understand." Walker rubs his sideburns thoughtfully. "Perhaps a change of subject is in order. I've learned the Scala will perform an iconigration soon."

"Really?! Will you sneak me in?" Iconigrations are when the Scala transfers souls in a huge group. So cool.

"Of course." A wisp of a grin rounds his mouth. "And where would you like to go now?" He opens a portal.

I soak in Walker's warm smile. A knot of emotion forms in my throat. "Thanks again, Walker. For everything."

"No need for thanks." Walker sets his hand on my cheek, his touch is warm and grounding. "You're very important to me, Myla." He glances at the black portal. "Now where to?"

I check my watch. "Well, school ended an hour ago. Can we go to the Ryder library?"

"Absolutely." Walker takes my hand in his. Together, we step into the portal. For once, I actually don't feel ill as we tumble through space. We step out right by the mansion's front door.

I give Walker's hand a little squeeze. "See you at the iconigration."

Walker nods. "Until then." He steps into the dark portal and disappears.

CHAPTER NINE

A

I take a deep breath, walk up to the front door of the Ryder mansion and knock. No answer.

I jiggle the handle. It's unlocked. I turn the knob and step inside.

"Cissy? Zeke?" I nervously bite my lower lip. I'm totally late after that fiasco at the Arena with Adair. If after all that, I can't go to the library today, I will definitely need to kill something. Hopefully, not Zeke.

Soft giggles sound from behind the corner to the West Wing.

"Zekie, don't!" It's Cissy.

Oh, they're here alright. Ick.

I stand in the center of the reception hall. "Cissy, I'm going over to the library. Is that okay?"

More giggles.

"I'll take that as a 'yes.'" I walk down the hallway to the East Wing and hike up the stairs. I stop at the second floor.

This is the exact spot I saw in my dreamscape. This is where Mom met up with her family–my family–before she was sworn in as Senator. I stare at the closed door, knots of nervous energy forming down my spine.

Here goes.

I slowly set my fingertips on the knob and twist. It's open. I step past the threshold and flip on the lights. Inside is an ornate wooden conference room with mahogany tables and chairs. Huge paintings of the Oligarchy hang from the walls.

I frown. None of this looks like it did in my dreamscape.

Another door stands ajar at the back of the room. I walk through it and enter a long, open space dripping in cobwebs. My breath catches. This is the old senate offices, exactly the way they were before the war. My heart starts beating like crazy.

"Hey, Myla."

I jump a bit and gasp. "Oh, Cissy. I didn't see you there."

"Didn't you hear me calling you on the way over?"

I run my finger along a dusty desktop. "I guess I was a little distracted." I peep at the empty space behind her. "Where's Zeke?"

Cissy shrugs. "I told him I'd meet up with him later." She eyes my fighting suit. "Another Arena match today?"

"Of sorts."

"You're going once or twice a month now." She shakes her head from side to side. "I'm worried about you."

I open my mouth, ready to tell her everything, then close it just as quickly. "I'm fine, Cissy."

"You're always saying that lately." She steps around the dim space. "What are you doing in here? This is nasty old office space they used before the war. It's been boarded up for ages."

"Mom was a Senator in the old Republic. Her team worked in this office."

Cissy's tawny eyes open wide. "Wow." She sets her hand on her rib cage. "How long have you known that?"

"Since I first visited the library. I found a book about it."

"Why didn't you tell me?"

"I don't know. It's private stuff." Guilt worms its way around my belly. *Am I so proud that I can't tell my best friend I'm part-ghoul?*

"You never used to feel that way." She steps to my side and gently sets her hand on my shoulder. "We've gabbed about your Mom's pre-war 'mystery history' since we were kids. Remember that time we made sand castles at Canus Beach? You pretended your Mom fought demons in a tall tower. I said your father was the dragon King."

My voice cracks when I speak. "Yeah, I remember." I slowly lower myself into a rickety office chair, setting off a poof of cobwebs and dust. I cover my face with my hands.

Cissy kneels beside me. "Come on, Myla. There's something bothering you and it's more than your Mom being a Senator. You can tell me."

I hug my elbows. "Here's the thing. The Lewises used to be a huge family. Everyone was murdered in Armageddon's War because Mom was a Senator. That's why she's so overprotective of me. She lost everyone she loved." I stare at the floor. "I never even got to meet them."

Cissy pats my hand. "I'm so sorry."

"For so long I wanted to know the truth. Now I want to forget everything I've learned." A warm tear rolls down the bridge of my nose.

"I understand, sweetie."

I slump into the old office chair and watch dust motes float through the beam of light from the opened door. Somewhere an old-fashioned clock ticks away. I stare into the shadows, imagining ghostly Lewis eyes peeping at me in fear. My skin puckers into gooseflesh. Cissy gently rests her hand on my arm.

"Hey, I might have something to cheer you up." She slides an envelope out of her pocket. "I totally shouldn't do this."

I look at her out of my right eye. "Do what?"

"Everyone's freaking out in the East Wing. The thrax reserved the mansion for some event to celebrate autumn, but the ghoul minister's kicking them out. No one wants to tell a bunch of demon fighters that they can't use the house." She taps the sealed envelope against her palm and looks at me expectantly. "I'm supposed to give this to one of the other Furor fighters to deliver."

Thrax? Message? I smell payback.

I shoot Cissy my most innocent grin. "You're right. It would totally cheer me up to go on a little errand."

"That's my Myla." Cissy starts to hand me the letter, and then she pulls it back. "Don't be surprised if they're a little cranky about the change."

"Oh, I can handle it." I scoop the envelope from her hands. Zipping down my fighting suit, I set the letter against my collar-bone, then zip it up again. "I'm on it."

"One more thing. The thrax are really into their traditions. To get into their compound, you have to wear a dress and ride a horse." Her face lands somewhere between a wince and a smile. "This could be a nice change of pace for you. Getting dressed up and all."

I open my mouth to spill the truth: I'm not dress-girl or horse-lady. Sure, I love sneaking into the Ryder stables to kill Doxy demons, but I have no idea how to touch a horse, let alone ride it. But then I shut my yap. Screw it. I'd say just about anything for this payback fiesta. "That sounds like such a nice idea, Cissy."

"And won't tell anyone I let you do this, okay?"

"Never."

"Good." She rocks back on her heels, setting her golden ring-lets swinging. "There are some thrax horses in the Ryder stables. I guess they're enchanted or something. I hear they basically ride themselves, if you know what I mean."

Some little part of me feels guilty for misleading Cissy here when she's trying to be nice, but my inner demon has that little part of me in a sleeper hold. "Sounds like a plan."

Cissy and I leave the mansion, hike past the hedgerow maze, and head toward a long and thin building on the outer grounds: the Ryder stables. A great wooden door marks the entrance; Cissy hauls it open. Inside, there's a long central aisle with about a dozen stalls on either side.

I walk up the main aisle, peeking in the different stalls. Dry hay crunches beneath my feet. "I've always wondered. Why do the Ryders have stables anyway? Zeke never talks about riding and his parents only seem to love tennis."

"It's for guests. Thrax aren't the only ones who like to travel by horse. Some ghouls and demons do it too. Normally, there are only a few horses in residence, but with the thrax in town, the stables are almost always full these days."

I look at the different horses, reading the names printed above the stalls. "Moon Shadow. Firelight. Eugene."

"That last one is a demon horse. Don't go near it."

My brows arch with admiration. "You're a fountain of diplomatic information, Miss Frederickson."

Cissy grins. "Zeke's parents have taught me all sorts of stuff. It's really interesting."

A horse with a bluish-gray coat steps out of a nearby stall. She prances up to me and whinnies.

I smile. I'd know this horse anywhere. She's been a target of the Doxy demons for months. They love to snarl her mane and tail; I love to play her personal demon exterminator. I run my fingers through the horse's silky black mane. "What's your name, lovely?"

Cissy steps up to the now-empty stall. "She's a thrax horse. Her name's Nightshade." Cissy peeps inside. "I wonder how she got out of her stall."

I shrug. "You said the horses were enchanted. Maybe they can do magic."

Nightshade couches onto the stable floor. Her big black eyes stare at me in a way that says 'climb on.'

My body buzzes with excitement. I quickly slip onto into Nightshade; her back feels warm and steady below me as she rises to her feet. The next moment, Nightshade begins walking toward the stable doors. A sense of calm and ease washes over me. I feel as if I've ridden on her all my life. Grinning, I loop my fingers through her mane and whisper in a low voice. "Take me to the thrax." She rears on her hind legs.

Cissy frowns. "Not yet, Myla. You're supposed to wear a gown!"

Nightshade gallops toward the stable exit. I look over my shoulder and wave. "I'll figure something out!"

I'm pretty sure Cissy screams something at me, but I can't hear her. Okay, maybe I could hear her if I tried, but I'm riding a freaking horse! Nightshade's muscles shift beneath me in drum-roll rhythm. The wind whirls across my face, roars in my ears and dances through my long auburn hair. It's nothing less than glorious.

Nightshade and I pound over the rolling hills behind the Ryder mansion. Exhilaration bubbles through my bloodstream. We thrum across vast fields of high grass. After a short ride, her pace starts to slow.

A trio of purple tents appears on the horizon. They're all large and held in place by sturdy poles, more like circus tents than camping stuff. A line of tall pine trees looms to their right. Nightshade slows to a halt.

"Are we here, Night?"

The horse nickers.

I release my fingers from her mane, slide down the horse's barrel and pick my way toward the nearest tent. Everything looks deserted. A girl in a yellow gown steps out from the line of trees. She's tall and willowy with long blonde hair.

I wave my arms. "Hello, there!"

The girl stops, eyeing me from head to toe. "Are you lost too? I've lived here for months and I still can't find my way around. This place is huge."

I step closer. "Yes, I'm lost. Kind of."

She grins. "Forgive my bad manners." She curtsies. "I'm Lady Avery. Who are you?" She blinks her large eyes, one green and one brown.

"I'm Myla." I stare at her for a moment. "You look familiar."

"I'm the younger sister of the Great Scala Heir."

"Yeah, that's it." I flash my most winning smile. "I'm looking for Prince Lincoln. I have an important message for him."

She shifts her weight onto her right leg. "He's at a thrax-only event. You're not supposed to go unless you're invited." She scans my black fighting suit. "And unless you're wearing proper dress."

"Of course, I was invited to today's…" I look at her encouragingly.

"Battle practice with the young Lords?"

Not a bright one, that Avery.

"Exactly. That's totally what I was invited to. And I got an official exception for the dress thing."

Avery frowns. "I've never heard of an official exception."

"I have a skin condition. This suit was, uh, prescribed by my doctor." I hold out my hand. "You should stand back. It's kind of contagious."

"Oh, my!"

"Where's the practice again?"

"That way." She points to a rocky hill across from the tall pines. "I'm heading there myself. Now that my sister's the Scala Heir, I'm the Great Lady for the House of Acca." She beams and tosses her hair. "Isn't that wonderful?"

I plaster my smile back on. "It sure is." I take off at a run. "I'll see you there!"

"Okay. Goodbye, Myla!"

I speed up the rocky incline, my heart thudding with anticipation. I summit the small hill and scope out the ground below. A flat patch of green field opens before me. Lincoln stands in its center, surrounded by four men in velvet tunics of bronze, yellow, purple, and blue. They all look in their late teens. The Queen waits on the sidelines, motionless and regal in her black velvet gown. The Great Ladies encircle her, still wearing their multicolored dresses from the initiation. Adair has changed into a simple white robe.

In the center of the field, Lincoln flips a wooden practice sword in his hand. Raising his arm high, he demonstrates a slicing technique to the young Lords. Everyone's attention is focused on the lesson. I picture what'll happen once I introduce myself. My mouth winds into a semi-evil grin.

Now's my chance.

I stride down the rocky hill and raise my arm high. "Hello, there! I have a message for the–"

The Acca Lord shakes his blonde head. "A demon! I shall protect you, my Prince!" He races toward me, arms outstretched.

I watch my opponent, shaking my head in disbelief. This is his total plan? Run up and grab me? That's way too easy. I wait until he's close, then leap up into the air and kick my heels forward. My boots connect with his chest. The Acca Lord tumbles onto his ass, gasping for breath. I somersault backwards, land on my feet and keep walking.

My grin stretches even wider. I love that move.

I keep a steady stride toward Lincoln, scanning the field as I go. The Queen and ladies stand immobile and stunned on the sidelines. The three remaining Lords bob on their heels, waiting for their turn to attack. Lincoln stares at me, his mismatched eyes filled with cool menace.

Good.

"Stop now, foul demon!" It's the Horus Lord this time. His 250 pounds of solid muscle barrel straight for me.

I size up his approach. This one will be a little more interesting.

Once the Horus Lord is almost upon me, I bend over at the waist. My tail wraps around my attacker's neck, spinning him 360 degrees. With a heavy thud, he lands back-first onto the field. A low groan fills the air.

I wince. Okay, that might be a concussion. Oops.

I resume my forward march. Lincoln's only a few yards away now. Lord Kamal takes up the cry. At least he has the sense to grab a wooden sword.

Weapons. That mixes it up.

I stop, set my weight on my right leg and cross my arms over my chest. Kamal races up to me, his sword raised high above his head.

"Die, you demon sc—"

My tail punches him in the gut. At least I think it was the gut. Eh, I wasn't really paying close attention. Lord Kamal crouches into a fetal position and falls over onto the ground, moaning.

I step up to the Striga Lord. "Are you gonna try anything?"

The young Lord shakes his head vigorously, causing the purple beads in his hair to jingle. "No, your ladyship."

"Good."

I turn to Lincoln. His stance is rigid; his face is still as stone. Raising my hand, I unzip the top of my suit. Gasps sound from the Great Ladies. I can't help but smile just a little bit. I slide the envelope out from under my suit and hand it over. The Prince grips the letter, his face unreadable.

"Message for you from the Ghoul Minister. It's urgent." I bow slightly. "If you'll excuse me, I'll leave you *real warriors* to fight it out." I walk away, and maybe I shake my hips a wee bit more than necessary.

As I cross the field, I scan the faces of the Great Ladies. All their mouths curl in unflattering looks of shock and disgust. Adair looks especially ugly. Sweet.

The Queen watches me too, but unlike the Great Ladies, a satisfied grin rounds her mouth. My tail waves goodbye to her. She nods slightly in return.

Avery appears at the top of the rocky hill. "I'm here, everyone!" She waves. "Did I miss anything?"

I shoot her a hearty thumbs-up. "Not much. Catch you later."

Avery curtsies. "Goodbye, Myla. I hope your skin condition improves."

"Oh, it has." I feel tons better already.

I hike over the hill, finding Nightshade waiting for me by the nearest tent. She paws the ground with her front hoof in a move that says 'let's vamoose.'

"I'm ready to go, too." I wind my fingers through her mane and haul myself onto her back. Nightshade gallops over the fields and hills. All too soon, we're trotting down my street. Nightshade stops by my front door; I slide off her barrel.

"Thank you, Night." She nuzzles into my neck. I brush her mane with my fingers and sigh. Nightshade is the best. "I'm so glad you found me, girl."

She whinnies softly and takes off at a gallop.

When I walk through my front door, the house is quiet and empty. I roam the rooms until I find a note from Mom on the kitchen table. She's running errands with Walker and won't be home until late. I make myself a quick bite to eat and slip into bed, a peaceful smile on my face for the first time in recent memory. You don't get many chances to kick ass like I did today. The only thing that could've made it better would be video.

.A.

Once I close my eyes, my dreams return me to the Gray Sea. I stand on a familiar stretch of dark sand beside a tall stonewall. Crouching low, I set my hands onto the desert floor. A circle of white fire erupts from the ground. From its center rises the form of my mother made from sand. She sits at a desk.

The earth continues to rise, the granules building into the shape of an office.

The circle of fire flares higher, then disappears. The moving sand transforms into flesh and blood. The scene before me comes to life.

Mom looks up from her desk. "Hello, Tim." She runs her fingertips along the neckline of her blue suit.

Tim's gaze follows the movement of her fingers across her chest. "You should call me TIM-29." His voice comes out a little husky.

I'm no lust expert, but it's possible that Tim has a thing for my Mom. My stomach lurches. Could this guy be my father?

"I've been calling you Tim for six months now, that isn't going to change." She smiles. Her face looks animated, alive, and dazzling.

I scratch my neck, my head wagging from side to side. I still can't believe this is the same person who conducts my Maternal Inquisition each morning.

Tim bows again. "As you wish, Senator."

"For the hundredth time, call me Camilla."

Tim shakes his head. "No, that wouldn't be right, Senator." He gingerly sets a cup of coffee onto her desktop.

"Thank you."

Tim leans over Mom's head and inhales deeply. He whispers one word: "Lavender."

Hair-smelling? That confirms it. Tim definitely has a thing for Mom.

"What did you say?" She scribbles away on a pad.

"Nothing, Senator." He takes a few quick steps backwards. "Xavier Cross is in the waiting room, again. He insists on seeing you."

Mom sighs. "He has an appointment in a *month*."

I've heard that sigh, many times. Whoever this guy is, he's getting on Mom's last nerve.

Tim grips his hands at his waist. "He wants to see you *today*."

A rotary phone on the desk begins to ring. Mom sets her hand on the receiver and looks to Tim. "Please tell him to wait *one month*." Tim nods and leaves the room.

Mom picks up her phone. "Senator Lewis speaking." She swivels her chair so she faces the wall. "Yes, Ambassador. I understand the complaint."

On the opposite side of the room, the door swings open. A man slides through. He's tall and fit with short brown hair, piercing blue eyes and skin the color of milky cocoa. He adjusts the lapels of his gray suit.

Still facing the wall, Mom continues her phone call. "I understand the demand, but we cannot guarantee that a particular soul will go to Hell. I'll certainly pass the request to Senator Myung."

Damn, she's not taking shizz from that caller. My brows arch. This is the same woman who now spends an hour to choose a frozen dinner from the freezer. I never imagined she could be so decisive.

The stranger walks around the room, studying the pictures lining the walls, his long arms clasped behind him. He moves with a calculated grace that I find oddly soothing.

Mom kicks at the base of the wall, her features cringing into her 'exasperated face.' She takes a deep breath. "Senator Myung holds the Afterlife Management seat, I head Other-Realm Diplomacy. As I've told you before, I have no formal say in this matter but I promise to make your request known." She pauses, listening. "Excellent, goodbye." She slams the receiver onto the phone. "Hells bells! That's the fourth time this week." She twists about in her chair, seeing the stranger in her office for the first time.

Mom's chocolate eyes narrow into slits. "And you are?"

The man reaches out his hand. "Xavier Cross."

Mom doesn't flinch. "You have an appointment in one month, Mister Cross. Tim should have stopped you."

Xavier seats himself in a chair across from Mom's desk. "It won't take five minutes, I promise." He smiles. His face is handsome with a square jaw and high cheekbones.

Mom stares at him, her lips pursed. "Five minutes." She glances at her watch. "Go."

I click my tongue. Nice move, Mom!

Xavier taps his knee with his pointer finger. "You're new to the Senate, aren't you?"

"My family's held the Senate Diplomacy Seat for eight hundred years, but yes, I've served in this particular role for six months."

"I saw your pictures on the walls. Annual Lewis family picnics."

"Yes, we're a close group. Four minutes."

"And you have a ghoul assistant." The look in his eyes says 'and that's the stupidest idea ever.' My eyes flash with anger. *Leave my Mom alone.*

Mom drums her fingers on the table, her face the picture of cool. "I drive connections across all the five realms: Heaven, Hell, Antrum, the Dark Lands, and Purgatory. Most of my staff are members of the Lewis family, but I'm extending my team to other realms as well. Three minutes."

"Do you trust that ghoul?"

A muscle twitches along Mom's jaw. "Mister Cross, what exactly is this about?"

There's something in her tone that's protective of Tim, maybe even loving. My possible ghoul dad. Barf.

"I'll tell you." He leans back in his chair. "I am the lead angel Ambassador and you don't seem to know who I am or why we need to meet. I wonder if you're more suited to duties outside the Senate. Perhaps your interest lies closer to the ghouls?"

I let out a low whistle. *Now he's asked for it.*

Mom's eyes flare red. "I take great exception to that, Mr. Cross." She whips open a drawer, pulling out a heavy file. With a thwack, she sets it on her desktop. "I've been researching you." She whips open the manila folder. "Xavier Cross, Lead Ambassador for the angels." She points to a line on the sheet before her. "For some reason, no one seems to remember seeing your wings. Your race is listed as 'unknown.'"

He shrugs. "I wonder often myself."

"Whatever you are, you've been angel Ambassador to my government for three hundred years." She eyes him with a wary look, and I have to agree, this guy seems a little sketchy. A protective urge coils up my spine.

Xavier gestures around the room. "I helped design this Senate building, in fact." His eyes flash bright blue. "I know things about the quasi government you couldn't guess at."

Correction: he seems a LOT sketchy.

"Obviously, you've more than your share of secrets." Mom lifts a red sheet of paper from the file. "Here's a summary of the grievances against you over the years." She gives the paper a shake. "Using angelic influence seems to be your favorite way to get work done. That tactic is illegal in and will no longer be tolerated in this office."

Xavier hitches his ankle onto his knee and smiles. "There's never been a formal complaint. What's the nature of the problem, exactly?"

Mom slams the paper into her folder. "Angelic influence. You know, mind control? When angels find the good in a mortal soul and use it to change their behavior."

My brows pop up. Angelic influence? Who knew they could control minds?

Xavier makes a tsk-tsk noise. "Perhaps you're thinking of dreamscaping. A handful of angels and demons have this gift. They can send visions to others' dreams, sometimes even communicate with them in their sleep. You must be confused."

Uh-oh. I've tried that 'you're confused' line on Mom before. It only makes her angrier.

Mom raises her hand. "Please. We both know that angelic influence is nothing like dreamscaping. You connect to non-angels and inspire them into your so-called good deeds." She slaps her hands onto the desktop. "I'm not a fool. Most of my angelic requests have one goal only: to prevent fully evil souls from entering Heaven through trial by combat. And why's that? Angelic influence doesn't work on the truly evil, so you could never control them."

Mom's spot-on with this one. In my Arena matches, I fight their worst souls for that very reason: pure evil would be uncontrollable in Heaven.

Xavier frowns. "Nonsense."

I roll my eyes. He's so full of it.

"I knew that would be your position. That's why I've been spending the past months gathering evidence to the contrary. In our first meeting, I'd like to lay out the facts, clear and simple. After that, we'll have an honest discussion about how our offices will interact going forward." She rises to her feet and steps in front of Xavier's chair. "Are you ready for an honest discussion today, Mister Cross?" Her eyes flash red.

I grin. That was the verbal equivalent of a gut punch. I never pictured wrath as having a place anywhere outside the Arena, but Mom brings it to a whole new level. Go, Mom, go!

Xavier rises to his feet. "Senator Lewis, if it means we can actually get to work, then I'll promise anything."

Mom grips her elbows. "Anything?"

His eyes flare blue. "That's what I said."

"Then repeat after me. I will not use angelic influence."

A muscle twitches along his jaw. "I will not use angelic influence."

"Promise noted, Ambassador Cross." She steps back to her desk and retakes her seat. "I'll see you in a month."

Xavier eyes her closely. "No, you'll see me Monday." Turning on his heel, he stomps out the door, slamming it behind him.

Spinning her chair around, Mom kicks the wall. "Exasperating!"

I sigh. *I feel your pain, Mom.* Nothing's worse than a handsome guy with a snarky mouth and superiority complex.

Tim slowly opens the door and steps into the room.

"Is everything alright Senator? I heard noises."

"Where've you been the past few minutes, Tim?"

"At my desk." His forehead creases. "Filing, I think."

"You didn't see anyone walk past you?"

"No."

Mom speaks in a low voice. "He used angelic influence. Hopefully for the last time."

I rub my chin. It makes sense that angelic influence would work on anyone with a smidgeon of goodness in them, so long as the angel was powerful enough.

Tim frowns. "What did you say, Senator?"

"Nothing. I'm fine, Tim. Thank you for checking." Mom watches her assistant step back toward the door. "Oh, Tim?"

"Yes, Senator?"

"There's a cocktail event in the ballroom downstairs after work. Would you like to go and have a drink with me?"

Tim smiles. "Yes, Senator Lewis. I would."

Ugh. That might answer the whole 'which ghoul is my Dad' question.

They continue to speak, but their bodies become sand again and slip back into the earth. For the rest of the night, I dream that I keep trying to cook the perfect worm soufflé. It's freaking nasty.

CHAPTER TEN

A

When I open my eyes, one thought flashes through my mind: my dad may be a ghoul named Tim-29. It lines up with everything I learned from Mom and my dreamscapes. It's just really depressing.

I step into the kitchen, ready for this morning's Maternal Inquisition. Mom sits at our scratched Formica table, sipping her coffee. She eyes me carefully. "Did you have another dream?" The Inquisition beginneth.

"Yes, I did."

"Do you want to talk about it?"

I almost say no. This whole 'journey of discovery' has been a bit of a bust. Taking a deep breath, I slide into the chair across from her. "I think I saw my father in a dreamscape last night." I nervously drum my fingers on the tabletop. "Is he a ghoul named Tim-29?"

Her face is a cool mask. "Yes, that's him."

I cross my fingers. "You're lying."

"Never. Tim-29 is your father."

Mom's words hit me like a punch to the gut. It's one thing to suspect your dad's a ghoul, it's another, much nastier thing for your Mom to confirm it. I shake my head from side to side. "That can't be right."

She purses her lips. "It was a one-night thing. A woman has needs."

Okay, that's downright disgusting. "Way too much information, Mom!"

"You seemed to be having a hard time understanding. I wanted to give you a little context."

I drum my fingers on the tabletop. Something about this doesn't add up. "I don't know."

Mom looks directly into my eyes, her gaze steely and firm. "Have I ever lied to you, Myla?"

I swallow past the knot in my throat. "No."

"Tim is your father. I realize it's unconventional. That's why I kept it from you for so long."

I twist my lips into a yuck-face. "I still can't believe you got busy with a ghoul."

"Attraction comes in many forms. Take Walker, for instance. His grandmother was an archangel."

I groan. More disgustingness. "You do realize I haven't eaten."

"Come on, now. Be open-minded. This kind of thing happens all the time. It's nothing to get mopey about."

I frown. "I'm not mopey." I just want to eat ice cream and cry like it's my job, that's all.

Mom raises her eyebrows.

"Okay, maybe I'm a little bit mopey." I lean back in my chair, letting the news wash over me. "How come I don't look like, you know?" I pull the skin back on my face.

"You won't look like a ghoul until you die as a mortal."

"So, instead of dying, I'll become a gray-skinned zombie some-day. I guess that's kind-of a bonus." My head's officially spinning. "Anything else you want to share?"

"I think that's enough for one morning, don't you?"

"Yes, totally." I hitch my thumb toward the door. "I'm going to play depressing music and get ready for school."

"I'll get out the Frankenberry."

"Thanks, Mom." I slink back to my room, blast Taylor Swift, and change into the rattiest sweats and t-shirt I can find. Ghouls are some of the grouchiest, most overbearing pains in this astral plane. And they are my people. A gloomy weight settles over me.

I walk back to the kitchen. Every step's an effort, like my limbs are loaded down with rocks. My mind's sluggish too. I barely notice breakfast, the long drive to school, or walking through the front doors to Purgatory High. I meander through the sea of students.

It's official. I'm in the midst of an epic self-pity-fest.

From down the crowded hallway, Cissy spies me and waves. "Hey, Myla!"

I step up to her locker, my brain still a blur. "Morning." I'm pretty sure Cissy gabs on about some change to gym class. I can't process her words, so I do my best to smile and look interested. Then, I hear something that sounds like blah-blah-blah *Ryder library* blah-blah-blah.

I blink and shake my head. "What did you say, Cis?"

"You're going to the Ryder library after school today, right?"

"Yup." Maybe I can read up on being a half-ghoul. Yay.

"Great. See you later!" She steps into the crowd. I start the long slog over to History class. Looking up, I half-expect a little black storm-cloud to hover over my head.

I reach my classroom and settle into a chair in the last row. Zeke slides into the seat across the aisle from mine. Blech.

"Hey, Myla."

"Hi."

A genuine grin warms his chiseled features. "Did I tell you what Cissy did the other day?"

"No." I'm pretty sure he starts talking about Cissy, but I'm having issues with my attention span today. I can't understand a word. Instead, I focus on his cheery face and animated hand gestures. It's like watching a kitten chase a ball of string. He's so happy; I can't help but smile. After a while, his words become clear.

"My parents really like her." Zeke tosses his mop of golden hair. "They're showing her the ropes of diplomacy; she's a natural. Like at this political dinner, she smiled and made small talk with some of the most boring losers ever. It was great."

Miss Thing claps her hands. "Your attention, class!" She strides across the front of the room, her long robes swaying with each step. Unfortunately, she's decided to wear her hood down today, and the combination of her bright red lips and bald gray head is downright spooky.

"I've a very important lesson for you today." Miss Thing stalks back and forth before her desk, her red heels click-clacking with each step. "You may have heard terrible rumors about demons." She laces her long red fingernails under her chin. "I won't mince words. Some say the demons may one day attack *us*, their beloved ghoul allies."

I lean back in my chair, my brows rising. *Anti-demon rumors? That's new.* Normally it's all demon-love, all the time.

Miss Thing sighs. "Demons are poor, misunderstood creatures that are true friends to ghouls. Maybe not so much to quasis." She taps her chin with her long gray finger. "But since you're our minions, that means they're really *your* friends too!" She glances about the classroom expectantly.

I scan the faces as well. Everyone looks at our teacher with open, accepting stares. My chest tightens with frustration as the word 'minion' rattles around my brain. We used to rule ourselves, sistah, and did a damn good job of it too.

Miss Thing gazes at one of the many Oligarchy glamour shots she's taped to her wall. "Besides, our brave and handsome leaders tell us demons will be our allies forever. And we know the Oligarchy could never lie or make a mistake." Her eyes flutter as she exhales. "So, there's nothing to worry about."

Huh. That was a lot of explaining for something not to worry about.

Miss Thing walks up to the board. Using super-screechy chalk, she starts listing examples of how demons have been trustworthy through the ages. Twenty minutes go by and she's reached one and a half items.

Zeke shifts his weight; his chair lets out a soft squeak. I turn to him and realize he's been whispering to me about Cissy this whole time. I smile and pretend I've been listening all along.

"It's been so awesome having Cissy around," says Zeke. "My parents don't get a lot of support from the ghouls. Basically, they let us keep our house and that's it. We have to pay for all the diplomatic events. It adds up."

"That's too bad, Zeke. I had no idea."

"My parents are pretty picky, too. They worry about every little thing. Cissy's really good about the details, though. Like at dinner, she figured out how to get floral centerpieces that were periwinkle instead of cerulean. Mom was pumped."

Wow. I have no idea what he just said.

"That's totally cool, Zeke. I'm happy for you."

"Anyway, she's a great girl." He smiles. "And you've done an awesome job adjusting to our relationship. I know it must be hard, seeing us together all the time." He arches his eyebrow and winks.

Just when you think it's safe to have a conversation with Zeke Ryder, he turns back into the Lust Monster. My voice drips with a healthy dose of venom. "I've adjusted, Zeke. You should too."

The rest of the day zips by and before I know it, I'm driving my green station wagon over to the Ryder mansion.

Betsy putters up the long curve of the mansion's driveway. Cissy and Zeke stand outside the front door, their bodies stiff with rage. Both their mouths are set into thin lines. I wave through the closed window. They glare in reply.

Ick. The thrax must have whined to Zeke's parents. Not good.

I park Betsy and step up to the mansion, all innocence and smiles. "Hey, guys! What's going on?"

Zeke taps his foot. "What in blazes did you do at the thrax compound the other day?"

I unzip my hoodie and try to look casual. "Oh, they mentioned me?"

Zeke's eyes almost pop out of his head. "Mentioned you? They howled about you. It's a diplomatic nightmare."

I roll my eyes. "It is not."

Cissy frowns. "Is too. You flattened three of their Lords."

I did, didn't I? Sweet Satan, that was fun.

Cissy points at my mouth. "I see that self-satisfied smirk. You're getting in deeper by the second."

I force my face into neutral-mode.

Zeke rubs his temples. "When you were said you knew the thrax Prince, we thought you were kidding."

"Hmmm. Let's take a step into the way-back machine here. I told you both that the Prince and I fought; you refused to believe me because you thought...what was it you thought again?" I give my chin a dramatic tap. "Oh, yeah. You thought that I had a huge crush on Zeke. Well, for the record, I don't give a crap about Zeke."

"Fine, we believe you now." Cissy half-frowns. "But that's not the point, Myla. The *point* is that you fought back against the Prince in a mean and sneaky way."

I keep my face carefully neutral. Mostly. "*I* fought back? How's everyone so sure it was me?"

"Hmm." Now it's Zeke's turn to tap his chin. "How many Arena-quality fighters are there out there who got honorary swords from Prince Lincoln? It's a short list. You."

"Hey, I did what you asked and delivered the note. Case closed."

Zeke frowns. "Not by a long shot. The thrax want you to make things right. My parents say if you agree to whatever they ask, we're all good. You can even keep using the library." His brows raise. "*If* you agree, that is."

The chill of shock envelops me. No library means no way to find out more about my father. I hadn't thought about that. Cissy sniffles miserably, her bottom lip trembling. I hadn't thought about how I could hurt her, either. My cold shock solidifies into icy guilt.

"So, what do the thrax want me to do?"

Zeke screws up his mouth. "Uh, we don't know yet."

"So, can I go to the library today anyway? I can't really agree until I know *what* they want." I shift my weight from foot to foot. "Plus, I really want to research–" I stop myself before saying 'my ghoul heritage.' "Uh, things."

"I don't know." Zeke slaps on his Mr. Smarmy grin. "We really shouldn't let you go until everything's worked out."

Disappointment lands on my shoulders. "I get it." I jam my hands into the pockets of my sweats. "I'll head home." I turn toward Betsy.

Cissy grabs my arm. "No, you can still use the library." She starts blinking madly, a sugary grin forced onto her face.

Uh-uh. Cissy's working some angle here.

Zeke wraps his arm around her shoulder and winks. "Of course! Mom and Dad said it was fine, just for today. Only promise to stay in the library. No roaming around."

I eye their forced chipper-ness carefully. They're *definitely* up to something. I shrug. What do I care? I want intel and now I can get it. "I'll stay in the library, no problem."

Cissy opens the front door with a long creak; then she gestures toward the West Wing. "See you later."

"Have fun, you two." I speed down the West Wing hallway and up to the fourth floor library. Stepping out of the stairwell, I'm greeted by the familiar labyrinth of tall wooden bookcases. I wind my way through the maze of shelves, finding the ghoul section in the far right corner. After scanning a few dusty volumes, I find the *Libra Ghoul*.

My muscles tighten with nervous energy. Here's the master encyclopedia on all things ghoul-ish. I pull down the four-inch thick book and eye the hefty leather binding. Across the cover, a hundred ghouls are listed as authors, their letters and numbers all in glittering gold script.

I haul the *Libra Ghoul* over to my favorite window seat. I sit down, open the book, scan the index, and find the section on ghoul half-breeds, reading:

Ghouls may mate with creatures from other realms. The offspring will appear in human form throughout their mortal lives, a phase which is known as the larvae stage.

I stick out my tongue. Yuck, I'm a larvae right now.

Upon death, the larvae mature into their wondrous ghoul form. In their mortal state, half-breeds are notorious for failing to follow rules and procedures. Once dead, however, they develop a natural appreciation for Group Think and process.

Whoa. I'll turn into some rule-loving nincompoop one day. I shiver, fight the sense of nausea in my stomach, and return my attention to the book. A section called Group Think catches my eye.

Mature ghouls are not isolated organisms like other unfortunate creatures. They share a single consciousness led by the most perfect of our kind, the Oligarchy. This superior form of connected living is called Group Think. Thanks to it, the thoughts of our great leaders constantly pulse through the minds of every ghoul.

I snap the book shut with a sneer. Someday I'll have the Oligarchy in my head 24-7? That sucks with a capital 'S.' Maybe I'm better off not knowing my heritage.

Footsteps sound from the other side of the Library. "You'll find her in here, your Highness."

My stomach spirals with shock. There aren't a lot of your Highnesses running around Purgatory. Suddenly, Cissy and Zeke's offer of the library makes perfect sense. Those little creeps. Okay, it was totally sneaky of me to hit the thrax compound with every intention of causing trouble. But Cissy and Zeke are being pretty sneaky here, too. If they want me to play nice with others, an ambush isn't the way to do it.

"Thank you." The voice is definitely Lincoln's. I can tell by his clipped tone that I'm in for it. Ugh.

I re-open the *Libra Ghoul* and pretend to be super-interested. Footsteps march in drum-roll rhythm across the library floor, then pause nearby. I look up. Lincoln stands before me in his leather pants and velvet tunic, his mismatched eyes glowering. A jolt of adrenaline races through my bloodstream.

Bring it on.

"Hello, Miss Lewis." He sets his feet apart; his broad shoulders stiffen. Battle stance.

"Hello, Mister The Prince."

"I had an official audience with the Ghoul Minister today. It seems he didn't approve your delivering his message."

I close my book. "And?"

"So, you admit you raided the thrax compound without authorization?"

I tap my cheek. "So, *you* admit that a lowly quasi girl successfully raided your super-awesome demon-hunter compound?"

"Your actions were rude and startling. The Lords were not prepared."

I sniff. "They were wearing chain mail, carrying weapons, and in the middle of battle training. I call that a fair fight."

He shakes his head from side to side. "My men don't expect strange girls in unitards to appear out of nowhere."

I raise my pointer finger. "One, it's a dragon-scale fighting suit, not a unitard." I raise another digit. "Two, what exactly *do* they expect girls to do when they're attacked? Half the best Arena fighters are women."

"That's not how it is in Antrum."

"What's an Antrum?"

"Where I live, where all thrax live. Back on Earth, deep underground."

"That makes sense. Not knowing girls fight; it figures you all live under a rock."

Closing his eyes, he takes in a deep breath. "No one speaks to me like that." A muscle twitches along his jaw.

My eyes narrow. He's not the only one who doesn't like back-talk. "Welcome to Purgatory."

"The Earls demand you attend a tournament of demon fighting prowess to celebrate the autumnal equinox. As senior members of the thrax nobility, they will battle on the field of honor."

"Humph." No way am I joining that sausage party. They can prove their manliness on their own time. "Sounds like a 'we'll show her' kind of thing."

"The Lords have a right to display their skills under traditional circumstances."

"Well, there's one thing they need to do first."

Lincoln folds his arms over his chest. "And what's that, in your experience?"

"Say. Please."

The Prince rakes one hand through his brown hair. "Disrespectful."

He thinks *I'm* disrespectful? "Funny, I was about to say the same thing to you."

Lincoln inhales slowly, his fists open and close. Turning on his heel, he stomps away. Leaning back in my perch, I lace my fingers over my belly and watch him retreat. He's got a strong back, long arms roped with muscle, and a bottom half that does justice to those black leather pants. Though the front side of him is pretty tasty, too. His mouth, I must say, is particularly yummy-looking.

Whoa there. I should not stare lustily at snobby Princes. Come to think of it, since when do I stare lustily at guys, period? I shake out my hands and shift my head from side to side. That fight threw me out of whack, big time.

I hop to my feet, a broad grin rounding my mouth. *That fight threw me out of whack because I WON.* I'm so proud of my bad-self, I almost dance out of the library and down the steps, mentally replaying every word of my verbal ass-whooping. I reach the reception hall and freeze.

Cissy and Zeke stand by the front door and, dang, they look mighty peeved. Again.

Cissy sets her fists on her hips. "The thrax High Prince just left his meeting with the Ghoul Minister. He was not happy."

I put on my innocent face and blink. "What makes you say that?"

Cissy frowns. "He just blew past us."

Zeke points to the West Wing. "And the diplomatic conference room is right below the library. What do you say about that?"

"I say that's sure strange." I shrug. "That Prince is pretty temperamental for a demon hunter, huh?"

Zeke folds his arms over his chest. "Did you two fight again?"

"Fight?" I scratch my neck. "We never fight." Technically. We *yell* at each other a lot, though.

Cissy turns to Zeke. "Can you give us some girl-time? Myla and I need to talk."

Zeke glares at me for a full minute. "Sure."

Cissy opens the reception hall's back door and gestures to the hedgerow maze behind the mansion. "This way, Myla."

I walk through the doorway and onto the yellowing grass. Cissy follows me, closing the door behind her with a soft click. The muscles along my jaw tighten with determination. I will *not* feel guilty this time around. She and Zeke totally ambushed me.

Cissy spins around to face me. "Spill it."

"I don't know what you're talking about."

"It's me here." Cissy rolls her eyes. "You're not leaving this spot until I get some information. I know you two fought. Honestly, you're causing like, huge inter-realm incidents here."

I let out a dramatic gasp. "Come on! Who sent the Prince of Pissed my way with no warning? What did you think would happen?"

Cissy stares at her toes for a minute. "That was Zeke's idea. I told him it wouldn't work."

"Well, it didn't." *Leave it to Zeke to come up with a lame plan like that one.*

Cissy sighs. "So, what exactly *did* happen?"

I puff out a breath. "The Prince demands I attend a tournament so his steak-head Earls can show me how awesome they are."

"And you said?"

"I said they had to say 'please.'" I fold my arms over my chest. I'm totally in the right here; no way am I backing down.

Cissy groans. "What is it between you two?"

"Uh, hatred?"

"No." Cissy slowly scans me from head to toe. "No, it's not."

I roll my eyes. Cissy can be so thick sometimes. "Uh, *yes-yes* it is."

"You can't see it, but I can. You *care* about this guy." Her eyes flicker red with envy. "More than you care about me."

Her words slam into me, knocking my breath away. Sure, I think about Lincoln a lot, but only because he's being such a dick. She's wrong. Totally wrong. "I care about kicking him in the head, that's about it. You're my best and only friend."

Cissy's voice turns low and menacing. "He fights you and holds his own. You can't resist a good battle, Myla." Her irises blaze with scarlet light. "But you should be *my* friend first."

Anger boils up my spine. "What a coincidence! I'd like it if you were *my friend first*, too. I totally came clean about the Prince and you laughed it off. Then you ambush me in the library. Not okay, girlfriend."

Cissy's eyes narrow into fiery red slits. "You're right. I should have believed you when you said you fought with the Prince and didn't care about Zeke. I never should have sent you to the library unprepared. For that, I'm sorry. Truly." She speaks in a super-low and creepy voice. "Now prove you're more *my friend* than *his enemy*. Go with me to the tournament."

Uh-oh. My heart sinks to my toes. Cissy's envy demon is kicking in, big time. Sure, she shows demonic jealousy when girls like Paulette talk about Zeke, but that's small stuff. Her full-blown envy attacks don't happen often, but when they do, I don't want to be anywhere near the blast radius.

My mouth brightens into what I hope is a convincing smile. "I'm your friend first, last, and always, Cissy." I chuck her on the upper arm. "You know that." Out of the corner of my eye, I scan the mansion's grounds, looking for safe lines of exit.

Cissy's eyes keep burning red with jealousy. "Then prove it." Her mouth compresses into a straight line. "Go with me to the tournament. Show me that I'm more important to you than *he* is."

I raise my hands to shoulder level, palms forward. "Look, I know I caused trouble delivering that message, but you and Zeke totally set me up too. In the library, you didn't—"

"Stop right there." Her voice stays creepy-calm as her eyes flicker with fire. "I don't care about the message. I don't care about

151

the library. I care about one thing." She steps closer. "What's. Mine."

My mouth contracts into a tiny 'o' shape. I've never, ever seen Cissy's envy demon this riled up. She's a little scary right now, and I *know* scary. My mind freezes with shock. "I'm not sure what to say."

She steps even closer. "Say you're going to the tournament."

With my palms still at shoulder-level, I waggle them from side to side in the universal sign for 'calm down.' "Let me think about it." I cock my head to the right, considering. A tournament could be cool—I'd love to catch some new demon-fighting tricks. Then, I picture Lincoln's face. Anger boils through my body, melting away all thoughts until I can't remember why I was contemplating this stupid tournament in the first place. "Not a chance."

Cissy bares her teeth, her eyes flaring with an almost blinding red light. She turns on her heel and marches away.

Oh, no.

This hasn't happened since the third grade, and it's the kryptonite to my super sassy-mouth:

The silent treatment from Cissy.

Once she's a safe distance, I rev up Betsy and putter home, assessing my new friendless state along the way. Cissy's out of control right now, but she can't stay fired up forever. At least, I don't *think* she can. I bet she'll return to her normal, sweet self in a few days, tops. *Yeah that's it.* I march through my front door, say my hellos to Mom, and plunk onto the couch to spend some quality time with the Human Channel.

Half-way through a *Scooby-Doo* marathon, I fall into a deep sleep. Within seconds, I'm dreaming of the Gray Sea.

CHAPTER ELEVEN

A.

In my dreamscape, I return to the dark sands of the Gray Sea. I stand on the warm ground, the stench of sulphur thick in my lungs. Kneeling to the earth, I set my hands onto the desert floor. A ring of white flame appears. The sand within the circle rises, forming into the shape of my mother. More of the desert crawls upward, creating the outline of a room surrounding her.

The ring of fire flares brighter, then it fades away. Before me, the figures change. Instead of being made from sand, they're now flesh and bone. I scan the scene, seeing a busy Senate chamber made of white marble. Wooden benches line the floor, all of them filled with quasis in purple robes, their many different tails swaying in the same slow rhythm. In the front of the space, my mother stands behind a tall wooden podium. The Senators watch her from the benches, their attention fixed.

Mom grips the podium's edges. "My proposal with Senator Myung is an important step forward in fair after-life treatment for human souls. Too often, souls reach Purgatory without any comfort or support from the guardian angels who protected them during their lifetime."

Xavier slips through the back door of the Senate chamber and stands along the far wall. He wears a gray suit with a blue tie that highlights his turquoise eyes. As he watches Mom, his stern face softens into a smile. A warm feeling spreads through my chest. The two of them must have worked out their differences. *Nice job, Mom.*

My mother scans the crowd. "This bill will help guardian angels find their human's soul after death, just as previous legislation helps their tempting demon find them today. Please respect our sacred role in keeping Purgatory a neutral and fair space for souls."

Mom scans the senate floor. All eyes are fixed on her.

"Next week, remember the human souls entering Purgatory every day, every moment. Vote in favor of the Myung-Lewis bill. Thank you."

The chamber's silent for a moment, then members of the Senate begin to clap. The applause quickly swells. I join in and cheer, every cell in my body bursting with pride. *Go, Camilla!*

Bowing slightly, Mom steps away from the podium. The room echoes with low chatter as everyone rises to their feet and moves on with their day. A small group of Senators encircle Mom, asking questions. Tim rushes through the back door of the room, his long robes fluttering with each step. He gently touches Mom's upper arm.

"Senator Lewis, we must depart for the committee meeting."

"Thank you, Tim." She rests her hand on his shoulder. He shivers.

Together, they leave the chamber. Xavier watches them go, and then he follows a short distance behind. They step through a series of long marble passageways until reaching a small wooden door. Xavier hangs back in the busy hall.

I watch Xavier as he keeps a careful distance from my mother. His movements are protective, almost possessive, but not in a creepy-stalker way. Hmm. I might be starting to like this guy.

Tim holds the door open. "The committee will meet in here today, Senator Lewis."

Mom steps inside. "Thank you." She and Tim walk to a long wooden table surrounded by heavy leather chairs. As they take their seats, two new figures step into the room. One's a familiar-looking ghoul in a long black robe. The other is Armageddon.

My body goes on full alert. Armageddon's here? I want to break through the dreamscape, grab Mom's hand, and run for it. Instead, I feel rooted to the spot, unable to do anything but brace myself against jolts of panic.

Mom scans the newcomer, her face rounding into a polite smile. "Good afternoon, Ambassador."

Wait a second. Mom used to work with Armageddon? Whoa. I scan their faces. No one seems affected by his greater demon aura. They should be slammed with fear, but all of them—especially Mom—appear genuinely calm. My mind whirls until the reason's clear: Armageddon turned into a greater demon when he became King of Hell. Clever. There's more to his takeover of Purgatory than I first suspected.

Armageddon's long black face wears an unreadable expression. "Senator."

Mom turns to address the ghoul. "Greetings to you, O-72."

O-72 nods. "We thank you."

Suddenly, I realize where I've seen that ghoul before. Slap a red robe on that guy and he's one of the Oligarchy today. I've seen him at matches a dozen times.

Armageddon, Mom, and an Oligarchy ghoul? What in blazes is going on here?

My sleepy mind struggles to understand what I'm seeing. I've adjusted to the concept that Mom was a Senator. In fact, it's been awesome seeing her in action. But finding out that she dealt with Armageddon drives a lead feeling into my stomach. I know how this story ends, and it can't be good that Mom was in the middle of it.

Xavier walks into the room. "Good afternoon, everyone." He slides in to a leather chair across from Mom.

Armageddon eyes Xavier's every move, his face unmoving, his irises flaring bright red. "Ambassador Cross." His upper lip twists, exposing a sharp canine. Shivers of anxiety rattle my spine. Clearly, Armageddon hates Xavier with a vengeance. What happened between these two?

Mom motions to Tim. "Let's begin." He pulls a manila folder from within the folds of his robes and hands it to her. "Thank you, Tim." She sets the folder before her on the tabletop. "Our first item of the day is a diplomacy tour of—"

Armageddon leans back in his chair. "No. I have unfinished business here." He steeples his three-knuckled fingers under his pointed chin. "You know what I want."

O-72 lets out a long breath. "I've heard it many times, Armageddon. Maybe someday you'll become the King of Hell, but right now you're a common demon, fourth class."

Armageddon visibly cringes at these words. "So you keep telling me."

Beads of black sweat appear on O-72's forehead. He adjusts the neckline of his ghoul robes. "The rules are the rules. Only two categories of demons go to iconigrations and Arena matches: the first class and the King of Hell. Not fourth class demons. Not you. Be thankful you've been appointed delegate to this Council. It's a great honor for someone with your humble background."

Armageddon's eyes narrow. "But not the honor I want. My son moves souls at the Arena. I want to be there."

Mom stays unflappable. "We appreciate that your son is the Great Scala. Perhaps you could arrange to see him outside of the Arena?"

Armageddon bares his teeth. "The thrax poisoned his mind against me. You all know this." He pounds the table with his fist. "I want Arena access to my son." He scans the table with a predatory glare. "I wish to see him move souls."

I inhale a stunned breath. I knew the Scala was Armageddon's son, but I didn't realize the old demon wanted anything to do with his child. A tremor of fear rattles my shoulders. Armageddon's calculating something, weaving his invisible plans. He did this when he schemed his takeover of Purgatory; it gives me the creeps.

O-72 wags his massive gray head. "This is not possible. Ghouls only allow certain demons into any Arena event. The rules are the rules."

"I see." Armageddon laces his three-knuckled fingers together by his long neck. "We all bend the rules. Sometimes." He skewers O-72 with a look that speaks of hidden secrets that Armageddon has stockpiled for just such an occasion. "You, of all of us, should understand that."

O-72 clears this throat. "I'll see what I can do."

Armageddon lowers his hands, his mouth curling into an evil grin. "That's all I ask." He rises to his feet. "We're done here."

Mom points directly at Armageddon's chest. "Where are you going?"

I gasp. *Damn, Mom!* Going toe-to-toe with the future King of Hell. My chest tightens with bands of worry.

Xavier raises his hand. "If Armageddon wishes to *retreat*, he may." Something in his tone says the word 'retreat' is laced with some particular memory, one that Xavier is flaunting in the demon's face.

Armageddon twists his head to glare at Xavier, a low hiss sounds from his throat. "Your time will come."

Xavier's blue eyes flare brightly. "We'll see."

Mom knocks on the tabletop with her fist. "We have important matters to discuss here today." She taps the manila folder with her pointer finger. "Let's get back to it."

Armageddon curls his finger to O-72. "Come with me."

O-72 dutifully rises to his feet and follows Armageddon from the room. He couldn't be more under the demon's control if marionette strings trailed from his robes. Mom watches the pair leave, her face still as stone.

I bite my lower lip anxiously. Not a good look from Mom. She's about ready to lose her freaking mind on someone. At least, it's not me.

Mom rounds on Xavier. "Why didn't you back me up? Armageddon should never have been able to leave the meeting early." She pushes her manila folder away from her, and it flies halfway down the table. "We can't let him collude with ghouls and override the authority of this office."

Xavier laughs. "Please. I've watched ghouls and demons fight each other for thousands of years. They'll plot for a time, and then they'll fight over some nonsense and go home. Demons are chaos and destruction. Ghouls are rules and regulations. Oil and water don't mix."

"I've told you a hundred times, Armageddon is different." Her eyes flare red. "We can't let him go unchallenged."

Every cell in my body screams that she is right. I want to jump into the dreamscape and start shaking Xavier by the shoulders, telling him to listen to Mom or I'll kick him in the shins. But I can't do anything.

But Xavier doesn't seem to hear my mother, let alone me. He leans back in his chair, his head gently shaking from side to side. Standing behind them both, Tim looks so mousy and frightened, I'm surprised that he doesn't duck under the table to hide.

Xavier drums his fingers on the tabletop. "I've seen Armageddon's type before. He doesn't have the staying power to really change the system."

Ha! Armageddon tears down the whole freaking system singlehandedly. Please, listen. Please, please, please!

Mom rubs her neck with her hand. "Have you heard him go on about his son? It's strange. He wants access to Maxon and will do anything to get it."

Xavier laughs. "Do you hear yourself? A demon loves his son. It's insane, Camilla."

"I didn't say he loves his son." Mom sets her palms on her eyes. "He's plotting something, something big, and he needs Maxon for it." She lowers her hands until her gaze meets Xavier's straight on. "Armageddon is dangerous. We're all at risk."

Her look of worry sets my stomach churning. I so want to jump to her side, wrap my arm around her shoulder, and tell her that I'll be with her soon.

Xavier has the same general idea. He leans forward, his blue eyes searching Mom's face. "I'd never let anything happen to you, Camilla. You have nothing to worry about."

Mom reaches across the table, wrapping her hand around Xavier's. "I hope you're right, Xavier." Energy flares around them when they touch.

Tim looks just about ready to puke or scream, I can't tell which. I watch his tortured face and realize one thing: if this ghoul is my father, then he's definitely the jealous type. His mouth presses into such an angry line, I'm shocked he doesn't break a tooth. Maybe that's why he isn't part of our lives. My heart sinks to my toes. Or maybe Mom lied to me about Tim being my father in the first place. I wag my head from side to side. Not possible. Mom's a lot of things, but a liar? Not one of them.

Mom gives Xavier's hand a little shake. "But unfortunately, I have *a lot* to worry about." She tilts her head to one side. "First on the list is you, Xavier Cross. I'm doing my job without backing from the angels. We need to be strict with Armageddon right now, and to do that we must stay in lock step–"

Xavier's eyes gleam bright blue. "No, you don't need to worry about Armageddon." He grips her hand more rightly. Tim watches the movement and gasps.

Tim's not the only one who's shocked. Why-oh-why isn't that angelic whatever-he-is not listening to the truth? As Xavier's eyes glow brighter, Mom's turn glassy and dead. My body goes on full alert. Xavier's using angelic influence on her, the dirt bag. I want to jump into the image and kick his ass across the room. Maybe twice.

Mom rubs her forehead with her free hand. "Yes, there's nothing…" She pauses; then she shakes her head vigorously. Her eyes flare demon-bright. "How *dare* you try to use angelic influence on me!"

Alright, Mom! Way to shut that move down. I exhale a ragged breath, my alert level returning to something like normal.

Mom rises to her feet. "This is outrageous. I'm placing a formal request for a new angelic Ambassador and for a censure of Armageddon."

Xavier frowns. "They won't listen to you like I do, Camilla. You'll be committing career suicide. Your ideas will sound insane."

"That may be, but my paperwork will be filed by week's end." She storms from the room with Tim behind her. Xavier watches her go, his face turning white with worry. The look on his face is so loving and gentle, I want to give him a hug, even though he is a bit of a nut job.

Before me, Xavier's body transforms into sand once more. With a low hiss, the entire scene melts back into the desert floor. I sit back on the gray sand. My mind runs through every detail of what I've just seen. Armageddon's obsession with Maxon...how the first of the Oligarchy was controlled by Armageddon...And Mom's battle to get the threat taken seriously. Sulphur sears my lungs, wind pelts my body, but none of it seems to matter.

I wake to the sound of scraping metal. I open my eyes, seeing gray sky outside my window. I yawn, slip out of bed, and walk into the kitchen. Mom stands before the table, holding a flat block of wood with a long metal arm: a fabric slicer. She pulls the razor-sharp arm up and down, making long cuts on black cloth.

"Hey, Mom."

"Good morning, Myla." I examine her face. Mom's skin is creased with lines. Her hair is coarse and streaked with gray. Her once-vibrant smile is now a look of constant worry.

What did the war do to her?

Mom makes another cut with the slicer. "I hope I didn't wake you up. It's faster to cut hoods this way."

I lean against the chipped countertop. "It's fine."

"How'd you sleep?" The way Mom asks the question, I think what she already knows the answer.

"Not so good. Verus sent me another dreamscape. I saw you in some Senate committee meetings. Did you really know Armageddon before the war?"

"That I did. For thousands of years, ghouls and demons had never trusted each other enough to team up. That all changed with Armageddon."

"I see him at matches sometimes." I picture the long pointed face, blade-like nose, black stone skin, and fiery eyes. "He's terrifying."

"He was *always* frightening, but once Armageddon became a greater demon, he hit a new level of awful." She shivers. "I've heard that now, no human, angel, or ghoul can stand to be near him for more than a few minutes."

"I'd believe that."

She makes another slice with the chopping arm. "He black-mailed or bribed all the ghouls who became the new Oligarchy. Purgatory's defenses allow only a handful of demons to enter at a time. Armageddon convinced the ghouls to open enough portals for an entire demon army to enter our lands."

"Wow. They didn't teach us that in school." Frowning, I angrily pick at the chipped counter with my thumbnail. School sucks.

"I'm not surprised." Mom makes another slice. "The demons routed our defenses and set up a puppet government of ghouls. Since then, as long as the ghouls send extra souls to Hell, the demons support their rule." She shivers. "But I don't think Armageddon will be happy with a puppet government in forever. It's not in his nature."

I lace my fingers behind my neck and let out a long breath. Let's sum up the awfulness here. I have a ghoul for a dad, a silent treatment for a best friend, and a Mom with a ton of depressing history to think through. My vision turns hazy at the edges.

Mom eyes me closely. "Why don't you stay home from school today? You don't look well."

I picture facing Cissy and the silent treatment at school. I feel a little sick to my stomach.

"You're right, Mom. I'm going back to bed." I've been awake for less than an hour, but it's already been that kind of day. I slump into my room, curl under my covers, and fall fast asleep. A contented smile curls my lips as I fall off into a dreamscape-free sleep.

𝒜.

I stay home the rest of that day, and the next, and the next. Mom's really cool about it. She makes me frozen dinners and lets me watch all the television I want. A full week goes by before I trek back to class.

As I putter along the familiar route to school, my face stretches into a confident grin. After a whole week, Cissy must feel sorry for her super-sick best friend, transforming her envy demon into ancient history. In fact, I bet she'll just say hello and chat away like nothing ever happened.

Yeah, that's it.

I park Betsy, step into school and scan the crowded hallway. Cissy stands beside by her locker. I walk to her side and slap on my most winning smile.

"Hey there, Cissy."

Silence.

"I'm feeling much better, thanks for asking."

Cissy slowly turns to face me. The moment her eyes meet mine, her irises flash so brightly, I shield my eyes from the glare. With a low growl, she slams her locker and stomps off down the hallway.

My stomach twists with disappointment. So much for chatting away like nothing happened. Damn, her envy demon is a bitch when it's up.

I go to class and pretend to look interested at whatever garbage the Old Timer has to say, but actually I'm brainstorming awesome one-liners for Cissy. I know if I can get her to laugh at lunch, she'll crumble (and I'll avoid the thrax tournament). My favorite line is: "Talk to me and I'll brush your tail." I nod silently. This will work for sure.

That's when a thud sounds at the class door.

Everyone freezes as all eyes turn to the stranger. A dark figure looms through the door's small glass window. The intruder's skin is black and smooth as polished stone. My body tenses.

That looks like Armageddon. Hells bells. He's coming to kill off the ghouls, just like Mom predicted. My tail arches over my shoulder, ready to strike.

The Old Timer waves the intruder away. "Come back later. I'm in a very important lesson."

The stranger knocks again, this time hard enough to set the doorframe shaking. "Inspection!" The voice sounds like hundreds of people whispering at once.

My mind races through the different types of demons. Which one would have a voice like that? The sound is grating, mysterious, and completely terrifying. Demonic wrath curls up my belly, preparing me to fight.

The Old Timer crinkles his nose, making his handlebar moustache twitch. "I wasn't informed of any inspection."

"*Demon* inspection."

The Old Timer straightens his robes and rushes over to the class door, swinging it wide open with a flourish. "Welcome to my classroom, oh mighty demon."

The figure lurches into the room. Tall and slender, it looks like a smaller version of Armageddon, right down to the fitted black tuxedo. The Old Timer speeds to the demon's side, gesturing to the room full of students.

My inner demon growls with anger. The Old Timer's showing us off like it's dinnertime and we're so many sides of beef. My mouth stretches into a dark smile. Just try something, you two. Anything.

"Mighty demon, this class is called Lessons in Servitude. Is there a particular skill you'd like to see? Robe cleaning, massage, bowing and scraping?"

"I'm not here to *see* anything." The edges of the demon's thin red mouth twist into a smile.

The Old Timer coils the end of his moustache with one finger. "Then, what are you here for?"

"This." A bit of the demon's cheek peels off into a butterfly-like creature with a blood-red body and thick black wings. The creature's tiny face has bright red eyes, a turned-up nose and an itty-bitty mouth lined with gleaming black teeth. Its dark wings pump furiously, causing its gangly arms and legs to sway in mid-air.

I let out a breath. Now I know exactly what monster this is: a Papilio demon. It's nasty, but nowhere near as awful as Armageddon.

The demon's body peels off into more evil butterflies. In no time, little flying demons flutter through the air in one great dark cloud. The humanoid demon's bulk shrinks into a misshapen lump, and then disappears. In its place, a swarm of Papilio zoom about the classroom, upending chairs and startling students. Some of the little nasties get their arms tangled in my hair. Gross.

A bunch of kids start to scream; their sad cries set off my wrath reflex in a huge way. My eyes burn with rage as I start planning attack vectors and the best ways to skewer Papilio with my tail. It's bad enough we have to sit in this school and listen to ghoul lies all day long. Demon attacks are off the curriculum.

The Papilio whiz about, pulling stuff out of backpacks, pockets, and purses. They shred books, crush coins into lumps of metal, and pull out hair by the handful. I rise to my feet, my hands balling with rage.

The swarm whips about me, then flips their focus, heading toward the Old Timer's desk. He stands in front of it, his back against the desktop, his arms stretched forward.

My tail relaxes. The Old Timer gets a turn. Nice.

"Per Article 7 of the Spectral Treaty, inspections are limited to quasis only. This is a ghoul *teacher's* desk."

The Papilio encircle the Old Timer's desk, tearing through his stuff with a vengeance. The floor quickly becomes littered with pens, papers, and shredded books.

The Old Timer sets his fists on his bony hips. "These are my personal items! I'm a ghoul! *I have rights!*"

The little demons titter with a hundred whispery voices. A group of them grab one end of the Old Timer's moustache and pull, hard. It breaks loose with a rrrrip.

The Old Timer's gray hand pats his upper lip. "How *dare* you!"

The demons chuckle even louder, then swarm out the room and down the hall. The Old Timer follows after them, shaking his bony fist shoulder-high.

I slip back into my chair, a satisfied grin rounding my mouth. All our failed test papers and bad report cards lie in shreds on the classroom floor. That's good, but it's even better to watch a ghoul find out what demons are *really* like.

Like I've said all along, they're anything but our noble allies.

CHAPTER TWELVE

A

I march across the greenish-yellow lawn at school. Setting my thumb into my mouth, I bite down on my nail and wince. Yowch. I've chewed every fingernail to a nub. The stupid thrax tournament is coming up this weekend. It's been one week, four days, and six hours since I last spoke to Cissy.

I'm starting to crack.

I glance at my watch. I'm due at the muddy field behind school in two minutes. I step around the back of the building and scan for my class. My eye twitches as I spot a group of kids standing in the center of the sloppy green.

Jogging up to my gym class, I jam my hands into my hoodie pockets. I don't say hello to anyone and no one greets me, either. You'd think after almost two weeks, I'd start to make new friends. Sure, I tried talking to other kids, but we form groups by our deadly-sin powers, and wrath's pretty rare. And Furor-wrath, like me? Rare to the level of freaky.

I tried chatting up the few wrath-quasis at school, but they just wanted to kick my butt. It's a wrath-thing; you like to see how you rank in the hierarchy. Unfortunately, that would've ended with them in the hospital, not a new best friend for yours truly. Zeke's lust-bunny buddies always ask me to join their lunch table, but Cissy's there too. And every time we make eye contact, her envy demon roars to life. It's just weird. All in all, I've spent a lot of quality time eating Demon bars in a corner.

The Old Timer and Tank step into the center of the group. Tank blows a long tweet from his whistle. Everyone falls silent.

Our gym teacher sets his monstrous hands on his hips. With his skyscraper build, bald head, and solid chin, he's a tower in his black robes. Beside him, the Old Timer looks like a gray stick in a blanket with half a moustache.

"We've big news for you today," says Tank. "OT-42 wanted to combine our classes for this special announcement because…" He looks down at the Old Timer. "Why are we doing this again?"

The Old Timer pats the raw skin above his lip. "Security." He scans the field nervously. "You never know who'll stop by."

I hide a snarky smile under my hand. After the Papilio demon attack, the Old Timer hasn't been the same ghoul, in a good way. The obnoxious lessons on 'serving our masters' have disappeared, replaced by study halls where we read demon self-defense books. He doesn't even give tests anymore.

Tank slaps the Old Timer on the back with such force that the rickety ghoul almost tumbles into the crowd. "That's right," says Tank. "Safety in numbers. Very important." He presses his huge hands together. "As you know, quasis are tested Senior Year and assigned a lifetime service. Testing hasn't yet started for this class." A low groan rises from the group of students. Tank raises his arms. "Don't worry. There'll be no tests today."

The Old Timer wraps his cloak around him more tightly. "In fact, we're here to tell you there won't be *any* testing this year."

The groans change into happy chatter.

No testing? I pump the air with my fist. That's freaking awesome!

Tank folds his huge arms over his barrel chest. "Now, quiet down." The students instantly fall silent. "The Department of Quasi

Learning has decided that this year, all students will be assigned the same service. Everyone will join the new Ghoul Protection League. Going forward, gym class will train you for this service."

In the back of my mind, I remember Cissy telling me something about gym class changing. Fighting in a Protection League sounds pretty cool.

I raise my hand. "What battle skills will we learn?"

The Old Timer wags his bald head. "None. The GPL teaches you how to best lay down your lives for your ghoul masters, giving us time to escape in case of attack."

A stunned silence falls over the group. No one moves.

Holy Hades! Sure, I wanted ghouls to realize demons aren't allies, but I assumed they'd do something logical with the information, like leave Purgatory or build up some kind of army. But asking us to lay down our lives while they portal their asses out of here? Incredibly lame.

"OT-42 is exaggerating," says Tank quickly. "You'll learn other things too. Angel warriors will teach you some defense skills."

My brow arcs. Angel warriors? Battle skills? This class just got upgraded to somewhat lame.

The Old Timer nods vigorously. "Angels have been giving us advice on how to prepare for, well, just to prepare in general. They'll help with training."

A memory pops into my mind: the day the Old Timer asked me to make worm soufflé. Cissy pointed out angels on the lawn. Everyone was shocked, but I was too excited about avoiding squishing worms to think about it too much. My eyes stretch wide with understanding. So *that's* why angels were hanging around school. They're helping ghouls to—what did the Old Timer call it again—to 'prepare in general?'

Of course. The angels are here to help the ghouls prepare for another demon invasion. A shiver runs across my shoulders. Mom said Armageddon would never be happy with puppet-rule of Purgatory, and she was right. Again.

Cissy raises her hand. I feel a pang in my chest; I miss her. There must be some way to snap her out of this demon envy thing. She clears her throat. "Who exactly are we protecting and preparing for? Demons?"

The Old Timer sets his arms out, palms forward. "No, no, no. Nothing like that. Demons are our friends. Everyone knows that." His eyes glow bright red.

I roll my eyes. Suuuuuuuuuure they are.

"Let's get started." Tank blasts his whistle again. "I want you all to practice running around the yard, flailing your arms, and screaming 'Take *me*! Take *me*!' On my mark. Set. Go!"

The other kids break up into small groups and start walking around the field. Some get into the exercise and really ham it up. Cissy and Zeke stroll nearby, chatting and smiling. My heart finally cracks.

I walk over to Cissy and stand directly in her walking path. Our gazes meet. Her irises flare bright red.

Zeke scratches his neck with his hand. "I'll leave you two to talk." He quickly slips away.

Cissy keeps glaring at me, her eyes flaring brighter. This has so got to end, and much as I hate to do this, I think there is only one way to get her envy demon to go bye-bye.

"I may possibly consider going to the tournament. Maybe." I flip my finger back and forth between her eyes. "But I need to talk to my friend Cissy and not envy-demon girl."

Cissy inhales a long breath, her eyes slowly turning back to their original tawny brown.

Good. Now we're getting somewhere.

She shakes her head from side to side. "That's better, now." She lets out a few breaths. "I think my envy demon got a little out of control there."

I plant my fists on my hips. *Now it's time to let loose.* "A *little* out of control? You didn't talk to me for two weeks. You've been a bitch on wheels. And about what? Some guy." I waggle my finger at her. "I've been totally patient with you through the whole Zekie-poo lovey-dovey boyfriend festival. All I do is get into a few fights with a guy and you LOSE IT. For the record, you totally and completely suck as a friend right now."

Her hands pop over her mouth. "Oh my goodness. I do suck."

"Completely."

"I don't know what to say, Myla." Her eyes are lined with tears. "I lost control." She wags her head. "You don't have to go to the tournament if you don't want to."

I scratch my neck and frown. "No, I'll go to the stupid tournament."

Cissy grins, bouncing on her heels. "Thank you, Myla, thank you!" She wraps me in a big hug.

I stand stone-still, allowing her to hug me but not returning the motion. "On one condition."

"Name it."

"I want some serious apologizing for this totally unreasonable fit of extended jealousy."

Cissy nods sagely. "You're right. Way over the top." She wags her eyebrows up and down. "How many, then? Two? Three?"

"Five." I fold my arms over my chest. "You make me five pans of brownies. Different flavors. And no conning your Mom into doing it."

"You got it. Thank you. So. Much." She moves to give me another hug; I raise my palm, stopping her.

"And one last thing. If I'm going, I'll do it my way."

⅄

I slip out of my room and tiptoe to the front door of my house, the keys to Betsy in the pocket of my hoodie. Holding my breath, I wrap my fingers around the door handle.

Mom pops her head out of the kitchen. I'm so snagged.

"Where are you sneaking off to?" She steps toward me, her shoulders slumping. "Are you going to meet other top Arena fighters?" Her tail wraps around her hand. "I know they're all part Furor demon too."

Meeting Furor fighters on the sly? Where does she come up with this cockamamie stuff to worry about?

"I've met the other Arena fighters." I shrug. "They're fine."

She sets her hand on her hip. "So, you're not sneaking off to meet them?"

"Why would I do that?" I spin the keys around my finger. "Don't get me wrong, they're okay fighters, but…"

"Not as good as you."

"Something like that." They're actually a bunch of washed-up has-beens, in my humble opinion. Don't get me wrong, they could kick anyone's ass in Purgatory, just not mine.

"So, what are you up to?"

"Look, I'm not going to meet any Furor fighters." But I *am* going to the thrax tournament. I'm such a bad liar, I was hoping to sneak out without a Maternal Inquisition.

Her chocolate eyes narrow. "So, where are you going?"

"Hanging out with Cissy." At a thrax tournament, but I leave that part out.

Mom stares at me for a long moment, then nods. "Okay, have fun."

"Thanks, Mom. I'll be back soon." Because once they see I'm wearing sweats instead of some stupid ball gown, I'll get to leave. My grin stretches extra wide.

My plan's so freaking awesome.

I drive Betsy to the thrax compound, park her on a dry patch of field, and follow the crowd. Everyone's in traditional thrax dress and glaring at my ratty sweatpants and gray hoodie. I glance at my watch. If I leave in the next ten minutes, I can still catch reruns of *I Love Lucy* on the Human Channel. Sweet.

I follow the thrax crowd. We hike through the trees and onto a wide meadow covered in mud. By the forest's edge stand five large tents. Each one's bigger than my house and in a different color: yellow, bronze, purple, blue, or black. Beyond the tents lies an oval tournament green—it's the only place around that *is* green—and it's surrounded by a shoulder-high wooden fence. Two long spectator pavilions overlook the green, one on each side.

Squinting, I take a closer look at the pavilions. They're raised platforms covered in stepped rows of seats. Wooden poles hold a cloth ceiling over the audience's heads. Flags and lanterns hang everywhere.

Cissy stands near the tournament green, looking lovely in a simple medieval dress of emerald fabric with long loopy sleeves. I wave. "Hey, Cissy!"

Her jaw drops as she runs to my side. "Myla, you showed up."

"That I did." I gesture to my sweats. "And this is what I'm wearing. Who do I talk to so I can get kicked out?"

"You're supposed to be in a traditional gown. Like me."

"Drat." I snap my fingers and make my 'aw shucks' face. "I guess I'll have to go home."

Cissy chuckles, her head shaking from side to side. "You're not getting out of this so easily. They have emergency dresses around here."

"They do?" I freeze.

"Oh, yeah. Unlike you, I did some homework on the thrax." She sighs. "Why didn't you call the dressmaker I gave you?"

I frown and kick the dirt with my sneaker. "Because I came up with this awesome plan." Okay, maybe my plan isn't *that* freaking awesome.

Cissy grips my hand and leads me to the Rixa tent. Bands of tension grip my shoulders. Lincoln could be in there. I grit my teeth, waiting for the familiar waves of rage to pour through me. They don't appear. Instead, I feel charged with nervous energy, my stomach doing flip-flops.

What the Hell is wrong with me?

My friend pauses beside the fabric flap that serves as the tent's door. My breath hitches.

Cissy clears her throat. "Hello!"

An elder woman's voice sounds from inside. "Yes?"

"We're two maiden guests for the house of Rixa. May we enter?"

The tent flap opens. A portly woman in a simple black gown peeps her winkled face at us. "No one's in here but me. Come on in."

My body relaxes a bit. No close encounter with Prince Pompous. Whew.

Cissy guides me inside. "My name's Cissy and this is Myla. She needs a gown of welcome."

The woman sets her plump hands on her hips and looks me over. She has brown hair streaked with gray, a round face, and mismatched eyes of ice-blue and wheat-brown. "Is she the one who's Lincoln's, ah, guest?"

I raise my pointer finger. "Technically, I'm more of a prisoner."

"Behave, Myla." Cissy stifles a smile. "Yes, she's the one."

"I'm Queen Octavia's handmaiden, Bera."

Cissy curtsies. "Nice to meet you." She elbows me softly in the ribs.

"Nice to, uh…" I scan the tent's interior. My mouth opens wide with surprise. This place is packed with every sort of armor and weapon you can imagine, including baculum. I point to a line of silver swords with zigzag blades. "Those are for killing Viperons, aren't they?" I bounce on the balls of my feet. "I wasn't sure they really existed."

Bera's plump cheeks round into a smile. "Actually, they kill Viperons *and* Simia demons."

Okay, I've heard rumors of these blades but I thought they were legends, like a flying carpet or Excalibur. I watch the weapons glimmer on the tent walls, my fingers itching to touch them. "Wow. Can I hold one?"

"No, you can't," Cissy shoots me a look that says 'focus, Myla.' "We just need a gown of welcome and we'll be out of your way." She glances meaningfully to the tent entrance.

She's right. Lincoln could walk through any second. "Yes, a gown would be great."

Bera nods. "I think we have something." She waddles over to a large trunk along the back wall of the tent. Cissy follows her and releases my arm. Bera pulls up the trunk's heavy wooden lid and sorts through layers of fabric. She pulls out what can only be described as a big pile of white pouf. "Here you go."

Cissy grabs the garment. "Thank you."

Bera bends into the trunk again, pulling out a pair of white heels. She eyes my feet. "These should fit."

Cissy holds up the gown. It's a huge marshmallow of a dress covered in layers of puffy lace.

My upper lip curls. "I am *not* wearing this."

"You have no one to blame but yourself, Myla."

A voice sounds from outside the tent. "I am a warrior for the House of Rixa. May I enter?"

My body freezes. Damn. I'd know that voice anywhere: Lincoln. The tension-bands cinch around my spine and creep their way up my neck.

Wearing sweats today? Officially my least-most awesome plan, ever.

Bera waddles over to the tent entrance. "Just a moment, your Highness." She holds the flaps of fabric together and turns to me. "Be quick about it now. The tournament's about to begin."

There's no point arguing. If I'd done a little research, I wouldn't be in this mess. I whip off my sweats and slip on the marshmallow monstrosity. My tail quickly punches a hole through the back and whips around the dress, patting the fabric like it's a strange beast. I slip my feet into the white heels and shoot a glance at Cissy. "I'm not even going to ask you how I look."

She winces. "Don't."

I wave to Bera. "I'm all set. Is there another way out of here?"

"No." Bera releases the flap of fabric and whips open the tent door. She holds up her hand. "Just one moment, your Highness. A few maidens need to leave first."

I've only one option: smile and work the gown like it's the best thing ever. I plaster on a huge grin, saunter up to the tent flap, and step outside. Lincoln stands there wearing black body armor with an eagle crest insignia on his chest. Our eyes meet; the air around us crackles with some kind of energy. He looks me over from head to foot, his face unreadable.

"Miss Lewis." He bows slightly.

"Your Highness." I try to curtsey and end up dragging the gown through the mud. Behind me, Cissy steps outside.

"Excuse me." Lincoln disappears into the tent, closing the flap behind him.

Cissy links her arm with mine. We walk forward a few paces, then she leans in, her voice barely a whisper. "So, how did it go back there? Any yelling, kicking, spitting?" She doesn't need to add 'with the Prince.'

"No, we said hello and that was it."

Cissy frowns. "Humph."

"What do you mean, humph?"

"I mean, if you want to keep my envy demon away, we should stop this conversation right now." She pauses, and then rubs her eyes with her knuckles.

I wince, dreading what I'll see when she pulls her hands away. I can't handle a major envy meltdown right now. I move a bit closer to Cissy. "Are you okay?"

My best friend lowers her hands. Her eyes are their regular tawny brown, thank badness. "Let's change the subject." She gestures to my gown. "Can you move around in that thing?"

I place my hand on my heart, raising my other palm to shoulder level. "I hereby solemnly swear to listen to Cissy's fashion advice from now on. This makes two monster dresses I could have avoided if I had taken help from you." I look down at the muddy hem of my gown. At least the weight of the dirt is holding down some of the puffiness.

"Next time we have to go fancy for something, we'll get ready *together*." She winks. "We can still do some damage control today, though. I say we sit in the pavilion." She eyes my gown again. "Back row."

"Excellent idea. Lead on."

We hike through the mud to the nearest pavilion. I pause by the stairs to the seats, seeing nothing available in the back row. My heart sinks. There is, in fact, only one open chair in the entire pavilion, and it's next to the Great Ladies. Yuck.

I turn on my heel. "Maybe we should check out the pavilion on the other side."

A whiny voice calls out. "Miss Lewis, come sit by us!" I look up to see the Scala Heir wearing white robes and waving in my direction. I squelch the urge to chuck my shoe at her head.

Seating etiquette at a thrax tournament is diplomatic stuff. Girly-girl stuff. Cissy stuff. I lean over and whisper in her ear. "Help?"

Cissy nods, speaking in a low voice that only I can hear. "I got this." Turning to the Great Ladies, Cissy curtsies low. "We thank you for the kind offer, but Myla and I need to sit together. It's a quasi tradition." She whispers in my ear. "That should shut them up. Thrax have all sorts of rules about following tradition, theirs and those of other realms."

Adair rises to her feet. "To our people, no tradition comes before the desire of the Scala Heir. And I very much desire to speak with Miss Lewis." She snaps her fingers. Three blonde girls in yellow gowns appear by our side. "These are ladies of my House. They'll accompany you to an excellent seat at the opposite pavilion. Miss Lewis stays here."

My upper lip curls with disgust. I speak to Cissy out of one side of my mouth. "Options?"

Cissy lets out a low groan. "I got nothing." She gives my hand a squeeze. "I'm so sorry, Myla. I'm new to this diplomacy stuff. The tradition excuse was all I had."

Panic rips through me. Sitting next to a bunch of girly-girls for who-knows-how long? I've lived this nightmare a few times at school. They'll want to talk about stuff like eyelash extensions, panty liners, and cuticle cream. It's torture.

Cissy tightens her grip on my arm. "Let's make a run for it. This tournament is a whole lot of dumb, anyway."

Run for it? That sounds like a *great* plan. I'm about to say 'yes, yes, yes' when I catch Adair's gaze. Her mouth rounds into a self-satisfied smirk while her left eyebrow quirks with a look that says 'I knew you'd crack, you lowly form of life.'

I freeze. A challenge lurks in her eyes, and I'm always up for a challenge. Straightening my shoulders, I plaster on a wide grin. "I'd love to join you, oh Scala Heir."

Her nasty smirk collapses into a disgusted sneer. *Nice.* "How wonderful of you to join us." Adair gestures to the open chair besides her. "Please, sit here."

I turn to the trio of girls surrounding my best friend. "Take good care of her or I *will* hurt you." I chuck Cissy on the shoulder. "See you after the match."

Cissy grins. "Go get 'em." Her escorts guide her away; I watch her meld into the crowd. Taking a deep breath, I re-plaster on my smile, walk up the steps, and take my seat next to the Scala Heir.

"Hello, I'm—"

"Miss Lewis," finishes the Scala Heir. "We all know that part, silly." She smiles and tosses her head, sending her long blonde hair in a perfect arc over her shoulder. "And you know me. I saw you at the ceremony."

Yeah, when you were calling me a lesser form of life. What's changed since then? My face warms into a genuine grin. That's right. I held my own against all those Lords. Now I'm getting a little thrax respect.

"Let me introduce you to everyone else." Adair gestures to a girl sitting next to her in a purple gown. She's bone-thin with olive skin and a strong jaw. Her long brown hair is held back in a net of purple beads. "This is Lady Gianna from the House of Striga."

A familiar blonde head waves to me from the end of the row. "Hi, Myla!" I shoot a friendly wave at Avery. She bounces a bit in her seat. "Isn't it great how Gianna and Adair are friends now? Typically, Acca and Striga hate each other."

The other Great Ladies share a knowing look while Adair grits her teeth, a muscle twitching along her jaw-line. "Quiet, Avery! I'll get to you in a second." The Scala Heir inhales a deep breath, and then gestures to the girl seated next to Gianna.

"This is Lady Keisha from the House of Horus." Adair points to a girl in a bronze gown with ebony skin, large mismatched eyes, and dreadlocks down to her waist. Keisha sends me a smile that's somehow warm and icy at the same time.

Adair nods to the next girl in line, who wears a blue gown. "Here we have Lady Nita from the House of Kamal." She has creamy cocoa skin, striking bone structure, long brown hair, and nasty sneer on her face. Adair doesn't bother to point to the girl at the end of the row. "I guess you already met Avery. She's from the House of Acca, like me."

Avery waves again. "Hello, Myla! So nice to see you again."

I force on my best smile. "Hello, everyone."

Adair turns her attention to my gown. She eyes me from head to toe. Twice.

I bite my bottom lip. *Here it comes.*

"You look very festive, Miss Lewis." The rest of the Great Ladies snicker.

I'm about to cause another inter-realm incident when an older, plump man with receding red hair steps onto the tournament green, a crossbow in his hand. His barrel chest almost bursts out of his black-and-yellow tunic. Avery claps her hands and points. "Look, there's father!"

The Scala Heir shares a snide glance with Gianna. "We can all see him, Avery."

The Earl of Acca raises his thick arms high. "Welcome to the autumn tournament and exhibition! This display of fighting skill prepares us for the *real* event, the winter tournament, where the greatest warrior in Antrum will be named!" The crowd breaks out into wild applause. "Of course, I'm hoping it will be Acca's honor this year." The applause dies down.

The Earl lifts his crossbow. "I'll begin today's exhibition with a display of my own fighting skill against a dreaded Limus demon!"

I grimace. I sure hope it's not Sheila.

The fence on one end of the tournament grounds swings open. A Limus demon floats through, its body a towering mass of green goo. I scan the face. Not Sheila, whew.

The Earl of Acca loads a metal bolt into his crossbow and starts firing. The missiles fly harmlessly through the goopy demon and thud into the wooden wall around the field.

I nudge the Scala Heir with my elbow. "He's not really using a crossbow against a Limus, is he?"

"What's a Limus?" She frowns. "Oh, that green thing. Father knows what he's doing. He's a *thrax*, Miss Lewis."

The Limus speeds toward its victim. The Earl of Acca firms up his stance, shooting bolt after bolt through the demon's body. I glance around me. A lantern hangs from one of the posts that hold up the pavilion's fabric ceiling.

Yeah, that would do it.

The Limus slams into the Earl. Green goo encases the man whole. Inside the demon, the Earl of Acca flails, trying to whack his way out with the crossbow. Next to me, the Scala Heir and Gianna continue chatting. I nudge her in the ribs again.

"Your father's in big trouble."

She looks at me and arches her eyebrow. "No, he's not. And if you keep interrupting me, Gianna'll put a hex on you." She turns to face her friend, showing me as much back as possible.

On the tournament grounds, the Earl of Acca feebly kicks and punches from inside the Limus demon. Some thrax stand up in their pavilion seats, their faces twisted with worry. The Earl stops moving altogether.

That's it.

I rip the lantern off the post and hurl it with all my strength. The fire slams into the demon's skin. The Limus bursts into emerald flames. The thrax in the pavilions gasp. The fire dies down, leaving the Earl standing alone, wheezing and covered in green goop.

He points at me, slime dripping from his finger. "YOU! How dare you!"

For a few long minutes, there's a lot of confusion, gasping, and cries of 'how dare you' from the Earl. It's all a big blur until a familiar hand grips mine. I turn to see Cissy standing beside me. She tugs on my arm. "Let's get out of here."

"Sounds like a plan."

She pulls me past the tournament field, stopping behind one of the tents. Her eyes grow large with alarm. "What happened back there, Myla?"

"I saved that guy's life."

"Everyone said he was doing fine."

"Everyone's wrong. A Limus demon was about to digest him whole. He was *not* doing fine." I fold my arms over my chest. "He's just a pompous blowhard who didn't want to get showed up by a girl, even if that girl saved his life."

Cissy grinds her teeth. "The House of Acca is freaking out. I need to do some damage control." She winces. "This could take a while." Cissy's forehead creases with concern, the same expression she wears when feeding stray cats or tending her shoebox of moth cocoons. She doesn't want this blow-up to cause trouble for Zeke and his family. Which, since I'm associated with them and their house, it very well could.

I won't let her face this alone. "I'll go with you."

"No, best if you stay scarce. Every Acca flunky within yelling range is screaming how you dishonored them for a second time."

Dishonored, really? I pause, rubbing my neck with my hand. After hanging out with Adair, it's not actually all that surprising. That House of Acca is bad news. I chuck Cissy gently on the shoulder. "No worries. I can just head back."

She tilts her head to one side. "Are you sure?"

"Sure, I'm sure." If I can ever find my way back to the parking lot and Betsy. That was a hike.

Cissy gives me a peck on the cheek. "Thanks." She lifts up her skirt a bit, spins about and speeds off. Once she's gone, I scope out the grounds, trying to picture the long path back to Betsy. Not really sure how to begin.

That's when I hear it. Angry Acca voices calling for the 'foul demon,' 'scum fighter,' and 'quasi whore' who humiliated their Earl. I saved the guy's life, and this is what happens? My throat tightens. Sadness and disappointment wind about my ribs. What have I been trying to prove by fighting these people? Did I think they'd realize a quasi girl has as much value as a thrax warrior? No matter what I do, they'll never see me as anything but a foul demon.

My eyes sting. *He'll never see me as anything but a foul demon, either.*

A bitter gloom settles into my bones. *I need to head home, now.* I try to slog my way back to the parking lot, but I'm not used to the puffy dress and heels. I slip in the mud, landing on my bum with a thump. Warm tears blur my vision.

Footsteps slosh up behind me. Even in the mud, I can't miss the military precision of the owner's walk. Lincoln.

I lift my hands, watching mud drip through my fingers. "Look, buddy. If you're here to complain, I've already heard it. The House of Acca yells much better than they fight."

Lincoln clears his throat. "On behalf of myself and my people, thank you for saving the Earl's life."

I shake my head, not sure if I heard him correctly. Was that actual niceness from the Prince's mouth? I watch his outline as he walks away.

My head cocks to one side. "You're welcome."

I slowly haul myself to my feet. My gown's so loaded with mud, it now weighs a ton. I frown. It's going to take me forever to slog back to Betsy, even if I can figure out where I parked her.

A whinny sounds from a nearby line of trees. I scan the dim forest. Nightshade's bluish-gray coat gleams in the shadows. I smile.

"Perfect timing, Night. I could sure use a ride."

CHAPTER THIRTEEN

A.

Cissy's chipper voice carries from my front door into my dingy bedroom. "Hello, Momma Lewis. Is Myla home?"

Sitting upright in bed, I slam shut the schoolbook in my hands. *Cissy's here. Sweet.*

I glance at my Darth Vader alarm clock; the thrax autumn tournament ended hours ago. In a feat of super stealthy-ness, I was able to sneak home without Mom seeing me or my muddy dress, thanks in large part to the world's biggest bathroom-window-slash-emergency-entrance. Since then, I've been waiting on pins and needles for some news from Cissy.

Mom speaks next. "I thought you and Myla were at *your* house."

Leaping to my feet, I rush through my bedroom door. "Hi, Mom! Hey, Cissy!" I find both of them standing in the opened doorway. Cissy's in sweats and a t-shirt; Mom wears a look that says 'you two are up to something.'

Mom's chocolate eyes narrow. "What are you doing home, Myla?"

I sidle up to the front door and try to act cool. "Oh, I came back here a while ago to do some homework. Didn't you hear me come in?"

"Ah, no." Her Mom-radar is now scanning the situation, full throttle. I'm sure she suspects something's off here, but hopefully she won't guess what it is.

I grab my best friend's hand. "Cissy's here to help with the rest of my homework." I drag her toward my room. "See you later, Mom!" We rush through the bedroom doorway, closing it quickly behind us.

I'm bursting with curiosity. "So, what happened after I left?"

"That Earl is a piece of nastiness. All he did was whine about how you humiliated him." Cissy rolls her eyes. "He wanted to file an official diplomatic complaint."

"That douchebag! I saved his freaking life!" My eyes flicker red with anger. An official complaint could cause me, Mom, and the Ryders a whole lot of trouble.

She rubs her chin thoughtfully. "Everyone in the House of Acca was screaming for it."

"I heard them." My voice hitches. "Someone should wash their mouths out with soap." The memory of their cries echoes through my mind. My chest tightens with humiliation and rage.

Cissy shoots me a sly grin. "Don't take that part too seriously. They were complaining, but *not complaining*, if you know what I mean."

Huh. "That's clear as mud."

Cissy looks around the room, as if searching for the words. "It's like the Earl's people don't respect him, but they're too afraid of him to push back when he's being a loser." She frowns. "The Earl is not very *thrax*, if you know what I mean."

I snap my fingers. "Now *that* I understand. For a leader of demon hunters, he acts like a total wuss. Plus, he doesn't know dick about fighting demons. A crossbow with a Limus?"

Cissy chuckles. "I don't think a lot of them knew that."

I raise my pointer finger. "A lot of them aren't an Earl."

"True." She eyes me carefully. "Anyway, you won't have to worry about an official complaint. Lincoln stuck up for you."

My heart beats so wildly, I think it could break free from my chest. "Oh, he did?" I decide that now's a really good time to straighten everything on my dresser. "What did he say?"

"You saved the Earl's life and they owe you thanks, not a complaint. He shut down the discussion like *that*." She snaps her fingers.

Suddenly, I feel like doing a happy dance around the bedroom. "Did he say anything else?"

"He said it's not the thrax way to repay your kindness with cruelty, even if…" Her hand pops over her mouth.

My heart beats even more excitedly, if that's possible. "Come on. Even if *what*?"

"Even if you *are* a demon." Cissy winces.

There's that word again: demon.

"Oh." I plunk down at the edge of my bed and fold my hands into my lap. Sadness wraps about me like a heavy blanket.

Cissy sits down beside me. "Don't let him get you down. You're from totally different worlds, that's all." She wraps her arm about my shoulder. "Look, I'm glad you're interested in someone, but really? It shouldn't be him."

Ouch. That hurt.

"I didn't say I was interested." My eyes start to sting. *Whatever you do, don't cry, Myla.*

"Come on, sweetie." She gives my shoulder a gentle squeeze. "A ton of guys would give anything to date you. The fact is, you're a quasi, not a thrax. There's nothing wrong with that." Her voice takes on a joking tone. "It's not like you're part ghoul or something."

And then I lose it: a full on, snot-strings-out-of-my-nose festival of balling my eyes out. It takes Cissy a while to calm me down enough so I can explain why I'm so upset.

"Here's the thing. I think my dad's a ghoul."

Cissy gasps. "I'm sorry, Myla."

My face flushes with embarrassment and pain. "For so long, I wanted to know two things: what Mom did before the war and who my father was. Now, I wish I'd never asked."

184

Cissy twists so she can see me face-to-face. "If it makes any difference, it doesn't change how I feel about you or our friendship. Not one bit."

My mouth rounds into a shaky smile. "Thanks, Cissy. That does make a difference."

𝒜

I stand on a rolling dune of the Gray Sea, the warm grains of sand heating the tender soles of my bare feet. Wind whips my long cotton nightgown about my legs. Although I'm deep asleep, I'm awake and alert inside this dreamscape. It's my first since the thrax autumn tournament took place one week ago.

One week ago? That disaster is as fresh as if it were yesterday.

I set my hands onto the dark ground, creating a circle of white flame. My mother's form rises from the earth, her body made from granules of sand. The ring of fire flashes higher, then vanishes. Mom now appears in flesh and blood. She wears her purple robes and stands before the speaker podium in the Senate chamber.

"I stand before you today to address an issue that many of you will find hard to accept." Mom clears her throat. "Many believe that the differences between ghouls and demons run so deep, there could never be an alliance between them." She scans the chamber floor. Most Senators whisper in small groups. A handful watch her with mild interest. Xavier leans against the back wall in his gray suit, his face creased with worry. Tim stands in the doorway, his eyes large with fear.

Mom slams her fist on the podium. More Senators glare in her direction. "I won't mince words. I believe Ambassador Armageddon is creating an alliance with ghouls for the invasion of Purgatory. We must act!"

A gray-haired senator with a lanky body and an elephant tail takes to his feet. "Senator Lewis, we've been over this before. These allegations are not the work of a sane mind. You've been warned about this. If you continue on this path, we must move for your impeachment."

My breath catches. My mother…Impeached? The word rattles around my brain, sending jolts of shock and alarm though my system.

The Senate chamber springs to life. All attention glues to Mom as she starts a shouting match with the elder Senator.

Xavier rushes forward to stand beside Mom. "The issue of Armageddon will be tabled for the day, thank you." He wraps his long arm about Mom's shoulder and guides her to the back wall of the Senate chamber.

My body relaxes. Disaster averted.

Mom and Xavier huddle by the chamber wall. She shoves his hand off her shoulder. "Why did you do that?"

"Senator Adams was about to start impeachment proceedings."

Her eyes glow red. "And *I* was about to start calling for *your* replacement."

He grins. "I suppose I should send Senator Adams a gift basket, then." His eyes flare blue. "Do you think he likes peanuts?"

Mom's frown warms into a sad smile; her eyes fade to chocolate brown. "If you're going to say 'I told you so,' get it over with."

"I won't." Xavier pauses. "How about taking a break? I hear there's a lovely garden behind your diplomatic offices. We could get ice cream on the way." He leans in closer, whispering in her ear. "When's the last time you ate ice cream?"

Okay, this guy is a total cutie. Why couldn't Mom have hooked up with him? Part of me wonders if she did at some point. My rock-solid faith in Mom's inability to lie is officially starting to crumble.

"It's been a long time, that's for certain." She blushes. "I don't know, Xavier."

I can see Mom's knees turning into Jell-O from here. I purse my lips, considering. Maybe she *did* hook up with him.

"Come on, leave the Senate building for just one afternoon. I *am* Ambassador after all. We can talk about nothing but work, if you like."

Their gazes meet for a long moment. Mom licks her lips. "Alright."

I smile. *Ice cream and a walk.* That's so cute, I want to pinch their cheeks.

The pair head toward back door of the Senate chamber. Mom waves to Tim. "I'm so glad you're here. Can you clear my schedule for this afternoon? The Ambassador and I are going out."

Tim nods. "Yes, Senator Lewis." A muscle twitches along his neck. He watches them leave, his irises flaring demon red.

So, Tim definitely had jealousy issues. I consider asking Mom about that, and then rule against it. With my luck, I'll find out he went berserk and shot up the Senate chamber over her.

Before me, the scene in the Gray Sea turns back into grains of sand. The figures of Mom, Xavier, and Tim disintegrate into the ground.

I awake to the sound of Mom humming a nonsense tune. I stretch and yawn, then slip out of bed and pad into the kitchen. Mom stands by the stove, clicking on the gas burner below a frying pan. She smiles. "What do you want in your omelet?"

"I'll eat cereal, thanks."

"Let's take a break from Frankenberry. How about peppers and onions?"

"Yum." I slide into my favorite seat at the kitchen table. "I had another dreamscape last night."

Mom whisks some egg whites in a small bowl. "Do you have any questions for me?"

I squeeze my eyes tight. *I won't ask the question, I won't ask the question, I won't ask the question.*

I open them. Eh, I'll ask the question.

"Did you hook up with that Xavier guy?"

Mom holds still for a moment, then pokes at the omelet with her spatula. "Yes."

"Xavier's not my real—"

"No." Her tone says this is not up for discussion without a fight. And this morning, I'm not in a fighting mood.

I sigh. Oh well, it was worth a try.

"Why don't we see Tim ever?"

I wince. Here comes the bad news. He's dead or berserk or joined Hell's evil clown pavilion.

Mom hums and pours the egg mixture into the pan. "He and I had a falling out. He wanted more from our relationship. I told him it was a one-time thing."

"That's it? He doesn't want to see his awesome daughter?"

"No, I'm sorry Myla."

I brace myself, waiting for the waves of sadness because ghoul-dad doesn't want in on my life. But my feelings can be summed up in one word: meh. I'm strangely okay with this whole thing. I shrug.

Mom jiggles the pan with one hand. "Now *I* have a question for *you*."

"Shoot."

"The other day when you went to hang out with Cissy, what'd you *really* do?"

I scan the room as if a good story will be written on the wallpaper. "Ah, nothing." Could I be a worse liar?

Mom picks up an envelope from the counter. "Walker delivered a letter early this morning. From the Queen of the Thrax."

Dang.

"What's Walker doing playing mailman for the thrax?"

"Don't change the subject." Mom sprinkles spices into the pan. "Are you sure there's nothing you want to tell me?"

"Yup."

"I see." She turns down the burner. "The Queen of the Thrax is a diplomatic issue. Maybe I'll give the Ryders a call; perhaps they'll have some insight." She shoots me a sly grin.

I'm so nailed. The last thing I want is her chatting with the Ryders and finding out about the three Lords I flattened, my yelling match in the Library, and who knows what else.

"Okay, I went to this demon hunter tournament with Cissy. The thrax are a bunch of quasi-phobic girl haters and I can't wait until they crawl back under the rock they came from. That's it."

Mom sets my plate in front of me. The omelet sure smells yummy. "The Queen wants you to attend another tournament.

This one celebrates winter and names the greatest warrior in Antrum."

I stuff a bite of omelet into my mouth. "This tastes really good, Mom." I swallow. "I don't know why the thrax bother to celebrate the seasons in Purgatory. We have two of them: muddy and not-so-muddy."

Mom slips into the chair across from mine. "That wasn't an answer to my question."

Dammit. She's in awesome form today. "I'm not going."

She lets out a low whistle. "You really hate the thrax, huh?"

"You got that right." I chow down on more of my breakfast.

"Myla, it's unprecedented for thrax to be in Purgatory at all, let alone interacting with quasis. Normally, they kill anyone with demon blood on sight."

"So you're taking the thrax side in this? You haven't been through the play-by-play. That thrax Prince has been totally insulting." I remember how he said I deserved to be thanked for saving the Earl, even though I'm a *demon*. Thanks for nothing, asshat. I tap the tabletop with my pointer finger. "And another thing. Even when you think he's *not* being insulting, he ends up being insulting. I don't care what his title is, he's going to treat me with respect."

"We're not talking about the Prince here. For someone like the Queen to reach out to a quasi is unheard of. Refusing her invitation could set back diplomatic relations with the thrax for decades."

"Boo hoo."

"This isn't just about you, Myla. Suppose we need thrax allies down the road? You have to think of the greater good."

I picture the demon inspections at school. Things have never been this rough.

"Fine." I frown. "But I hate it when you make sense."

Mom smiles. "I'll try not to in the future." She taps the card on her chin. "She must be a clever one, this Queen."

I freeze with a bite of omelet half-way to my mouth. *Lincoln's Mom is sneaky?* "What makes you say that?"

"She had the invitation hand delivered to you, care of me. She must have known you wouldn't attend without some encouragement." She flips the card over. "She also wrote a note that a dressmaker would contact us. I'm guessing you need motivation in that area as well?"

As I munch my omelet, I consider the two dresses I've worn in the last decade: the neon carrot and the great white pouf. What a pair of disasters. If I could wear my fighting suit 24-7, I would. "When it comes to dresses, I have one thing to say: blech."

"I'll take that as a cry for wardrobe help. I'll give the tailor your measurements."

I let out a long breath. "Thanks, Mom." I grit my teeth in frustration. Another thrax tournament. More sitting around in overly large formalwear, trying to talk nonsense with a bunch of nincompoops. If only Cissy could be there. I pause, an idea forming.

"Hey, can I see that invite?"

"Sure." She hands it to me.

"Cool, it says I can bring a friend. Cissy will be thrilled." And I'll have a wingman for the event. Nice.

Mom rises to her feet. "I need to run some errands today, so I'll drop you off at school." She glances at the wall clock. "We better leave soon."

I set my plate in the sink. "Can't Walker take you around?"

"I can go myself. There's no need to keep bothering Walker."

I grin. Mom's showing some of her old spark and independence. "Sounds good to me, Senator."

As Mom drives me to school, she talks about working with the thrax as Senator of Diplomacy. Basically, they only bothered her office if something happened that could make them leave Antrum or, even worse to them, compromise their over-the-top security systems. They live underground for a reason: the demons would love to wipe them out and try to, often.

I fiddle with Betsy's air vents. "Do you remember anything else?"

"Let's see. The current ruling family came to power in the Middle Ages."

190

"Makes sense. They got a little stuck there, I think."

She chuckles. "This was seven hundred years ago, I think. Demons had just invaded Antrum. The archangel Aquila was called in to help."

"Why her?"

"Archangels are very rare, very powerful. The story is that Aquila fell in love with a thrax and her children became the House of Rixa. They're the only ones who can use these special weapons, I can't remember the name."

I picture Lincoln with his fiery broadsword. "Baculum."

"That's it. The Rixa drove out the demons and have ruled Antrum ever since."

I let out a breath with a frustrated huff. Back at Zeke's party, I was excited that Miss Thing taught me how thrax had mismatched eyes. Who knew there was so much more I wasn't learning? "Wow. They don't teach us any of this stuff in school."

"Of course, not. They're too busy brainwashing you into being slaves."

My eyebrows pop up. That's rather sassy talk from Mom.

"I'll make you a list of books for your next visit to the Ryder library. I've let them fill your head with trash for too long." She pulls up to the drop-off area in front of school. "And here we are."

"Thanks, Mom. See you later."

"Bye, now."

As she drives away, I realize Mom said goodbye without hyperventilating and asking me to be safe. Awesome.

I walk into school and find my best friend leaving the little girl's room.

"Morning, Cissy."

"Hey, Myla."

I wag the invitation by my ear. "Have I got a surprise for you!" I place the envelope in her hand. "And *you're* going with me."

Cissy opens the letter, reads, and jumps up and down.

"This is amazing! The Queen of the thrax, wow. The Ryders will be so excited. Can I show Zeke?"

"Sure, knock yourself out. I'll catch up with you later."

My first class is with my worst teacher, Miss Thing. I pick a seat in the last row, pull out my notebook, and scribble 'I hate Prince Lincoln' over and over.

Miss Thing raises her arms. "Class, today we'll learn about Earth's most important holiday. It's a month-long celebration of ghoul superiority called Halloween." She pulls open her top desk drawer. "I've some precious artifacts of this sacred celebration that I'll pass around. But first, who can tell me why Halloween's important to quasis?"

The room is silent.

"How about you, Paulette?"

Paulette looks up from her Prada purse. "What?"

Miss Thing groans. "Why's Halloween important to quasis?"

"Because it's about ghouls?"

"Exactly! And what's important to ghouls is important to you."

I frown. I've seen enough reruns on the Human Channel to know Miss Thing is wrong on this one. I raise my hand.

"Yes, Myla?"

"Isn't a Halloween a human holiday where they dress up in costumes and go door to door for candy?"

She lets out an exaggerated gasp. "You've been watching that clap-trap human channel on public access television." She shivers. "That's all a pack of lies and you're a fool to believe a word."

I smack my lips. *I'm the fool here?* This from the same woman who says all the Oligarchy are hotties. I return my attention to my very important notebook scribbling. Screw her.

Miss Thing lifts a bag of tiny yellow and orange candies from her desk. "Can everyone see these? They're called *candy corn*. Every Halloween, humans fill large bowls with candy corn and do not eat any. Why? The corn symbolizes the gold nuggets they'll one day give to ghouls." She hands the bag to a nearby student. "Pass these around and be careful about it."

Zeke saunters into the room and winks at our teacher. "Hello, lovely."

"Hi there, Zeke." She makes goo-goo eyes at him, which is just disgusting.

I slump lower in my chair and grit my teeth. When I'm late, Miss Thing practically skins me alive.

Zeke slips into the chair next to mine. "Hey, Myla."

"Hi, Zeke."

Miss Thing brings out a plastic pumpkin. A basic face is painted on it with geometric shapes. "Class, this is called a jack-o-lantern." She holds the pumpkin reverently above her head. "On earth, humans carve likenesses of their favorite ghouls out of pumpkins. This one is me."

I eye the jack-o-lantern. The bald part is spot-on, but it needs red lipstick.

As Miss Thing goes through more items in her desk, Zeke leans over the aisle. "It's so great that you're finally being a grown-up about all this."

"About what?"

"The thrax. You know, going to the winter tournament and taking Cissy along. It means a lot to my family. Thanks."

"Well, it's all about you, Zeke." I smack my lips. "Per usual."

Zeke taps his desktop with his pen. "Hey, it's me." Not sure if he's ignoring my sarcasm or not catching it. Either way, it *is* him. "So, you'll order a regular gown this time?"

My upper lip twists. This isn't my favorite subject. "Yup."

"You'll have to order soon. The event's in three weeks."

"My mom's on it."

"And you'll get ready with Cissy so there's no funny business?"

My blood starts to boil. "I'll get ready with Cissy because she's my *friend*."

"And you'll—"

"Excuse me, Zeke, but I'm missing a really important lecture right now on Zagnut Bars." I point to Miss Thing. "Let's just stop talking and start paying attention to Miss Thing, okay?" Otherwise you'll end up with another black eye.

"Whatever." Zeke turns to face our teacher. I watch him for a moment, wondering if I did the right thing to invite Cissy at all.

Oh, well. I'll find out soon enough.

CHAPTER FOURTEEN

A

I step up to a typical-looking ranch house in Middle Purgatory and ring the doorbell. Outside, the place looks just like my home: a one-story gray ranch house on a bland street of other one-story gray ranch houses. A few seconds pass before a beautiful blonde couple opens the door.

A willowy-tall woman tilts her head to one side, setting her blonde ringlets jiggling. "Hello, Myla."

Damn, Cissy's mom totally hates me. "Hi, Mrs. Frederickson."

"I'm here, too." Cissy's dad's handsome face droops into a frustrated frown. He hates me too. It's the tail. Most quasis don't see Furor as demons per se, since they have two deadly sins and all. We're more like freaks of nature, which is how Mr. Frederickson is glaring at me right now.

"Hello, Mr. F." No point using his full name; he loathes me anyway. I pop onto my tip-toes and peer over their collective shoulders. "Is Cissy home?" I look beyond her parents, seeing the familiar interior of oriental rugs, gilded furniture, and modern art.

"Myla!" Cissy bursts through the wall of her parents, grabbing my hand. "The gowns arrived last night!" She drags me past the parental gatekeepers and through their elaborately-decorated house. I've been here a hundred times, but I'm still shocked that any walls can hold so many tiny shelves, statues, and pricey knick-knacks. Cissy leads me into her bedroom and kicks the door shut behind us. "I had to empty half my closet to make room for them."

Something colorful on the wall catches my eye. "Hey, you got a new painting." I stare at it and wince. "What is it?"

"Some kind of human modern art thing my dad scared up. Jackson Polly-somebody. Dad got a deal on it." She tilts her head, setting her blonde ringlets bouncing. "I think it may have fallen off a truck, if you know what I mean."

I scan her room, looking for anything else that's different. My bedroom's standard ghoul issue: drab carpet, blah bed, and non-descript dresser. It hasn't changed since I was two years old. Cissy's room looks like a decorator show house from the old quasi republic days. There's a matching bed-set, plush carpet, and line of funky paintings on her walls. Her dad is constantly adding new goodies from his black-market deals.

My best friend pulls the cover from her gown. It's an emerald-green sheath with long looping sleeves that's trimmed with black velvet.

I lean back on my heels and stare. "That looks lovely. What do the colors mean?"

"Green means I'm a single woman in a relationship. The black ribbon says I'm a guest of the House of Rixa." She pulls the cover off my gown. It looks like the first one, only it's blood red.

"What does red mean?"

"That you're a single lady who's unattached."

"Why don't they have me carry around a price list too? Sheesh." A pair of stacked boxes catch my eye. "What's in there?"

"Shoes and stuff." Cissy holds her gown against her torso and models in the mirror. "This is even nicer than what I wore to the autumn tournament."

I step over to the boxes and pull out my matching shoes. Inside the box I also find a complex set of winding strips like mummy wrappings. I pick mine up with two fingers. "What the heck are these?"

Cissy glances over her shoulder at me. "Your underwear."

"You've got to be kidding."

She sets one hand on her hip. "See? If you'd gone with me to the tailor instead of having your mom send in measurements, you'd know all this stuff. Thrax are nuts about their traditions, and those are traditional thrax undies."

"I'm not wearing them." Dropping the strips back into the box, I look at them out of my right eye. "I don't even know how to get these things on."

"You're wearing them and I know exactly how to put them on you." Cissy glares at me. "They look like typical underwear when they're on, don't worry. From what the Ryders told me, thrax are insane about this kinda stuff. If someone saw you in the bathroom wearing anything else, it could turn into a diplomatic horror story."

My upper lip curls. "I don't know, Cissy."

"Oh, stop being a baby and put on your free gorgeous gown. We don't want to be late."

We slip on our dresses and I have to admit, I really like mine. The last two gowns I wore were the neon carrot and the marshmallow nightmare. This one's simple, pretty and actually fits me.

And yes, I wear the traditional thrax undies. Whatever.

I drive Betsy over to thrax central. Cissy complains the entire ride how my beautiful green station wagon has barely-functioning air vents and sketchy radio. I remind her of Betsy's loyalty and her own lack of car. Once we get to the thrax compound, it takes for-bleeding-ever to find a parking space. The winter tournament's a much bigger shindig than autumn. I find a spot for Betsy, and then Cissy and I follow the crowd through a winding forest path that opens onto a large field.

Cissy shakes her head. "They must have cut down half a for-est." Compared to the autumn tournament, this field is huge and covered in fancy tents. There must be two dozen total, all in different colors.

I nudge Cissy's arm. "There are five major houses, so the other tents must be the lesser ones."

She smiles. "You've done some research."

"Mom gave me some books."

We approach the tournament green. It's now surrounded by more and larger seating pavilions. A network of wooden walkways keeps everyone from sloshing through the mud. The thrax really went all-out this time.

With all the extra crowds and hassle, Cissy and I are really late. The pavilions are packed; there's no chance to get a seat. We decide to stand by the tall wooden fence that surrounds the tournament green.

I settle into a spot, set my elbows atop the fence and scan the fighting field. The Earl of Acca stands in the center, his crossbow held high. He's bashing it into a ghoul. My breath catches.

I tap Cissy's shoulder. "I know that ghoul. It's XP-22. I see him at Arena matches."

Her pretty mouth sags into a frown. "Why's the Earl fighting a ghoul?"

"I'm forced to fight in the Arena. It's a job for XP-22. They must have paid him to appear." I watch the Earl hammer away at XP-22 as he tries to run away. Anger careens up my spine. "This isn't right. Even you could kick XP-22's butt. And he clearly isn't attacking the Earl."

"Shh, Myla. It's not our place to judge."

"Fine." I grit my teeth and look away. The crowd breaks out into wild applause. "Is it over?"

"Yes."

"Is the ghoul dead?"

Cissy sucks in a breath. "Oh, yeah."

The Earl of Acca struts off the field. Some thrax lackeys clear off the body. My eyes flare red with rage and horror. XP-22 didn't deserve to end his afterlife that way.

Across the tournament green, the wooden fence swings open. A dragon creeps onto the field of battle. Its body is large as a cow, with a tail twice as long. It has stubby wings, red eyes, a long thin snout, and black scales that glitter purple in the light. It's a shadow dragon, a rare demon that's incredibly hard to kill.

I let out a low whistle. I feel sorry for whatever sucker goes after that thing.

The sucker in question steps onto the field of battle: Lincoln. He wears black body armor with the Rixa crest, his baculum broadsword gripped in one hand. He marches toward the dragon, tossing his blade from hand to hand, eyeing up his opponent.

The dragon rears up on his haunches, arcs his head toward the sky and spits out a stream of red fire. With deliberate steps, Lincoln closes in on the beast's mouth. Raising his baculum high above his head, he blocks the dragon's stream of fire with his sword. A shower of red-hot sparks cloud the air. The dragon gags, shakes its head, and hops backwards. Its neck becomes level with the tournament green.

Lincoln crouches into a body roll and slides under the beast's belly, reappearing by the beast's tail.

My eyebrows pop up. That's a pretty neat move.

Baculum sword in hand, the Prince scales the dragon's back, the beast howling and flailing beneath him. I watch the play of muscle on Lincoln's chest and legs as he climbs up the dragon's body. My skin flushes with desire and heat. Damn, that's one gorgeous man, even if he is a creep sometimes.

Cissy touches my shoulder. "Are you okay, Myla?"

"What do you mean?"

She points to the wooden fence. I've gripped it so hard, there's now a crack in the wood. I loosen my grip and shrug. "Yeah, I'm fine. That's just a really cool demon."

"You and demons." Cissy sniffs. "Well, be careful with that fence. It doesn't look too sturdy."

"Sure." My gaze sweeps the crowd. Queen Octavia sits in the front row of the largest pavilion, her mismatched eyes fixed on me. I shiver and return my focus to the fighting grounds. The Prince still rides the dragon's back as the beast twists and rears.

"Nat!" Lincoln waves to a sturdy thrax at the sidelines. "Toss me a muzzle!"

The man throws at Lincoln what looks like a thick leather net. The Prince slips it over the dragon's mouth and pulls on the attached leash. The animal quiets. Shaking his head from side to side, Lincoln slides off the dragon's back, the fire-sword still firmly in his grip.

A cry rises up from the pavilions. "Kill! Kill!"

Lincoln steps around the dragon, checking its jaw and hind legs. He raises one hand; the crowd goes quiet. "Nat, come here!"

The barrel-chested man jogs onto the tournament green. Sturdy and fit, he wears black body armor like Lincoln's.

The Prince nods his head to the dragon. "Nat, how old do you say this beast is?"

Squinting, I take a closer look at the dragon's body as well. *He's right.* That dragon's way too young for tournament fighting. No true warrior takes on anything but a fully-grown opponent who's in attack mode. A lesson the Earl of Acca should learn, pronto. I tilt my head to one side. It takes a lot of control to stop in the middle of a battle. I almost hate to admit it, but I'm impressed.

I return my attention to the fighting grounds, where Nat checks the creature's teeth. "The beast is four, maybe five years old, My Prince. Still a pup."

Lincoln pats the beast's hindquarters. "What would you say about these marks?"

Nat whistles through his teeth. "Stinging nettle, very painful. Would have driven the poor beast wild."

Stinging nettle? That's cruel stuff. Even some demon communities forbid it.

Lincoln raises his hands, addressing the crowd. "This beast is not yet of age and has been mistreated. Killing it would be dishonorable." The crowd responds with a grumpy murmur. Lincoln passes the muzzle's leash to Nat. "Take him back to the Menagerie. Tell the Master of Creatures I'll speak with him shortly."

I watch Lincoln march off the tournament green. Unlike the Earl of Acca, Prince Pompous knows there's no glory in pummeling a weaker someone who's not attacking you. Who would've thought?

Another touch brushes my shoulder. "Hey, Cissy." Turning around, I see that it isn't my best friend beside me, but Bera, Queen Octavia's handmaiden.

"The Queen would like to speak with you."

Shock explodes through my body. "The Queen wants to speak with me?" I shoot a startled glance at Cissy. Her tawny eyes stretch wide.

"Aye." Bera grips my sleeve, yanking me away from the wooden fence. "Now."

My hand wobbles at Cissy in a half-hearted goodbye. "Catch you later, I guess." What in blazes does the Queen want with me? Anxiety zings through my nervous system.

Cissy's voice comes out as a squeak. "Sure, see you."

Bera turns toward the royal pavilion. "Follow me."

The crowd parts for us as we walk along. My heart hammers anxiously in my chest. What in unholy hell is going on? I hike up the steps to the pavilion's main platform. King Connor and Queen Octavia sit side by side in throne-like chairs. The Scala Heir lounges beside the Queen, a nasty scowl on her face.

"Come here, Miss Lewis." The Queen snaps her fingers and glares at the Scala Heir. Adair scurries away. Octavia nods to the now-open chair. Her crown slips forward a bit with the movement.

I slip into the high-backed seat beside her. "Hello, your Highness." I wave to the King. "And your Highness."

The King nods his head slightly. "Miss Lewis." He looks regal with his shock of white hair and silver crown.

The Queen's mismatched eyes narrow. "You may call me Octavia." Up close, I notice her porcelain skin, high cheekbones, and delicate laugh-lines. Her sandy-brown hair is wound into a braided bun at the base of her neck.

"Thanks. Call me Myla." I scan the scene. The Great Ladies stand near the steps to the royal pavilion. They all cluster around Adair, pointing at me and giggling. *Ugh.* My hands ball into fists.

With long fingers, the Queen lifts a golden wine goblet from a nearby table. She looks out over the crowd. I can almost see the wheels of her mind spin. "The Great Ladies stare at you, Myla."

I turn in their direction and glare, my eyes flaring demon-red. Their faces whiten. Quick as a heartbeat, they all turn away.

I smack my lips. "Now they've stopped."

Octavia stifles a smile. "I wish I could do that trick." She gestures across the tournament grounds to where Lincoln must be stalking around. "My son doesn't look at you at all."

I make a point of *not* gazing in the direction of her point. "That's fine with me."

"I see." She sips her wine, watching me closely. "Are you enjoying the tournament?"

"Honestly, no. I knew the ghoul who fought the Earl of Acca. Killing him was not—" I clear my throat. "He wasn't a worthy opponent, that's all."

A smile curls the queen's lips. "Spoken as a true thrax."

My back teeth lock with anger. "I'm a quasi-demon…As the Earl of Acca was quick to point out." *And your son, too, although I won't say that to your face.*

"I know. I've seen your tail." I glance at her mismatched eyes. Behind them, mental gears whirl and spin even faster. I have the weird feeling she knows exactly what I was thinking about Lincoln.

I sigh. It's bad enough sitting through another of these boring tournaments, let alone making small talk with Lincoln's calculating and somewhat creepy Mom. I fidget in my chair and watch the gate swing open on the tournament green. An Arachnoid demon crawls out onto the field of battle. Arachnoids are ten-foot tall daddy-long-leg spiders with extra armor and a bad attitude. They have tiny bodies, thread-thin legs, and giant pincer mouths with a poisonous bite. Across the green, the Earl of Kamal marches onto the field, a tiger by his side.

I shake my head. "He should've brought a falcon."

Octavia sips her wine. "And why's that?"

"The tiger can fight the Arachnoid's legs all day; it won't make a dent. They have light armor that's good as dragon scales. But the demon's body is pretty unprotected, especially from the top. A bird could go after it pretty easily."

In the edges of my vision, I see my tail straighten Octavia's crown. That thing so needs a leash. Frowning, I give it a smack.

Octavia arches her eyebrow. "I was about to thank you for doing that."

"It wasn't me. My tail has a mind of its own sometimes."

Her lips purse. "Interesting." She eyes me from head to toe. Suddenly, I understand how animals feel in the zoo.

I let out an exasperated sigh. "Why'd you invite me here, Octavia?"

She chuckles. "I wondered if you'd ask the obvious question. Would you believe me if I said it's a matter of quasi-thrax diplomacy?"

"No."

"That's wise." She sips her wine, examining my face, and then sets the goblet down. "I brought you here because I think my son finds you interesting."

My eyes almost pop out of my head. I look behind me. Someone else must have snuck into the pavilion. "Me?" I tap my ribcage.

She nods.

"You don't know your son very well." He's a pompous jerk who would never be interested in a 'demon' like me.

"Perhaps." The corners of her mouth round up slightly. "I think I know *you*, however." Octavia snaps her fingers. Bera rushes to stand before her.

The handmaiden bows. "Your Highness."

"Escort Myla to my family's tent." She pats my hand. "I gave your measurements to my smithy. He's made you a suit of armor. I'd like you to fight in the tourney under the crest of my homeland, the House of Gurith." She gestures to the tournament field, where the Earl of Kamal battles the Arachnoid. "Whoever kills that demon first, wins the tournament and is named the greatest warrior in Antrum. I think it will be you."

My heart leaps in my chest. "Yes!" I jump to my feet and stand beside Bera, then pause. I scan the queen's mask-like face. The wheels of her mind still whirl and churn. "Why're you helping me?"

"Bera, will you wait for Myla at the base of the stairs?" Her handmaiden nods and steps away.

The Queen curls her finger in my direction. "Come closer."

I lean forward; Octavia whispers in my ear. "I'm helping you, my dear, because you and I are the only two females in this vicinity who aren't nit-wits."

My face stretches into a wide grin. "I like you Octavia."

"Do you?" A smile dances in her eyes. "Go put on your armor."

I meet Bera at the base of the stairs. She leads me through the crush of the crowd to a small golden tent decorated with a Viking-style dragon's head. Bera pulls up the entrance flap; we step inside. It's an empty and snug space filled with small store of weapons. A great wooden trunk lays against one wall.

"Come here, girl." Bera pulls up the trunk's lid. Inside sits a fitted suit of under-armor made from brown leather along with a golden breastplate. I brush my fingers over the dragon's head insignia hammered into the metal. "It's so beautiful."

Bera beams. "It's like the one Octavia wore when she battled in these very games so many years ago. The House of Gurith's one of the few that allows women warriors."

"Did she win the tournament?"

"Second place. Connor took first." She winks. "But you'll win today, girl."

I gently pull the armor from the trunk. "If not, I'll look great fighting." I stare into my reflection in the shining gold and grin. I'm about to fight in the tournament. Me, demon girl. My tail swishes in an excited rhythm. I know exactly how to down that Arachnoid too.

I quickly put on the armor. It fits perfectly. Bera ties back my long auburn hair with a golden ribbon.

"There, now. You're all set." Bera gestures to the store of weapons. "What would you like? A blade? Crossbow?"

"Nothing, just me."

The blood drains from Bera's face. "What will you fight with?"

My tail pops over my shoulder and waves in her direction. "One guess. Let's go."

We march out of the tent and through the crowd. Stares and whispers surround me. It's awesome. Bera guides me to one end of the tournament green. On the field, the Earl of Horus battles the Arachnoid. He's going after the legs too. Dumbass.

"Now, wait here, girl. The Earl has a few more minutes of time. If he doesn't kill the demon by then, it's your turn."

I watch the Earl of Horus hack away at the Arachnoid's shin. It'll be my turn.

While I wait, I stretch and crack my neck. Cissy steps up beside me, her eyes big with shock.

"Myla, what are you doing here? What're you wearing?"

"Armor."

"You're supposed to wear traditional dress."

"I am following tradition. The Queen told me to fight the Arachnoid, and it's tradition to do what the Queen tells you, right?" I wag my eyebrows up and down.

Cissy grabs my upper arm. "You mean that nasty spider monster out there? You'll get killed!"

"No, I'll have a good time." I pinch her cheek. "You worry too much. Arachnoids are easy-peasy."

A silver trumpet blares. The Earl of Horus walks off the tournament green to encouraging cheers from the crowd.

Bera steps forward, sets one hand on the wooden fence and swings it open. "Your turn, girl. Make Gurith proud."

I stride onto the tournament green. The crowd falls silent. Somewhere in the distance, a cow moos. Worried voices whisper that I'm not carrying a weapon.

I smirk. That's what they think.

The Arachnoid charges at me, its long legs a flutter of movement. I wait until it's a step away and jump high, gripping the upper half of its nearest leg. Arachnoids keep the top of their limbs level; you can use them like a gymnast's parallel bars. I haul myself up until my belly rests on the spider's upper thigh. Swinging my body 360-degrees, I spin about the spider-leg and into the air. I somersault upwards, landing on the demon's tiny body.

In the corner of my vision, I see Lincoln standing by the edge of the tournament ground, an empty muzzle in his hand. He stares at me intently, his face unreadable.

What the blazes does he want?

I lose my footing, slide straight off the demon, and land on the ground with a whump. A gasp sounds from the crowd.

Focus, Myla.

I hop back onto my feet and wait for the Arachnoid to make another pass. It scurries around to face me, its legs moving in an odd rhythm. The limbs are now angled so they aren't level. Clever spider. I can't vault onto its body anymore.

I need a new strategy.

The Arachnoid scampers toward me, two long pincers flexing in its hungry mouth. My inner demon goes into overdrive. Volts of anger shock my system. My tail flicks eagerly by my shoulder.

As the spider scrambles nearer, I drop to the ground, rolling to the demon's outer left side. My tail loops around two of its eight legs. Bounding to my feet, I run straight under the creature's belly, flipping it onto its back. The Arachnoid lays stunned and immobile. I quickly step about the spider's small body, weaving my tail around its eight limbs.

With a swish of my hips, I cinch all the spider's legs together.

Gotcha.

Trumpets blare. The crowd cheers. A chant of "Kill! Kill!" erupts from the pavilions.

I fold my arms over my chest. "Why kill it? It hasn't done anything to me."

The Arachnoid recovers from its shock and starts fighting my tail. One of the demon's legs breaks free, slicing through my leather armor and scratching my back. Pain rips up my spine. My eyes blaze demon-red.

"Okay, now it's done something." I spin about, hauling the Arachnoid with me. Once the demon has enough momentum, my tail releases it, launching the spider to the other side of the tournament grounds. The monster slams into the protecting wall with a thud, leaving a long smear of yellow goop as it slides to the ground.

I frown. "Well, now it's killed. Yuck."

The crowd erupts in another cheer. Cissy races out onto the green and gives me a big hug.

"Myla, that was amazing!"

"Thanks, Cissy." It's tempting to say 'I told you so,' but I don't want to be a sore winner.

The Queen waves me toward the royal pavilion. I walk over and stand before her and King Connor.

Octavia grins. "You did well." She and the King share a look that's an entire conversation in itself.

King Connor raises his arm. "I hereby declare Myla Lewis from the House of Gurith to be the greatest warrior in all Antrum!" The crowd lets out a hearty round of applause.

Octavia addresses the crowd, a golden swath of fabric in her hand. "As is our tradition, I award a silk handkerchief to the winner." She offers me the garment. "I thought you might prefer this, however."

I take the fabric in my hand. It's a delicate golden shawl with tiny pearl beading. "Thank you, Octavia. This is lovely."

The Queen smiles. "The armor is yours to keep as well."

"Wow. Thanks, again." I rub the delicate fabric between my fingertips. The Queen planned this all along. My eyes sting, but not with rage. I'm not used to mom-figure types who have such confidence in me.

King Connor lowers his arm. "It is tradition for the winner to accompany each House on one demon patrol throughout the next year. I hope that meets with your approval?"

Demon killing on earth? My heart and mouth both kick into overdrive. "That would be sweet!" I clear my throat and take a deep breath. "I mean, I would be honored to join demon patrol, your Highness."

Connor's laugh lines curl up with his smile. "The winner may also make a single request of the King and Queen. As long as it is within reason, your boon will be granted."

There's no question what I want. "I'd like to keep Nightshade."

A smile quirks the Queen's mouth. "A kindred soul, eh?"

I shift my weight from foot to foot. I hope this isn't a rude request. "Yes. Nightshade is very special."

The King and Queen share a long look.

"Granted." Octavia motions to a nearby servant. "Please make sure Myla's horse is saddled and ready for her to ride home tonight." She gestures to the open chair beside hers. "Now join me for the closing ceremony." I step into the pavilion and take my place at her side.

The rest of the tournament is a lot of falderal and marching around. Trumpets play, lords parade, and ladies giggle. The Earl of Acca struts around like a peacock with a new set of feathers. Everyone stops by to say 'good evening' to the Queen and 'congratulations' to me. Finally, the guests go home, the sky turns dark, and Octavia rises to her feet. She pats my hand.

"Well done, Myla. You are a tribute to the House of Gurith."

"Thank you."

"Was I right to assume you'd ride Nightshade to the Ryder stables tonight?"

"I'd like to."

"Of course. You'll find her beyond that line of trees." She gestures across the tournament grounds. "Good night, my dear."

"Good night, Octavia."

The Queen walks to the other side of the pavilion. Connor's sturdy form waits there by the exit stairs. The King nods in my direction, winds Octavia's arm through his, and the pair step away.

It takes a bit of meandering in the dark, but I find the stables easily enough. It's a long wooden building set into the trees. The front gate lies open. I step inside, seeing a central aisle lined with a dozen stalls on each side. Nightshade stands at the building's end. An oil lamp casts a circle of light beside her as she nuzzles a crouched figure. Whoever-it-is sits half inside the final stall.

The stranger rises to his feet, and I see the familiar outline of Lincoln: broad shoulders, earthy-brown hair, and military bearing. My stomach twists. With his back to me, he scans a shelf of jars at the far wall. Nodding, he pulls out a white container. He crouches on his heels, leaning over something in the last stall.

I step closer. Nightshade brushes her muzzle against Lincoln's back. Reaching behind him, the Prince absently pats the horse's cheek. "I know you're there, Night. I'm happy to see you too."

I freeze in place. Nightshade is Lincoln's horse? My mouth starts talking on its own. "Hi, there."

Lincoln rises to his feet. "Oh, hello." He stands straight and alert, his black body armor open at the neck. Candlelight casts shadows on his full mouth and scooped-out cheeks.

"I'm here for Nightshade."

The horse leans her blue-gray head toward Lincoln. "She knows. We've been saying good-bye."

"Is she your horse?"

"One of them. The House of Striga breeds them; I raised her from a foal. Every Striga horse is enchanted, but Night takes it to a new level."

I smile. "I know, she keeps me on her back without a saddle. I don't even have to ask, she takes me where I need to go. Or she's waiting for me when I get there. I think she does magic." Night turns to me, her black marble-eyes blinking in a way that says 'no kidding.'

Lincoln runs his fingers down her mane. "The House of Striga specializes in witchcraft. Nightshade casts spells for everything you described. She also has the power to make small things appear and disappear. Oh, and she loves to send fireballs at enemies during battle." The horse whinnies; Lincoln grins. "We've gotten out of some close scrapes that way."

"Look, I never would've asked for her if I knew–"

"It was a fair request. You fought well today." He rubs Nightshade's neck in long strokes. "My mother comes from the House of Gurith. It's a lesser house, but one of the few that allow women warriors. She's wanted a female tournament champion for years. You've made her very happy." He sighs. "Besides, Nightshade chose you, didn't she?"

"Yes. At the Ryder stables."

"I rode her there to meet the minister. Normally, she comes back on her own." Night tosses her head and snorts. "I don't take it personally, girl."

Reaching into his pocket, Lincoln pulls out a few small biscuits. Nightshade eats them from his outstretched hand. I watch him closely, my forehead knit in confusion. Is this the same guy who insulted quasis and yelled at me in the Ryder library?

Lincoln gently strokes Night's forehead. "I've never seen anyone fight the way you did today. Your eyes turned red."

"That's my demon side. All quasis have a power with one of the seven deadly sins. Mine's wrath."

"Have you any battle training?"

"Nope. I started fighting death matches in the Arena when I was twelve. I sorta learned on my feet."

A low moan sounds from the stall behind Lincoln.

I take a step forward. "What's in there?"

"The Shadow Dragon. He was too sick to haul back to the Menagerie." Lincoln opens the white jar, sniffs the contents, and winces. "This may smell bad, little man, but it'll help." He crouches down.

I step closer. The dragon's black scales look chalky white. His fiery red eyes are now dimmed. My tail strokes along his back, his slowing heartbeat thrums through me like it was my own. The connection between us can mean only one thing. "This isn't a Shadow Dragon. He's Furor." Although they can take the form of a dragon, Furor are part human too. It's against inter-realm law to fight them in the Arena, let alone a tournament like this one.

Lincoln scoops more ointment onto his fingers, rubs it into the beast's flank. "How do you know? It's never changed into human form."

I turn to him and arch my brows. "One guess." My tail waves at him over my shoulder.

He chuckles. "Okay, I'll take your word for it." He leans back onto his heels. "Why do you think he hasn't changed form?"

"I think he's too frightened." I pick up the back leg, look at the talons. "His first talons haven't come in yet. He can't be five years old." The creature in the stall shoots me a sleepy look. "Poor little thing."

"I'll send a message to the Furor ambassador tonight." He pats the dragon's back with long strokes. "Are you absolutely certain?"

"Yes. By now, a Shadow Dragon would have tried to spear us with its tail. That's how they consume your soul." I smile. "Or try to."

He grins back. My knees go a bit wobbly. "You know a lot about demons."

"Arena fighters like me see all the matches they want. Last month, I saw a horde of Cellula."

"Really? I haven't seen that breed in years." He closes the ointment jar and sets it aside. "So that's how you knew."

"Knew what?"

"How to save Earl of Acca from the Limus. He's a pompous blowhard, but he *is* one of our most important Earls." He looks at me intently. His wheat-brown and slate-blue eyes shimmer. "Thanks again for saving his life."

I shift my weight from foot to foot. It feels weird to do anything but yell at this guy. "You're, uh, welcome." I turn my attention to the wounded creature. "Poor little guy."

Lincoln grits his teeth. "Shadow Dragons are rare, the Master of Creatures wanted something to dazzle the crowd. But any creature this young, it's not–" The dragon flinches, Lincoln pats his side. "Calm down, boy."

I finish the thought. "Honorable."

"Yes." Lincoln's mismatched eyes find mine again. My stomach lurches with something I don't know how to name.

It's time to leave.

"It's late. I better head out." I reach for Nightshade, she whinnies and prances away. I follow her down the stable's main aisle. "Come on, girl."

"Myla, what did you do to your back?"

I look over my shoulder. "Oh, that was the Arachnoid. I forgot it got one good lick in."

Lincoln rises to his feet. "Come over here."

What a worrywart. "It's fine, really."

Lincoln steps up behind me. "That looks bad. Arachnoids are poisonous. Wait one minute." He rushes over to the shelves on the far wall, pulls down a white towel, and jogs back to my side. "I'm going to pat the wound, all right?"

"Okay." I barely feel the fabric on my skin.

Lincoln steps in front of me, the towel in his hands. It's covered with green and yellow pus. "See, what I mean? Bad."

"Hells bells! But I don't feel anything."

"It's the neurotoxin." Lincoln jogs back over to the shelf of jars. "By the time you feel the pain, it's too late." He pulls a yellow jar from the shelves and inspects the hand-written label. "Don't worry, this one'll do it."

"How do you know that?"

"I've hunted demons since I was six years old. I've seen every injury you can imagine. That's an Arachnoid cut, and this ointment's the cure." A green horse blanket hangs from a peg on a nearby wall. Lincoln pulls it down with his free hand. "You'll need to take your upper armor off. Cover up with this."

He tosses the blanket to me; I catch it with my right hand. I look at the once-white towel lying on the stable floor. It could be my imagination, but the gooey stain seems to slowly creep along the fabric. Lincoln's right; this is bad.

"Give me a minute." I step into a nearby stall and strip off my breastplate and under-armor. I wish I'd brought my fighting suit—that Arachnoid would never have gotten through dragon scales. Oh, well. I hold the blanket to my chest and step back into the main aisle.

Lincoln steps closer. "You better sit."

Bending my knees, I fold my legs beneath me on the stable floor. Lincoln crouches behind me. He leans forward, his breath tickling the shell of my ear. "This is going to hurt at first."

I hear the scrape of the jar's lid, then sense Lincoln's vague touch on my back.

"I don't feel anything."

"Give it a few seconds."

Suddenly, the skin on my back blazes with pain. Hurt explodes from my shoulders until every nerve ending in my body screams in agony. "Son of a bitch!" I jam the blanket into my mouth and bite down hard. I crouch forward, my head almost touching the stable floor.

"You're doing great. Just a bit longer."

The agony blasts through me again, then one by one, my nerve endings return to normal. The pain melts away. I pull the blanket from my mouth and exhale slowly. "Okay, it's better now."

Lincoln leans in closer. His warm breath glides down my bare neck. "Good."

That's when it hits me.

It's the middle of the night; I'm half-naked in a deserted stable; the guy I hate most in the universe is massaging my back; and damn, his touch feels crazy-awesome.

I try to stand up. "I'm totally fine now."

Lincoln's hands grip the bare skin at my waist, pulling me back to the floor. The touch sends fire through me; I shiver.

"You're *not* fine. Stay still." The Prince's fingers move in a relentless rhythm, starting at my shoulders. There my muscles flush with heat and loosen. His palms slide down the sides of my torso, then press against the small of my back. I bite into the blanket again, but not with pain. Heat and desire pool into places where I didn't even know I had nerve endings. My inner Furor demon howls with a new sensation:

Lust.

The situation's quickly heading into uncharted territory for yours truly. Massage skills aside, this guy's still a pompous jerk. And since when do I get lusty about anybody? I only inherited the wrath side of the Furor lust-and-wrath combo, didn't I? With every expert flick of the Prince's fingers, another image flashes through my mind: Lincoln's hands cupping on my breasts, gliding across my belly, sliding up my thighs. What the Hell is happening to me? I flat-out panic.

"I think I can—" I try to stand again. Waves of nausea hit me. The world turns fuzzy, then everything blurs into a white haze.

CHAPTER FIFTEEN

For a long time, my mind hovers in an empty space between sleep and dream. The pain in my back is gone. The tournament and stables seem a thousand miles away.

My dreams finally come into focus. I find myself standing on the windy floor of the Gray Sea. Dreamscape. A circle of white flame flickers on the ground by my feet. Within the fire, sand rises into the form of my mother in her senate robes. The ring of flames flares higher, then disappears. Mom's sand-made body transforms into living reality.

Mom sits on a bench in the marble senate chamber. She clasps her hands tightly in her lap, her back is stiff and straight. Around her, senators, aides, and ambassadors cram onto benches and crowd along the walls. There's hardly room to breathe, let alone move. At the front of the chamber, Senator Adams stands before the speaker's podium, his elephant tail swinging slowly behind him. He speaks in a low and craggy voice.

"None wish to see Senator Lewis impeached, but her words against Ambassador Armageddon show a tenuous grip on reality. She needs treatment, not a role in government."

A handful of Senators leap to their feet, shouting for Mom's impeachment.

A stunned gasp escapes my lips. They're really going to do it: impeach my mother for telling the truth about Armageddon.

"Now, now." Senator Adams raises his withered hands to shoulder height. "Let's give Senator Lewis a chance to explain. Perhaps her words have been taken out of context." He gestures to Mom. "If you please."

Mom slowly rises to her feet, her mouth set into a firm line. "Thank you for the opportunity to speak before this chamber." She scans the room, her brown eyes filled with steely resolve. Xavier leans against the back wall in his crisp gray suit, his face pale with worry. Tim hovers by the chamber's exit. A muscle twitches along his gray neck.

Mom inhales slowly. "I've been asked to recant my words about Armageddon and the ghouls. If not, I'll be the first Lewis Senator in eight hundred years to be impeached." Mom scans the crowded Senate floor. "The truth may be something you choose to see as lunacy, but I won't back down. This is a legitimate threat. Whatever the cost, I accept it." She retakes her seat.

All the breath leaves my body. That's about the bravest thing I've seen anybody do, ever. I'm torn between wanting to give her a high five and curl her up into a comforting hug.

Senator Adams shakes his gray-haired head. "Then, it's the sad duty of this body to declare you, Camilla Lewis, to be—"

A low hum fills the chamber. A portal opens beside Senator Adams. Through it steps Armageddon, O-72, and a pair of hulking Manus demons. Standing six feet tall and almost as wide, the Manus are covered in shaggy black fur. Their hefty arms scrape against the floor. Pointed yellow tusks hang past their chins.

Holy Hell! I've seen Manus demons across the Arena floor before, but never *this* close. These beasts are the thugs of the demon world: massive, ruthless, and absolutely terrifying. They have one rule when in battle mode: *leave none alive*. Adrenaline courses through me. Run, Mom!

Senator Adams clears his throat. "Ambassador Armageddon, what perfect timing. We're removing Senator Lewis from office due to her unstable attitude toward you and our ghoul allies."

Armageddon's long black face curls into a smile. He folds his gangly arms over his thin chest. "Oh, there's no need for that."

Adams smiles. "You're too gracious, Ambassador, but we're concerned for the Senator's sanity."

Armageddon gently touches Adams's shoulder. "No, I'm not gracious at all. Senator Lewis is right. I'm about to attack Purgatory." Armageddon's eyes flare bright red, his three-knuckled fingers curl into the Senator's shoulder. Adams freezes in place. Little by little, the Senator's body and robes turn smooth and black as stone. "Starting with you." Armageddon lifts his hand. Adams crumbles into a pile of ash.

My limbs quiver with shock. I knew Armageddon drained the souls of his victims, but watching him do it? Something else entirely.

Screams erupt from the Senate floor. The crowd makes a mad rush for the exit. I try to spot my mother in the frantic mob, but can't find her. Terror crushes my rib cage, shortening my breath.

Armageddon's eyes flare bright. "Go to work." He waves his three-knuckled hands at the pack of Manus demons surrounding him. "Leave none alive."

The demons swing their heavy arms high, attacking nearby Senators. More portals open. Ghouls step out, red-eyed Manus demons beside them.

Somewhere in the crush of bodies, Xavier appears, his arm wrapped protectively around Mom's shoulders. I let out a ragged breath. She's alright, at least for now.

Xavier drags her through the frantic press of bodies and demons. There are so many people in a frantic rush, no one seems to move at all. A group of Senators struggle to press through the main exit, their bodies stuck as everyone ties to leave the chamber at once. Raising its massive arms high, a Manus demon smashes through both the Senators and the granite wall, creating a larger exit. Mom and Xavier squeeze through the new doorway and race down the marble corridors beyond. Tim follows closely behind.

I watch my father scurry behind my mom and Xavier, my upper lip twisting with disgust. When Mom needed him, Tim was nowhere to be seen. But now that she has a way out, he's the first to follow behind. It's humiliating to share DNA with this worm.

Mom, Xavier, and Tim race down the corridor as portals open all about them. Manus demons and ghouls stream into the hallways, attacking every quasi they can find. The air rings with thuds and screams. Xavier turns down a quiet corridor and presses on the marble wall.

"There should be a panic room somewhere around here." A marble panel pops open, revealing a small dusty space behind the wall. Xavier pulls Mom inside.

"Wait for me!" Tim squeezes in behind them.

I grit my teeth. *What a douche-move from Tim.*

Xavier slams the marble door shut. "You'll be safe here for a while."

Mom grips Tim's arm. "My family's waiting for me outside the cloak room. Can you portal to them and get them out?" Demon roars echo through the air. All the blood drains from Mom's face. "Hurry."

An image appears in my mind's eye: the smiling Lewis faces from Mom's swearing-in ceremony. My heart sinks. Of course, they'd be here today, supporting her through impeachment. *There must be some way to save them.* Mom's family can't die here.

Tim closes his large black eyes. "Our Group Think has changed. New voices claim to be the Oligarchy." His forehead lines with thought. "Demons are overrunning Purgatory. All the Senators and their families are being killed." His eyes slowly open. "I'm not authorized to open portals anymore." The Manus howls grow louder. The walls and floor shake as they prowl and attack. Tim steps toward the wall, his lower lip trembling with fear. "I'm sorry, Camilla."

I have the unladylike urge to spit at him. Coward.

"Fine. I'll get them." Mom turns to the marble door and starts prying it open with her fingernails.

Xavier wraps his arms around her shoulders, pulling her back. "The hallway's crawling with demons. You can't go out there."

"But I have to help my family!" Mom writhes under Xavier's grip. Her eyes are wild and brimmed with tears.

I hug my elbows. Pangs of sadness strike my body like so many stones. *There's no way to stop this.* Soon, Mom's family—*my family*—will be destroyed.

A young girl's screams echo in the outside hallway. Mom claws frantically at the door, her irises flaring red. "Dani!"

I remember the little wisp of a girl who was Vice President of Fun for the Lewis Family. The weight of my grief presses in harder and heavier, crushing something deep within me. Please, no.

Xavier wrestles Mom away from the door. "Camilla, you can't go out there. You'll be killed."

"That's my niece. She's just a child. You have to let me go!"

Dani's screams grow louder, then fall silent. The pounding and howls of the Manus demons fade.

Mom collapses onto the floor, sobbing. "They came here to support me through impeachment. What have I done?"

I grip my elbows so tightly, I'm surprised my bones don't crack. My arms ache to reach into that past reality and hold her close, whispering *I'm sorry, Mom, so sorry.* I never could have imagined the horror of Armageddon's war.

Xavier kneels beside her, his hand gently rubbing her back. "It wouldn't have mattered where they were. You heard Walker. Demons have overrun Purgatory. All the Senator's families have been targeted." He rises to his feet, setting his hand on the marble doorway. "My heart goes out to you, Camilla."

Mom looks up at him, tears rolling down her cheeks. "Where are you going?"

Tim cowers against the wall. "They'll kill you too, Xavier. You're a quasi sympathizer, an enemy of the new state." His voice breaks. "We're all enemies of the state now. I hear it in Group Think." His fingers shiver as they grip his robes.

I watch my ghoul-father tremble and realize that Tim did a brave thing in working with Mom. Most ghouls don't consider quasis a legit form of life, let alone a potential boss. He took a risk because he cared about her, and now his life's in danger.

Xavier presses his ear to the marble wall. "I helped build this place, remember? I know ways to leave without being seen. I'll go to Armageddon and see what can be done."

Mom looks up, her bottom lip quivering. "You mean the angels, right?"

Xavier shakes his head. "I don't understand."

"You said you'd speak to Armageddon. You must mean you'll talk to your people. The angels."

Xavier offers Mom a sad smile. "Yes, of course. The angels."

My forehead creases with confusion. Mom's way too upset to notice, but the way he answered her question was a little suspicious. What did he mean by saying that he would talk to Armageddon?

Mom rises to her feet. "I'm going with you."

"No, I do this alone or not at all." His fingers glide along the marble panel, looking for the mechanism to open the door. "I'll return as soon as I can."

The scene before me freezes. The figures change from flesh and bone back into sand. Little by little, their bodies crumble onto the Gray Sea. My dream fades into a place that's black and empty. Sadness seeps into my heart.

Mom's voice calls to me from the darkness of my dream. I awaken. "Myla, can you hear me?"

I open my eyes. I'm lying on a plush bed inside a small and sturdy wooden house. The room's filled with gilded furniture and delicate sculptures. Oriental rugs cover the floor. Mom stands beside me. The low chatter of many voices echoes in from the opened windows and door.

I shake my head from side to side, my brain still muddled with sleep. "Where am I?"

"The Queen's cottage," says Mom. "The thrax have been camping throughout this area."

I pull myself up to sitting. "How long have I been here?"

"Since last night. I came as soon as I learned of your injury."

My foggy brain tries to process Mom's words. I must have passed out after Lincoln healed my back. *And I'm just waking up now?* "What was wrong with me?"

"You ran a high fever fighting the infection." Mom presses her hand to my forehead. "But it broke about an hour ago. Did you sleep alright?"

Memories of Armageddon's attack flicker through my mind. I grip Mom's hand. "I had a dreamscape last night."

I might as well have set off a bomb in the Queen's chamber. At the sound of the word 'dreamscape,' the lively chatter of servants falls into perfect silence. The figures milling outside my window freeze. Expectation fills the air.

My mouth droops into a frown. Nice move, Myla. I'm in the Queen's bedroom because the High Prince put me here. Everyone must be dying to know why. Now I'm talking about dreamscapes, aka super-rare angel stuff. If I hired a carnival barker to stand outside my window and sell tickets, I couldn't have a more interested audience.

Bending over, Mom whispers in my ear. "Can it wait until we get home?"

She doesn't need to ask me twice. "Yeah, that's fine."

Mom stands up straight, her voice steady and strong. "You were very fortunate, Myla. The doctors said you could have died." She pauses, holding up one hand, waiting for any reaction from our hidden audience.

The silence around us turns deafening. Hells Bells. I'm still the marquee act in today's performance of 'what does the Prince want with that girl?'

Mom lets out a frustrated puff of air. "Show's over folks. Get back to work or I call the Queen."

Instantly, bodies begin to move again outside my window. Low chatter resumes in the hallway. I shoot Mom a hearty thumbs-up. She's acting more and more like her old self every day. It's awesome.

I flip off the covers and set my bare feet on the cold floor. "So, when do we leave?"

Mom rushes to my side, guiding my body back to lay down. "The doctors say you need to stay here and rest for a few days." She tucks the covers under my chin.

"I feel fine. Really."

Mom sits on the edge of the bed, her voice low. "Does this have to do with that thrax boy you were telling me about? I can't imagine you're thrilled to finish your recovery here."

"No, it's not about him." *But if I'm being honest with myself, it's totally about him.* After my weird lust-filled encounter last night, I want as much distance between us as possible. "I'm ready to go home, that's all."

Mom fluffs a pillow under my head. "Doctor's orders, Myla-la. I'll be back to check on you tomorrow. Maybe you can go home then." She rises to her feet. "Get some rest, promise?"

I snuggle under the covers and grin. "Promise."

Once Mom is gone, I slide out of bed and stretch, catching my reflection in a mirror. I'm now wearing a white linen nightgown. *When did that happen?*

I shrug. I suppose it's better than waking up in my armor. I step about the elegant space, running my fingers over the heavy wallpaper and staring at the delicate sculptures. I walk up to the opened window. Rows of cottages stretch off into the distance, followed by a much larger network of fancy tents.

A knock sounds at the door. "May I come in?" It's Lincoln. My breath hitches. "Sure."

The door opens and Lincoln steps inside. "Hello, Miss Lewis." My body turns gooey. This can't help my recovery.

"Hi." I scope out his outfit: jeans, a fitted black t-shirt, and leather boots. "Wow. You know about the twenty-first century."

"That's right, you've only seen me at official court events." He gestures down his torso. "Welcome to my day off."

"I like it." I make the same gesture over my white sheath. "Welcome to this random nightgown someone put on me." I frown. "That wasn't you, was it?"

He grins. "I'll never tell."

A dumb part of me wants to smile back, but I stop myself and look out the window again. He's still a creep.

Lincoln's voice sounds behind me. "I wanted to check that you're okay. Things were a little touch-and-go last night." He lets out a long breath. "And you look fine." There's a long pause where I keep staring out the window and not talking to Lincoln. *Don't forget that he's an ass, Myla.* Not to mention that weirdness in the stables last night. I must've had an allergic reaction to the neurotoxin. My inner demon is wrath only, end of story.

The floorboards creak softly as Prince shifts his weight from foot to foot. "I'll take my leave now."

His footsteps thud as he walks away. Something in my rib cage tightens. For some reason, I don't want him to go.

"Hey." I spin around to face him. He stands by door; his hand grips the handle. Our gazes lock. "Thanks for...You know."

He arches his brows. "Saving your life?"

"Yes, that." I half-smile and realize something: it's hard to hate someone who saved your life, especially if that someone gives a mean massage.

"No problem." He folds his arms over his chest. "We're running a special this month on magical horses and lifesaving."

I full-on grin. "You have a sense of humor. Somehow I didn't expect that."

He looks at me out of his slate-blue eye. "Well, it's not like I wowed you with my dazzling personality when we met."

I can't help but chuckle. "No, you didn't."

"In fact, I was closed-minded and awful for far too long. I'm very sorry."

I screw my mouth onto one side of my face. He's not getting off the hook that easily. "No more nasty 'demon girl' comments?"

Straightening his stance, he sets his hand over his heart. "Never again." He winks. "I got a stern talking to from my mother about that." His full mouth winds into a crafty grin. "And you know how she can be."

Dammit, he just got off the hook. "Yes, I do." I laugh.

He steps closer. "How about we start over?" He bows slightly. "Hello, I'm Lincoln."

I pause, eyeing him carefully. *Why not?*

"Myla Lewis."

He offers his hand. "Friends?"

I set my palm on his. "Friends." His skin feels warm and firm. I remember his touch on the small of my back, then quickly drop his hand. "I guess I'm stuck here for the next few days." I shrug. "I don't feel all that sick though."

"I have a very over-protective court physician." Mischief dances in his mismatched eyes.

I poke him in the shoulder. "Hey, now. Did you get me out of school?"

He leans against the wall, hitching his right leg across the left. "If I did, it would be justified as an extra tournament reward."

"So, what's there to do around here, *friend?*"

"Want to take Nightshade for a ride?"

I pause, tilting my head to one side. Memories of his touch simmer in the back of my mind. I need to be careful. No more bizarre lust demon episodes, particularly with guys who only just proved they aren't total jerks. But hey, friends do stuff like ride horses around. We can do that.

I nod once. "Sure."

"Good. I'll have some riding togs sent over."

"Pants, please." I've seen these thrax ladies riding side-saddle in long dresses. Not my thing.

He grins. "I'll make sure they offer you a wide selection."

"Great." I yawn and stretch. "See you at the stables in an hour?"

"You don't need more time to get ready?"

I sniff. "Do I look like that girl to you?"

He chuckles. "No, you don't." He swings open the door. "In an hour, then."

Lincoln steps out the door. An army of servants pour into the cottage, all wearing traditional gowns and tunics. They bring me food, things to wear and fill up a copper tub for a bath. I wash, have a snack, and decide to dress in brown leather pants, tall black boots, and a corseted red blouse. My long auburn hair is tied back with a black velvet ribbon.

I find the stables. Lincoln stands outside with Nightshade and a sleek black Arabian horse.

"I'd like you to meet Bastion." He gestures to the black horse.

"He's a beauty." I pat the horse's neck. "Another from the House of Striga?" I comb my fingers comb his silky mane.

"Yes. I didn't raise him, but we're still very close." He adjusts Bastion's saddle, and then runs his hand through the horse's mane as well. Our fingers brush; the touch is a shock of connection.

I pull my hand away quickly, my heart thudding at double-speed. I catch Lincoln's gaze, seeing intensity there. His hand didn't move against mine by accident. Suddenly, I can't stop thinking about what it would be like to kiss him. *Focus, Myla. You only want to be friends with this guy.* Time to change the subject. "How's the Furor?"

A smile dances in Lincoln's eyes. "Much better. He still hasn't changed form, but we moved him to the palace infirmary all the same."

"I'm glad."

Nightshade trots up beside me, tossing her bluish-gray head from side to side. I get the feeling she's anxious to run. Gripping her saddle, I haul myself onto her back.

Lincoln does the same with Bastion. "Ready?"

My heart decides that now is a good time to beat so hard, a whoosh of blood sounds in my ears. Ready for *what*, exactly? Friendship, trouble, something else?

I grip the reins more tightly and work hard at acting cool. "Sure. Where to?"

"Follow me." Lincoln clicks his tongue. Our horses take off at a gallop.

Nightshade's hooves thunder beneath me as Lincoln and I tear through the compound. Thrax poke their heads out tent flaps and windowsills as we ride by. They don't get cable out here, so I guess the Prince's afternoon ride qualifies as entertainment.

The ground opens up into rolling hills covered in greenish-yellow grass. Smooth gray clouds cover the sky. Nightshade and Bastion fall into in a slower rhythm, every breath and hoof-fall in perfect sync. A line of hedges looms ahead.

Lincoln glances over his shoulder, smiling in a way that I feel down to my toes. His wavy brown hair dances across his face, highlighting his strong cheekbones and firm jawline. He nods to the low wall of green. "Do you think it's too dangerous to–"

I dig my thighs into Nightshade's barrel. "Hyah!" My horse races toward the hedge.

Behind me, Lincoln clicks his tongue. The thrum of Bastion's hoof-falls sounds behind me, drawing nearer by the second. The hedges close in. Nightshade shifts her weight onto her back legs, and then springs forward. There's the weightless joy of flying through the air, followed by the heavy thud as we hit the ground. Lincoln lands a second behind me. I pull Nightshade's reins so we circle Lincoln and Bastion. "And that is *me* kicking your butt!"

He laughs. "I didn't realize it was a competition."

My face beams. Okay, how awesome is this? Normally, I hang with people who obsess that I'll hurt myself—*or them*—with the warrior stuff I do. Case in point: if Cissy complains one more time how I chipped her tooth in grade school, I'll scream. Now, here's Lincoln, trying to beat me over the hedge wall, then laughing when he loses.

I guide my steed so we're side by side. "To a warrior, everything's a competition."

Lincoln eyes me carefully. "Are you really prepared to all-out compete with me?"

I stick out my tongue. "Do your worst."

"Good. I will." Grinning, Lincoln clicks his tongue again. Nightshade and Bastion head off in a new direction.

We scale up a hilly path. The horses slow to a walk. The trail narrows, ending on a cliff that overlooks the Gray Sea. We dismount, guiding the horses to sip from a nearby pool. I plunk down at the cliff's edge, letting my feet dangle off the rock lip. The desert stretches off to the horizon, its charcoal-gray ground touched by a silver sky. I feel like I live in this place, I see it so much in my dreamscapes from Verus.

I shield my eyes from the updraft of sand. "How often do you come here?"

Lincoln sits beside me on the ledge. "Whenever I need a break from court. Maybe once a week."

"The Gray Sea is lovely in a…" I bob my head up and down, trying to find the right words.

"Bleak desert kind of way?"

"Exactly." I smile softly. No one's ever finished a thought for me before. It's kinda cool. "So, what's it like to hunt demons on earth?"

Lincoln winces. "A bit grisly. Most of the ladies in court ask that I skip the more gruesome bits, so I usually cut the description short and simply say that—"

"Well, if one of those ladies shows up, you can stop talking." I shoot him a sly look. "It's me here, Lincoln."

"Right." He jumps to his feet. "Let's say I'm the demon. I'm on earth's surface causing all sorts of trouble, only humans think I'm a storm or an illness breaking out or whatever."

My jaw falls open. "Humans can't see demons?"

"Nope." He points to his blue eye. "Thrax only see them as part of our angel nature, and you probably see them from the demon part in yours. You be the thrax."

I rise to my feet. "Grr."

Lincoln chuckles. "And a 'grr' to you, too." He gestures toward me. "So you find out demons are causing trouble somewhere, let's say it's a forest. You get your team together and suit up for demon patrol."

"Do you wear those tunics to fight demons?"

"Nope. The one place thrax go high-tech is on demon patrol. We have the latest in body armor, night vision goggles, that kind of thing. The Rixa bring one traditional piece of equipment." He pulls two small silver sticks from the belt of his jeans.

I break out into a grin. "I was hoping we'd get to this part."

"They're called baculum." He tosses them to me.

"This I know." I hold the two sticks in one hand, the way I saw Lincoln do at the tournament. I imagine the baculum turning into a broad sword made of white fire, they become one in my palm. I change the fire-sword into a net, spear, trident, and in general, have a jolly old time.

"These things are amazing." I jump toward him, wagging a trident at his chest. "Taste death, evil demon!"

Lincoln shoots me a sly grin, his right eyebrow arched. "Did you just ask me to 'taste death?'"

I blush. "I might have gotten carried away."

He grins. "No need to blush, although it looks good on you."

Fuuuuuuck. That comment only made me blush deeper.

"Taste death." He taps his chin in mock-contemplation. "I can work with that." Lincoln staggers about, clutching his heart. He falls onto his back, twitches dramatically, and lays silent.

"Excellent performance, your Highness." I picture the fire-trident disappearing and it does. Leaning over Lincoln, I set the silver sticks onto his stomach. Light reflects off the intricate runes carved into the surface. "Thanks."

He looks at me out of his right eye. "You're welcome." The Prince sits up, rubbing his chin. "How'd you do that? Only Rixa can use baculum."

I shrug. "I don't know. Did you ever test these with quasis? Maybe we've always been able to."

He nods slowly. "Sure, maybe."

I sit down beside him, the dry grass scratching against my hands. We don't speak for a time. Energy crackles around us. One thought keeps running through my mind: I reached my left hand out only a few inches, I could touch his thigh. My fingers twitch anxiously.

Whoa, there. Find something else to do with your hands, Myla. I pull up a fat, yellow blade of grass. Holding it straight between my thumbs, I blow through my palms. The blade lets off a blast as a make-shift trumpet.

Lincoln stares at my hands for a moment. After that, his gaze shifts to me. His look is heavy with desire, and my pulse goes through the roof. The Prince rounds his mouth into a sly grin, and I have the sinking feeling he knows exactly why I made a pretend trumpet: so I wouldn't reach out and touch him. I decide my best move is to play it casual. I let out another blast from my make-shift trumpet.

Lincoln pulls up his own blade of grass. "I didn't know grass could do that."

I wink. "You don't know a lot of things." This is getting too intense, so I lean back on the grass and stare at the cloudy sky. The extra distance between us feels better. Another change of subject could help, too. "So, what are you doing tonight?"

Lincoln lays down beside me, staring up at the same overcast view. There goes my safe zone of extra space. My fingers start twitching again.

The Prince sighs. "Official state dinner. Prince stuff. Boring."

I turn to him. "You got me out of school. The least I can do is return the favor." His face angles toward mine. We share a smile. My stomach lurches.

He raises his eyebrows. "What exactly will you do?"

My mouth curls into a Cheshire cat grin. Sure, I've had my share of lame master plans in the past. However, the one that's appeared in my mind is so incredibly awesome, it only needs that final touch of secrecy to make it absolutely perfect. "I have some ideas…But I want it to be a surprise."

"Fine. Just get us both in *big trouble*."

"You got it." I stare at him for a long moment, then I shake my head. "I can't believe you're the same guy I met before."

"I'm not." His mouth quirks into a different kind of smile. I blush.

He laces his hands behind his head. "I saw you once before the Ryder ball, you know."

I roll my eyes. "Sure you did."

He chuckles. "You were chasing a pack of Doxy demons through the woods by the mansion's stables, as I recall."

I shoot him a mischievous grin. When we met at the ball, *that's* why he asked me if I visited the Ryder stables. He knew I had a sideline killing Doxies. And why would *that* have made such an impression on him? One reason only. "I killed the demons first, didn't I?"

He mock-frowns. "Yes."

Ooooh, I love it when I win. "Let's see, now. That means I beat you in jumping the hedge and killing the Doxies. That makes not once, but twice."

Lincoln quirks his brow. "Is that a challenge, Myla?"

I roll my eyes. "With you? Always."

In the blink of an eye, he flips his body to rest atop mine. I gasp, feeling his firm muscles press against my soft curves in all the right ways. Warmth gathers in my core. His mouth hovers just above mine. "Are you sure?"

For a second, I consider kneeing him in the groin, jumping to my feet, and running for Nightshade, but only for a second. I'm Myla Lewis, and I do not back down. I can handle this. Friends wrestle and goof around. This is fine. "Sure, I'm sure."

He raises his hand, sliding his finger down my cheek. Heat pools between my thighs. "I don't mind the thought of you beating me, Myla." His arms are braced on either side of my head, his knees straddle either side of my hips. "Not at all."

I stare at his full mouth. Every cell in my body wants to touch him, kiss him. *What the hell is happening to me?*

He offers me sneaky smile. "Want to know *why* that doesn't bother me?"

A roll of thunder shakes the air. Maybe a storm is coming. Maybe I'll get blasted into a million bits by lightning. Maybe I could care less. My inner lust demon has kicked to life with a vengeance. I open my mouth, hoping something snarky and cute will come out. Instead, I just nod. Total fail.

Lincoln leans in closer, licks his lips. "I don't care because…" There's a moment where I'm sure I'll get my first kiss. "Because I'm about to beat your ass back to the stables." Leaping to his feet, he races up to Bastion and mounts his horse.

I jump to my feet, a mixture of sexual heat and rage flowing through me. "You bastard! You lying sneaky evil sonuvabitch bastard!"

Lincoln rears Bastion, the horse balances firmly on his hind legs. "Catch you later." He winks.

I stomp my foot and shoot him dirty looks, but all the almost-kissing-stuff has me flustered.

Lincoln leads Bastion onto the ground, then glances over his shoulder and grins. Setting his heels into Bastion's barrel, he takes off at a gallop.

That clears my head in a hurry.

I'm not letting some hottie Prince bastard distract me with nasty talk that totally makes me wonder what he looks like naked. And on that topic, since when do I think about *anybody* naked? Well, except for Lincoln, whose bare belly must be particularly ripped.

I shake my head from side to side. *Focus, Myla.*

I race across the open ground and hoist myself onto Night-shade. "Let's get him, Night." Before the words are out of my mouth, she's off at a gallop. I urge her onward, but we soon lose Lincoln and Bastion in the forest. I catch up with them both back at the stables.

The Prince stands by Bastion, an overly-satisfied grin on his full mouth. "Hey, loser."

I pull Nightshade's reins so we circle Lincoln and his horse. "Hey, cheater." *You're never getting away with that Mister Sexy trick again, my friend.* I point directly at his nose. "Besides, if I were you, I wouldn't poke fun at someone who's about to get you out of an evening of suck."

"True. And you're *still* one up on me, after all." He bows slightly at the waist.

"That's better." I bow my head. "Now, if you'll excuse me, I have a lot of prep work to do for tonight." I lean back in the saddle and twiddle my fingers at him.

He chuckles. "Have fun."

"I will." I pat Nightshade's neck. "Girl, take me to—" She's off at a run before I finish my sentence. As we speed across the countryside, I keep thinking one thing: this is going to be sweeeeeeet.

CHAPTER SIXTEEN

A

It's dark by the time I return to the thrax compound. I settle Nightshade into her stall, then steal over to the mead hall, my evil cargo in tow: a cooler filled with the Reperio demons from my Biology class.

This is so awesome; I can't stand myself.

I tiptoe up to a long wooden building with an arched roof. The only windows are two high vent-holes, one on either side of the building. I pause and adjust the collar on my fighting suit. Light flickers in through the window-holes. From inside the hall, the air echoes with the chatter of voices and clinking of silverware. Thrax are feasting inside.

Taking a deep breath, I position myself under one of the vent-holes. Using the thick outer planks, I scale up the building's side and settle myself onto the window's ledge. In front of me, the ceiling is filled with a network of heavy wooden beams.

I smile. It'll be easy-peasy to crawl along the main beam.

I scan the hall below, careful to hide in the ceiling's shadows. Two long wooden tables line the floor, both surrounded by thrax.

The men wear crested tunics; the ladies are dressed in formal gowns of their house's color. At the far end of the building, a minstrel sits beside a crackling fireplace, playing a soft tune on his lute. Servants bustle around, refilling wine glasses and plates. Mid-way along the far-right table, the King, Queen, and High Prince sit in throne-like chairs. Lincoln wears his black leather pants, silver chain mail, and black tunic.

The Earl of Acca rises to his feet. He runs his plump hand through his thinning red hair. "Perhaps the Scala Heir will honor us with a song?"

"Of course, Father." Adair slides off her bench and walks over to the minstrel. She wears a long white cloak, just like the old Scala. The room grows quiet. "I know you're all wondering what it's like to be the Scala Heir." She glances dramatically about. "Of course, it represents a massive power shift for the House of Acca." She gestures to her father. He grins so hard his cheeks must hurt.

Adair folds her hands into her cloak's long sleeves. "I'm now more than a thrax, maybe even more than a mortal."

I roll my eyes. This is worse than the 'can I feel your muscle-y muscles' line. This girl needs a healthy dose of reality.

"Tonight, I wanted to share my personal Scala journey with you all." Adair inhales a long breath and looks to the minstrel. "I've written a song to the tune of 'Are you going to Scarborough Fair?'" She gestures to the lute player who plinks out a quiet melody. All faces are locked on Adair and her song.

Now's my chance.

I creep along the dining room's main ceiling beam, my evil cargo in hand.

Adair clears her throat, then sings with a warbling old-lady voice:

Who will worship the Scala Adair?
All the thrax if given the time
My powers are great, my face is so fair
Who won't want the love that is mine?

She stares directly at Lincoln's face when she sings the 'love that is mine' part. His features subtly twist into a 'yikes' face, a movement that makes him raise his eyes. He sees me and winks.

Warmth blooms through my chest; a smile curls my lips. Lincoln's way different than I thought. Funny, handsome, sexy, and— let's not forget my favorite attribute—able to hold his own and compete with me. Part of me wonders if I'm going too far, too fast, feeling things for a guy who I thought was a major jerk only a few days ago. Good thing another part of me takes the worrying part out back and kicks the shit out of it.

The lute player strums another few bars, then Adair sings again.

My powers are great, my face is so fair
Who won't want the love that is miiiiiiiiiiiiiiiiiiiiine?

Lincoln glances in my direction and mouths the words 'no way.' I grin. A weight falls off my shoulders that I didn't know I carried. I guess part of me was worried what it meant that Lincoln and Adair were angelbound. I'd hate to think of him as stuck with that dingbat forever.

Speaking of the dingbat...I smile, then mime showing off my arm muscle to Lincoln. I soundlessly move my lips while saying 'Can I touch you?'

Lincoln scowls, his head shaking from side to side. Angling his forehead in my direction, he pointedly smoothes his eyebrow with his middle finger. I have to bite my fist not to laugh out loud.

Adair raises her arms. "Thank you, my people!" The room breaks into enthusiastic applause, no one more than the Earl of Acca. Lincoln claps politely. After that, he gulps a mouthful of wine.

Waving, I catch his attention. I point to the box in my hands, and then to the small window at the other end of the wooden beam.

Lincoln nods slightly and stifles laughter, his cheeks still full of wine. He tries to swallow his gulp and starts coughing instead.

Avery rushes to his side. "Are you alright, your Highness?"

Lincoln clears his throat. "I'm fine, thank you."

"Was there something in the rafters that bothered you?" She tilts her head upwards. I freeze.

Crap, I'm going to get caught.

He grabs Avery's hand. "No." Her attention locks on his face. "There's a question I've been meaning to ask you, um, Avery."

Avery's already-large eyes open wider. "Oh, my. Whatever you want, your Highness."

"How are you..." He bites his lips together.

"Yes? Yes?"

"Enjoying...Your dinner?"

"Oh, it's very good, your Highness. I always like brisket."

"Well, okay then." He releases her hands and nods gravely.

Grinning ear to ear, I open my little case of Reperio demons.

Here it comes.

The nasty little buggers skitter across the ceiling beams and down the walls. The tiny paper men hop onto the feasting tables, kicking over wine glasses and stomping through brisket. The pencil-ladies twist the silverware into little lewd sculptures.

The thrax go completely berserk. No one brought weapons and everyone's sworn to fight demons, even though Reperio are more mischief than danger. There's a lot of fork chucking and potato-throwing.

I quickly scoot across the beam, jump out the opposite window and land outside the hall. Lincoln easily slips out the door in the confusion. I grab his hand and run for it. His grip is warm and firm, sending prickles of excitement through me. We reach the stables and pause.

I laugh so hard, I wrap my arms over my stomach so I don't fall over. "Did you see the look on Adair's face?"

"Adair? I was watching the Earl of Acca. I think he was going to cry."

"Do you need to go back and help?"

"Absolutely not. I've been sprung. Is there a part two for this plan?" His brows raise and that warmth curls back into my belly with a vengeance.

"Of course." I gesture to Nightshade and Bastion, all saddled and ready to ride. "We're going to break into the Ryder botanical gardens." There's a pause where Lincoln's face is unreadable, then his mouth winds into a smile.

"Nice."

We gallop over the darkened countryside to a great greenhouse that's three stories tall and made entirely of glass. A huge tree pops through the building's ceiling, ending in a massive canopy of leaves.

"Here we are." I slide off Nightshade and try the door. It's locked.

I frown. "Well, I should've seen *that* coming."

Lincoln turns to Nightshade "Do you mind helping us out, girl?"

The horse whinnies and the doorknob disappears. That's right; I forgot Nightshade does magic.

I push open the door and step inside. Moonlight glints off the trees, vines and shrubbery that line the greenhouse floor. My mouth winds with a satisfied grin. This place is closed to the public, so, of course, I've wanted to break in for ages. I steal a glance at Lincoln; my heart kicks. *It's nice to have a partner in crime.* Tiptoeing around the greenery, I lead him toward the massive tree at the building's center, all the while thinking how we're alone, it's dark, and he looks mighty handsome in the moonlight. My heart rate goes through the roof.

"And here we are." I bow slightly. "The very rare and beautiful Tumtum tree." Reaching out, I brush my hands down the old tree's gnarled bark, feeling the life and energy under its skin. "You only find them in Purgatory."

Lincoln nudges me with his elbow. "You're trouble, Myla Lewis." He leans forward, his mouth curling into a snarky grin that turns my insides into goo.

My eyes narrow. I'm not gooey enough to let that comment slide, however.

Stepping back, I fold my arms across my chest and slap on a look of righteous indignation. "I am *not* trouble. We're here on a mission of mercy."

"Really now?"

I point to a white sign nailed to the center of the trunk. "See? This poor thing has a huge 'do not climb me' sign, and that's just not right. If anything ever screamed 'climb me now,' it's this particular tree."

Lincoln leans back on his heel. "You have a point."

"Of course, I do." I grip the knobby trunk and start to climb. Lincoln scales the opposite side.

I swing myself so I balance standing on a horizontal branch. "First one to touch the ceiling wins."

Lincoln finds a new toehold in the bark and scales upwards. "You're on."

A jolt of excitement runs through me. He's not telling me to leave and be safe, he's not chickening out; he's actually racing me to the top. I'm so distracted and happy, I almost tumble off the branch, catching myself at the last second. I return my attention to the trunk and begin to climb.

As we race along, I know this is one competition I should win easily: I have an extra appendage, after all. But I keep holding back, angling for a better view of Lincoln's firm thighs and muscled back as he scales higher. Bands of heat writhe within my core. Finally, I stop moving altogether and admit the obvious truth. My inner Furor demon is wrath *and* lust. For some reason, Lincoln's the guy who brings them both to life.

Man, am I in trouble.

Voices sound from the countryside. "Prince Lincoln!" I look out the greenhouse window. Torch-light appears on the horizon.

There's a search party out for Lincoln. Yipes.

Lincoln slides down the trunk, landing at the base of the tree. He turns to me and reaches upwards. "Do you need a hand, Myla?"

Honestly, I'm perfectly capable of jumping off this tree all by my lonesome. I stare at Lincoln's ropy arms and firm chest, my lust demon roaring ever louder inside me. Suddenly, I want to touch him so badly, I'd use any excuse at all.

"Sure." I scale down for a bit, then step off the trunk and into Lincoln's arms. My body slowly slides down his. Each contour of his chest brushes against my breast and belly. Desire ricochets through me, heating my core.

Hellooooo, lust demon.

I lick my lips slowly. "Thanks, Lincoln."

"You're welcome." Up close he smells earthy, all forest pine and leather. He winds his hands around my waist. "I meant what I said today, Myla."

My face flushes with surprise and heat. He's not talking about *that* again, is he? Our almost kiss? "You mean when we were talking about beating?"

His hand slides up my back; a shiver of desire runs through me. "About beating as *challenging*. My subjects complain, but no one pushes me to be better. You did that, even when you hated me." He smiles. "*Especially* when you hated me." His fingers weave through the hair at the base of my neck. "Does that make sense?"

I meet his mismatched eyes and realize yes, I know exactly what he means. I've spent my life hoping the way my world runs would be *tolerated*, not looking for someone to race me. Who knew anyone like Lincoln was possible? I want to say all this, but my throat tightens. I only manage five words: "Yes, it does. Very much."

His eyes almost glow with intensity. "I like this. Feeling like I have a peer, a partner." He cups my face in his hands. "I like *you*, Myla." My knees turn watery beneath me. *I like you, too.*

He pulls my mouth onto his and damn, it feels good. His lips are soft and the touch of his tongue along mine is electric. My heart starts thudding like crazy. I grip his t-shirt and ball the fabric in my fists. Our kiss deepens. Off on the horizon, a bolt of lightning strikes the earth, followed by a low roll of thunder. The flash of light snaps us out of the moment. We step apart.

I shake my head. "That's weird. It's not supposed to storm tonight."

"Prince Lincoln!" The voices outside grow louder.

Lincoln sighs. "We better go."

We leave the greenhouse, remount our horses and ride back to the thrax compound. All around, voices call for Prince Lincoln.

More torches flash in the darkness. Lincoln rides up beside me and grabs Nightshade's reins. "Your cottage is past those trees. You should go; I'll take care of Night."

I give Lincoln a silent thumbs-up and tiptoe to my cottage door. The room is cozy, warm, and inviting. I change into my new nightie, slip under the covers, and quickly fall asleep, smiling my face off the entire time.

A.

I awaken the next morning to the sound of Mom's voice. She's not happy, which means one thing: I'm in trouble.

"Myla." Mom taps my shoulder. "Come on, wake up."

I open my eyes, looking as innocent as possible. "Good morning, Mom."

Her mouth thins to an angry line. "What happened yesterday?"

She's getting right down to business. Correction: I'm in *deep* trouble.

"Nothing. I just sat in here, minding my own business." I force myself to cough. Twice. "Recovering. Why?"

"Reperio demons were released at the Scala winter feast last night. The same ones that went missing from your school yesterday. It caused quite a ruckus."

"A ruckus, huh? They should have better security." I do my best to shiver. "I heard the screaming around dinnertime. It was so frightening; I stayed in here and did homework."

Mom's brown eyes narrow. "I see. What kind of homework?"

"Very important...Homework." I'm not exactly a wiz thinking on my feet, unless it involves killing something.

"Humph. The Ryders reported that someone broke into their botanical gardens last night too."

"No way. That's shocking!"

"You're a terrible liar, Myla."

I shoot her a grin and maybe it's a bit too cocky. "Hey, I have my story and I'm sticking to it."

"We're going home. Now."

My smile fades. I guess I knew it would end this way all along, but it's still a bummer to leave early.

Mom grabs my little pile of things and walks out of the cottage. I slip into my sweats and follow her outside. Everyone's awake and peeping their heads outside their windows or fancy tent-flaps. Lincoln stands in front of his cottage, leaning against the door-jamb. He wears a fitted white t-shirt and flannel pajama bottoms. My hands itch to touch his chest. Now.

Mom marches over to Betsy and revs her engine. I follow her to the car, feeling Lincoln's eyes on me. I shoot him a glance as I slide into the front seat. He winks; I blush. Damn, yesterday was a lot of fun.

We drive past a long line of cottages. The Great Ladies stand outside them, each one wearing a long nightgown in her house's color. If looks were needles, I'd be a pincushion right now.

I'm going home a day early, but that was worth it. Absolutely.

Mom taps the steering wheel with her nails. "If you're well enough to cause trouble, you're well enough to learn. I'm dropping you off at school."

I open my mouth, ready to explain why I need to spend the afternoon recovering and watching TV. "Well, I…You have to understand, it…"

Mom purses her lips. "I can't want to hear this."

"You know what?" I lean back in my seat. "I've got nothing. Drop me off at school."

Mom cracks the tiniest smile. "They shouldn't have demons in a classroom anyway."

"Does that mean I don't have to go to school?"

"Nice try."

I hit school sometime after lunch. Cissy spots me the second my sneakers hit the hallway. "It's good to see you feeling better, sweetie." She plants a quick kiss on my cheek.

"Thanks, Cissy."

"So I thought you weren't coming back to school until tomorrow. What happened?"

What happened? Lincoln happened. Heat climbs into my cheeks as I remember the Prince's kiss and his sweet words. *Not that I'm telling Cissy anything about that.* The last thing I need is the return of the envy monster. I clear my throat. "I felt better."

Cissy sets her hand on my arm. "Are you okay? You look flushed."

I force a cough. "Yeah, I'm fine. Still recovering." Hells bells, could I be any more suspicious?

Cissy gives my arm a gentle pat. "Don't push yourself, sweetie."

I exhale. "You're so right." And so not suspecting anything. Sweet.

"Oh, you won't believe what happened at school. Someone stole all the Biology demons."

"No. Way." I grin, my eyes flaring red. Talking about kissing Lincoln? A bad idea. Bragging about stealing Reperio? A requirement.

"Hells bells! Myla, did you have something to do with that?"

"I most surely did." I wag my eyebrows up and down. "I totally stole the Reperio and released them at a thrax dinner. Isn't that the best idea in the history of ever?"

Cissy sighs. "I won't lecture you on why that was completely insane. If you'd been caught, it would have been another diplomatic nightmare. Not to mention the fact that stealing from school is illegal."

I click my tongue. "This is one of your non-lecture-lectures, isn't it?"

Cissy tries to grimace, but smiles instead. "You are trouble, Myla Lewis."

Funny, that's what Lincoln said too. I remember the Prince's kiss and feel all fuzzy inside. I must have a pretty goofy look on my face, because once I return my attention to Cissy, she's now suspecting something, big time.

"Why'd you release demons at a thrax dinner?" She smacks her lips. "Does this have anything to do with Prince Lincoln?"

Play it cool, Myla. "Oh, him? He's just a friend." A friend that I kissed once and now want to strip down and lick, that's all.

"Are you holding out on me?" Her eyes flare red.

Wooo-ee. I need to vamoose before she goes all envy demon on me. "Sorry, Cissy. I gotta run or I'll be late." Turning on my heel, I rush off before she has a chance to stop me.

Whew. That was close.

CHAPTER SEVENTEEN

A

"Good morning, Myla. You're called to serve."

I open my eyes and yawn. "Hey there, Walker. I haven't seen you in ages." In fact, the last time I saw him was three months ago, when I fought Deacon in the Arena and almost tackled Lincoln. Who knew I'd end up kissing the guy? Since then, I've gone to both the thrax autumn and winter tournaments. Time has flown.

Now it's just a few days after celebrations for the New Year. Too long, really, between visits from my honorary undead older brother. Normally he sneaks me in to see someone else's match at the Arena at least once a month.

I mock-frown. "I've missed you, Walker."

My heart thumps sadly. *I miss Lincoln, too.* I haven't heard a word from him since the winter tournament two weeks ago. It's really bumming me out that I was some kind of one-kiss-stand for him. Nightshade's now a permanent resident at the Ryder stables; I take her out for regular jaunts near the thrax compound. Each time, I hope to run into a particular someone, but no such luck. I'm too proud to do more than that.

I let out a low sigh. Okay, I'm actually *not* too proud to do more than that, but the thrax have their little campground on some kind of mega lock-down these days.

Walker sizes me up carefully. "I've missed you as well." He rubs his long sideburns. "I hear congratulations are in order."

I flip off my covers and set my toes on the chilly floor. "Why's that?"

"You're the greatest warrior in Antrum."

"Oh, yeah." I step over to my dresser, open the top drawer and pull out my golden breastplate. "Queen Octavia hooked me up with armor and a spot in the tournament." I set the breastplate over my gray nightgown and model it for Walker. "I took out an Arachnoid in this thing."

Walker grins. "I wish I could have seen it."

I wink. "Perhaps another time." I carefully set the breastplate back into my drawer. "So, who am I fighting today?"

Walker lowers his voice. "I have a surprise for you. We're actually seeing an iconigration."

I clasp my hands. "No. Way." Iconigrations are when the Scala moves multiple souls to Heaven or Hell at once. I've only seen these a few times. Mega cool.

"Oh, I found a way." He sets one finger over his mouth in a 'shh' face. "Just don't tell your mother what we're up to."

I mime zipping my mouth shut. "Got it." Mom freaks out when I do anything different. I have a feeling an iconigration would send her through the roof.

"See you in a bit." Walker steps out my bedroom door, careful to close it behind him.

I shower, change into my fighting suit, and walk into the kitchen, a smarmy smile on my face. Iconigrations are the best.

Mom sits at the table, holding a mug of steaming coffee. She takes one look at me and frowns. "What's going on, Myla?"

I put on my best 'innocent face': eyes wide and blinking like mad. "Walker's taking me to the Arena for another death-match. You know, the usual." A pile of Demon bars sit on the counter. I grab one and dive in.

"Did you have any strange dreams last night?"

"Nope."

"Make any new friends?"

Besides the thrax High Prince?

"Cissy's still my best friend, Mom." Misleading but true.

Mom rounds on Walker. "What soul is she battling this morning?"

"The CEO of a financial conglomerate back on earth. Nasty fellow." Unlike me, Walker's a really good liar.

Mom eyes me carefully for a full minute. Her fingers slowly drum the tabletop. "I suppose it's all right."

Sweeeeeeeeeet.

I swallow my last bite of breakfast. "Let's get going."

Walker lowers his head. A crackling sound fills the air as a portal opens by our fridge. I take Walker's hand in mine.

"See you later, Mom."

She looks at me out of her right eye. "Uh-huh." After my little performance with the Reperio demons, she's on constant sneak-alert for everything I do. Not that I blame her.

Walker and I step into the portal, tumble through empty space, and walk out again into a darkened archway off the Arena floor. I'm actually starting to like portal travel.

I lean against the stone wall and look out across the stadium. Everything's deserted.

"There used to be great ceremonies before an iconigration," says Walker. "Now the Scala shows up, creates soul-columns and leaves."

A low hiss echoes through the air. A portal opens along the Arena's top level. Through it steps the tallest ghoul I've ever seen and someone I never wanted to see again: Armageddon.

I turn to Walker. "What's tall, dark, and demonic doing here?"

He shrugs. "He comes to see his son sometimes."

My tail arcs over my shoulder. My body goes on full alert.

Another figure steps out from the portal: a tiny woman in a high-necked red silk gown with a bustle on the back. She looks like something from earth in the 1800s, except for her pink skin, pig-snout nose, and tiny black eyes. Her hair's a long piggy tail that winds into a bun behind her head. In her hoof-hand she holds a silver briefcase.

Armageddon, a ghoul and a few Manus demons all seat themselves in the black marble balcony. The King of Hell snaps his fingers over his shoulder. "Clementine. Now." The pig-demon rushes onto the balcony, taking her seat beside Armageddon's black stone throne. She opens the briefcase in her lap and fiddles with whatever's inside. A high-pitched buzz rings softly in the air.

I nod to Walker. "What do you think Armageddon's up to?"

"Who knows? He's always doing strange things. I wouldn't worry about it."

Humph. That attitude got Purgatory overrun in the first place.

A long portal opens in the center of the Arena floor. Through it steps six ghouls carrying a fancy stretcher. The old Scala lays atop the makeshift cot in his white robes, fast asleep. A thin white blanket is tucked beneath his chin.

One carrier-ghoul gently touches the Scala's thin shoulder.

The old man's cloudy eyes open a crack. "Ah, J-27."

The ghoul bows. "It's time to call the souls to Heaven, Great Scala."

Walker taps my hand. "He just said–"

"I understood him." My body freezes. *Hey now, I just understood freaking Latin.* "How in Hell do I understand Latin?"

Walker seems awfully interested in staring out at the Arena floor. "When he wants to, the Scala can make the crowd understand him."

I smack my lips once. *That sounds mega-fishy.* I never heard the Scala had that power. I tilt my head to one side, trying to figure out if Walker's telling the truth. "Are you lying to me?"

He turns to me, his face the picture of cool. "Why would I lie?"

Okay, he has a point. Back to watching the Scala.

On the Arena floor, the Scala feebly raises his right hand. A flurry of igni lightning bolts swirl about his palm. Two dozen ghosts appear on the stadium's floor. I examine the one closest to me. Its shape quickly morphs between thousands of different faces and body types. *Icons*. Each one contains thousands of human souls.

I watch the icon bodies transform in a blinding flicker. It's beautiful.

The Scala drops his shaking hand. The igni disappear. He gasps for air, his bony rib cage heaving up and down. The ghouls prop him upright. He catches his breath.

I shake my head. That is one really old dude. He looks like he could cork any second.

"In the quasi republic, the Scala moved hundreds of icons to Heaven at a time. Now it's rare to see more than a few dozen." Walker sighs. "Today, it's the iconigrations to Hell that are packed to overflowing."

I glance to Armageddon and Clementine. A soft scarlet glow shines from inside her briefcase. Strange red shadows crawl under her cheeks and snout. The buzzing sound grows louder.

J-27 touches the Scala's shoulder again. "You must move them."

The old man nods, his breath coming in rough gasps. He raises his wrinkled hand again; tiny lightning bolts whirl about his palm. The igni fly from his fingertips and whiz around the Arena floor. They settle around each icon, circling the morphing spirits in ever faster loops. The igni multiply, becoming pillars of white light.

I love to see those in action. Soul-columns. How the Scala moves spirits.

The Scala gasps; his eyes roll back into his head. The soul-columns become blindingly bright, then disappear, taking the icons with them.

The Scala drops his trembling hand. His breath comes faster and rougher than ever. Is he going to drop dead right here?

J-27 sets his fingers against the old man's withered throat. The ghoul's gray face turns pale as milk. "We must visit the healer right away."

Armageddon leans forward, resting his elbows on his knees. He stares into the briefcase in Clementine's lap and grins. The light inside the case now blazes bright red. The buzzing grows louder.

I don't care what Walker said. Whatever's in that briefcase isn't harmless plotting from Armageddon. It's B-A-D. My skin prickles with alarm.

The King of Hell rubs his three-knuckled hands together. "Let's see if this contraption is worth the price we paid."

The six ghouls grab the Scala's stretcher and bow their heads. The air crackles with energy. The edges of a portal appear and fade. Back sweat streams down the ghoul's cheeks.

I shoot Walker a look. "What's going on?"

Walker closes his eyes. "I don't know. There's no Group Think. That's strange."

"Do the Oligarchy talk in your head non-stop?"

"Always." Walker's face creases in concentration. "Though I can shut them off if I wish." His focus grows more intense. "I'm not shutting them off now."

Armageddon chuckles. "That's enough, Clementine." The pig-demon snaps her briefcase shut.

A portal immediately appears on the Arena floor. The ghouls smile nervously, lift the Scala's stretcher and step through the black door-hole.

The demon leader takes to his feet. "We leave. Now." He marches back to the stadium's top level, orders his ghoul to open a portal, and vanishes into it along with Clementine and his Manus demon guard.

I frown. "He's scheming again."

Walker waves his hand dismissively. "He's always scheming. I've seen strange things from him for twenty years now. I find that worrying about it isn't productive."

I open my yap, ready to argue my point, but decide not to bother. Normally, I'd fight with Walker on this for another ten minutes, minimum. But being in the Arena reminds me of Lincoln awarding my sword. Closing my eyes, I remember his mouth on mine in the botanical gardens and feel like a total fool. If he wanted to be in touch with me, he would have done it weeks ago.

Gritting my teeth, I bite back the urge to mope. "We should head back."

Walker leans against the archway wall, his eyes glowing with a bit of red. "I hate to see the two of you like this."

I absently pick moss off the uneven stones lining the wall. "The two of *who* like *what?*"

"You and Lincoln. Miserable."

Wait a second. *Did Walker say what I thought he said?* "You know Lincoln?" My body goes on high alert.

"I do." Walker's mouth droops into a frown. "But I swore to never breathe a word of it." A muscle twitches along his jaw. "It's the artist in me. Too soft a heart."

I step closer to him, careful to make every inch of me look as pleading and pathetic as possible. "Come on, don't leave a girl hanging."

He inhales a long breath. "I've known Lincoln as long as I've known you, Myla. I can't explain how or why. Not yet, anyway."

First of all, it's totally annoying that he's still being secretive. *Tell me already!* But somehow I can't summon up my typical angst about Mom's code of silence with everyone in my life. Besides, other topics are far more interesting.

"Did you say Lincoln's *miserable?*" My face breaks out into a huge smile.

"Yes. And he's been that way ever since he first set eyes on you."

I remember Lincoln and I chatting on the bluff overlooking the Gray Sea. "He said something about that once. He saw me fighting Doxy demons." But he didn't share any ongoing Myla-related misery. Although, come to think of it, that could explain his whole 'what a lowly demon you are' attitude when we first met. Over-compensate much?

Walker nods sagely. "He saw you soon after his arrival in Purgatory. You burst out of a lake, I believe."

"That's right. I was fighting Doxy demons from the stables. They were getting too bitey, so I led them to a lake in the woods." My voice turns low and dreamy. "Water neutralizes their sting." *And the Prince was there too?* I blink three times, trying to force myself to process this information. Lincoln's been thinking about me for months; he's still thinking about me.

Walker cocks his left eyebrow. "In truth, he's been a wee bit obsessed with you."

I was right. We connected. Warmth blossoms through my chest. "No. Way." My tail pushes his shoulder, slamming him against the wall.

"Careful, Myla." He grins. "I'm not wearing armor."

"Eh, you're way tougher than you look, Walker." I pace the stone hallway, a combination of excitement and anxiety pulsing through me. *Lincoln's just as miserable as I am. He cares about me, is even a little bit obsessed with me.*

That. Is. So. Cool.

Pausing, I turn to Walker. "This is the best news I've had in weeks." My brow furrows. Something about this doesn't add up. "Hey, if he's so into me, why haven't I heard a peep out of his majesty?"

"That's why I wanted to talk to you."

Uh, oh…I know that tone from Walker. He's about to unload something awful. My body automatically goes into battle stance, bracing for the impact.

Walker inhales a long breath. "The two of you are perfectly matched." He shakes his head from side to side, frowning.

My stomach constricts. "That's normally said like it's a *good* thing."

Walker's black eyes fill with sadness and empathy. "You're from different realms. He's a Prince. Your fighting skills are critical to the smooth functioning of the Arena." He points to Armageddon's seat in the Arena. "And you live in a realm that's essentially ruled by the King of Hell. Not a stable situation." He sighs. "Match or not, the chances of you two having a future together are slim."

Says you. I grimace. He's doing that Walker-thing where he *acts* like he's answering my question. "Why hasn't he been in touch?"

Walker eyes me for a long minute, then speaks. "Since you left, Lincoln's been in non-stop negotiations with the House of Acca. They want war. The Prince is the only person the Earl listens to."

A cold shiver whirls up my body. Here comes the bad news. "And why's that?"

Walker folds his arms into his loopy sleeves with an air of finality. "Until you came along, Lincoln and Adair were about to be betrothed."

Reality slams into me like a fist. What did I *think* was happening with Adair cooing over Lincoln all the time? Choosing him to be angelbound? Not to mention all that weird muscle grabbing. They were getting engaged.

No, that can't be right. Shaking my head from side to side, I kick the wall, hard. I remember Adair singing at the Winter feast. She said Lincoln was her love; he almost barfed. "Lincoln doesn't seem to think he has to marry her."

"Perhaps he's right." Walker frowns. "But there's far too much stacked against you both. Believe me, I've no joy in saying this. You need to move on now, before your feelings grow too deep."

I roll my eyes. "Please. I kissed the guy once, that's all."

Walker's eyebrows almost jet off his head. "You kissed someone?" His mouth hangs open. "You. Myla Lewis." He sighs. "I see my warning comes too late."

I cross my arms over my chest. He needs to calm down. "Look, I appreciate your playing older brother and all, but you're worrying about nothing. If Lincoln were really that into me, he'd find a way to get in touch." Case closed.

Walker slips his hand into the folds of his robe. "He already has." He sets a silver envelope onto my palm. My name is written on it in black ink.

My heart kicks in my chest as I tear open the letter and pull out a card. It reads 'Tomorrow, the Ryder mansion ballroom, 4 PM. Dress casually. Lincoln.' I grin and shake my hips in a little happy dance.

Walker rolls his eyes. "Never play poker, Myla."

I fix him with a half-frown. "What's *that* supposed to mean?"

"I've never seen you hide an emotion in your life." He sets his hands back into the folds of his robes and sighs. "Clearly, you already have feelings for Lincoln."

I tilt my head to one side, considering. The Prince is funny, handsome, smart and kicks serious demon ass. Why shouldn't I like him? "Maybe I do." I stick out my tongue at Walker. Nyah.

"Oh, my." Walker works hard to hide his smile, but I can tell that secretly, he's totally digging this. "The two of you together are going to be trouble."

My face breaks out into a wide grin. "I certainly hope so."

A

Tank stands on the muddy back lawn of High, motioning students closer with his beefy hands. "Everyone, gather around. Class is about to begin."

I glance at my watch. Once this class is over, I can go to the Ryder mansion for my mystery whatever-it-is with Lincoln. Anxiety burns through my chest.

The Old Timer lurks by our gym teacher's elbow. His fingers tremble as he twiddles his half-a-moustache. Cissy and Zeke chat nearby.

The Old Timer smoothes his palms over his receding gray hair, guiding the frizzy strands into a tiny pony tail. "We have special guests today." He gives his moustache-half an extra-long twirl. "Angel warriors. They'll arrive any minute."

My mind empties of all thought except pure joy. I jump up and down. "Yes! Yes! Yes!" I've never seen angels fight. The entire class turns in my direction, their eyes large and mouths small. Tails stop wagging.

Cissy slides up beside me and whispers in my ear. "You might want to cool it. The other kids are scared of angels. Everyone else is—"

I raise my pointer finger. "I'm *not like* everyone else and I don't want to *be like* everyone else."

Cissy chuckles. "I noticed. Okay, jump up and down. Knock yourself out."

The Old Timer starts blabbing about how to act in front of angels. The other students stand google-eyed and twitchy, hanging on his every word.

I elbow Cissy, trying my best to look super calm and cool. "So, any luck with that research project?"

"You mean finding out what Prince Lincoln wants with you at the Ryder mansion today?"

"That's the one."

"Nope. I think Zeke's parents know, but they won't say a word." She glances at her watch. "Class ends in forty minutes. You'll find out soon enough."

Two angels appear on a nearby patch of muddy lawn. A man and woman, they're tall and trim with white-blond hair that hangs straight and loose down their backs. They have milky skin, pale blue eyes, and large white wings. Their silver armor is delicately carved with runes of protection. The students gasp as the pair steps up to Tank and the Old Timer. I don't think anyone breathes, let alone talks.

The woman angel is the first to speak. "Good afternoon, everyone. I am Rhiannon and this is Levi. We're members of the new personal guard for the Angel Verus."

Verus got an armed guard? That's never happened before. There must be a new level of danger in Purgatory. That and Armageddon's strange behavior today at the Arena? Something is very, very wrong.

Levi sets his hands on his hips. "We're here to show you how to defend yourselves against demons."

The Old Timer clears his throat. "Excuse me, but this is the Ghoul *Protection* League. I'm sure you'll teach the students how to *defend ghouls*." A spasm rolls across his upper lip. "Especially from Papilio demons." His head jerks. "They assailed my personal possessions. I've filed numerous complaint forms with the Oligarchy but they won't even acknowledge the attack." He slams his fist into his open palm. "You should show the students how to fight them." His irises flare scarlet.

I silently whistle. Those Papilio demons really messed with his undead head.

Rhiannon meets the Old Timer's stare, her irises flaring with blue light. "No. This is defense training, not instructions on revenge." Righteous power rolls off her in waves.

The Old Timer bows so low, he almost falls over. "Of course, teach whatever you like."

Levi rubs his hands together. "We'll begin with Manus demons." He raises his palm level before his mouth and breathes onto his skin. His hand magically fills with clear water. He breathes once more. The water bursts into white flame.

"Let's look at a Manus." Levi tips his hand over. The burning water pours into the shape of a massive Manus demon, only this one's clear as glass and encased in white flame.

A few of the students yelp, more inhale sharply. Angels are so freaking cool. I punch the air with my fist.

Rhiannon walks around the demon. "As you can see, Manus are at least six feet tall and almost as wide." She points to different parts of the demon as she speaks. "Distinguishing marks are powerful arms, yellow tusks, black fur, and short legs. They're extremely strong and often used for heavy work, such as smashing into buildings or through crowds. Their most vulnerable point is here." She points right below the rib cage. "A blow to the gut will stun them, giving you time to escape."

Tank folds his thick arms over his chest. "How should the students fight them?"

"They shouldn't," says Rhiannon. "That falls under the category of 'sacrificing your life for your masters.' Today, we're learning defense. Whatever the demon, your best defensive move is to run." She scans the small group of students. "Any questions?"

Silence.

Levi tilts his head to one side. "Would you like to see more?"

I shoot my hand into the air. "Yes, absolutely."

A few kids nod.

"Excellent," says Rhiannon. "Next, we'll take a look at Armageddon."

The Old Timer squeaks. "Armageddon is our friend."

Rhiannon smiles. "Of course, he is."

I grit my teeth and kick at the muddy turf. *Of course, he isn't.* I can't believe someone like Rhiannon has to give lip service to the Old Timer's stupidity. He invaded Purgatory once. Why wouldn't he do it again?

Rhiannon moves beside the burning Manus demon, raises her palm and blows across her open hand. More magical water appears, white flame licking across the surface of her skin. Rhiannon tips her hand, the water pours into the shape of the King of Hell. He stands seven feet tall with smooth skin and a gangly body. A blade-like nose divides his long face.

I swallow. Yup, that's him alright.

Levi walks around the model of Armageddon. "Take a close look, everyone. Armageddon is a greater demon. They're heartless, rare, and incredibly powerful. Each develops a preferred method of attack. For Armageddon, it's touch. If he can get his fingers on your bare skin, he'll pull out your soul."

I remember the dreamscape where Armageddon turned Senator Adams into a pile of ash. I shiver.

Levi's jaw sets into a firm line. "Armageddon's body is invulnerable. Only another greater demon can fight him. Simply put, your best defense is to run. If you can't escape, cover up any exposed skin."

The angels pour more demons from their palms. Other students start asking questions and stop acting terrified. Even Tank and the Old Timer join in. The lawn fills with monsters made of clear water and white flame.

So. Freaking. Cool.

I almost pinch myself. This can't be real: I'm at school, talking about how demons fight, and no one's glaring at me like I'm a nut-job. Awesome.

Rhiannon and Levi end the lecture. I watch them leave and check my watch: 3:45 PM.

Unholy moley. Class ran over and I'm late for my mystery encounter with Lincoln. I wave goodbye to Cissy and Zeke, race over to Betsy, and drive off to Upper Purgatory.

CHAPTER EIGHTEEN

.A.

It takes at least a million years to putter over to the Ryder mansion. I park the wagon, jog up to the front door, and test the handle. It swings open.

I step inside the reception hall.

"Hello? Anybody here?" I check my watch. Almost 5 o'clock. They must have left. "Hells bells." Frustration bolts through my arms and legs. My gaze rests on the dainty porcelain statues lining the reception hall's gilded tables. Damn, I'd love to smash a few of those against the wall. My hands ball into fists.

Voices echo in from the East Wing ballroom.

My fists loosen. Maybe I'm not too late.

With halting steps, I follow the sounds down the hallway. At the end of the corridor, the arched gateway to the ballroom lies open. I peer inside.

Lincoln stands at the center of the ballroom floor, a square of padded mats beneath his feet. He faces Nat, the man who inspected the Furor dragon at the Winter Tournament. The pair run through battle moves with wooden swords. Lincoln wears black knee-length spandex shorts and, well, nothing else. I watch the play of muscles across his back, arms, and legs. Damn, he looks tasty. My lust demon purrs inside me.

I raise my arm. "Hello!"

Nat pauses and waves. "Hello there!" He has a square face with a round nose, mismatched button eyes, and grizzled chin. Both his barrel-shaped chest and stocky limbs are firm with muscle. Like Lincoln, he wears compression pants, only his are paired with an olive green t-shirt.

With his opponent distracted, Lincoln drops onto his knee, swinging his free leg against Nat's shins. The elder man falls, hitting the mat face-first with a thud.

Lincoln hops to his feet. "Always stay mindful of the battle, Nat. You taught me that." He jogs to the edge of the mats, pulls on a white t-shirt and waves in my direction. "Hello, Myla!"

"Hi. Sorry I'm late." *To whatever weirdness this is.*

"No problem. It gave me and Nat a chance to practice." He gestures to the older man beside him. Nat's back on his feet and smiling. "I don't believe you two have officially met. Myla, I'd like to present Nathaniel Archer, my Master at Arms."

"Master at Arms?"

Nat half bows. "That means I teach the young Prince how to fight demons, milady." He has a gravelly voice with a cute cockney accent.

Lincoln winks. "And stay alive in the process." He steps up to the edge of the mats, then pauses. Our gazes lock; energy zings in the space between us. We share a slow and warm smile. *I missed you too, Lincoln.* I ache to wrap my arms around him.

Nat steps between us. "I'm also here as royal chaperone." He clears his throat. "In case any ladies should stop by what's officially a boys-only work out."

I tilt my head to one side. "You've never had a chaperone before, Lincoln."

His smile droops. "We'll get to that in a bit."

"Good." I've zero desire to hear about the Earl of Acca right now. There'll be plenty of time for that nightmare. Later.

Lincoln rubs his palms together, his full smile returning. "I've a surprise for you first. Nat here will teach you how to fight with something besides your tail."

My heart feels like a balloon about to float to the ceiling. "Really?" I race up to the edge of the mats and bob on the balls of my feet. I've never had actual combat training.

Best. Surprise. Ever.

Nat sets his hands on his hips. "Now, be fair, my Prince. I never agreed to attack the young Miss."

"I told you, Nat. She's not like the ladies of the court." He picks up a wooden sword and flicks it straight at my head. I catch it in my left hand, an inch away from my nose. Lincoln grins. "It's a shame that you missed her at the tournament. She was amazing."

My skin flushes something fierce. "Thanks." I turn to Nat. "I fought in the Arena since I was twelve." I set the blunt point of the sword on my fingertip and balance it there. "Hand-to-hand combat, to the death."

Nat points a meaty finger at Lincoln. "I won't do it, no matter you're the Prince and the young miss says it's all fine and dandy. Ladies don't stand a chance fightin' a thrax and that's the truth." He stares at me and frowns. "Look at her, such a lovely young thing. You can't be serious, my Prince."

Humph. A lovely young thing that could snap your neck in four seconds or less. Showing this guy how girls can fight? Sounds like a challenge. My lips curl into a mischievous grin. I'm always up for a challenge.

Lincoln flips his sword into his right hand, his mismatched eyes finding mine. "Is that what you think, Nat?" He firms up his footing, his back arching into battle stance.

Nat crosses his heavy arms over his barrel-chest. "It's not what I think, young Prince. It's what I *know*."

Peeling off my sneakers, I step onto the practice mats in my bare feet, the wooden sword gripped tightly in my hand. My heart thuds so hard, my pulse throbs through my throat and temples. At this point, I wouldn't care if we were practicing open heart surgery, as long as I got closer to Lincoln. I hold the Prince's gaze, giving him the barest of nods.

"Here's what *I* know, Nat." Raising his sword level with his shoulder, Lincoln lunges straight for me.

My mind clears as the Prince's sword streams toward my head. Battle mode clicks into my brain. Lincoln's no longer the guy I wanna kiss, he's six feet of solid muscle streaming at me with a weapon and a plan.

Fortunately for me, his plan kinda sucks.

I lean over at the last second. Once his body slams into my side, my tail grabs Lincoln's neck, flipping him over. He spins 360 degrees through the air, landing flat on his back with a thud. He looks up at me, raising his right eyebrow.

"You're using wrestling moves in a sword fight, Myla."

I sniff. "Says the guy on the mat."

Arching his back, Lincoln springs onto his feet. My mind calculates the possible moves from this stance. The Prince lunges at me again with his wooden sword; I block his strike with an upward thrust. As he slices from different angles, I keep blocking.

No matter what I do, I stay stuck on the defensive. Grr. I need to break through his hits and get on the attack.

When Lincoln spins around for another strike, I see my chance. For the millisecond his back is turned to me, I leap into the air and kick out feet-first, looking to connect with his shoulders and slam him face-first onto the mat.

Lincoln senses my move, dodging before I strike. Instead of pummeling into Lincoln's shoulders, I kick empty air and tumble onto the ground, landing flat on my back. Lincoln springs forward, pinning me to the mat, his hands holding mine immobile.

"I warned you about wrestling moves, Myla."

"And I should have warned *you* about my tail." With all my focus, I will the arrowhead end to curl, giving Lincoln a good punch in the gut.

But my tail has a mind of its own. Ignoring my commands, the arrowhead end slides up Lincoln's arm and begins mussing his hair. Long brown strands fall over the Prince's slate-blue and wheat-brown eyes. Half his mouth quirks with a grin.

"Some secret weapon you've got there."

I groan. "My inner demon and I don't always see eye-to-eye."

Suddenly my brain slips out of battle mode, entering into the very pleasant sensation of Lincoln's body atop mine. I twist my wrists; he holds me firmly to the mat. Damn, that's hot. I stare at his mouth. *Kiss me.*

Nat steps up beside us. "You've proved your point, my Prince. I'll fight the young Miss." He nervously scans the room. "The pair of you need to be getting up."

My eyes stay locked on Lincoln's. "No." My voice comes out a low whisper. "Just one." I shift my hips so my leg brushes between his thighs. *Come on.*

Lincoln grins, then he leans in closer. His mouth presses onto mine and damn, he tastes better than I remember. Our tongues slide and explore while he holds me firmly to the mat. Desire burns through me, body and soul.

Somewhere on the mansion grounds, a lightning bolt strikes the earth, followed by a deep roll of thunder. I actively ignore the fact that this is the second time lightning has struck the moment I feel strong emotion for Lincoln. Kissing him is just too good.

Nat leans over, pulling on Lincoln's shoulder. "That's quite enough, you two."

The Prince rolls to the side, then we both slowly rise to our feet. Damn, damn, damn. After feeling his touch, being this far away from him almost hurts.

Nat guides Lincoln off the practice mats. "Let's begin the lesson." He picks up a wooden weapon from the floor, tossing it between his hands. He pauses, eyeing me closely. "You're a little bit of hellfire, aren't you, young Miss?"

I grin. "I hope so."

Nat and I shift into battle stance. He shows me some basic moves, and then we slide into a rhythm of thrusts and parries with our wooden swords. After a few minutes of lusty thoughts about Lincoln, my head clicks back into battle mode. There's nothing but challenge and counter-challenge, dodge and strike. Lincoln watches from the sidelines, his arms folded over his chest. The hours fly by.

Nat pats me on the shoulder. "That's all the time we have, little Miss. You done well."

"Thanks, Nat. That was great."

He raises his meaty pointer finger in my direction. "Don't forget to practice. An hour with the sword, every day."

"I won't." Stepping across the floor, I sit with my back to the ballroom wall, panting for breath.

Nat heaves the practice mats about, stacking one onto another. Lincoln sits down beside me, his hands gripping a water bottle way too tightly. My inner battle mode instantly ends. Worry, desire, and affection duke it out inside me.

I know what's coming now. Bad news.

"Want some water?" Lincoln tilts the tall plastic bottle in my direction.

"Yes, please." My tail slides the water from his hand. "And thanks for setting up training with Nat. He's amazing."

"I'm glad." Lincoln drums his fingers on his knees. "I asked you here for another reason as well." His voice is low.

My breath hitches. *I won't make him do this.*

"I know what you're about to say, Lincoln." I take a swig from the bottle, hoping some water will steady my nerves. "Walker told me about the Earl of Acca. About Adair. It's pretty obvious why Nat's playing chaperone today." Lincoln was only allowed off compound with some anti-Myla protection.

"Walker *told you?*" The muscles along his jaw tighten. "I'm gonna kill that guy. I told him to deliver a message, that's it. He doesn't even know you."

Um, actually he does. Not that I'll get into that right now. "He was only trying to help."

Lincoln turns to me, his eyes stretching wide with disbelief. "And you still came here today?"

"Of course, I did." I elbow him in the arm. "Besides, Walker said you had a master plan to defeat the Earl."

He winks. "That I do."

"See? Nothing to worry about." If I lose Lincoln, it won't be to some pompous windbag who shoots crossbow bolts at a Limus demon. Sheesh.

He stares at me for what feels like a million years. "Most people crumble in front of the Earl, my parents included." He angles his head to one side. "How are you possible?"

"I've wondered the same thing about you." I curl my finger toward him. Lincoln leans in for another kiss.

From across the ballroom, Nat clears his throat. "Come on, you two."

Lincoln chuckles. "Nat's taking his role as chaperone rather seriously." His mouth thins to a straight line. "There's one more thing you need to know. For my plan to work, my people must return to Antrum immediately."

Sadness wraps around me, heavy as a blanket. "When do you leave?"

"Next Saturday."

I nod, processing the news. "If these are our last days together," I straighten my shoulders, "then I want to have *fun*." I wag my brows up and down. "Maybe get into some more *deep trouble*."

He laughs; the sound curls my toes. "More Reperio demons?"

"No way. That's so two weeks ago."

"I have it." Lincoln rises to his feet. "There's a party Thursday night, a kind of official send-off. We could be troublesome there." He offers me his hand.

I slide my fingers into his palm. The warmth from his skin is yummy. "Sounds like a plan." Lincoln pulls me to my feet.

Our bodies are only inches apart now. Our hands are still entwined; neither of us is letting go.

"Excellent. I'll have you added to the guest list."

"Can you add my friends Cissy and Zeke too?" If I go without her, I'll never hear the end of it.

"Of course." He releases my hand, and this time the loss of his touch hurts even more. "The Great Ladies of the court are organizing this event; it'll be traditional thrax attire. Someone will be in touch about making you another gown."

I wince. "I went through all that with the tournaments. I'm not really Ball Gown Girl. Maybe we can break-in somewhere again?"

Lincoln chuckles. "With the scrutiny I'm under, I'm afraid that won't be possible. But I'd really like to see you at the ball." Tilting his head, he looks at me from his slate-gray eye. He slowly runs his pointer finger down my jaw-line. "Say yes, Myla."

A warm blush crawls up my neck. "Yes."

⅃.

The Old Timer paces the classroom, a massive set of nail clippers in his fingers. With his free hand, he twiddles what's left of his handlebar moustache. Cissy sits nearby. A few days have passed since Lincoln invited me—plus Zeke and Cissy—to the thrax ball. They won't shut up about it, which makes this nervewracking event wrack my nerves all the more. I'm starting to wonder if I should have invited them at all.

"Class, please note the proper equipment for overgrown cuticles."

A few students glance in his direction. The rest are busy whispering.

"Have you sent your measurements in?" Cissy has appointed herself event manager for Lincoln's going-away ball. She's already bugging me about wearing thrax undies.

"Yes, Mom did it right away. I'm a guest of the House of Gurith, so I'll be in red and gold."

"I'm a single lady for the House of Rixa, so I'm in green and black."

I drum my fingers on my desk. "It's weird having your life colorcoded. Do you think the thrax ever want to wear plaid and tell everyone else to stick to it?"

Cissy raises her eyebrows. "Ah, no. I think they're really-really-really into their traditions, period."

I sigh. Cissy's right. And top of their list-of-traditions is forcing people to marry when they're eighteen. Not that I'm bitter.

To demonstrate proper clipping techniques, the Old Timer peels off his black boots and tattered socks. His feet are green and bumpy with long yellow toenails. It's beyond disgusting.

The PA system buzzes to life. The Headmaster's voice blasts through a tiny speaker on the classroom wall. "All students report to the gymnasium immediately."

Our Headmaster's famous for hour-long announcements that go into painful detail about his youth on Earth in some place called Buffalo. It's basically ghoul central and he misses the spicy chicken wings. For him to shut his yap after all of seven words is unheard of.

Something's going on.

We file out of the classroom and into the gymnasium. Within minutes, the student body sits in neat rows on metal folding chairs, our multitude of tails poking through the back-openings. Before us, the faculty stands in a straight line along the gym's front wall, their coal-black eyes staring blankly forward. It could be me, but they look especially gray and undead right now. If I didn't know better, I'd say they were scared.

Cissy sits next to me. "What do you think this is all about?"

"Nothing good."

Our Headmaster steps up to a small wooden podium beside the line of faculty. He raises his long bony arms. He's tall, skeletal and gray-skinned; a Neanderthal-style forehead hangs over his beady dark eyes. Although he wears standard-issue ghoul black robes, he always tops them with a red and slightly-cockeyed bow tie.

"Greetings to the DL-19 School for Quasi Servitude." Lowering his hands, the Headmaster tries to straighten his bow tie. He makes it a wee more skewed instead. "I'd like to begin by introducing–"

"Me." An unforgettable voice booms from the back of the gymnasium. Three hundred students turn around, all their faces twisted in confusion. All the faces, that is, except mine. I know exactly who's entered the room: Armageddon.

The King of Hell looms seven feet tall and pencil-thin; his short torso, gangly arms, and long legs all fit into a perfectly-sized tux and tails. His pointed face scans the gym, two crimson eyes blazing over a blade-like nose. Beside him stand a pair of Manus demons, their bodies covered in shaggy black fur. Long yellow tusks hang past their chins.

Armageddon steps slowly down the gym's main aisle. On either side of him, students cringe and huddle, their faces twisted in fear.

Wrapping my hands around Cissy's, I speak in a low voice. "Remember, greater demons have an aura that causes fear and panic."

She nods quickly. "The angels said that in class the other day."

Armageddon steps closer to our aisle. I shoot Cissy what I hope is a calming look, but I'm not sure I'm ready for this, either. I've only been close to Armageddon a handful of times. And each one sucked. "Brace yourself."

Then, it hits. A wall of terror crashes into my body, freezing me in place. Cissy's hands tremble violently under my own. Unable to turn away, I watch Armageddon speed to the front of the gymnasium, his legs and coattails a blur of movement. Behind him, the Manus demons lumber along on their stumpy gorilla-style legs, knuckles dragging.

The hairs on the back of my neck prickle. This is bad, very bad.

The Headmaster cowers to one side as Armageddon approaches the podium. Between us, there's now enough distance that I no longer feel the terror of a greater demon's presence. I scan the teacher's stiff bodies. Some of their brows are pockmarked with black sweat. Their turn to feel the full force of Armageddon.

The King of Hell grips the edges of the podium. "This is a demon inspection." He scans the room, his upper lip bent with a sneer. I might be imagining things, but he seems to find me in the crowd, his gaze glowing red with recognition. "I'm Armageddon."

My terror-level kicks up a few notches. No way am I imagining this. Twice I've stopped Armageddon from getting a purely evil soul into Heaven—first, with the Choker and then Deacon—and he sure looks like the type to hold a grudge. The thought crosses my mind that I might not leave here alive. I grip Cissy's hands more firmly. A thin sheen of sweat coats our skin.

Armageddon's three-knuckled fingers grip the podium so firmly, it looks ready to snap in two. "You all look...Ready."

Miss Thing sniffles a bit, her face lined with long black streaks from her tears. Armageddon struts over to her, pausing before her in the long line of teachers. Her shoulders visibly shake. "Do I frighten you?"

Her voice comes out a ragged whisper. "Yes."

Armageddon's mouth winds until an evil grin. "I see." The King of Hell grips Miss Thing's shoulder; she gasps. Red light blazes from under her gray flesh, causing her skin to char and crack.

An odd chill creeps over my body. *This can't be real.* The King of Hell cannot be sucking the soul from a teacher in front of the entire student body. Why aren't one of the teachers doing something to protect her? Or better yet, the Oligarchy?

My teacher's face twists with terror, her long red nails clawing at her glowing skin. *This is all too real.* Waves of nausea crash through me, each one worse than the last.

A moment later, her body flares into a column of red flame. It all happens so quickly, she barely has a chance to scream. Once the fire dies out, Miss Thing has transformed into a frozen image of herself, only one that's made entirely of gray ash.

The gymnasium takes on a dream-like quality. No one speaks. No one moves. A charred smell hangs in the air. I cover my nose and mouth so I don't barf.

Armageddon removes his hand from our teacher's shoulder; her body crumbles. The King of Hell stares menacingly at the pile of ashes on the gymnasium floor. He bares his teeth slightly, showing shining, blade-like canines in a face of smooth black stone. "Thank you for your answer."

Whirling about, Armageddon rounds on the student body, seeming to stare into all our eyes at once. I have the strange sensation he's reaching into our souls, testing our strength, our ability to fight him. A satisfied grin curls his wide mouth. "My inspection is complete."

Turning on his heel, Armageddon marches out the gymnasium's back door, the Manus demons skulking along behind him. The group lumbers across the threshold, followed by the unmistakable hum of a portal opening in the hallway beyond. The gym door slowly swings shut with a long creak.

I exhale. *He's gone.* Tension seeps from my shoulders. My stomach unwinds.

Seconds tick by. The gymnasium stays silent. All at once, students break into sobs. Others scream. A teacher collapses. More kids stare about the room, wide-eyed with panic. The headmaster steps back to the podium.

"Everyone will return to class. Until further notice, History class will report to TNK-XJ64 for extra lessons in the Ghoul Protection League. That is all." He marches around the gym, comforting the most hysterical students and encouraging everyone back into their routine.

Huh. My eyes flare red as I stare at the headmaster. Didn't take long for him to decide that the solution for their Armageddon problem was more Ghoul Protection League classes for us. Asshole.

Cissy grips my hand, her voice is low and ragged. "Stay close to me, sweetie." We follow the crush of kids out of the gym. I scan the terrified faces around me. Something's coming, and it's not a new era of friendly relations between ghouls, angels, demons, thrax, and quasis. It's Armageddon.

The rest of the day is a mish-mash of stuttering teachers and tear-streamed faces. Cissy joins me for the rest of my classes. She keeps asking me how I'd fight a Manus demon. For once, I'm not thrilled to answer.

Somehow I find Betsy, drive home and stuff my head with Mom's homemade spaghetti. Throughout dinner, my mother watches my every move with interest.

"How was the pasta?"

I set my plate in the sink. "Yummy, Mom. Thanks."

Her chocolate eyes narrow. "Can you help me with some robe alterations?"

"Sure."

We step into her room. I stand on a stool in front of a multi-paneled mirror. Mom slips a ghoul-robe over my head and examines the hem. I stare into the reflective glass, seeing the large brown eyes, high cheekbones, and full mouth that convinced so many human souls that I was harmless.

Mom sits at my feet, a silver push-pin held firmly between her lips. She speaks from one side of her mouth. "Want to talk about it yet?"

I can't help but smile. *Mom noticed I'm upset.* She's done that a lot more lately. "Wow. How long have you known?"

She bobs her head from side to side. "Since you walked through the door, pretty much."

"Don't take this the wrong way, but I can't believe you haven't asked me a million questions by now."

"I haven't, have I?" She leans back on her heels, her gaze lost in thought. "The dreamscapes from Verus have been good for me." She nods, decisively. "I didn't realize how much I needed to talk about things." She pokes my heel with her pointer finger and smiles. "More importantly, they've been good for *us*."

I return her grin. "Yeah, they have." Half the time, Mom skips her grueling morning question-and-answer sessions. That alone has been a huge relationship builder. "Maybe we should reach out to Tim, bring the family together."

She eyes me carefully. "Maybe you should tell me what happened today?"

She's got me there. I inhale a long breath. "Things have been weird at school for a long time. It started back in September when angels started hanging around our Headmaster and Superintendent. Turns out, they've been giving advice on how to protect against demons. That's why the school started the Ghoul Protection League."

Mom rolls her eyes. "I remember you telling me about that silly League."

"I didn't take it too seriously at first, either."

Cocking her head to one side, Mom eyes the drape of the robe. Pulling the pin from her mouth, she sets it into the fabric's hem.

"The demons aren't acting like the good little allies they once were. The rank-and-file ghouls know something's going on, even if their leaders don't."

Rising to her feet, Mom gently grips the robe's shoulders. "We're all set. Let me pull this off you." The fabric slides over my head. "Watch the pins." She lays the new robe over a nearby chair, then sits at the foot of her bed. "So, strange things were happening, and you didn't take it seriously. But now you are. Why?"

Stepping down from the stool, I sit beside Mom. "Armageddon 'inspected' our school today." I make little quotation marks with my fingers when I say 'inspected.' "He killed one of the teachers for no reason."

"Oh, my. Did the Oligarchy show up?"

"No."

"It's what they should have done. With their Group Think, they knew exactly what was happening by the second. Armageddon was testing them."

"Well, they failed that test, big-time." What a bunch of bozos the Oligarchy are.

"Those four, let's just say they don't like facing unpleasant realities."

I fidget. "If the demons ever do attack, what would we do?"

Mom looks around the room for a time, then she nods. "Back when I was Senator, we built a series of bunkers where the government could hide out. In there, we had everything we needed to keep working: food, water, armor, communications equipment, and even Senate robes. The bunkers were top secret and built so that no pure demon could get in or out."

"That sounds great, only they didn't really work last time, right?"

"The Senate thought it would be ghouls *or* demons who attacked, never that they'd team up into a single demon-and-ghoul-army. But they did unite. The ghouls created portals to bring in the demon army. It was all over before anyone reached the bunkers. The Angels and thrax came to fight for us, but in the end there wasn't too much they could do. All we got were slightly better terms in the final peace treaty."

"You know what, Mom?" I rest my head on her shoulder. "I think we may need one of those bunkers soon." Anxiety prickles over my skin.

Mom pats my hand. "I think so too, Myla-la."

CHAPTER NINETEEN

$\mathcal{A}$

Cissy rushes through the opened door of her lavish bedroom, two huge garment bags gripped in her left hand. In her right, she holds a pair of boxes wrapped in string. "Our gowns are finally here!" She gently sets the packages onto her pink bedspread. "The Great Ladies dropped them off."

I check my watch. Only a few hours to go before Lincoln's farewell ball begins. Good thing I'm not one of those types who needs a million years to get ready. I glance at the gowns and frown. "That's strange. You'd think they'd have something better to do."

Cissy hangs the gowns side-by-side in her closet. Hers is green and black, mine's red and gold. "How do you know? Maybe it's an ancient thrax tradition."

"Maybe." With the thrax, you never know. I wouldn't be shocked if they had a tradition for which way toilet paper falls off the roll.

Cissy claps her hands. "Let's get dressed!" She quickly shuts the bedroom door, then she and I peel down to our underwear.

A portal appears by Cissy's closet; Walker steps through. "Good evening, Myla. You have been called to serve."

Cissy yelps, quickly grabbing her clothes and holding them over her front. I do the same.

"Walker!" I roll my eyes. "There's a new fad called knocking. Ever heard of it?"

Walker shifts his weight from foot to foot. "You were, um, concerned that I haven't given you advance warning before a match. You have one this Saturday morning, 5 AM. Since it's Thursday night, I thought you'd be pleased to know."

"That's nice, Walker. You can go now."

If Walker had blood, he'd be blushing at this point. "I must, um, apologize for the intrusion. I will go inform your mother of the match."

Cissy nods toward the stack of boxes. "Be sure to say the gowns arrived in time."

"No!" I try to kick Cissy in the shins and miss. "She thinks we're hanging out at Zeke's again, she doesn't know about the ball." I turn to Walker, my eyes pleading. "Please don't say a word to Mom. You know how she gets."

Walker scans the gowns with an expert eye. "Lincoln invited you to the ball tonight." It's not a question.

"They're friends," says Cissy quickly. I've spent an inordinate amount of time convincing her of that fact. No point awakening her envy demon when Lincoln leaves in a few days.

"I'll keep your secret." Walker pulls up his hood. "I only wish I had an invitation to this evening's festivities." He closes his eyes; another portal appears by Cissy's closet. Walker starts to leave, then pauses. He angles toward me, his eyes glowing red under his hood. "You two will cause a lot of trouble, you know."

"One can only hope." I stick out my tongue at him. "I'm not worried about a certain dopey Earl ruining my life."

"Only you, Myla." Stepping through the portal, Walker disappears.

Cissy tosses her clothes back onto the floor, her focus moving laser-style in my direction. "What was *that* all about?"

"Do you promise to keep a lid on your envy demon?"

Cissy grits her teeth. "Yes."

I hold my pointer finger and thumb before my nose in the hand signal for 'little.' "There may be a wee bit of sexual tension between me and Lincoln." Best to ease her gently into reality. "And that Earl guy still hates me because I doused him in green demon goop."

"Oh." Cissy screws her mouth onto one side of her face. "But Lincoln's going back to Antrum, isn't he?"

"Yup. Saturday." Normally this fact would be incredibly depressing. But since I'm seeing Lincoln in minutes? Couldn't care less.

"Got it." She bobs her head happily, her attention returning to the gowns. I let out a long sigh.

Stepping over to the boxes, I pull out my matching shoes and thrax undies. Mine look like mummy wrappings with thick black lines sewn onto them. "These look even weirder than last time. Do I *really* have to wear this?"

"Do you *really* think you're leaving my room in anything else?"

Well, that's the truth.

There's a flurry of makeup brushes and hair spray, then we both slip into our gowns.

Cissy sets her hand on her hip, scanning me up and down. My dress is red and gold brocade with a fitted bodice that leaves my shoulders bare; the low pointed waist has a hole in the back for my tail. The gown's skirt is floor-length and cut into sections that shimmer as I move. My long auburn hair hangs loose about my shoulders.

I suck in a shaky breath. I'm a curvy girl, and usually I wear sweats that pretty much hide that fact. But in this dress, I'm all hourglass. In fact, the bodice has this corset thing inside it that gives me a waspish waist. Add it all up and I'm feeling mighty awkward. I turn to Cissy. "Okay, what do you think?"

"Myla, you look stunning."

I exhale. She may be exaggerating, but I need it right now. "Thanks." I gesture to her dress. "Let's see yours." Cissy spins about, showing a shimmering black under-gown with a green velvet overdress and long looping sleeves. The velvet is loosely tied up her chest with long green ribbons, then it falls open at her skirts to reveal the black gown beneath. Her hair hangs in golden ringlets to her shoulders. Her tail swings happily behind her. I grin. "You look lovely."

"Thank you." She curtsies. "We better get going. We're already cutting it close on time."

We say our goodbyes to Cissy's parents and take our seats in my green station wagon, careful not to crinkle our new gowns. Betsy's especially cranky today, spewing out extra smoke and noise before the engine finally starts humming. Finally, we start the short trip from Cissy's to the Ryder mansion. With every passing mile, my blood pressure ratchets up a few points. Can't. Wait.

"Why don't you get that car fixed?" Cissy pulls down the rear view mirror, checking her make-up.

"Are you kidding?" I steer Betsy down the back roads to the Ryder mansion. "Filling out paperwork for an official maintenance request takes weeks." I pat the dashboard. "As long as Betsy moves, she's fine."

Squinting, I stare through the windshield. Off in the distance, the Ryder mansion lays perched on its gray-green hill, its white bricks glittering in the haze of twilight. All around lay a sea of dark and boarded-up houses. Excitement blooms inside me.

Myla and Lincoln…Partners in crime on a new mission to rain trouble onto tight-assed thrax everywhere. Yay.

We drive closer, seeing hundreds of horses lining the cobblestone path to the mansion. Each beautiful animal carries a lovely lady in a flowing gown. Velvet bridles hang from all the horse's heads; colored ribbons are woven into their lady's hair. Beside every rider stands a man in brown leather pants, silver chain mail, and a velvet over-tunic with a colored crest.

"Wow." I slow the car to a crawl.

"I know, thrax are nuts about horses. The Ryders say they built all those cabins and stuff in the woods so they could have their four-footed friends close-by."

273

The station wagon nears the driveway. Its exhaust system kicks, letting out a huge puff of black smoke. Some horses whinny, causing their riders and escorts shoot me the evil eye.

I scan the roads. No other cars are around for miles. "Are we the only non-thrax at this shindig?" My heartbeat kicks into overdrive.

"Yup. This isn't a diplomatic event; they basically asked to use the house for a private party." She flips down the visor, checking her make-up. "I thought Lincoln would have told you all this stuff."

What do I say here? It took Lincoln two weeks to figure out how to sneak off and wrestle me for a few hours; long chit-chats and party planning are out of the question. I frown. "I said sexual tension, Cissy, not besties."

The station wagon spits out another mushroom cloud of smoke. More stares follow. We putter past the main parking lot. It's been corded off to make room for make-shift stables.

Where am I supposed to park this monster?

"Tell me there's another way to park than driving this clunker past every member of thrax nobility."

Cissy frowns. "Do you want me to tell you that…Or do you want the truth?"

"Ugh."

"The lot's your first right after the main entryway. We're almost there." The exhaust system kicks again; I wince. Another horse whinnies, rearing slightly on its back feet. I get even more glares this time. "Drive slowly, Myla. I think you're scaring the horses a little."

I lock my back teeth and focus on the road. The horses aren't the only ones getting a little scared.

I park the car in the empty lot beside the mansion. "That sucked."

Off in the distance, trumpets sound. Cissy whips open the car door. "Introductions have started. We're going to be late!"

Cissy and I rush to the mansion's front door. A few thrax linger by the entryway, their footmen leading the last of the horses down the cobblestone drive. We line up behind the final partygoers, smoothing out our dresses and trying to slow our breathing.

A male voice bellows from inside the reception hall. "Miss Cecilia Frederickson, escort to Mister Ezekiel Ryder."

Cissy gives my hand a squeeze. "That's my cue." She steps through the opened doorway and into the reception hall. The room is packed with thrax in their colored outfits. Cissy glides to the center of the room and waits. Zeke saunters out from the crowd, wearing a black velvet tunic over chain mail and leather pants. He takes Cissy's arm; they march off into the ballroom to the trill of silver trumpets.

I hover in the doorway and watch them leave, a nervous stitch eating into my side. The trumpets grow silent, followed by a pause that lasts a million billion years, minimum. My heart beats so loudly, I'm sure all of Upper Purgatory can hear it.

The herald lowers his silver trumpet. "Miss Myla Lewis without escort."

I stifle the urge to groan. Without escort? Really?! How about *with* the ability to kick ass? They need to leave the Middle Ages, STAT.

Straightening my shoulders, I step through the doorway and head to the center of the reception room. Maybe it's me, but it seems like the hall suddenly turns super-silent. Each click-clack of my heels on the tiled floor sounds deafening. Although hundreds of eyes stare at me, I only focus on two: one slate-gray and the other wheat-brown.

Lincoln stands within the sea of faces, his body flanked by a group of beautiful young ladies. He's wearing black leather pants, silver mail, and a black velvet over-tunic. A glimmering eagle is sewn onto his chest; a silver crown glistens atop his mop of brown hair. He stares at me with fire in his eyes, his full mouth slightly open.

A minute passes before I realize that I should do something other than stand in the reception hall looking like a dumbass. The guests pass anxious looks and giggles. I scan for Cissy and some direction on what to do next, but she's already disappeared into the ballroom.

The herald blares his trumpet once again. "Miss Myla Lewis *without escort*." My brain freezes. I have a feeling he's hinting at something, but can't guess what.

The giggles grow louder, the stares more disbelieving. I glance toward the front door, calculating how long it would take to sprint to my car.

Lincoln steps out from the crowd, offering me his arm. If I thought the giggles were loud, that's nothing compared to the outright gasps that now echo through the room. Smiling, I grip his arm tightly, feeling the warmth and solid muscle under my palm. We step into the ballroom.

"I think we shocked your nobility."

Lincoln grins. "They need to be shocked every so often; keeps them on their toes." He nods toward the dance floor. "Speaking of which…"

I stare at the synchronized lines of dancers on the floor. While a violinist plays a jig, the thrax all jump about in a medieval hoedown of complex movements.

"I don't know that dance, Lincoln. I'll sit this one out."

"Let's see what we can do about that." Lincoln snaps his fingers at the violinist. The musician instantly looks our way. The Prince makes a slicing motion across his throat. The lively jig transforms into a sultry tune.

"Ah, a slow dance." Lincoln leads me toward the floor. "Anyone can do that."

I stifle a grin. "That's a neat little trick."

He arches his brows. "It's good to be the Prince." We reach the center of the dance floor. "Shall we?" Bit by bit, Lincoln pulls my hands up to his neck; I weave my fingers through his wavy brown hair. Sliding his fingertips down my back, his hands settle about my waist. I shiver, remembering his touch in the stables, his kiss in the botanical gardens. My skin flushes. Our bodies sway to the slow tune.

A new sea of faces stare at us, but I only see the Prince's eyes and the play of light on his high cheekbones and strong jawline. The room feels empty, only us two. A smile tugs at Lincoln's full mouth. "I have a secret for you, Myla."

"Really? What is it?"

"I can't whisper it when you're all the way over there. Come closer."

I move my body nearer to his; we're almost touching. "How's this?" I tilt my head so he can speak in my ear.

"Closer."

Smiling softly, I press my body against his, sensing every firm contour of his chest and hips. We freeze. My breath catches. I scan Lincoln's face, feeling the intensity of his stare. His palms stroke the small of my back and we sway to the music once again. It's taking everything I have not to kiss him.

I tip my head to one side. "And now?"

Lincoln's breath tickles the shell of my ear. "A girl like you… In a dress like that…Should always dance this close."

I glimpse around the room, finding a lot of wide eyes, loud whispers, and not-so-polite pointing in my direction. The Earl of Acca looks red-faced and ready to burst with rage. Adair sits at a nearby table, her gaze locked on me and filled with loathing. "I'm not sure the thrax agree, Lincoln."

The Prince slides his hand up my back. His fingertips brush the bare skin on my shoulders. I bite my lip, stifling the urge to make an 'mmm' noise. The Prince sets his lips by my ear. "Time to start causing trouble, don't you–"

"Prince Lincoln!" It's Gianna, rushing toward us in a purple gown. "It's urgent! A demon patrol's under ambush!" As soon as there's an inch of room between us, Gianna inserts herself, grabbing Lincoln's hand and trying to pull him from the dance floor.

A man with a purple-crested tunic steps up to our group. "If it pleases your Highness, I'll keep the young lady company tonight."

"Thank you, Aldo." Lincoln turns to me. "If the patrol's under attack, I'll be unable to return." His face turns stony and solemn. "Making the trip to Earth takes some time."

"I understand." My body and mind feel numb. "Protect your people, of course." I watch him leave the room with Gianna, my forehead knit in confusion and not a little measure of shock. How did things change so quickly?

My skin prickles with awareness. Something about this doesn't feel quite right. I scan the ballroom, finding the Earl and Avery standing nearby. Both look downright happy now. That can't be good.

Before I can figure out what's happening, the slow music kicks back up to a furious jig. Grabbing my hand, Aldo spins me around the dance floor. As I twirl and sway, I'm handed off to a succession of men with yellow, blue, purple, and pink crests. Adair, Nita, and Keisha always seem to be nearby. Either those Great Ladies are the worst dancers in Antrum, or they're purposely stepping on the back of my dress every few seconds. This goes on for a while until I realize something.

It's very chilly in the ballroom...But just on my backside.

I reach around to test the back of my dress, only to find out that it's no longer there. I gasp. All the back panels of my gown are gone. Those little multi-colored creeps figured out how to pull out the stitches on my dress. No wonder they were playing around with it until a few hours before the ball. Adair, Nita, and Keisha stop dancing and start laughing their silly little heads off.

Twisting about, I try pulling the two side panels of my gown together to hide my bum, but there simply isn't enough fabric. The entire dance floor starts laughing. My face turns at least eighteen shades of red.

Cissy appears out of nowhere. Standing behind me to cover my backside, she sets her hands on my shoulders and shoves me toward a bank of windows along the far wall. Once there, she points to an arched panel of glass. "This is a door to the hedgerow maze. Flip up the lock and twist that handle."

I do as she instructs; we quickly step outside. Grabbing my hand, Cissy leads me to the mansion's opposite wing. There, in the safety of the shadows, she sets me onto a bench by one of the maze entrances.

"I'm so sorry, I didn't think." Cissy frowns.

My body feels numb. Did that really happen? Who pulls out the backs of dresses, honestly? "Don't beat yourself up. How could you have known they'd do something like that?"

"It's not that part, it's…" Cissy bites her bottom lip.

A chill crawls up my spine. "There's more to the story, isn't there?" I press my palms to my eyes, feeling my stomach tumble to my feet. "Lay it on me."

"Well, you know how your thrax underwear had black lines on it this time?"

"Yeeeeeeeeah."

"When yours were on, they spelled something in Latin."

"Latin?" *That lying, sneaky, backstabby Adair and her doofus father.*

"Yeah. I guess all thrax can speak it."

I open my fingers to look at her out of my left eye. "And what exactly is written on my ass right now?"

"Cunnus. C-U-N-N-U-S. I heard the thrax talking. I guess it means…"

"I know what it means." I rebury my head in my hands. "Cissy! You should have said something!"

"Okay, it totally looked strange. But you were so twitchy about the underwear. I didn't want another diplomatic snafu." Cissy crinkles her bottom lip.

I grip the edge of the bench like I'll snap it in two. Rage boils through my bloodstream. "I love you Cissy, but you've been nothing but a high maintenance nightmare for months now." I tick off her misdeeds on my fingers. "First, you go crazy with envy that Lincoln'll get my attention when you're waaaaaay too into Zekie. Second, you give me the silent treatment for what's basically no good reason. And third, you neglect to mention that I'm walking out the door with CUNNUS written on my butt. This hurts in a serious way and it's got to stop." My eyes flare red. "Not to mention the fact that it's ruined my last night with Lincoln."

Cissy's eyes grow large; she pops her hand over her mouth. "I'm soooo sorry, Myla." Her bottom lip quivers. "You're right; I've been a really bad friend." She sits down beside me on the bench. "Talk to me. Please. What can I do to make it up to you?"

I speak through gritted teeth. "Go back to the ball and have Zeke drive you home. I want to be alone for a while." A weight settles on my chest. Lincoln's off on demon patrol, somewhere on Earth. We had a fun night planned and now *this*. Man, do I ever need to kill something.

Cissy gnaws on her thumbnail. "I'm really sorry."

"I know." My voice drips with frustration and rage. "I need some time, that's all."

"Okay." She glances toward the mansion's distant lights. "If I ride home with Zeke, you're *really* fine driving Betsy back alone?"

"Yup." *Leave already.*

She takes a few hesitant steps away. "Call you tomorrow?"

I ball my hands into fists and nod. If I say anything else, I'll lose my temper for sure. Then Cissy'll have a black eye to match the one I gave Zeke all those years ago. Cissy's footsteps slop in the muddy grass, growing more distant with each stride. Soon they disappear altogether.

I jump to my feet. *That freaking sonuvabitch Earl and his dippy daughter, ruining everything.* The fires of wrath spark and coil inside me. Resting my weight on my right leg, I kick the bench with all my strength, breaking the wooden planks in two neat halves. That makes me feel better.

"Nice kick," says a familiar voice. I scan the shadows, seeing a figure step into the clearing: Lincoln.

I'm pretty sure I gasp. Loudly. What in blazes is he doing here?

"Hello, Myla." He rakes one hand through his brown hair. He left his crown back at the mansion. I have a feeling that means something, but I'm not sure what.

I grin from ear to ear. "Shouldn't you be on Earth right now?" My rage melts away, replaced by a tingly feeling in my stomach.

"Why ever would I do that?" He smiles, and the butterflies in my belly turn rowdy. "That was the worst fake emergency I've ever seen." Switching his stance, he scopes out my dress, or lack thereof. "Looks like there was more to their master plan, though." He lets out a puff of air. "I'll be honest. I didn't see *that* coming. Rather elaborate scheme, don't you think?" His gaze rakes over my backside, desire flaring in his eyes. "Not that I'm complaining."

The fire in his eyes rouses my lust demon. She purrs inside me, pumping heat through my veins. Then I remember what's written on my ass. Ugh.

"No fair peeking." I spin about, trying to cover my bum with what's left of my dress. Not that I mind Lincoln checking out my butt so much, but the CUNNUS sign is a little awkward. Okay, a *lot* awkward.

"They did us a favor, you know." He taps his temple. "That's why I played along."

I roll my eyes and chuckle. "I'm so sure."

"Think about it. We could have spent a few hours at the ball, irritating certain people. But this way, we can be alone." He steps closer. "It'll be some time before they figure out I'm not on Earth." His full mouth winds into a mischievous grin. My insides get all gooey. "Want to get in trouble?"

Yes and no. "I'm not going anywhere dressed like this, except home." No way am I walking around the mansion grounds with CUNNUS written on my bum. The entire thrax nation is lurking nearby, not to mention Cissy, Zeke, and his parents. Nuh-uh.

Lincoln purses his lips. "So, if you had something to wear, you'd be interested in a little stroll?"

"I would." Not sure where he's going with this.

Lincoln leans forward, pulling his velvet tunic over his head. "This should work fine." He only wears silver chain mail over black leather pants.

"What?" I poke at the long over-shirt with my finger. "You want me to wear that?"

"Why not? You'll be covered." He winks. "Mostly." Extending one hand, he offers me the garment.

I eye it carefully. It could actually fit me pretty well. I screw my mouth onto one side of my face. "Where would I change?"

"How about behind the hedges?" He tosses me the tunic, then turns his back to me. "I promise not to peek."

I jog beyond the wall of green and swap out my gown for Lincoln's tunic. I spin about, eyeing the fit. It looks good, but I'm showing a lot of bare leg.

I bite my lower lip. "I'm feeling a bit exposed, Lincoln." I kick off my heels. The ground chills my bare feet.

"Don't worry, you'll be fine."

I tiptoe past the line of hedges. There I see Lincoln standing in his black leather pants and…Nothing else. They hang low on his hips, showing off the vee of muscle below his stomach. Whoa. Desire zings through my system.

Lincoln eyes me from head to toe, his gaze lingering on my legs. "Now we're both a bit exposed."

I gesture to him in a 'hey you're not wearing a shirt' kind of way. "Are you sure that's a good idea?" It's not like half the thrax aren't partying nearby.

"Why not? I won't return to the ball." True, and I'm probably about to ruin his tunic to boot.

Grinning, Lincoln kicks the pile of chain mail with his bare foot. "Plus, this stuff weighs a ton." He links his arms across his chest. "And I was promised some trouble, remember?"

That settles it.

I bow slightly. "Alright, you got me. Where to?"

"I have a specific spot in mind." He laces his fingers with mine. A thrill of connection zings in my palm. "Let's go." His mismatched eyes twinkle in the moonlight. My tummy goes all tingly again.

At this point, I'd follow him pretty much anywhere. As we walk along, my heart thumps a mile a minute, my breathing turns low and shallow, and my lust demon definitely wants to come out and play. Lincoln steps into the hedgerow maze, picking his way with uncanny accuracy. We soon reach the fountain at the labyrinth's center. It's turned off now, so it looks like one large, still pool of water.

My brows arch in confusion. Out of all the places in the Ryder grounds, why would Lincoln take me here?

The Prince guides me to sit on the lip of the fountain. I hop up onto the edge, feeling the warm stone beneath me, my legs dangling below. Stepping back, Lincoln examines me, his eyes glistening with wonder.

"There." He hooks his thumbs into the waistband of his leather pants. "That's how you looked when I first saw you by the lake."

I nod. That's right; he found me fighting Doxy demons in the water. "So, that's why you brought me here?" I scratch my cheek. That's a little strange.

"Well, I think about that night all the time. Maybe too much." He shoots me a shy smile. "That sounds kind of crazy, doesn't it?"

"Depends." I move my mouth to one side, considering. "What's the interest?"

He rubs his neck with his hand. "It's a bit of a story, actually. I was chasing down some Doxy demons at the Ryder stables. I thought you were another thrax, tracking the same pack."

I mock-frown. "Another *guy*, of course."

He sets his hand on his bare chest. "Guilty as charged." He steps closer, my heart thuds harder in my rib cage. "You disappeared into the water. I thought you'd be drowned, but you came out fighting." He pauses before me, setting his warm hands on my bare knees. A thrill of heat whirls about my belly. His palms are calloused in all the right ways for a warrior.

With gentle pressure, Lincoln guides my legs apart. My heart rate goes through the roof. "You were fighting like a demon yourself, eyes glowing red in the darkness. And you were laughing." The Prince presses his firm body against my soft curves. My breath hitches. Damn, that feels good.

Lincoln notices my little gasp and smiles. "I saw you were a woman, a warrior." He leans in close, his mouth a breath above my own. "A force of nature. From that day on, I've thought of you, that night, and the water."

I inhale deeply, ready to say 'I never met anyone like you before, either. You make me crazy, too. In a good way.' I speak, but two words only: "I understand."

His voice comes out low and husky. "Good."

Our mouths meet, fierce and rough, every flick of the Prince's tongue driving more heat between my legs. My arms slide about Lincoln's bare shoulders, sensing his velvet-soft skin over solid muscle. Suddenly, I want to run my hands over every inch of his body. Lincoln's fingers press around my thighs, tracing the hem of my tunic. Desire rockets through me.

A thin bolt of lightning strikes the ground a few yards away. Low rolls of thunder shake the air.

My head snaps to the spot of grass where the lightning hit. It's a smoldering patch of black by the fountain's edge. "Did you see that?" This is the third time lightning strikes when I feel strong emotions around Lincoln. Even *I'm* having a hard time pretending it's a coincidence.

"No." Lincoln kisses my neck, then gently bites my earlobe. My legs go wobbly beneath me.

"But Lincoln, aren't you worried about the–"

He frames my face with his fingertips. "No." Fire burns in his mismatched eyes. "Kiss me, Myla."

A smile tugs at the edge of my mouth. *That's one helluva good idea.* I lean in and taste him, my need flaring hotter. Lincoln grips my waist, grinding our hips in rhythm. I feel his length, hard and ready, pressing against me through his leather pants. Each new thrust is a jolt of raw pleasure. The world collapses until there's nothing but our mouths, our bodies, and longing. He leaves in two days for Antrum. Who knows when I'll see him again, taste him again? *No time to wait.* My lust instinct runs wild, its power overriding anything else.

I slide off the lip of the fountain, landing on the cool grass. Looking down, I curl my hands around the bottom of my tunic, ready to strip it off.

That's when I feel it. Heat around my eyes. *My irises are glowing red.* That's never happened before when I've felt lust, only wrath. Although, come to think of it, I've never really felt lusty about a guy before.

I stop moving, careful to keep my head down. This is the dark side of inheriting both the classic Furor traits: wrath *and* lust. I stare at my fingers as they clutch the tunic's hem. "I think we should stop now." My breath is low and shaky. I'm no wiz at controlling my wrath, and I've been working at that all my life. Now lust? My first kiss was weeks ago. Tonight, I almost stripped down and did who-knows-what with Lincoln. That's not who I want to be.

Lincoln sets his hand on my arm. "What's wrong, Myla?"

I bite my bottom lip, careful to keep my head down and eyes hidden. Part of me wants to run for it, the other part wants to kiss him again. Badly. Stupid lust demon.

Lincoln sets his knuckle under my chin. With a gentle nudge, he tries to guide my gaze to his. I'm having none of it.

"That's not a good idea, Lincoln."

The Prince leans over, twisting so he can peep into my face. A smile tugs at the corner of his mouth. "Your eyes are changing. It's beautiful."

"It's my Furor lust side." My voice shakes a bit. "I've only ever felt wrath before."

He links his fingers with mine, his voice gentle. "Let's take it slowly, then. We have all the time in the world."

I exhale. "Yeah, that would be good."

He tilts his head to one side, listening. "Especially since they haven't sent out a search party yet." He grins. "Shall we find another way to cause trouble?"

"Sure." I give his fingers a squeeze. "How about exploring more of the maze?"

He kisses the tip of my nose. "*That* is a great idea."

CHAPTER TWENTY

A.

I sit in Betsy's shabby front seat, still wearing Lincoln's tunic. The evening sky is giving over to morning; a soft glow lines the horizon. I think through last night with Lincoln and smile my face off. We walked through the maze for hours, talking. I now know his favorite kind of music (jazz), least favorite word (moist), and nastiest all-time fear (invasion of Antrum). We debated which demons are hardest to fight, easiest to track, and have the worst personal hygiene. I explained to him at length why Frankenberry cereal rocks, Cissy and Zeke can get annoying, and reruns on the Human Channel are the bomb. Poor guy doesn't even have a phone, they're so nuts about security in Antrum, let alone television. I felt it my moral duty to educate him.

I bang the steering wheel with my fist. Damn, I forgot to ask him how he knows Walker! Note to self: ask that next time for sure.

Twisting the key in the ignition, I rev the engine. Betsy doesn't buck or cough smoke as I drive off. I grin. Sometimes, everything goes your way.

The good luck continues once I get home. I tiptoe around the back of the house and fiddle with the bathroom window. It slides open without a hitch. *Awesome.* I shimmy inside and sneak into my bedroom. Slipping off Lincoln's tunic, I throw on a gray nightie and slide into bed.

I'm feeling quite proud of my sneaky self when my bedroom door swings open. Mom's outline appears in the darkened threshold. "Where have you been, Myla Lewis?"

She's using my full name. I'm in trouble.

"I went to a party with Cissy." I fluff my pillow under my head. "I know I should've told you."

"Yes, you should have."

"Now I'm back and safe. I have school tomorrow. Can we talk about it in the morning?"

Mom pauses, then lets out a long breath. "I suppose so." She wags her finger at me. "But you're in big trouble, young lady."

Her threat bounces off my wall of inner bliss. "You got it, Mom. We'll talk in the morning." I close my eyes and drift off to sleep.

In my dreams, I return to the Gray Sea. A circle of white fire blazes on the sand by my feet. Mom's figure rises from within the flames. The walls of our living room build around her.

The fire flares brighter and vanishes. The sand sculpture turns into real life. The living room looks exactly as it does today, only the couch is less threadbare, the carpet's plusher, and the walls show fewer cracks. Mom piles bolts of black fabric onto the couch, a terrycloth robe wrapped loosely around her. I sigh. She's already looking like a shabby, house-bound version of her former self. Sadness creeps into my bones. Senator Lewis is gone.

Someone knocks on our front door.

"Just a second." Mom walks up to the door and swings it open. Xavier stands outside in his gray suit. A muscle twitches along his neck.

Mom waves him inside. "Xavier! Come in. Have a seat." She moves a bolt of fabric off the couch and steps into the kitchen. "Do you want some ice cream? I don't have anything as good as the old days, but I found this." She stands in the kitchen doorway, squinting at a tiny package in her hands. "They're called 'Frozen Milk Product Bars.'"

"No, thank you." Xavier's eyes stay glued to the floor. Something about him is off, but I can't put my finger on it.

"You're right. I don't know what I was thinking." Mom steps back into the kitchen. "By the way, my service paperwork was approved. I'm officially a seamstress as of today."

"I heard. Quasis with a service can't be terminated. You're safe now."

"Thanks to you and your people." Mom steps back into the living room, pulling her robe tighter around her.

Xavier inhales a ragged breath. "We need to talk, Camilla." The hollow tone in his voice sets my teeth on edge.

Mom's face creases in confusion. "Sure, won't you sit down?" She gestures to the empty spot on the couch.

Xavier shakes head. "You were right all along. About Armageddon, the Oligarchy, everything." He glances toward Mom, his eyes dim. Could he be sick? I have the overwhelming urge to rush to his side, take his temperature and pat his hand. Poor guy.

Mom's forehead knits in confusion. "Why bring that up now?"

"I should have backed you up. I want you to know that."

Mom shrugs. "If you'd agreed with me, it wouldn't have made any difference. The Senate didn't believe a word I had to say, just like you predicted. They almost had me impeached." Her voice cracks when she says that last phrase. "You did what you thought was right, too."

"No, I didn't." Xavier's left hand balls into a fist and he punches his leg. "I wasn't thinking about right and wrong. I just *felt* things. I felt the need to protect you."

I purse my lips and frown. Hmm. That's an awful lot of lovey-dovey talk out of Xavier. I turn my attention to Mom, who's doing way too much blushing and retying her robe. Definitely some attraction there.

Xavier steps closer. "This shouldn't happen to someone like me."

Mom looks up from her robe, her head cocked to one side in her 'confused look.' She isn't the only one. I'm stumped as well. What's all this 'someone like me' stuff? He's a common angel, right?

Mom sets her hand on her throat. "What're you talking about?"

Blue light flares in Xavier's eyes. "I'm an archangel."

I stagger back a few steps, my body reeling from the shock. A freaking archangel? They're rarer than greater demons, and totally badass.

"An archangel? But there was nothing in your record."

"That's why I came to Purgatory. Few know me here. After the first few millennia of celebrity, I've chosen a low profile." He closes his blue eyes. Points of white light sparkle around his shoulders. Great golden wings appear on Xavier's back.

Mom's fingertips brush the long gleaming feathers. Her voice is low and breathy. "So beautiful."

Xavier shivers and opens his eyes. The wings disappear.

"An archangel." Mom slides her hands into the pockets of her robe. "I didn't know there were any left."

I sniff. What Mom doesn't know about angels and demons is a *lot*. A greater demon can be born or made. Armageddon became one when he was crowned the King of Hell. But archangels? Limited supply from the beginning of time. They're so old and powerful, they rarely hang out with mortals at all. Most common angels never meet one. My eyes almost bug out of my head.

I can't believe Mom worked with an archangel. *Cool.*

Xavier sets his hand on the living room wall, leaning onto it for support. "There aren't many of us. I led our armies in the Battle of the Gates, the one that drove demons from Heaven. Armageddon was the general on the opposing side." A sad look washes across his face. "He was a common demon then."

I remember Xavier and Armageddon in the Senate committee meeting. That pair hate each other's guts. I shake my head in disbelief. They fought in the War of the Gates, a thousand years ago. That's one long grudge.

Mom examines his face for what feels like years. "Why are you telling me this now?"

Xavier smiles. "I knew you'd ask that question." His grin slowly fades. "I must leave, but not before I say something, just once." He steps up to Mom, gingerly setting his hand against her cheek. She leans into his touch. "I've been around a long time. I've seen mountains form, stars appear, oceans give birth to life. I've witnessed wars and weddings, mercy and hatred, greed and sacrifice. In all that time, I've never loved a woman." His fingers curl, drawing her mouth toward his. Xavier's lips brush hers once, gently. "Until you."

Holy shit.

I knew there was a flirty spark between them, but this? Whoa. And the way Mom stares at him all slack-jawed and wide-eyed, it's pretty clear she didn't see this coming either.

Xavier lowers his hand, turns on his heel, and walks away.

Mom steps into his path, blocking his exit. Her eyes take on a steely look, the one I know means she won't back down. "Where are you going?"

He stares past her and opens the front door. Mom sets her body firmly in the threshold. "Where, Xavier?"

"Let me go." He stands tall and unflinching, every inch of him filled with stony resolve.

Mom searches his face, her eyes opening super-wide. "Wait a minute. Why wasn't I killed in Armageddon's War? Why was I–of all people–given a service?" She closes the door behind her and glares at Xavier.

"That's not important, Camilla. All that matters is your safety."

My mind whirls. Mom once said that someone made a great sacrifice to keep us safe. At the time, I was pretty sure that mystery someone was my father. Now here's Xavier, doing something huge for Mom's safety.

My skin erupts in gooseflesh. *Could Xavier be my dad?*

The gears of my mind stall out. Mom said my dad was Tim, and whatever other faults she has, she doesn't lie. Hide the truth and strong-arm everyone else into doing the same thing? Sure. Outright lie? No. At least, that's what I used to think.

Mom steps closer to Xavier, her bottom lip trembling. "What did you do, Xavier?" She grips his hands in her own. "WHAT DID YOU DO?!"

Xavier stares at their clasped hands, his eyes glistening. "I traded your life for mine. As of midnight tonight, Armageddon takes me to Hell."

Mom sets her hand on her throat. Her breaths come in rough gasps. "When are you coming back?"

"I'm not, Camilla."

"But the things they'll do to you. You can't go." Her face hardens. "I never agreed to this. I won't allow it. They can kill me instead."

Her words hit me like so many stones. When mortals go to Hell, demons consume their souls. But Archangels heal from any injury. If Xavier goes to Hell, it's for one reason only: *an eternity of pain.* I shiver. The things they'll do to him, indeed.

Xavier wags his head from side to side. "It's all done and irreversible. I made the bargain with Armageddon the day he invaded Purgatory. A ghoul will act as your guardian when I've gone. His name is WKR-7. You can trust him, he's part archangel."

Mom grips her hands at her waist. "There must be something we can do."

"No, I made my choice and I'm at peace with it." He looks at her, his blue eyes filled with love and longing. "Let me go, Camilla."

Mom scans his face. Her breathing slows. "Not a chance." Stepping closer, she rests her hands on his shoulders. He doesn't move nearer, so she arches her bare feet to stand on tiptoe. Their mouths are an inch apart. "I love you too, Xavier." Little by little, she sets her lips on his. He doesn't respond to the kiss.

Mom pulls back. "What is it?"

"This will only make things harder for you."

"Nonsense." She slowly runs her tongue along his bottom lip. "Be with me."

My eyebrows rise. Damn, Mom. That's quite the move. Who knew she had a little lust demon in her after all?

The archangel returns her kisses slowly, tentatively. Mom's fingers slide to Xavier's shoulders, wind around his lapels, and push his suit-coat to the floor. He groans, grips her waist, and pulls her against him, hard. Their kiss turns hungry and wild. Xavier unties the belt of her robe.

Mom takes his hand, pulls him into her bedroom and closes the door.

I nod once to myself. I am so having a 'who's my daddy' discussion with Mom in the morning. This is ridiculous.

The image of Mom and Xavier disappears into the sand. Another scene rises in its place: our front doorstep at night.

Mom opens the front door, her robe wrapped tightly around her. "Hello? Anyone out there?" She scans the yard, her face pale with worry.

I grit my teeth. I know who's she's waiting for: Armageddon. I glance through the opened door to our living room's wall clock. 5 AM. The King of Hell was due at midnight.

Mom watches the empty yard for a time, the muscles along her jawline taut. Insects chirp in the darkness. A soft breeze rustles the browning leaves on our front-lawn trees. After a few minutes, Mom lets out a long sigh, the edges of her mouth softening.

My body relaxes as well. It's almost morning. Maybe Armageddon isn't coming after all.

Cracking her neck from side to side, Mom turns back to the house. She takes a step toward the door and freezes, every muscle in her body turning rigid.

I gasp, knowing that particular movement all too well. Mom was hit with greater demon aura, and that means one thing. Armageddon is here.

The King of Hell steps out of the line of trees. "Good morning, Camilla. I've come for Xavier." I fight the urge to jump into the dreamscape and kick the crap out of him, or at least try to. *Get off my lawn, asshole.*

Mom spins about slowly, her face still as stone. She meets Armageddon's gaze head-on. "You can't have him."

The King of Hell strolls up the walk to our house, pausing at the foot of the steps. His wide mouth twists with a sneer as he eyes her from head to toe. He says one word in a rumbling voice: "Xavier."

The archangel steps out the front door and stands beside Mom. She grips his hand. "Don't do it, Xavier. Just get out of here." The archangel shoots her a sad smile. After that, he slowly walks to Armageddon's side.

My body stiffens with shock and rage. This can't be happening.

The King of Hell sets his three-knuckled hand on Xavier's shoulder. "Let's see those wings you hid from everyone for so long."

Xavier stands stoic and still.

Armageddon's long red tongue flickers over his smooth black lips. "Perhaps if you were in a little more pain, it would break up your concentration." He grips Xavier's arm and snaps it with a loud CRACK. The archangel's face writhes with pain; his golden wings appear.

My anger hits the breaking point. *Verus and her dreamscapes can kiss my ass; I'm not standing by.* My tail arcs over my shoulder; my body snaps into battle stance. I race toward dreamscape, the warm sand sliding beneath my bare feet, my gaze locked on Armageddon. *You are so going down, buddy.*

I get within a few feet of the King of Hell when my body slams into what feels like a brick wall. It's some kind of force field, keeping the past away from the present. My back teeth lock. All I've accomplished is to give myself a better view of Armageddon's gloating smile and Xavier's overwhelming agony.

"Ah, I remember those wings." Armageddon chuckles. "You showed them when you rallied the angels and drove my army from Heaven." The King of Hell rounds on Mom. "Does it pain you to watch me hurt him?"

Mom glares at Armageddon, her arms folded over her chest.

I press my palms against the invisible wall. Every cell in my body wants to break through and stand beside her. *Stay strong, Mom.*

The King of Hell twists Xavier's broken arm. The archangel sucks in a breath, gritting his teeth. Mom's eyes slowly bead with tears. Mine do, too.

"It *does* pain you." Armageddon's mouth bends into an impossibly-large smile. "Good. Because I'll be doing this for all eternity. Whenever you think of the Senate or your murdered family or sewing one of those silly robes, I want you think of Xavier and how I'm torturing him at that exact moment. Just for you."

I slam my fists into the force field; it doesn't budge. I need to kill Armageddon, save Xavier, and help my mom. *Let me in!*

Mom's shoulders slump, worry lines appear around eyes. I notice a few gray hairs I hadn't seen before.

I freeze in place, unable to do anything but watch her sorrow beyond the invisible barrier. Mom steps back, leaning against the outer wall of the house for support. She sets her hand on her rib cage and I can almost hear her heart crack with grief. This is when the weepy, over-worrying version of my mother came to be. *I'm so sorry, Mom.* I never dreamed this is what happened. I understand now.

Armageddon waves his long and bony hand. "Goodbye, seamstress." He and Xavier disappear. For a moment, Mom stands still on the front stoop, and then she crumples onto the concrete landing, her shoulders heaving with sobs.

Mom's body turns back into sand before dissolving into the desert floor. The rest of the scene does the same. The dreamscape ends. Somehow, I know this is the last one.

For what feels like eons, I stare at the Gray Sea, watching the rolling dunes of charcoal-colored sand touch a blue and gray sky. The wind howls through me; sulphur chokes my lungs. I could care less.

One thought keeps churning through my mind: at this moment, somewhere in Hell, Xavier's being tortured. All because he saved my mother's life; my life too. Even though I'm deep asleep, I know my face streams with tears.

CHAPTER TWENTY-ONE

A

I wake up to the electronic howl of my alarm clock. Bit by bit, I open my eyes and stretch. My pillow's damp against my cheek. That was one hell of a dreamscape. How do I even *begin* to talk to Mom about this?

My backpack's propped against my bedroom wall. I stare at it for a moment. This chat should wait until after school, for both our sakes. I take a deep breath, throw on some sweats and walk into the kitchen. Mom sits at the table, a steaming mug of coffee in her hands. Her mouth is a thin line.

I forgot. I'm in deep trouble.

"Good morning." I speed across the room and pretend to be super-interested in the cabinet on the opposite wall.

Mom's fingernails tap her porcelain mug. "What happened to you last night? This had better be good."

I remember Lincoln's kisses and smile. *It was 'wake up your lust demon' good.*

"Like I said last night, Cissy and I went to a party." I move cereal boxes back and forth on a shelf. "It was at the Ryder mansion. Things ran late. I didn't want you to worry, so I didn't tell you everything about it." I cross my fingers and set them on my belly. *Please let her move on without asking the obvious question.*

"And what *exactly* didn't you mention?" My shoulders slump. She asked the obvious question.

I start organizing the cereal boxes in alphabetical order, careful to keep my back toward my mother. If she sees my superguilty face, I'm done for. I steel my shoulders. "Cissy and Zeke were the only other quasis there."

Mom gasps. "So, who *was* at the Ryder mansion?"

My face screws up into the mutha of all winces. "Thrax." Here it comes.

A thunk sounds as Mom slams her coffee cup onto the table. "Not that thrax boy you met at Zeke's some months back?" What a memory she has. She must keep a list of every angel and thrax I've ever laid eyes on. "Did he touch you?"

I can't help but smile. "We kind of touched each other, Mom. And it was Prince Lincoln. He's the same boy I met at Zeke's party."

"Noooo!"

Mom's scream rattles my spine. I grip a box of cereal so hard, some of it spills onto the counter. I force myself to breathe slowly. *Remember what she's been through, Myla.* My voice comes out calm and level. "Verus showed me why you worry, Mom. I know you're scared someone will drag me off like Armageddon did to Xavier. But Lincoln would never do anything like that."

Mom's voice is raw and low. "Verus told you NOTHING." She rushes over and grips my arm, spinning me about.

I inhale a sharp breath. "Calm down, Mom. You're scaring me."

"Please don't let it be happening." She grips my face between her palms, forcing me to stare directly into her eyes. Her face contorts with panic. "Sweet Satan, no!" She releases me and staggers back a few feet, her hand at her throat.

My shoulders knot with fear and frustration. I've never seen Mom act this way before. Maybe she's having some kind of an episode, like a heart attack or stroke? I rush to her side. "What is it, Mom? Are you okay?"

Mom covers her mouth with her left hand, her right points to our bathroom. "Go see for yourself."

My body numbs with shock. I have never, ever seen Mom this extreme before. The skin along my neck prickles. "Okay, Mom. I'll look. It'll be fine." I guide her to the couch, and then walk into the bathroom.

As I step across the ratty living room carpet, the world seems to move in slow motion. My heartbeat thuds in my ears. Every breath feels forced and tight. *Don't let Mom freak you out. This is another nothing she's worrying about, just like all the rest.* I step into the bathroom and glance at my image in the mirror.

Now it's my turn to start hyperventilating.

Shaking my head, I blink over and over, testing my senses. But the image in the glass does not change. I claw at the reflection, trying to scrape away what I see. It can't be right:

My eyes have always been chocolate brown. This morning, they're both turquoise blue. *Angel blue.*

Unholy Hell.

I stagger back into the living room. "What's going on, Mom?" My mind speeds through possibilities, each one worse than the last. Did Gianna cast a spell on me at the ball? Is my lust demon short-circuiting my eye sockets? Panic zings through my nervous system. Whatever this is, it is B-A-D.

Mom leaps to her feet. "Walker, where are you?" She paces the grimy carpet, screaming for Walker like she'll bust her windpipe. My pulse quickens.

A portal opens by the front door. Walker steps through, his long black robes swaying. "This is highly irregular, Camilla. What do you require?"

Mom points at me, her arm trembling. "Look at her, Walker."

Lowering his dark cowl, Walker steps to my side. His black button eyes stare directly into mine for a moment, the ghost of a smile winding his mouth. "We knew it would happen sometime, Camilla."

I exhale a long breath. Whatever weirdness this is, it doesn't scare Walker. I scan his face, seeing a combination of excitement, concern, and pride. If this isn't a totally bad thing, what is it?

Mom rounds on him, her eyes flaring red. "No, Walker. We did *not* know this would happen. In case you haven't noticed, I've lived *my life* to avoid this day."

Hmm. Mom's in fury mode while Walker is concerned but pleased. This mystery morning is getting downright annoying. I set my fists on my hips. "Will someone please tell me what's going on?"

Walker turns to Mom. He speaks in his own version of the 'I'm so very very caaaaaaalm' voice. "Camilla, I'm unable to break my vow of silence without your permission. May I have it so I can explain things to Myla?"

"Absolutely not!" A muscle twitches by Mom's mouth. "Don't say a word, Walker. Just portal her out of here." Mom's words remind me of something she said in my dreamscape last night. *Don't do it, Xavier. Just get out of here.*

I freeze.

Memories whirl through my brain. The casual way Mom invited Tim for drinks. The calm words she used to describe their falling-out. The lack of kisses, goo-goo eyes, and any flirty energy between them, period.

So not like Xavier. A shiver rattles my shoulders. Suddenly, it's obvious why my eyes are angel blue. *Xavier is my father and Mom lied to me in a big way.* My blood boils with anger. I turn to my mother, my voice low and creepy-calm.

"Tim is not my father. You two never even kissed, did you?"

Mom's voice catches in her throat. "That's not true." She half-collapses onto the couch. "TIM-29 is your father, Myla."

Rage whirls up my spine. *Enough already.* "I know you're lying to me, Mom. Xavier *is* my father."

She chokes out one word. "No."

My blue eyes narrow. "Let's see, then. All quasis have brown eyes that flare red. Angel eyes glow blue." I give my chin a few dramatic taps. "My eyes turn red when I'm in wrath-mode. If my father's an angel, then they'll glow blue when I feel love."

Mom clutches the couch's frayed armrests. "Myla, don't do anything silly."

That settles it. Closing my eyes, I picture Lincoln standing at the Ryder fountain, describing how I burst out of the lake, killing Doxy demons and laughing. *From that day on, I've thought of you.* I remember how his mismatched eyes glistened, how delicious his mouth felt on mine. A pleasant chill settles onto my skin. Odd electric sensations zing about my fingertips. I open my eyes once again.

"Myla, stop!" Mom gasps. "No one can see you like this."

Mom lectures on and on about hiding my glowing blue eyes, but I barely hear her. Instead, my attention's locked on the now-pleasant feeling of power that lingers around my fingers. The electric sensation expands and changes until it's a thousand tiny voices calling to me, some singing, others laughing, all of them aching to be brought to life. It's hypnotic. I glance around the room; Mom and Walker are lost in conversation. Only I can hear the little voices.

I'm dimly aware that Walker sits down beside Mom. Some of his words break through the haze in my brain. "Camilla, there's no point pretending any more. Her eyes are glowing bright blue."

Mom lets out a ragged breath. "Yes, Myla. Your father is Xavier. You were right about Tim. We never even held hands."

It's the confession of my lifetime, but I only half-hear her. My focus is still drawn to those little voices and the power behind them. I raise my hand before my face, flipping my palm front to back, over and over. My mouth seems to speak without my willing it. "I have the blood of an angel, demon, and human in me." Memories flip through my mind: using the baculum with Lincoln...Understanding Latin during the Scala initiation...Lightning strikes when I felt strong emotions...And my eyes turning blue after kissing someone with angel blood.

The voices grow louder, wrapping my consciousness in their calming words and lovely music. Their desire to take physical form becomes almost overwhelming. Suddenly, it's clear who they are: igni.

And who I am as well.

My voice comes out low and dreamy. "I'm the Scala Heir." At those words, an igni materializes before my palm: a single small bolt of white light that shimmers with beauty and strength. Part of me knows I should be terrified at the sight. Instead, I'm calmed as more and more igni appear by my hand, and then swim around my palm like a school of fish.

Around me, the world fades into a dreamy haze as the igni multiply, soaring and diving around each other in their dance around my fingertips. Their many songs unify into one voice, taking on clear words and meaning. They sing of souls soaring to a Heavenly afterlife that's beyond even the angels. They soothe me with calm words, helping me to accept their power and light. And they warn me: 'now you must discover how and why your powers hidden for so long. Your next step will then be clear.'

After that, they all disappear.

I lower my hand, staggering backwards until I lean against the living room wall. My breathing is ragged and tight. I can't seem to suck in enough air. My body turns numb with shock. Did that really happen? I force in slow breaths until my mind clears. The living room comes back into focus. Mom and Walker sit side by side on the couch, neither one moving.

Minutes pass until Walker bows his head, his voice solemn and low. "The Scala Heir."

Mom grips her hands at her waist, her eyes wild with panic. "It's not too late, Myla. Maxon Bane has lived almost a thousand years; he may live a thousand more. You always had the potential to become the Scala Heir, but you did *not* need to be awakened, let alone angelbound. Now that it's happened, you can still hide. Go anywhere. Run. Now. No one will know that you've changed."

I stare into her red-rimmed eyes, emotions battling inside me. There's frustration that she's still treating me like a child. Anger at having been lied to for a lifetime. Pity for everything she went through with the war and Xavier. Fear at what will happen now that I've changed into the Scala Heir. Tension crawls up my body.

One thing is for certain: no matter what path the future takes, I'm in for a long fight.

At that realization, my mouth rounds with the smallest of smiles. A fight like that? Sounds like a challenge. And I'm always up for a challenge.

Mom leans forward, resting her elbows on her knees. "Did you hear me Myla? You have to hide. Anywhere."

Stepping away from the wall, I move to stand before Mom and Walker. My voice comes out low and strong. "That's not your decision anymore, Mom. From now on, *I* make the choices about my future. And to do that, I need some answers." I remember what the igni told me: I must understand why and how all this happened.

Mom slumps further into the couch; her eyes lock on the floor.

I kneel before her, taking her hand in mine. "How long have you known I was the Scala Heir?"

Mom looks away, biting her bottom lip. My eyes narrow. I'm not taking 'no' for an answer this time.

I give her hand a squeeze. "I understand what happened with Xavier and Armageddon. Verus showed me in a dreamscape last night. I know you're frightened about losing me the way you lost my father. But I need you to be strong now, like you were as a Senator. I need you to answer my questions. How long have you known I was the Scala Heir?"

Mom's lower lip trembles. "After Armageddon took Xavier, I never saw your father again. Three months later you were born."

"Three months?" I wince. "That can't be right."

Mom inhales a shaky breath. "The Scala Heir develops faster than other children until age three. It's the earliest they can transfer souls. I knew you were the Heir before you were born." I imagine Mom in a post-war world, pregnant and alone. I let out a long sigh. At least she had Walker. I turn to him.

"Did you also know I was the Scala Heir?"

"Yes. Your mother told me." He sets a comforting hand on her shoulder. "I'd sworn to your father to protect her and follow her orders in all things."

I nod softly. Walker probably took some kind of sacred angelic oath. Those are unbreakable. I swing my attention back to Mom. "And that's when you decided to hide me?" She must have been terrified that my true identity would be revealed. No end to the list of nasties that would want to control me. Or in Armageddon's case, kill me.

"I tried to conceal you." She smiles. "But from the time you were little, it was clear you had your father's nature. Battle-ready. Fearless. Drawn to demon fighting like steel to a magnet. You were always sneaking into Arena matches, keeping notes on different types of demons and how best to kill them." Her brown eyes brighten with pride. "Your father cast the last demons from Heaven, you know."

I smile. "Yes, I learned that in a dreamscape."

Crouching back on my heels, I try letting the truth soak in: my father's an archangel. That's a mind blower. I would've been thrilled to *meet* an archangel in my lifetime, let alone be related to one. And now I'm the only child that Xavier has fathered in all of eternity. Whoa. Mom starts to speak, interrupting my thoughts.

"I needed to keep you safe. From Armageddon. From the ghouls. From everyone. I knew what they'd do if they found you." Her hands tremble beneath mine.

I give her fingers another gentle squeeze. "That's *not* going to happen." Fear rattles in my stomach. Honestly, that could totally happen. *Focus, Myla.* Remember what the igni said. You need answers and sitting around scared won't get you any. I refocus on my task, my brain whirring through information. "Besides you and Walker, who else knows I'm the Heir?"

Mom lets out a long breath. "Verus. She saw it in a vision."

I bite my thumbnail. "Everyone calls Verus the oracle angel."

Walker shakes his head. "Her visions don't always come to pass. Sometimes she fights against a particular future. In other cases, she works to ensure it happens."

Rising to my feet, I plunk into the high-back leather chair across from the couch, my forehead knit in concentration. With all my energy, I sift through everything I've learned. "I don't get it. The angels attend Arena matches. Why didn't they have me awakened and angelbound before?"

"The awakening part is fairly easy." Mom forces a smile. "You breathe in angelic stardust and it's done. But you didn't get near angels very often, except for Arena matches. And Walker guarded you there."

My eyes grow wider with understanding. "So that's why you had a coronary whenever I was called to serve. If I got too close to an Angel, one could toss stardust my way and activate my Scala powers." I picture the white cloud at the Adair's Scala initiation ceremony. The air tasted so sweet. That was the moment I awakened.

Walker steeples his fingers under his chin. "On the other hand, being angelbound is incredibly hard to do."

Mom nods. "You can't fake your way around it with magic or angelic influence. The Heir must feel genuine, intense love for someone with angel blood. Most often it's a parent." She shoots me a sad smile. "But you never met your father."

I half-roll my eyes and let out a high-pitched 'ooooh.' "So *that's* why you didn't want me anywhere near angels, thrax, or the Scala." It seemed completely insane at the time, but actually, she had a pretty good plan going there. Most likely, I'd never have gotten angelbound if I hadn't met Lincoln.

Mom's mouth forms a thin line. "Out of all the threats against us, angels were the worst. I lived in terror that you'd get angelbound." She wags her head. "The way you hated thrax, I thought you'd be safe at that winter tournament. You loathed Prince Lincoln in particular. Then when you released demons at a royal dinner, I thought it was to antagonize him further."

My mouth curls into a sneaky grin. "No, Lincoln was my partner in crime on that one." Thinking about him gives me a nice jolt of positive energy. "So years go by, then the angels raise the question of the Scala Heir."

Mom groans. "Yes, Verus asked my permission to do that. Like a fool, I agreed. I figured some simpleton would crawl out of the woodwork for the title, and that could only deflect attention from you."

My head tilts to one side. So, Verus set all that up. I'll have to come back to the topic of her sneakiness later. "I get why you did it, Mom. But the ceremony awakened *me*, not Adair. My powers should've started after that." I remember the lightning whenever I felt strong emotions for Lincoln. *Hey there, I was the one who set off those lightning strikes.* It was all Scala power. Excitement balloons in my chest. "And that's exactly what happened. I think I set off a lightning bolt or two."

Walker clicks his tongue. "If the ceremony didn't name Adair, it was an amazing forgery. Her eyes changed blue in front of everyone."

Mom rubs her forehead with her fingertips. "When Walker told me about it, I hoped there were two Scala Heirs." She exhales slowly. "Wishful thinking."

I close my eyes. *Think, Myla.* My brain nervously churns through facts about Adair. A minute passes before my eyes pop open again. "Gianna."

Mom leans back on the couch. "Who's Gianna?"

I scratch my temple, my mind still whirring. "She's a Great Lady of the thrax who's a powerful conjurer. The House of Striga is known for witchcraft; they breed enchanted horses. Gianna stood right beside Adair throughout the ceremony, whispering to her. I bet she was casting spells to change Adair's eyes. And then to fake her Scala powers."

"So foolish." Mom's mouth melts into a disapproving frown. "Lady Adair knew all along that she wasn't the real Scala Heir."

"She's the type." I stare hard at my palms, trying to think through what's an already unthinkable morning. A new question emerges in my mind. "Did Verus also ask your permission to send me dreamscapes?"

"Yes, I appreciated that she wanted to help us rebuild our relationship."

"It *was* helpful." I grimace. *Here it comes.* Time to revisit the whole question of Verus and her sneakiness. I drum my fingers on my knees. "Let's recap here. Verus talks *you* into letting me go to Adair's initiation, but *I'm* the one who's actually awakened.

Then, she gets you to agree to dreamscapes and, sure, those help us get along, but they *also* prepare me to become the Scala Heir. What's up with that?" My stomach churns with anger and frustration. Mom, Walker, Verus…Who *hasn't* been lying and manipulating me for years?

Mom purses her lips, choosing her words carefully. "Angels don't lie exactly, but they do tell just enough truth to achieve their goals. Take the initiation ceremony. Verus said a fake Scala Heir would be falsely awakened and angelbound. She didn't say you *would* be awakened as well."

Walker groans. "Angels. I'll never understand them."

Mom rises, walks over to my chair, and takes my hands in hers. "I've been so overwrought, I haven't said I'm happy for you. If you're angelbound to Lincoln, that means you love him, deeply." She pulls me to my feet, wrapping me in a warm hug.

"It does, doesn't it?" I rest my head on her shoulder. "Thanks, Mom."

Wow…a semi-normal mother-daughter interaction. Sure, it's about my part-angel demon-fighting maybe-boyfriend, but it's still progress.

Mom retakes her seat on the couch. I curl back into my chair as well. "Let me get this straight." I tick off the chain of events on my fingertips. "First, I'm awakened and get some basic Scala abilities, like setting off lightning strikes. Second, I get angelbound to Lincoln. Now my powers are stronger, like how I can create igni around my hand. Then, third–"

Mom finishes my thought. "Once Maxon dies, his powers pass on to you." She rubs her forehead. "You'll become the full Scala."

I inhale a breath so deeply, I feel it in my toes. Full Scala. That means everyone in the five realms will be *fully* focused on controlling *me*. Suddenly hiding out doesn't seem like such a sucky idea. I turn to Mom, ready to say just that, when the igni's advice reappears in my mind: I need to understand everything before deciding what to do. I press my palms into my eyes, trying to think, think, think. My brain almost hurts from this much concentrating.

I frown. "There are still some things I don't get. Lincoln said angels invited the thrax to Purgatory; they'd never have left their homeland otherwise. This may sound crazy, but I wonder if they wanted me to meet Lincoln. If they wanted me to be angelbound to *him*."

Mom bobs her head. "Could be. Although, it was only a matter of time before you fell for a quasi boy." She smiles. "I always hoped it would be that Zeke Ryder, but Cissy got him first."

Okay, I just threw up a little in the back of my throat. Quasi boys? Zeke Ryder?

I shoot a plaintive glance at Walker. He's biting his lips together, trying not to laugh.

"Trust me, Mom. I wasn't about to snuggle up with a quasi boy any time this millennia. It's too convenient that right after Verus puts out a call for the Scala Heir, she orders a gaggle of thrax boys to park their carcasses at our doorstep."

Walker nods. "I'm sure Verus wanted you to connect with Lincoln. You're too perfectly matched."

True. But what does that *mean*? Anxiety tightens my skull. I rub my temples with my fingertips, trying to release the pressure as well as some new insights. Finally, some appear. "That leaves two big questions. Why Lincoln? And why now?"

"Why Lincoln?" Mom pulls a few frayed threads from the arm-rest. "Angels are always hatching secret plans to fix the universe, Verus especially. If you're in one of her visions–and that vision says you must love Lincoln–you'll never know the reason until it's too late."

I nod. That sounds true. Incredibly depressing that I may be Verus's next vision-victim, but true.

Walker folds his long arms into his longer, loopy sleeves. "And why now? Perhaps the angels want to launch a war. It's no secret they want ghouls out of Purgatory. Having a Scala with a back-bone would help them in their fight."

"To battle the ghouls, angels would attack an unarmed foe." Mom frowns. "That they'd never do." Her jaw drops slightly. "But they *would* prepare for a counter-attack if they thought demons were about to invade."

I picture the angels giving advice to our headmaster, training my gym class and sending me one awesome dragon-scale fighting suit, free of charge. I point to Mom. "That's it. The demons must be preparing to invade. Soon." The moment the words leave my mouth, it's like the temperature in the living room drops below zero. Another war? I've seen what Armageddon can do. Fear twists in my belly. This is a new level of suck.

Walker lets out a frustrated sigh. "They've been saying that since Armageddon's War ended, and it's never happened."

"I don't know Walker, there's been strange stuff at school." I wince. "Extra inspections. Teachers being attacked or even killed. It's bad out there." I picture the pile of ash that once was Miss Thing and shiver.

Mom taps her cheek. "We need an exit plan."

I raise my hands to shoulder height, palms forward. "I won't run and hide." Despite my best intentions to sound badass, the words come out as more of a question.

"Think about it, Myla." Mom rises to her feet. "Only angels have blue eyes like yours. If you stay here, the ghouls and demons will figure out who you are, fast. They'll try to control you. Unlike Adair, you don't have an army nearby for protection. It's me and Walker, that's it."

I can't help but smile. Something in that speech reminded me of the Senator Lewis I saw in so many dreamscapes. I slump into my high-back chair, thinking through this crazy morning: finding out Xavier is my father, that I have Scala powers, how Verus connected me with Lincoln, and that demons could invade Purgatory any minute. I suppose I now know what happened to me and why, as the igni instructed me to do. Grim determination seeps into my body. Unfortunately, my next step is all too obvious.

Mom moves closer, her fists on her hips. "What do you want to do?"

I look up and meet her gaze. "Get the hell out of here."

Mom grins. "Yes, but where to go?" She paces the room. "Earth, Heaven, Antrum, somewhere else?"

I tilt my head from side to side, weighing the options. I'm about to run away and leave my entire life behind. The worn-out gears of my mind spin, circling back to the same name again and again. "Verus can be sneaky, but I'd go wherever she said it was safe."

Walker laces his fingers together at his waist. "It will take a bit to get an audience with Verus. You'll need a safe place to hide in the meantime." He taps the pads of his thumbs in a fast rhythm. "There's a bunker from the old quasi regime, a secret place where leaders went in times of trouble. It's in the Gray Sea." He turns to Mom. "We can take Myla there now, then I'll portal to Verus for advice."

Mom nods. "I know that bunker. It's right under a—"

I finish her thought. "—wall of black stone." Unholy Hell. That's the very spot where all my dreamscapes have started. My body turns cold. That can't be a coincidence.

Walker eyes me carefully. "You know this place?"

"I see it in my dreamscapes all the time." I hug my hands against my body. Suddenly, I've never been so cold. "That's a good sign from Verus, I guess. I'll go there, no problem."

Mom sits up straighter. "Agreed, but not now. You have a match tomorrow. If you don't show up, the ghouls will look for you right away. Walker is right. We need time to contact Verus and come up with a plan. I don't want you rushing off into worse trouble than you leave behind."

I try to meet Mom's gaze, but can only stare at the floor. Worse trouble, right. Not sure what that would be, but with my luck, it'll find me. "Agreed. I'll hit the match. With my hood on, no one will see my eyes have changed." Plus, that'll give me a chance to say my goodbyes tonight. A grim weight sets in around me. All my friends, school, Arena battles…Everything is about to change.

"It's settled then." Walker grips his hands behind his back. "I'll portal Myla right after the match."

"Sure thing." I give Walker a half-hearted nod. Tomorrow morning at 5 AM I'll be suiting up to leave Purgatory, possibly forever. I blink hard, trying to keep up with events. I just went from being an Arena fighter and homebody to 'Scala Heir on the run'. I grab a blanket from the couch and wrap it around me. Suddenly, I need a nap like it's my job.

Mom smoothes back her hair. "I remember that bunker from my days as a Senator. It takes some time to set up and at least four people to open. Is there any way I can get there earlier?"

"Another ghoul could portal you," says Walker. "How about TIM-29?"

I pull my blanket around me and roll my eyes. *TIM-29 is a dip.* "This plan has enough stupid in it without inviting that guy around."

The look on Mom's face says she agrees. "I haven't seen Tim since before Myla was born."

Walker shrugs. "But do you trust him, Camilla?"

She pauses. "Yes, completely."

"Then I'll approach TIM-29." Walker frowns. "You still need two more people."

My eyes half-open. My overwhelmed brain has just enough functioning cells to spit out one last idea. "If you only need folks to open a door and transport back, Cissy and Zeke can help."

"Good." Walker rocks back on his heels. "I'll speak with your friends as well. We'll all meet back here before the match tomorrow." He turns to me and grins. "Angelbound to Lincoln, eh?"

I curl deeper into my blanket and blush. "Yeah."

"You better tell him about the…" He points to the general area of my eyes.

Rising to my feet, I hunch-walk toward my bedroom. "I'm not doing anything until I've had a nap." I let out a puff of air. *What a bitch of a morning.*

Mom folds her arms over her chest, a smile twinkling in her eyes. "I'll call school and tell them you're sick."

I loop the top of the blanket over my head. "Thanks, Mom."

"And Myla?"

I take little shuffling steps to turn around and see her, the blanket still curled around my ears. "What, Mom?"

"I'm very proud of you."

My face breaks out into a huge smile. I didn't expect it'd feel *that good* to hear her say those words. "Thanks, Mom. I'm proud of you, too."

CHAPTER TWENTY-TWO

A

Sometime after lunch, Nightshade and I start the long ride to the thrax compound. Mom gave me a ghoul robe to wear; I'm careful to keep the hood drawn low to hide my eyes. As Night and I gallop along, a light drizzle falls over the browning trees and yellow grass. The clouds hang low and dark in the sky.

I sigh. The weather's as gloomy as my mood. Walker was right. Lincoln and I have a lot stacked up against us, and that was *before* I became the Scala Heir. Now I'm off to who-knows-where so I can hide for no-one-knows-how-long. I can't imagine this being good for our relationship.

Night and I soon cross the rolling hills to the open fields of thrax lands. I'm too nervous to enjoy the ride much. My thoughts keep turning over the realizations of the morning and how they probably spell doom and gloom for me and Lincoln. Night whinnies, breaking me out of my funk. I glance about, finding us stopped in front of the thrax feasting hall.

I lean forward and pat Night's neck. "In here, girl?"

Night whinnies again.

"Thanks." I slide off her back, step up to the hall's door and pull on the wooden handle. It opens with a long creak. I step inside, finding everything to be quiet, empty, and dark. My stomach somersaults with nervous energy. How do I even begin to explain everything to Lincoln?

"Hello? Anybody in here?"

No response. In a corner, I hear the clickity-clack of mouse claws on the wooden floor. No one's around. I stand by the feasting table, drumming my fingers on the rough wood. Anxiety spirals up my spine. The only thing worse than having to explain this to Lincoln? Having to hunt around the thrax compound first and find him. Maybe Nightshade made a mistake.

The door behind me slowly swings open. Adrenaline pumps into my bloodstream. Moving quickly, I pull my hood low over my face, steal across the room, and flatten myself against a stretch of wall by the door.

A column of light slices through the darkened feasting hall. Lincoln steps inside along with two older men.

My body relaxes a bit. Night was right.

The trio step into the darkened room; I adjust my hood for a better look at them. Lincoln wears his traditional leather pants, chain mail, and tunic. An older man stands beside him with ebony skin, long dread locks, and the crest of an Egyptian eye on his chest. Probably, the Earl of Horus. Next to him stands a man with cocoa skin, high cheekbones, and short gray hair. His tunic's covered with the image of three blue claw-marks: the Earl of Kamal.

The door swings shut behind them, leaving the room in semi-darkness. Horus searches around the feasting table. "Curses, where are those blasted candles?"

"Never mind that," says Lincoln. "You said your need was urgent."

Kamal is the first to speak, his voice a rich baritone under a clipped accent. "We heard the House of Striga backed out of the Alliance."

My brows arch. Alliance? What kind of Alliance?

Lincoln folds his arms across his chest. "Striga has some questions, but I still have their seal on the Alliance parchment. If they back out—if *any of you* back out—it will mean the King's wrath." His voice becomes a low rumble. "You gave your seal. You gave your word."

I've never heard Lincoln get angry before, and I must admit I like him bossy. Desire starts pumping through my veins along with the adrenaline. The skin around my eyes heats up. Hells bells. My stupid inner lust demon's about to get me caught. Closing my eyelids, I force myself to think about saying goodbye to Lincoln. After a few seconds, I calm down enough to pay attention to the conversation again.

The Earl of Horus waves his hand. "This Alliance isn't worth the parchment it's written on. Even with Horus, Kamal, Striga, and Rixa together, we don't have enough strength of arms to face down the Earl of Acca."

I inwardly groan. Walker told me about this before. The Earl of Acca runs the most powerful House in Antrum. Now he wants the throne too, which in his mind means Lincoln marrying Adair. Reason number 439 why this relationship is probably doomed.

Kamal snaps his fingers, a falcon swoops from the rafters to land on his shoulder. I stifle a gasp, but Lincoln and the Earls barely notice the animal. I guess the House of Kamal must do stuff like this all the time. "Take my advice." Kamal runs his pinky down the falcon's head. "Give Acca what he wants."

Lincoln chuckles, but there's no humor in it. "Really? Is that what he wants this week? You've seen what happened with my father. Give in once and there's no end." He gestures between the two men. "We all know what's happening here. Acca sees my father as toothless, so now he's coming after my canines." He slams his fist into his hand. "I must stand my ground or I no longer deserve my crown."

His phrase, 'stand my ground,' echoes happily around my brain. *That means he won't marry Adair.* My mouth winds into a smile. Whatever happens, at least he'll never end up with that loser.

Lincoln stares coolly at the two Earls. "You speak of the great houses. But are they the only ones in Antrum? The Houses Gurith, Zerihun, and Alura are all loyal to the King, perhaps many more."

I remember reading about this in a Ryder library book. Thrax live deep underground. Lands below the old world—Europe, Australasia, Africa—are all ruled by Rixa. There are five major houses and hundreds of lesser ones. All follow the King's law but pretty much run their own show. Excitement strums in my chest. Lincoln plans to unite the lesser Houses and create one great army to fight Acca. I steal a glance at his mismatched eyes and smile. If anyone can do it, he can.

Horus points at Lincoln, the hint of a smile on his wide mouth. "You're a crafty one, I'll grant you. So much like Octavia."

Lincoln nods. "We return to Antrum tomorrow. I'll reach out to the lesser Houses the moment I return." He gestures from Kamal to Horus. "Don't forget why you signed this Alliance in the first place. Once Acca takes down my House, he'll come for you next. All I'm asking for is a little time."

Kamal frowns. "And your father supports this? Word is he bows lower to Acca each day."

Lincoln's upper lip curls. "Have you ever seen *me* bow?"

Kamal steps to the Prince's side. "No, my Prince. Never."

"Nor will you." Lincoln's gaze shifts between the Earls. "We leave for Antrum tomorrow. There's much work to do. If you'll excuse me." He motions to the exit.

The Earls pause, share a long look, and then nod. Lincoln opens the door. He's only a few inches away from me now, but so are the Earls.

Yipes.

Kamal steps toward the exit; then he stops at the threshold. My heart thuds so loud, I'm sure they can hear it. "I'll give you a month. I can risk no more with Acca."

The desperate look in Kamal's eyes sets my nerves on edge. The way everyone talks about Acca, you wouldn't think this dumbass shot crossbow bolts at a Limus demon.

Next, Horus steps up to grip Lincoln's arm, his features on edge. "You're the last chance we have."

The edges of Lincoln's mouth round with a grin. He's so not worried, it isn't funny. "And have I ever failed you?"

Kamal scowls. "Not yet." They finally leave; the door slams shut behind them. Lincoln exhales slowly.

That was close.

In one swift movement, Lincoln moves to face me, his mouth finding mine. The Prince's tongue plays across my lips, quickly driving deeper with need. Heat flows through my veins, pooling in my core. Lincoln's body shifts as presses me against the wall, the motion just rough enough to make me moan. Damn, that feels good. My legs tremble as I taste him over and over, his muscles flexing and releasing as me moves against me.

Lincoln sets his mouth by my ear. "You're lucky those Earls can't hunt worth a damn. I could hear you breathing from across the room."

I lick my lips and smile. "Lucky me."

The Prince stares at me for a long moment. "That was the part where I lose control because I didn't expect to see you." He shoots me a shy smile. "Next is the part where I say we take things slowly."

"Thank you." Although if I didn't have such an awful reason for visiting him, I'd talk him into returning to the first part.

Lincoln links his fingers with mine, and then leans back. "To what do I owe the pleasure of this visit?" Our arms swing in a happy motion. It feels insanely good to see him. I smile for the first time in what feels like years.

"Lincoln, what did my eyes look like yesterday?" I stay flush against the wall, careful to keep my head and hood in the shadows.

"Oh that." He frowns, remembering. "They were changing colors. Brown, blue, red. You said it was from your lust demon awakening for the first time." He leans in and nuzzles my neck. "Did I mention how much I liked red?"

I laugh. "That you did." Last night during our walk, we'd take breaks and kiss for a while before one of us would say 'taking it

315

slowly.' Over time, it turned into (what else) a competition to see how fast Lincoln could get my 'eyes to spark.' Hottie Prince pain-in-my-butt. "No less than six times, as I recall."

He purses his lips. "As long as I'm consistent, that's what matters." He looks at me out of his right eye. "Is that why you came here, to ask me that?"

I fidget against the wall. "No, I came here to show you something."

Lincoln's face creases with concern. "Okay. What is it?"

My stomach ties into knots. "What if I were different from who you thought I was?"

His voice stays calm, his face unreadable. "Like how, different?"

"What if I became someone who was a risk, a target?" Nervous energy zings through my body. I have the perverse desire to kick a hole in the feasting hall table. "Someone who needs to disappear for a very long time."

Lincoln moves closer, wrapping his long arms around me. "And you're afraid of what exactly?"

I close my eyes and snuggle into his shoulder, inhaling his scent of forest pine and leather. My body relaxes. This is what I've needed all day long. Here, with him holding me, I feel like I can say anything. "We've already got a lot stacked against us, Lincoln. Maybe you're better off with someone like Adair."

"Really?" He kisses the top of my head, gently. "Did you know Adair thinks Simia demons are cute?"

I roll my eyes. "You're lying."

"I wish." He slides one hand up my back. "You're hiding your eyes again, Myla."

Damn, he *is* a good hunter.

His fingers entwine with the back of my hood, slowly pulling it away from my face. "I already told you. I like it when your eyes turn red."

I grit my teeth and steel my shoulders. It takes everything I have just to keep my gaze level with his. Once he understands what I really am, this could be over, big time.

Lincoln's forehead furrows. "Your eyes are blue." His mouth thins to an angry line. "Did someone from the House of Striga cast a spell on you? So help me, I'll—"

"No, it's not that."

He cups my face in his hands, his features drawn with worry. "Are you sick?"

"No, nothing like that either." I open my mouth, ready to tell him I'm the Scala Heir. What comes out is a fragment of the truth. "My father is an angel named Xavier."

Lincoln's mismatched eyes stretch wide. "The *archangel* Xavier? I studied him at the citadel. Greatest warrior in history. Legend says he never loved anything but battle."

I let out a high-pitched humph. "Until he met my mother."

"I can see that. If she's anything like you." The Prince eyes me carefully for a minute, his face creasing with confusion. "I don't understand. That would make you—" He swallows. "That's impossible."

"I thought so too." I bite my lips together. How do you convince your kind-of boyfriend that you're a one-of-a-kind soul-swapping super being?

Only one way, really.

Inhaling deeply, I close my eyes and call the igni to return. At first, their music is tinkling and distant in my mind, then quickly growing rich and loud. Child-like laughter rings in my ears; my mouth quirks with a smile. Having them return is like welcoming an old friend home.

I raise my right palm to shoulder-height and open my eyes. In my mind I know Lincoln is near, but he seems blocked behind a white haze. The skin on my face cools; my irises glow bright blue. Igni materialize around my hand, appearing even faster this time than when I called them in my house. The tiny lightning bolts swirl about my palm before arcing to the ceiling in one great geyser. Once they hit the wooden rafters, the igni bounce and tumble to the floor like so many snowflakes, disappearing before they touch the ground.

I focus on Lincoln. When the haze around him clears, I find he's standing a few yards away, his face still as stone. I meet his gaze. "Possible or not, I *am* the next Scala."

"Myla, I—"

I raise both hands at him, palms forward. "No, I need to say something first. Now that my Scala powers are active, I have to go into hiding. I don't know when I'll resurface, if ever. Walker told me about all the things stacked up against us…How the Earl wants you to marry Adair. And I heard what you said to Kamal and Horus before. Unifying the lesser Houses? You've got enough to worry about without adding me to the list." I hug my elbows. *Here comes the yucky part.* "What I'm saying is, if you want to see someone else, that's okay with me." I roll my eyes. *What am I saying?* "Not that we're really dating in the first place."

I'd face-palm myself if it didn't make me look dumber. That was about the worst speech in the history of ever.

Lincoln's face is unreadable. "May I ask a question?"

I pretend that it's very important to check for dust on my ghoul robes. Anything not to look in his eyes at this point. "Sure."

"Do you love me?"

Holy cow! I did not see that coming, at all. "Um, well, I…"

Fuuuuuuuuuck. I have no idea what to say right now.

"Alright, I'll ask a different question." His face stays still as stone. I have no idea what he's thinking and damn, that's annoying. "When did this happen?"

Okay, *that* question I know how to answer.

"It's been happening for a while, but I didn't know it. The ceremony at the Arena actually awakened me, not Adair. Then, I was angelbound last night when we—" I bite my lower lip.

Lincoln watches me for a long minute, then his mouth does something impossible: erupt into the biggest grin I've ever seen. He rushes toward me, wraps his arms around my waist, and pulls me against him. "That's wonderful, Myla."

Wait a minute.

I look at Lincoln out of my right eye. This is unbelievable. "So, you're not worried about what I just said?"

"No. Should I be?"

Although it's not in my best interest, I'm not dropping this point for some reason. "But I have to go into hiding. Who knows when I'll resurface? Don't you want to, you know, move on?"

He grips my waist tighter, spinning me around in a circle. I can't help but laugh. He kisses me once, gently. "Of course, not. You've made me very happy."

At those words, the light bulb in my brain clicks to 'on.'

"You just heard blah-blah-blah 'getting angelbound means Myla loves me like crazy' blah-blah-blah. Am I right?"

"Yes." We're so close, I can feel his heart beat against my chest. "And I love you too, Myla. Like crazy." His mouth brushes along my jawline. Desire churns through me. "Now you say it back to me."

I stifle a grin. He can be such a hot bastard sometimes. "I love you, Lincoln."

"There now. The rest of it doesn't matter." His hand cups the back of my head, gently guiding my lips onto his. Our mouths meet in a slow kiss. My knees go all wobbly again.

"Ahem." A voice sounds from across the room.

Lincoln frowns. "That would be Mother."

Did he just say 'mother?' My face burns about a thousand shades of red. "I didn't hear anyone come in." I pull my hood low and take a huge step away from Lincoln. "Does she always sneak around like that?"

"Pretty much."

I pat my cheeks; my killer blush isn't going away any time soon. This wasn't how I pictured the Queen finding out about me and Lincoln. I was hoping for more of a 'let's meet up after battle practice' scenario versus her catching us snogging in the dark. Ugh. Not to mention my new powers. Lincoln may not mind that I'm the Scala Heir, but who knows what his parents will say?

Octavia stands by the closed door, her body stiff and tall in a black velvet gown, her brown hair pulled back into a twist. "It seems we've much to discuss. This way."

I stand in the center of the feasting hall, my body perfectly still. A knot of emotion forms in my throat. I keep telling myself to walk and my stubborn self keeps ignoring me. An official audience with the King and Queen? Right this very second? I've already had a 'very special' twenty-four hours as it is.

Lincoln steps up behind me, setting his firm hands on my shoulders. His mouth brushes the shell of my ear. "We can do this."

I wrap my fingers with Lincoln's, feeling the warmth of his skin. *Yes, we can do this.* Together, we open the door and cross the threshold, following Octavia to a massive tent made of black tapestry woven with silver eagles. Tall wooden poles hold the structure upright, each topped with a line of thin golden banners. A guard in black armor stands by the entrance flap.

Octavia wags a finger at him. "No one gets within twenty yards of this place, no matter what."

"Yes, your Highness."

The Queen turns to me. "We use this for official audiences." Flipping about, she disappears into the folds of the tent.

Once Octavia's gone, Lincoln grips my hand. "Just a minute, Myla." He pulls me out of earshot of the guard, stopping a few yards from the tent entrance.

I stare into Lincoln's mismatched eyes, my head tilting to one side. "What's wrong?"

He gently sets his hand on my shoulder, his thumb rubbing my skin in a soothing motion. "I don't want you to be surprised. My father may be a little gruff with you."

I suck in a fast breath. That little factoid was a shocker. Suddenly I'm very happy about the mini-shoulder massage I'm getting. "Why? He doesn't know me."

Lincoln smirks. "You're the greatest warrior in Antrum, everyone knows you."

I mock-frown. "That's not what I mean."

He glances about, searching for the right words to say. "My father's looking for a reason to give in to Acca."

Meaning he wants Lincoln to marry Adair...And me out of the way. Oh, he'll be a little gruff, alright. My upper lip curls. "Do we *have* to do this?" My voice came out a little whiny there.

Lincoln winds his arm around my back, the other wraps about my shoulder. Drawing me to him, he sets his mouth on mine. *Oh, yes.* His lips are everything soft, warm, and delicious. We kiss slowly, deeply. The rest of the universe disappears. Lincoln's hand pushes into the small of my back, then slowly slides around my waist to my belly. My mind goes blank. What was he was asking again? Why wasn't I saying yes?

Hey now, Myla. Way to think with your hormones.

I break the kiss and do my best to frown. "Is that your way of talking me into this?"

He eyes me with that sly grin. "Yes." His palm slides up the side of my torso, almost-just-maybe touching the swell of my breast.

Damn, damn, damn. He just talked me into this.

"Fine. Let's go."

He kisses the tip of my nose. "You won't regret it."

I try to swallow past the knot of emotion that just formed in my throat. "Can I get that in writing?"

CHAPTER TWENTY-THREE

$\mathcal{A}$

I stand inside a large square space filled with sturdy wooden chairs and tables. Iron chests and oriental rugs cover the floor. King Connor sits on a high-back chair in a black tunic, a sheet of parchment in his hand. His white hair hangs neatly to his shoulders. Octavia stands beside him.

The King rises to his feet, his face creasing into a smile as he greets his son. Connor's basso voice rings out: "Hello, hello!" He lumbers over to Lincoln, wrapping him in a bear hug. It feels like a million years eke by as the King slowly turns to me. I grit my teeth and try to plaster on a smile.

"What's this?" The King sets his meaty fists on his hips. "I wasn't informed of any strangers coming to visit." His voice drips with irritation.

Here it comes. The gruffness.

Lincoln grips my hand. "This is Myla, father. She's the girl I've been telling you about."

Telling you about? My heart kicks in my chest. Lincoln's been chatting me up with his parents. My fake grin turns into a real one.

Connor leans back on one heel. "Yes, I remember." His eyes narrow as he takes me in from head to toe. "You're the quasi-demon."

I open my mouth to correct him, but Lincoln gets there first. "Her name is Myla." His tone has a protective edge. My grin grows wider. His protective side is hot.

The King lumbers back to his table, and then plunks his burly frame into a high-back chair. Octavia slides into the empty seat beside him. Lincoln and I stand a few yards away, hand in hand.

Connor lets out a long breath. "If you're here, I assume the two of you are in *trouble*." The way he says 'trouble,' I know he's thinking one thing: I'm carrying Lincoln's child.

Anger shoots through my body. Whoa there, asshole! I'm a lot of things. Pregnant isn't one of them.

Octavia gasps. "Connor!"

He slaps the tabletop with him palms. "Well, they *are* in trouble, aren't they?" He turns to me. "Aren't *you?*"

That does it. What a nasty, arrogant, and insulting dickweed! My eyes flare red with rage. "That would be no, your Disgustingness." My tone drips with venom. "Keep your dirty mind to yourself."

Lincoln turns to me, his face twisted with worry. "Myla, what are you doing?" He leans in closer, his voice barely above a whisper. "No one speaks to my father that way."

My teeth grind. So we're back to requiring 'special words of reverence' when speaking with thrax royalty, eh? I did *not* fight about this with Lincoln for three months solid just to cave in with his dear old dad. He'll show me some respect, too.

I nod to Lincoln. "Don't worry. I got this." Closing my eyes, I pull back my hood, raise my hand, and call out to the igni. They appear faster than ever before, their music and laughter quickly drowning out anything else in my head. Their tiny bodies whirl about my hand, almost blocking my view of the tent's interior.

I watch their light swirl about my fingertips, then I order them to break free. *Let's show this King what trouble really is.* With a burst of laughter, they obey.

Moving in a small knot of bodies, the igni zoom about the tent, knocking over candlesticks and upending chairs. Like a great pinwheel, they spin about in the center of the room, faster and faster. A high-pitched hum fills the air and then—POOF—they all disappear.

I grin. How's *that* for trouble?

An icy chill freezes my skin; my eyes glow bright blue. Opening them slowly, I glare directly at the King, speaking in the nastiest voice I can muster. "I'm the Scala Heir, Connor. I'm not *in* trouble." My eyes blaze with blue fire. "I *am* trouble."

The tent's interior comes back into focus. Lincoln stands beside me, his body rigid and his expression unreadable. Octavia sits beside Connor's chair, her face a stony mask. The King stares at me for a long minute, his features blank. I have to consciously stop myself from sticking my tongue out at him. Nyah.

The King breaks the silence by slamming his fist onto the wooden table. My body snaps into battle stance, my tail arched over my shoulder. *Want a piece of me?* I'd like to see you try, big guy.

"Well, well." Connor's great head wags from side to side. "I'll be damned." He breaks into peals of loud, deep, and rolling laughter.

He's laughing? Really?!

I squint at the King. The igni must have short-circuited my senses; that can't be actual guffaws. I turn to Lincoln, my face wrinkled with confusion. "Are we good here?"

Lincoln nods. "Oh, yeah. He's loving this." The Prince leans in closer, satisfaction and pride shining in his eyes. "Well played, Myla." My insides turn all happy and squirmy as he gently kisses my cheek. I didn't know I was playing a game, but it looks like I hit the masterstroke.

Connor rubs his eyes with his meaty fingers. "Lincoln, my boy. What a treasure you are." The King points to me. "And you! A spitfire." He gestures to the empty chairs across from him. "Have a seat, both of you. Let's talk a bit, see what we can do here." He looks to his left. "Octavia, I'm sure you're behind this. At least in part?"

A ghost of a smile lurks about the Queen's mouth. "Always, Connor." She's a crafty one, that's for certain.

The Queen seats herself next to the King; I slip into the high-back chair beside Lincoln. Connor drums the tabletop with his palms. "It seems we have the Scala Heir with us today. What does that make Lady Adair?"

Octavia frowns. "A fraud. I can't believe I didn't see it before. Adair only showed Scala powers when Gianna was whispering nearby; such spells are nothing for the House of Striga." The Queen clicks her tongue. "Gianna's witchcraft could have changed Adair's eyes as well."

"The Houses of Acca and Striga have quarreled for centuries. Now they team up." The King sighs. "Dark news."

Lincoln's eyes take on a steely hue. I know that look: he's preparing to give bad news. "Their treachery has worsened. Striga asked to abandon the Alliance against Acca."

The King scowls. "And *when* did they make this request?"

Lincoln's features stay stone-cold calm. "Two days ago."

Connor grits his teeth. The jovial king from a few seconds ago disappears. "Interesting that you waited until now to tell me, boy." Little bits of spittle fly from his mouth as he speaks.

I sink a little lower in my chair. *Connor has serious mood issues.* One minute he's happy, the next? Spitting mad.

"You know why I waited, father." Lincoln positively oozes cool. "If I told you two days ago, you'd have done something rash. Now, we can consider the news about Striga in the context of what's *really* important." He laces his fingers through mine, and then sets both our hands on the tabletop with a thunk.

Whoa. Up until now, Lincoln and I have kept a friendly distance from each other in his father's presence. With that particular move, Lincoln couldn't have marked his territory more clearly than if he'd peed on a shrubbery.

The Prince's voice sounds with a low and dangerous edge. "I thought you wanted to talk about me and Myla?" Under my palm, his skin is slick with sweat. Poor guy. He puts up a good face but this must be killing him inside. I give his hand a little squeeze.

The King growls out one word. "Perhaps."

I hate to admit it, but I get how the King goes from happy to miserable to enraged to loving in sixty seconds or less. I know someone like that; I look at her in the mirror every morning.

The Prince and King launch into a mini-staring contest that lasts two excruciatingly long minutes. Octavia spends the time looking placid and Queenly. My face droops into an anxious frown as I rub my thumb in little circles on Lincoln's hand. After a lot of shifting in seats, huffing of breath, and staring, staring, staring, the King finally looks away. I'm no ace at playing these games of state, but I consider that a 'big win' in the Lincoln column. Connor turns to me, his manner turning gentle.

"The Scala Heir must excuse my temper." The King clears his throat. "Now that your powers are active, do you wish asylum with the thrax?"

Asylum with the thrax? It's a tempting idea at that, what with all the yummy Lincoln access. I glance around the table. Sadly, I don't know if these folks can protect themselves, let alone the Scala Heir. No, I have to go where Verus sends me. I shoot the King an appreciative smile. "I came here to see Lincoln. Mom and I have other plans for what happens next."

Octavia nods to Connor. "You remember Senator Lewis from the era of quasi rule?"

"Absolutely. Very capable. The only one who predicted Armageddon's rise, as I recall."

Octavia points to me. "This is her daughter."

My back straightens. So freaking cool to hear people talk about the awesomeness that is Senator Lewis. My mouth rounds into a proud smile.

"Interesting." Connor folds his hands onto the tabletop. "Very interesting."

The Queen eyes me and smiles. "Do you know how Connor and I met, Myla?"

The King lets out a lively chortle. "Not this story, Octavia." Clearly, he's back to a good mood. I feel like I need a scorecard to keep track.

Lincoln turns to me. "It was at the ball to celebrate the spring equinox."

"That's the *official* story," says Octavia. "It was actually at the winter tournament. I used to fight in those, you know."

I grin. "Yes, Bera told me."

I picture the golden breastplate Bera gave me to wear at the last Winter tournament. She'd said the Queen had one like it when she competed. I picture Octavia at that age, all spritely, wired with muscle, and absolutely lethal. Man, I would have loved to see that.

The Queen mimes shooting an arrow. "My skill lay with the bow. The tournament beast that year was a Manus demon. I shot it full of arrows—and was within seconds of winning—when I ran out of time. Connor waltzed onto the field of battle, ran the monster through with his sword, and won the tournament."

The King laughs his head off. "It was quite a bit more than that, Octavia." He shoots me a conspiratorial smile. "This was two hundred years ago and she still carries a grudge."

My eyes bulge. "Two hundred years?"

Lincoln nods. "Thrax live a long time."

I chew my lower lip, considering. The Scala lives a long time, too. I look at Lincoln's square jaw, scooped-out cheeks, and full mouth. He's so freaking awesome I can't stand it. If we can get through this nasty Scala-Acca-Armageddon stuff, we could have a very long and amazing time together. Lincoln seems to read what I'm thinking (with my skill for hiding emotion, it doesn't take a genius) and he rubs his foot against mine under the table. Pretending to scratch my nose, I hide my grin under my palm.

Connor curls his hands into mock-claws. "Never was there a worse tournament beast, and never a greater warrior to fight it than Octavia." His mouth winds into a cunning grin. "Afterwards, I went to visit my lady in her family's tent. I wanted to commend her valor on the battlefield, but I failed to announce myself formally."

Octavia smirks. "He walked in while I was alone and half-dressed. Appeared behind me out of nowhere."

Whoa. I know what I would do—what any warrior would do—in a situation like that. I wince. "What did he get? Elbow to the gut?"

Octavia arches her eyebrow. "Knee to the groin."

I grit my teeth. "Yowch."

Lincoln's shoulders rock with laughter. "You never told me that, father."

Connor chuckles as well. "It's not a memory I like to recall." He wraps his hand around Octavia's. "But after that moment, no one else would do. You see Myla, for the thrax, everything is about strength in battle."

I shoot Lincoln a knowing glance. "I've noticed." He starts another game of footsie with me under the table. I blush.

The King nods in my direction. "This, my dear, is why I'm willing to take a chance on you. You've some strength in you." He leans back on his chair. "But I get ahead of myself. If you're the Scala Heir, you need angel blood. Who's your father then?"

Lincoln's eyes positively twinkle. This would be his 'I'm about to drop a bomb of good news' face. "The archangel Xavier."

I think the royal couple's eyes almost blast out of their collective heads. The King lets out a low whistle. "You're first-generation archangel, then." He rubs his palms together. "And not just any archangel, Xavier!"

I frown, confused. "Why is first generation important?"

"More angel blood, more power," says Lincoln. "The current Scala is fifth-generation common angel. I'm third-generation archangel. Father's second. We descended from the archangel Aquila. Have you heard the story?"

"Yes, Mom told me how she founded the House of Rixa."

Connor grins. "I've heard of the Archangel Xavier. Amazing warrior turned diplomat. Led the final battle to drive demons from Heaven."

His words send an image into my mind's eye: the King of Hell twisting my father's broken arm. Pangs of grief and anger move through me.

Octavia's eyes narrow. "But he disappeared after the Wars, I believe."

I pick invisible lint off my robe. "I don't want to talk about that." I grit my teeth. Unholy moley. I sound exactly like Mom.

"Of course, of course." Connor folds his arms over his chest. "Now, what are your plans exactly?"

"I have an Arena match tomorrow morning. Right after that, I go to a safe house until we hear from the angels."

"I see." The King drums his fingers on the tabletop, his face lost in thought. All of a sudden, the atmosphere in the tent zings with tension. Both Lincoln and Octavia look particularly unreadable, which means something big is definitely going on.

I roll my eyes. I've had enough staring-and-not-talking for one day. "You're clearly debating something, Connor. What is it?"

He looks at me, his furry brows arching. "If you must know, it's whether to endorse Lincoln's plan to gather together the lesser houses."

My mouth starts speaking on its own. "I'll help him."

The King lets out a puff of breath. "And how will you do that from hiding?"

"I'll find a way." I bow my head. "Strength in battle, your Highness. If the Earl doesn't like it, I'll pull some strings and send him to Hell."

The King nods slowly. "I believe you'd do it, too."

I snap my fingers. "In a heartbeat."

"Fine, we'll wait." He points at Lincoln. "You've got a month, boy. Bring together the minor houses." His face droops. "I'll stall the Earl."

Lincoln's mouth curls into a satisfied smile. "Thank you, father." He gives my hand an especially long squeeze. Warmth and love bloom in my chest. Together, Lincoln and I can do this. We can do anything.

Octavia taps the tabletop with one fingernail. "We have other matters to discuss." She turns to me. "This match tomorrow morning. How will you compete without exposing your identity?"

"My fighting suit has a face-mask that hides my eyes."

The thought of my fighting suit is somehow calming. That thing is so freaking awesome.

"Very good." Octavia turns to her son. "And you'll be there as well?"

"It's not an official thrax event, but I'll contact the minister. I'm sure I can watch from an archway."

I turn to him with the biggest smile ever. "You'll be there?"

He winks. "Nowhere else."

I feel a weight lift from my body. Sweet.

Connor's brow furrows. "Will you bring extra soldiers with you?"

Lincoln leans back in his chair. Our joined hands slide off the tabletop to swing casually between us. "No, that would only attract unnecessary attention."

Octavia wags a finger at her son. "Be sure to wear full demon patrol gear: body armor, baculum, daggers…"

Lincoln nods. "I'll be safe, Mother."

I stifle a grin. *Glad my Mom's not the only one with an over-protective streak.*

The King rubs his chin. "And stay with her tonight."

Octavia gasps. "Connor!"

My jaw drops. "Whoa!" First, the King thinks I'm preggers. Then, he assumes Lincoln's sleeping in my bed? I so want to clobber this guy, it isn't funny. I may be part lust demon, but that doesn't mean I'm a slut. Sheesh.

The King wags his head. "I mean in a separate room, but ready for trouble."

I close my mouth into a scowl. So, I won't clobber him. Maybe. My blood still boils with anger.

Octavia clears her throat, trying to re-steer the conversation onto safer ground. "After the match, Lincoln will join our procession to Antrum."

Lincoln leaves tomorrow. That thought is one massive rainstorm on my angry parade. Suddenly, I no longer think about clobbering the King. Instead, I focus on how Lincoln and I will be separated, and for who knows how long? And Antrum's locked down so tightly, I don't even know when or how we can connect. A heavy sadness sets into my body.

My voice comes out barely above a whisper. "That's the plan."

Lincoln gives my hand a squeeze. "Let's get you back home. Did you ride Nightshade here?"

"Yes."

"Good. She's probably outside waiting for you now, along with Bastion." He gently kisses my cheek. "I'll meet you there in a minute. I have to get my stuff."

The sadness in my heart lightens a bit. At least I'll have Lincoln nearby until it's time for us to part.

I say my goodbyes to Connor and Octavia, giving her an extra-long hug. This may be the last time I see her for a long while. The Queen eyes me carefully, her mental gears spinning away.

"Don't worry," says Octavia. "We'll meet again, my dear."

I force a half-smile. "I'm sure we will." However, if I'm being honest with myself, seeing any of them again is far from a sure thing.

A.

It's dark by the time Lincoln and I near my house. Nightshade and Bastion step in perfect rhythm down the quiet streets. Sadness seeps into the air and our hearts. The two of us haven't spoken much since leaving the royal tent.

Without being asked, our horses stop on the stretch of sidewalk before my front porch. Lincoln and I dismount, telling Night and Bastion to return to the Ryder stables. Night stares at me, her over-large black eyes smooth and round as marbles, the look in them saying the horse equivalent of 'no kidding, sister.' Lincoln and I watch our mounts trot away, then stroll up to the front door, hand-in-hand. Mom opens it before we have a chance to knock.

"Myla! I've been worried sick."

I inwardly groan. She has her 'insanely overprotective and twitchy' face on. Not that I totally blame her, but yipes. This could get ugly.

I shift my weight from foot to foot. "Hi, Mom. This is Lincoln." I can't help but smile.

Lincoln's mouth warms into a shy grin. "Hello."

Mom taps her foot. "You're thrax?" She's in rare form: worried and anxious with a side order of crazy. Here comes the ugly.

The Prince nods. "Yes."

Mom eyes the heavy pack slung over Lincoln's shoulder. "You brought armor and weapons?"

"Yes."

"Good. Come in."

My mother, the charmer.

We all step inside. Mom closes the door behind us, then points dramatically to the couch. "*This* is where you'll be sleeping, Lincoln, the thrax." She fixes him with the exact same stare Lincoln's father gave me, the one that says 'I know what's on your oversexed little mind.' And hey, that's not untrue, but we've got it under control. Mostly.

He bows slightly. "Of course."

Mom wraps me in a long hug. "I'm glad you're safe, baby. Don't stay up too late." She glances at Lincoln and sighs. "Thank you for watching over Myla. It says a lot about your character." She kisses him gently on the cheek. "Good night."

I let out a long breath. That was a downright normal interaction between Mom and Lincoln. She's been bouncing back from her overprotective mode into her old Senator Lewis self faster and faster these days. What a relief.

Mom pulls her threadbare robe tighter and walks into her bedroom, closing the door behind her with a soft click.

Lincoln and I exchange a look that mixes shock and relief, the kind I normally reserve for near-miss accidents with Betsy. I half-smile. "I'm not sure who wins for weirdest parental interaction of the day."

"Come on. Me, definitely." He enfolds me in his arms. "I'm so sorry about that, by the way. Father should have focused on your safety, not a power play with the Earl. He used to be...Very different." He gives my back a gentle pat. "But enough about my family for one day." Leaning forward, the Prince moves to set his mouth on mine.

"I'm not sure that's such a good idea." Frowning, I glance at Mom's closed door.

Lincoln releases me and steps backwards. "I understand."

We're so close to goodbye. After tomorrow's Arena match, Lincoln returns to Antrum and Walker portals me into the Gray Sea safe house. The weight I felt on the ride home grows heavier, settling into every cell of my body. My eyes sting.

I wrap my fingers around Lincoln's hand and lead him into my room. Sadness hangs in the air like fog. Lincoln sits on my bed, his back against the headboard. I climb onto the mattress and curl up beside him. My cheek nestles onto his chest; his long arm wraps loosely about my back. My eyelids grow heavy.

A

That night I dream of an office decorated entirely in red. Crimson walls stretch off into the distance, with no end or windows in sight. My bare feet stand on a blood-red wooden floor dotted with small round carpets of the same hue. To my left, scarlet-colored leather chairs encircle a large table made of red crystal. At my right, there looms a massive cherry-red desk, and behind that desk sits Armageddon.

My breath catches. Armageddon is here! My body goes on high alert, preparing for a wall of terror to slam into me. It doesn't. I feel frightened, sure, but nothing like how it felt at school when Armageddon walked by me and Cissy.

What kind of dream is this anyway?

Armageddon folds his three-knuckled hands neatly onto the desktop, his mouth slowly stretching into an impossibly-wide grin. His long pointed face holds a knife-straight nose and two fiery red eyes. "Welcome, Maxon."

I say nothing, body frozen stiff. What the Hell is going on? Why does he think I'm his son Maxon?

The King of Hell drums his three-knuckled fingers on the tabletop. "Come now, boy. I've spoken to you in your dreams every week for the last thousand years. No need to be shy."

My eyes widen with understanding. Like how Verus sends me dreamscapes of the past, Armageddon must speak with his son in his sleep. I nod. It makes sense; greater demons have all sorts of odd powers. But why does he think I'm Maxon?

Armageddon arches the right brow on his stone-smooth face. "No need to show yourself or speak this time. I can smell the stench of your igni from here." He drops his palms onto the table-top and leans forward. "You're so very close, my son."

It's the igni. I've spent the last eight hours on a Scala Heir bender, showing my powers to Mom, Walker, Lincoln, and his parents. Igni must leave some kind of trace on my body and soul. Somehow it fooled Armageddon into chatting me up in my dreams. That's why I don't feel the terror of being physically close to him.

Armageddon leans back in his chair. "We both know what you're thinking. Long ago, I asked you to join me in ruling Hell; you refused. Now you carry my curse." His beady black eyes narrow into slits. "Go ahead. Ask me to forgive you, my son. Ask one more time. Perhaps I'll change my mind and offer you the mercy you so desperately seek."

There's a long pause where I know Armageddon's waiting for the mercy-begging to commence. That's so not happening. Ever.

"Not in the mood to grovel today, my boy? How tiresome." His eyes blare crimson red. "No matter. I will fulfill my curse and drag your body to Hell by force, and not to rule...But to suffer. Perhaps your soul will go to Heaven one day, but not before I torture your body *in Hell.*"

The demon pauses, and then snaps his fingers. "We're done here."

The office and Armageddon disappear. The rest of the night, my consciousness drifts about in darkness and silence.

Great. A crappy night's sleep right before my big match. Yet another reason to hate Armageddon.

CHAPTER TWENTY-FOUR

A

I awaken, finding myself alone in my own bed. Lincoln's left a small note on the nightstand beside me. 'Off to rumple the couch before your mom wakes up. See you at breakfast. L.' With a sad smile, I slip the note into the top drawer of my little table. It came from Lincoln; I can't bring myself to throw it away.

My bedroom door swings open. Mom steps inside, my fighting suit gripped in her hand. The worry lines around her eyes have deepened overnight. She pauses. "You're up."

I hoist myself to a seated position and set my feet on the chilly floor. "Yeah. I didn't sleep too well last night."

"It's 5 AM. Time to get ready for the Arena."

I rub my neck and stretch. "Thanks, Mom." Nervous energy twists down my spine. My hands tremble slightly.

Come on, Myla. This should be a match like all the others. Stay calm.

Tossing my suit on the bed, Mom gives my shoulder a gentle pat. "We're all in the kitchen. See you there when you're ready." She steps toward the door and pauses. "Do you want some Frankenberry?"

"Sure, Mom." The way my stomach churns, I may not hold it down, though.

I change into my fighting suit and step into our little kitchen, which is standing-room-only this morning. Mom, Cissy, and Zeke all sit at our tiny table. Lincoln and Walker stand nearby. Tim waits in a far corner, looking wide-eyed and twitchy.

The Prince winds me into a cozy hug. "Good morning, Myla."

Leaning into his shoulder, I inhale his yummy scent of forest pine and leather. "I'm glad you're here." I force on a grin.

His voice sounds low and soft in my ear. "You'll kick ass today."

A genuine smile curls my mouth. "Hells, yeah." Stepping back, I take in Lincoln's gear: black body armor, daggers holstered on his outer thighs, and baculum strapped to the base of his spine. "You look ready to kick ass too."

Lincoln shrugs. "Another day at the office."

Cissy and Zeke step closer; they're careful not to stare at my new blue irises. It's like those dreams where I show up to school naked, only instead of naked, I'm a blue-eyed, soul-swapping super-being. I'm sure they're trying to be sensitive, but sheesh. I feel like enough of a freak already.

"Morning, Myla." Cissy wraps me in an especially long squeeze. "Walker told us everything. I'm going to miss you, sweetie."

"I'll miss you too, Cissy." I picture the little shoebox of moths in her locker. I've always relied on Cissy to pick up the pieces and protect the endangered cocoon of weirdness that is my life. I honestly don't know what I'll do without her friendship. "Very much." My voice catches.

Zeke awkwardly punches my shoulder. "The next Scala, eh? Sorta explains why you never fell for any other guys at school."

Cissy breaks our hug, spins about, and elbows him in the ribs. "Be nice, Zeke. This isn't about conquests with your buddies. We're saying goodbye to Myla today."

"Oh, yeah." Zeke stares at his sneakers. "It's a bummer how you have to run off and everything."

"Thanks." Cissy, I'll miss. Zeke, maybe not so much.

Walker steps forward, his long robes swaying with the move-ment. He swings his arm wide, gesturing toward Tim. Compared to how Walker towers in his dark robes, Tim looks like a twelve-year-old in a black sheet. "Myla, I'd like you to meet TIM-29."

"Hello, Tim." It's weird being introduced to someone you've dreamscaped about for months. Especially when the someone in question is kind-of a douchebag. Too bad we couldn't think of anyone else.

"Pleasure to meet you." His large black eyes stare into mine. "I can't believe it. You really do have angel-blue irises."

"Yeah." I quickly shake his chilly hand. "I suppose I should get used to being the new freak show in town."

He taps his chin with his gray pointer finger. "Perhaps you could show us something. Do a trick or two with igni."

"Tim!" Mom sets her fists at her waist. "It's a risk for Myla to create igni here."

"Ah, of course." Tim chuckles, but there's no happiness in it. "It's so hard to believe, you having a child with Xavier. I mean, he's never fathered offspring in the history of time." His mouth snakes into a cunning smile. "I thought perhaps the girl's parent was Furor." He reaches toward my face. "There are spells you can cast to change eye color."

His hand moves closer to my eyes, but I'm too stunned to break his fingers. He thinks Mom's making this up? Like being the Scala Heir is such a hoot. What a doofus.

Mom bounds across the room, placing her body between me and Tim. "The subject is closed."

"Excuse my enthusiasm." Tim bows. "I'm overwhelmed to be back in the presence of Senator Lewis, as well as to meet her lovely daughter."

Wow. So he's a total suck-up *and* a douchebag. Yay. Lincoln shoots me a questioning look. I shrug. 'It is what it is' at this point.

Mom tries to smile. "Thank you for helping us today, Tim."

I nod my head, impressed. They're both acting pretty adult here, considering the history. Mom told me that when Tim discovered she'd hooked up with Xavier, they had a falling out. I'm guessing it was one of those 'You love me? Then it sucks to be you' conversations. Now he's coming back to portal Xavier's kid around. Awkward!

Walker unrolls a stack of maps onto the kitchen table. "Everyone, please take a look." We all gather around. On the top map, the dark sand of the Gray Sea stretches for miles. Here and there, lines of black rock break up the dreary desert. Walker points to one particularly large wall of dark stone. "Our bunker's hidden right here."

My stomach sinks. That's my new home away from home, for a few days at least. So. Freaking. Weird.

Walker's finger follows the line of dark stone. "Behind the rock wall, there's a huge dune." His fingertip starts at the top of the stone wall, slides down a long ramp-like dune, and ends far off in the desert.

Lincoln nods. "There may be good cover there, if we need it."

"Exactly." Walker taps the dune's crest. "This ridge was designed for snipers to protect the bunker entrance."

Walker points to the bottom of the rock wall. "The bunker's entrance is down here."

Images from my dreamscapes flash through my mind. "Is the bunker's door a kind of big circle in the sand that opens with fire?"

"Yes, it is." Walker's coal-black eyes focus on mine. "Was that in one of your dreamscapes?"

"In all of them, actually." Although what was so wrong with Verus sitting down and explaining everything to me like a normal person? I mean, other than breaking her promise to my mother, which she basically did anyway. Sneaky Verus.

Walker points to the spot on the desert floor where the bunker entrance is hidden. "We'll need four people to stand at each of the four points of the compass. When your four sets of hands touch the sand at the same time, a circle of fire will appear. The bunker door will slowly rise from there."

Cissy chews her fingernail. "Do we need gloves or anything?"

Walker shakes his head. "The bunker's encased in angel fire to block pure demons. It won't burn you."

I open my mouth, ready to say that the bunker's fire never burned me in my dreamscapes. Then I realize I'm a soul-swapping part-archangel super-being who may not be subject to the typical laws of physics. I sigh. My ongoing quest of personal discovery has officially hit a dead end. I know who I am, the Scala Heir, but I'm not too excited about that fact. Moving souls? Becoming a target for every creep who wants to rule the afterlife? Being more of a freak than I was already? Not sure I'm up for any of that. Staying hidden sounds like a great plan, maybe a permanent one.

Mom sets her hands on her hips. "The bunker protects from ghoul or demon attacks. If quasis and ghouls are inside, then ghouls can create portals in and out. If no ghouls are within, quasis open the main door manually."

Lincoln lets out an appreciative 'humph.' "Clever security system."

"There's more cool stuff here." Raising his hand, Walker flips to another map. This one shows the bunker's interior. "There's an antechamber and a main room inside. Both places have enough food, water, and clothing to last a few months at least. The main chamber also has a communications console and a periscope to the desert floor."

Walker points to Cissy and Zeke. "Once you open the bunker doors and get inside, Tim will create a portal to take you home." Walker turns to my mother. "Meanwhile, Camilla will set up the communications console so we're connected to the outside world. Myla, Lincoln, and I will meet you in the main chamber at 6 AM." Walker sets his long arms into the folds of his robe. "I believe that covers everything. Any questions?"

Only about a million. Where will the angels send me to hide? What happens if Armageddon invades Purgatory? When will I see Lincoln, my friends, and family again? And, my new personal favorite: Can we get someone *else* to be the Scala Heir?

Every muscle in my body overflows with nervous energy. I stare at my hands, opening and closing them over and over.

Walker clears his throat. "Myla?"

I snap out of my thoughts and look up. "Yeah?" That's when I realize it. Everyone in the room stares at me, and probably has been for some time. A flush creeps up my neck. Am I supposed to give a speech or something? This Scala Heir stuff is total bullshit. "I mean, what was the question again?"

Mom tilts her head to one side, her expression gentle. "Are we ready to go?"

Oh, I didn't realize that was my call. I slap on what I hope is a super-confident face. "Yes, absolutely. Let's go. Cissy, Zeke, Tim, and Mom open the bunker. Walker, Lincoln, and I go the Arena. Then Walker takes me to the bunker. Yeah."

Dammit. I remember the awful speech I gave to Lincoln at the fountain. That one looks like genuine oratory compared to the nugget of crap that just fell from my lips.

Lincoln slips his warm hand into mine. "Together, we can do anything, Myla."

I inhale a deep breath. *I hope so, Lincoln.*

A.

I stumble out of the portal, landing in one of the Arena's darkened archways. Light flickers in from the stadium floor, casting odd shadows on the rock walls. Lincoln and Walker step out next, appearing a few feet behind me.

The Prince sets his hand on Walker's shoulder. "Before we go further, I want to thank you for taking such good care of Myla and her mother. I only asked you to deliver a few messages, and you've gone above and beyond."

My heart warms. Walker's always so awesome and I never thank him enough. Stepping up to his side, I arch my feet onto my tippy-toes and kiss him gently on the cheek. "I can't believe it, this could be our last Arena match together." I look up at the ceiling, trying to calculate. "The first time you snuck me in here was, what, eight years ago?" I smile, remembering how Walker portaled me in on the sly, saying in that low voice of his: 'you may be called to serve one day.' Together, we watched a Viperon demon fight. I was instantly hooked.

Stepping backwards, I rock on my heels, smiling at the memory. Then I realize that it's quiet in the hallway. Waaaaaaay too quiet.

Walker and Lincoln face one another, their expressions unreadable. There's a long pause accentuated by gentle pit-pat of condensation off the uneven stone.

Huh. What's going on here?

I thunk my palm onto my forehead. "I forgot, you know each other too. How did that happen?" I smile. Story-telling time! Nice distraction.

Lincoln keeps staring at Walker and not saying anything. The temperature in the hallway becomes decidedly chilly. Something's up.

Walker turns to me. "You remember how my great-grandmother was an archangel?"

I nod. "Mom told me about it ages ago."

"She's the archangel Aquila," says Walker. "She also founded the House of Rixa. Lincoln and I are both members of the Aquilinea, a society for the descendants of Aquila."

I chuckle. "I should start a society for the descendants of Xavier. It'll give me something to do when I'm alone." I look between Lincoln and Walker, waiting for a response. That wasn't my best joke, but how about a courtesy laugh for the girl heading into an Arena death match? Speaking of that, my insides squirm with anxiety. The fight should start in a few minutes.

Walker's face is still as stone. "Your mother forbade me to mention my personal history, so I've respected her wishes. Now, however, it's time you knew about the Aquilinea."

"Thanks." My head bobs from side to side. "That explains why Octavia and Lincoln trusted you with their messages." I picture the ghouls who sometimes accompany Verus to matches; I always thought some of them looked like Walker. Must be Aquilinea as well. I glance out to the Arena floor. Maybe I'll see one of them out there today? The thought should be comforting, but it isn't. Thinking about the stadium only ratchets up my nerves.

Lincoln barely moves as he speaks. "That explains you and me. How about you and Myla?"

I eye him closely. *Oooooooh, I get it.* The Prince is never an easy guy to read, but I get the definite feeling he's ticked off about something or some*one*. The short list of options are Walker, Walker, and Walker. "You didn't know that Walker knew me?"

Lincoln's gaze stays locked on Walker. "Not beyond the few messages I gave him."

A muscle flickers along Walker's jawline. "I'm under an unbreakable oath. Myla's mother must approve anything I say about her."

"How about I act as proxy for my mother?" I twiddle my fingers in Walker's direction. "I release thee from thy oath." I want to hear how Walker ended up in my life too. Besides, the mega-tension in this hallway isn't helping an already-anxious morning.

"That should work." Lincoln's eyes narrow. "Speak."

Walker inhales a long breath. "Xavier was my instructor ages ago, in the Citadel. He became like a father to me. When he left Purgatory, he asked me to watch over Camilla. I took an unbreakable oath. When Myla was born, I watched over her too."

Lincoln's hands ball into fists. "So, Myla's the mystery girl you've been visiting all these years?"

My brows jet upwards. Who knew I was a topic of conversation between Walker and Lincoln? For years, no less.

Walker juts out his chin. "Yes."

My mouth rounds into an 'o.' It took my anxious brain a bit, but I finally get what's going on here. I move to stand directly in front of the Prince, cupping his face in my hands. His day-old stubble tickles my palms as he stubbornly keeps glaring at Walker. "It's not like that between us. Walker's basically my brother." I guide his eyes to look directly into mine.

Rage simmers behind the Prince's features. "So, you two never?"

"Sha!" I roll my eyes. "I appreciate the jealousy, but we're burning up valuable goodbye kiss time."

Lincoln finally grins and leans in closer. We share a slow kiss. It's sweet, intense, and over way too soon.

The Prince presses his forehead to mine. "Be safe."

My tail musses his hair. "I will." I kiss him one more time, just because I can.

I pull my mask over my face, suck in a deep breath, and turn to Walker. "Let's do this."

Walker turns to Lincoln, setting his fist on his chest. "Goodbye, Shield Brother." I'm guessing this is a traditional farewell for the Aquilinea, but the way Walker says it, it's more of a question: 'are we okay?'

The Prince pauses, then moves his fist in the same motion. "Until we meet again." The way Lincoln says the words, it's an answer: 'We're good.'

Walker smiles. Together, we step out onto the Arena floor, heading toward a group of quasis clustered around Sharkie. All of them have long black tails with arrowhead ends.

Arena fighters. All part-Furor. The best in Purgatory.

The last time we were all gathered together, it was the Scala initiation. My forehead creases with questions.

"Walker, is there a ceremony today?"

"Not that I know of."

"Uh-huh." My shoulders constrict with anxiety. Something about this feels off. Normally there's only one kick-ass quasi on the Arena floor, along with a bunch of lesser demons. Why are all the part-Furor Arena fighters in Purgatory—every top warrior we have—gathering in the Arena today?

I scan the Arena grounds. More weirdness is afoot. Usually, there's at least one extra ghoul on the stadium floor. Today, there's only Walker and Sharkie. The exit archways sit empty as well, except for the one directly across from me. In there, Lincoln paces in the shadows, his body tense as a coiled spring. He turns in my direction. Our gaze meets. There's no joy of lovers connecting, only the focus of two warriors waiting for…*What?*

Sharkie thumps his staff on the ground. At each of the four points of the compass, a member of the Oligarchy appears along the lip of the stadium. Turning as one, they open four massive portals along the Arena's top tier. Angels and demons pour into the stands.

I catalog the crowd. The angels look as they always do: white wings, linen robes, and blue eyes. I inspect the demons and gasp. This group isn't the usual grab bag of colors, shapes, and sizes. Today, the demons are all tall, bulky, and ripped with muscles. Great wings, as dark and angled as a bat's, hang off many of their backs. Without making a sound, they take their seats with military precision. At least five thousand of them pack the towering stands.

I'm used to a howling jumble of demons. Over the years, I've stopped noticing them. But today's silence sets my nerves on a knife's edge.

I look to Sharkie. He's panting out his nose-holes, black sweat dripping down his cheeks. Walker steps to my side, setting his hand on my shoulder. In the distant archway, Lincoln turns his baculum into a fiery broadsword.

Unholy moley. Whatever's coming, it's bad.

CHAPTER TWENTY-FIVE

A

The crowd of angels and demons take their seats in record time. Verus and Armageddon are last to process into the stadium. Angels in white armor flank either side of Verus. I recognize Rhiannon and Levi. Extra protection for Verus; not a good sign.

Squinting, I examine the dark balcony. Armageddon's surrounded by massive stone-skinned demons. Clementine sits there too, a satisfied smirk twisting her piggish face. I grip my hands behind my back to hide how I'm shaking.

The match is ready to begin.

Sharkie thumps his staff one more time. "Angels, ghouls, and demons, I bring you–"

Armageddon raises his pointer finger, his voice echoing through the stadium. "I request the presence of the Scala and Scala Heir." He shoots a snide glance at the Oligarchy. "Do you agree?"

Huh. As if they'd ever disagree.

The Oligarchy speak in unison. "Call the bearers."

Minutes tick by. I hop in place, cracking my neck from side to side. Man, I hate waiting around. Pisses. Me. Off. My inner wrath demon awakens, sending my tail in arc over my shoulder. New emotions—rage and frustration—combine with the terror that overwhelmed me before. Makes me feel better, actually. My shoulders loosen, getting ready to hit something.

Finally, a long portal opens in the center of the Arena floor. Out of it steps six ghouls carrying a stretcher. The Scala lies atop it, deep in sleep. Nearby stands the Scala Heir in her white robes. Her head is held high (a little too high, in the opinion of the *real* Scala Heir) as she scans the crowd.

Adair raises her hand. "I'd like to say something, if I may?"

Sharkie bows. "Of course, oh, Scala Heir."

"I was so touched when this random ghoul visited me and asked if I could join you people today. It really shows you've come to revere me. Thank you. Really."

I shoot a glance toward Lincoln. His gaze shifts between me and Adair; he shakes his head from side to side. I know exactly what he's thinking: she should never be here without any thrax to protect her.

Dingbat.

Sharkie pounds his staff onto the stadium floor. "Now we shall–"

Armageddon sniffs. Sharkie and the stadium fall silent. "I was not finished."

My muscles tighten as fear crawls up my spine. I don't like the smug grin rounding Armageddon's mouth. What could he possibly have to say? Get on with the match already.

Muscles twitch in the emcee's gray neck. In her balcony, Verus grips her throne, her blue eyes narrowing into slits. A long pause follows, then Sharkie stammers out one word: "Ye…Yes?"

Rising to his feet, Armageddon shoots his thin arms high. "ATTACK!"

My body freezes with shock. Fuuuuuuuuuuuuck.

What happens next takes seconds, but each one ekes by in what feels like years, beginning with demons streaming out of the stands and onto the Arena floor. I gasp, suddenly realizing why all the part-Furor fighters in Purgatory—every top quasi warrior we have—were brought together in the Arena today:

To wipe us all out at once.

I scan the top lip of the stadium. The Oligarchy stand stunned, their skeletal heads wagging. They stumble about for a bit, then step into their own portals and disappear. The main exit goes with them.

Thanks a lot, assholes.

In the white stands, the angels form an ad hoc group around Verus's balcony, but it's unclear if they want to protect her or look for escape. Either way, these aren't warriors. The demon fighters close in with military precision, slaughtering their way through the angel spectators to reach Verus and her entourage.

My body shivers with icy shock. I can't believe what I'm seeing.

Spreading her wings, Verus takes to flight. Some of her guard fight the demons in hand-to-hand combat, others take to the air and surround their Queen. A pack of demons pump their bat-like wings and rise into the air as well. The two sides claw, swoop, and stab each other in a dog-fight above my head.

The sight is surreal, overwhelming. The world moves by in super-slow motion. My heartbeat booms in my ears. I inspect the Arena floor, looking for the archway where Lincoln was waiting. He's no longer there.

Walker touches my shoulder, snapping me back to attention. "I've used Group Think to call my brothers and sisters in the Aquilinea. They'll transport as many angels as they can." He scans the crowd. "We need to get you out of here." He frowns. "There are too many people around to easily open a portal, but I'll have to try."

"What about Lincoln?" I scan the nearby crowd, seeing little past the close press of bodies.

Walker closes his eyes. "He's on the Arena floor." He grabs my hand. "I'll come back for him right after I move you."

"Got it." Bracing myself, I wait for the familiar buzz of a portal opening.

Nothing happens.

Around us, the stadium breaks out into full-bore pandemonium. Screams echo through the air. Demons, angels, and quasis scramble about, their bodies a jumble of bloody, hand-to-hand combat. Lincoln's caught somewhere in that tangle of war. My chest tightens. We all have to escape, now.

I search Walker's face, panic swirling through me. "What's wrong?"

His features contort. "Give it a moment, there are so many—"

But Walker's interrupted. Two dark and nasty Crini demons step in front of us, making for sixteen giant octopus legs to fend off at once.

Unholy moley.

The first Crini grabs Walker around the belly and squeezes. Now, Walker can barely breathe, let alone open a portal.

I round on the first Crini, my eyes blazing with fury. *How dare you lay a tentacle on my Walker?!* I dig in my heels, ready to leap up and kick in its face, when the second Crini takes a swipe at my back.

Dammit! Walker will have to wait.

I duck low while my tail goes to work, slicing through two of my attacker's arms. I quickly shoot a glance at Walker; his arms and legs are braced between the creature's long black beak and huge red eyes. It's taking all his strength not to get stuffed into the Crini's mouth.

That gives me an idea.

My Crini lunges at me again; this time I hold stock-still. The creature's arm wraps about me, pulling me toward its snapping jaws. I play possum until I'm inches away from its beak, then stab my tail through its eye and brain. The demon howls, then falls over dead. Hah!

I'm dropped in a heartbeat, only to get scooped up by Walker's monster. Fresh rage blasts through me. *This slimy monster picked the wrong girl.* The Crini wraps two massive arms wrap about my body; a third holds my tail firmly in place.

Dammit, this one's clever.

Panic zooms through me. I can't move my arms, legs, or tail. The Crini's great eyes flip between me and Walker, debating the better meal. Its gaze locks on me. Not good. With a curl of its tentacle, the demon moves Walker away from its mouth. After that, he pulls my head toward its jaws instead.

I writhe and struggle, but it's no use. The Crini opens its long beak. Green razor-sharp teeth line its mouth. Saliva drips from its huge pink tongue. Everything takes on a dreamlike quality. I seem to float outside myself as the monster drags my head deep within its jaws.

This is it. I'm about to get killed. Somehow I feel numbed instead of terrified.

I wince, my hands balling into fists. I struggle to break loose from the monster's grip, but it's no use. All I can do is wait for a CRACK as its teeth sink into my skull.

Instead of biting down, the creature's jaws loosen. Its tentacle-arms fall slack, allowing me to twist out of its grip. I gain solid footing and scan the Arena.

Holy crap, what happened there? I scope out the Arena's floor. Lincoln stands nearby, his baculum sword blazing. The Crini lies in two neat halves by his feet. I exhale a long breath, relief filling every cell in my body.

"I owe you one." I smile.

He grins, wagging his eyebrows suggestively. "I know."

I chuckle, more than thankful for the smile.

The Prince grabs my hand; his fire-sword disappears. "Walker's free, let's get out of here."

Relief washes over me. Walker's okay and we can leave! I scope out the stadium floor. Walker stands nearby, his arm gripping his belly, his face writhing in pain. A portal lays open beside him, its shape flickering in and out of focus.

We don't have long. Walker's so hurt, he can barely keep a half-portal open. We need to get him help and us to safety. Lincoln and I race toward the opened portal.

A high-pitched scream rattles our eardrums, freezing us both in place. Lincoln winces. "I know that voice."

"I do too. It's Adair." My heart sinks. *Why didn't that high-maintenance dip leave with the Scala?*

Squinting, I see Adair standing beside the lifeless hulk of a Manus demon. The creature lays face-down on the Arena floor, its body a mound of bloody wounds and matted black fur.

As I watch Adair scream and flail, my mouth scrunches onto one side of my face. This is what you call a 'classic moral dilemma.' On the one hand, I have Walker, clearly injured and struggling to open a portal so he can save himself, me, and the man that I love. On the other hand, I have Adair, who walked into this situation like a dumbass and arguably deserves to die. On top of everything, I'm part demon. Nobody *really* expects me to do the right thing here. I could grab Lincoln, shove us both through the portal, and easily talk my way out of it later. *Uh-oh, I totally panicked. My bad!* Inside my soul, my wrath demon growls, encouraging a fast exit.

A fast exit? Not a bad thought, really.

Once again, Adair screams like her head will explode and, damn it, I feel sorry for her lame ass. Nitwit or not, she doesn't deserve to die alone on the Arena floor.

Crap, I'm about to do the right thing again, just like I did for her father at the Winter tournament. Hopefully I won't live to regret it.

I motion to Walker. "Close the portal. We have to get Adair." Walker nods, the black door disappears. He stands still for a moment, grips his belly tighter and then crumples onto the Arena floor.

Hells Bells.

I kneel at Walker's side. "Are you alright?" My hands anxiously flutter near the general area of his belly. Playing nursemaid isn't exactly my strong suit.

Walker speaks through gritted teeth. "I'll be fine. The Crini demon caused some–" he winces "–internal damage. I have the gift of self-healing from my grandmother. I just need a little time." His face looks milky-pale.

Archangels have list of powers a mile long, their offspring usually inherit only one or two of them. I let out a long breath.

If Walker can self-heal, he'll be fine. I only wish Lincoln or I had that ability too.

I give Walker's hand an awkward pat. "Take as long as you need."

The Prince taps my shoulder; I rise to my feet. "What's up?"

He points across the Arena floor. "Tinea demon." A muscle twitches along his upper lip. "And it's heading straight for Adair."

"Of course, it is." My heart sinks. The Tinea's a humanoid worm about five feet tall with a sinewy body, greasy brown skin, and a great gaping hole of a mouth. Its head is an eyeless lump covered with fine, hair-like quills. Diamond-sharp claws shaped like rotors spin at the end of its rope-like arms and legs.

This thing is so badass, it isn't even funny. And I've never even *heard* of someone killing one. Knots of tension crawl up my legs and back. We are so screwed.

Tineas are the demon of choice if you want someone kidnapped or dead. Once they lock on your voice and gait, they never give up. Armageddon must have sent this one after Adair. I inspect the stadium floor, looking for the old Scala. There's no sign of him or his ghoul carriers. They probably high-tailed it out at the first sign of trouble and forgot all about the Scala Heir.

Well, Armageddon didn't forget.

"I'll stall the demon." Lincoln reignites his baculum. "Make sure she doesn't move or make any noise." I nod. Tineas hunt by touch and sound. If Adair stays quiet and still, it won't find her.

I bump fists with Lincoln and race off toward Adair. As I speed along, my gaze falls on the Arena's upper levels. An icy jolt of fear runs through me. The top lip of the Arena is covered with demons as they crawl, fly, and demolish their way out of the stadium.

They're off to overrun Purgatory.

Nausea overtakes me. Anyone I've ever known—students, teachers, and even the old mechanic who tries to fix Betsy—could be murdered today.

I shake my head from side to side. No time to think about that now.

351

Scanning the grounds around me, I find the Arena floor has mostly cleared out, only a half-dozen quasis and demons still battle it out nearby. A handful of Walker's Aquilinea brothers and sisters roam the grounds, opening portals for any angels that remain. Too many white-robed bodies lay lifeless on the stone seats. My throat tightens with grief.

I shift my gaze upwards. The skies are now clear; I can only hope Verus escaped while I was fighting the Crinis. I cross my fingers. *Please, let her live.*

Off in the stands, Armageddon sits still and tall in his dark throne. He licks his thin lips and catalogs the stadium. The seats are smashed, the archways shattered, and bodies of all kinds lay everywhere. His gaze lingers on the Tinea and he smiles. "Phase one is well in hand. Follow me." He and his entourage scale out of the Arena.

The tension in my back loosens a bit. At least that's one less thing to worry about.

Adair's only a few yards away now, looking willowy and bored in her white robes as she stomps about the stadium floor. I raise my arm. "Hey! Adair!"

Her tiny eyes glare at me over a pug nose. "Who are you?"

I stop before her and peel off my mask. "I'm Myla Lewis."

"Oh yeah, you're the one who stripped at the ball." She sneers. "Cunnus girl."

Normally, I'd knock her block off at this point. Instead, I take a deep breath and ball my hands into fists. "Look, Adair. You're in serious danger. There's a demon after you."

She giggles. "No, there's not." A Crini lurches past us on its way out of the stadium. "Watch this." She taps a tentacle with her finger. "Hello!"

The Crini examines me and Adair, its red eyes flaring demon-bright. The monster creeps closer, its long tentacles raised high. I move into battle stance, my tail arching over my shoulder.

Across the stadium floor, the Tinea fights Lincoln, its diamond claws sparring with the Prince's baculum sword. Angling its head-lump toward the Crini, the Tinea lets out a series of angry chirps.

I don't speak Tinea, but I'm guessing it's something like 'back off buddy, I got her.' The Crini pauses, shivers, and slinks away.

Adair grins. "See, what I mean? They won't touch the Scala Heir, although this thing–" she kicks the dead Manus demon "– almost crushed me when it fell over."

"The other demons avoid you because Armageddon sent the Tinea." I'm careful to whisper every word. "As long as you stand totally still and keep your voice down, the Tinea can't track you. So stay quiet and don't move, okay?"

"Sure, whatever." Adair glances around the stadium floor, her body language screaming 'she's not with me.'

Rage coils inside my belly. I'm trying to save Adair's life and, like her jackass of a father, she's too stuck-up and stubborn to see it.

Adair speaks in a full voice. "Look, all I'm worried about is a ride home. I should never have agreed to stop by the Arena this morning, only the ghoul asked so nicely."

Ride home? Is she serious? "Demons are attacking Purgatory, Adair."

"So?"

I'm about to say 'so your people probably evacuated,' but she's keeping her voice down (sort-of) and not moving. Why push it? "I'm sure someone will be here soon."

Adair freezes. "Lincoln!" She jumps up and down. "My Prince is here to save me."

Enough, already. My hands grip her upper arm. "What part of 'stand still and shut up' was unclear?"

"Lincoln! Oh, Lincoln!" She tugs us both toward the Prince and the Tinea.

I dig my heels into the Arena floor and hold her arm firm. "Adair, what did I say? Stay quiet and don't move. Lincoln is *fighting a demon* right now."

She squirms harder under my grasp. "Let me go!" She turns to me. "How dare you–" She freezes, her eyes carefully inspecting my face. "Hey, when did you get those blue irises?"

Unholy moley. I can see where this is going, and it's not a happy place.

"I don't have blue irises. You're seeing things." Not my best lie.

"Did you come here with Lincoln? You two disappeared at the party after your little Cunnus girl thing." Her tiny eyes thin to slits. "I need to talk to the High Prince. Now." She pokes my rib cage with her pointer finger. "I'll have you know, he and I are basically almost-engaged."

I take a deep breath. "Sure you are." I want to kick her. So. Hard. "Focus, Adair. Remember the nasty worm demon?"

"Lincoln!" She yanks against me with all her strength.

I speak in the loudest whisper I can manage. "Adair, *stay still.*"

She drags us both a few feet across the stadium floor. "I know what you're trying to do." Panic flickers in her eyes. "You're pretending to be the Scala Heir, aren't you?" She shoots a desperate look at Lincoln. "Well, you're not. I'm the Scala Heir. I'M THE SCALA HEEEEEEIR!"

Crap.

The Tinea stops. Angling its lumpy head, it sniffs through two jagged nose-holes. "Scala Heir."

Oh no, it smells the scent of igni on me, just like Armageddon did.

Lincoln hacks away at the Tinea's body, but the wounds heal as soon as they're made. The only way to kill a Tinea is to cut all four wormy limbs at once. Which is why no one's ever done it.

The demon plunges its arms into the ground, its body quickly burrowing under the soil of the Arena. It leaves behind a narrow hole in the stadium floor. I stare at the darkened pit, wishing I could jump in and hide for a little while. Maybe just until Adair's dead.

Lincoln sprints in our direction. "Don't move!"

"See, I was right. My Prince will save me." Adair's face twists into a haughty smile. "I'm thrax, and thrax know demons. That worm-thing was nothing to worry about."

Ugh, I can't believe she's this thick. Leaning my weight on my right hip, I watch her hop about and call for her Prince. Oh yeah, I believe.

"The demon will resurface any second." I grip her arm tighter. "Don't move or it will show up right by your—"

"Lincoln! I knew you'd come for me." She jumps up and down. Again.

I sigh. "Adair, you need to work on your listening skills."

Lincoln stands beside the false Scala Heir. I release her arm; she cuddles into his chest. "Oh, my Prince! I was so frightened."

Rage boils through me. Hands off, he's mine.

Lincoln pats her back. "Everything will be fine, Adair." His gaze shifts to me. "Myla, you said you'd keep her still."

Sweet Satan! No way are my Adair management skills getting critiqued here. I set my fists on my hips. "I tried. She's kind-of a bitch."

Laughter dances in Lincoln's eyes.

Adair rounds on me. At least she's detached her cheek from his collarbone. "No one speaks to the Scala Heir in that manner!"

That did it. I raise my hand to shoulder height, ready to bring down a whole lotta igni pain on her blonde head.

Before I can get too far, the Tinea starts to resurface. Near our feet, the soil of the Arena floor trembles and rises. Rotor-like hands break through the ground. A lumpy head and wormy body follow. The leathery skin shimmers with mucus.

Adair screams her head off.

The quills on the Tinea vibrate, then fall still. The creature sniffs through its thin nose-holes. My mind snaps into battle mode. Anger at Adair, worry for Walker, and fear about the future…It all disappears as my mind starts calculating possible attack vectors and defense moves. The dance of battle begins.

The Tinea's hole of a mouth stretches wide. Its lumpy head turns in my direction. "Scala Heir."

My body goes into battle stance, tail arched over my shoulder. Lincoln and I are on the same side of the Tinea. Not the best way to attack this thing.

"No, no, no!" Adair leaps between me and the demon. "*I'm* the Scala Heir."

Lincoln grabs her arm, trying to pull her out of the way. She won't budge.

The Tinea's wormy arms extend toward Adair, ready to stab through her belly, all in an attempt to get at me. My mind clicks through different moves and counter-moves.

Yeah, that'll do it.

Crouching to the ground, I swing out my leg, slamming my shin behind Adair's feet. The force of my kick takes her out at the ankles. Adair stumbles backwards, falling onto the dirt floor with a thump. The Tinea's arms whiz harmlessly above our heads.

Yes, that saved her life.

And yes, I totally enjoyed kicking her.

Adair's mismatched eyes look wide and glossy with fear. "That demon could have killed me." For once, she sits quietly and keeps her yap shut.

Lincoln and I stand side by side, the Tinea paused before us. The creature angles its head-lump toward me. "Scala Heir." It starts to burrow underground. Based on the angle, it'll resurface right behind Lincoln. Not good.

I stare at the burrowing demon and scratch my chin. The thing's pretty harmless in digging mode and there's no way to cut its limbs underground. We've got a little breather. "Lincoln, remember when I said I owed you one?"

"Clearly." Lincoln reignites his baculum. "I have big plans for how you'll pay me back." Before us, the Tinea has almost disappeared into the soil.

Shifting my hips, I spear it through the head with my tail. Spinning about, I slingshot the demon across the Arena floor. It slams into the opposite wall with a gooey thwack. "The Tinea was digging to resurface behind you. Now we're even."

Lincoln half-smiles. "Thanks, I think."

Across the Arena floor, the Tinea regains its footing and burrows into the soil.

Lincoln's eyes open extra-wide. "I've got an idea." He splits the baculum so his broadsword becomes two fiery short-swords. Standing at alert, he waits for the demon to resurface. "Get behind me."

Okay, I can see where he's going. It's easiest to finish the Tinea if we attack from opposite sides, but if we walk into position, the demon will know exactly where we are. We need the element of surprise.

I stand behind Lincoln, my body on high alert. Adair sits nearby, watching us with her jaw hanging open. My mind clicks back into battle mode, but this time with a difference. Now I calculate more than my own moves and counter-moves. I smile. Fighting as a team feels beyond awesome.

The ground before Lincoln rises. Rotor-like hands break through the surface.

My body tenses, a coiled spring ready to break free. Shifting my weight to the balls of my feet, I speak in a whisper. "Now?"

Lincoln's voice is calm and low. "Not yet."

The Tinea's greasy head-lump breaks through the Arena floor. I want to move so badly; it takes all my focus to wait. Next, the demon's wormy torso follows out of the hole. I shake out my fingertips, trying to release some of the tension. Finally, ropy legs pop out of the dirt and lock onto the ground.

"Now, Myla!" Lincoln bends over at the waist. Setting my foot onto his back, I launch myself into the air, somersault-twist over the Tinea's head, and land behind the demon in a crouch. Lincoln raises his short-swords high.

That's my cue.

As Lincoln brings his blades down through the demon's arms, I swipe my tail through the monster's legs. The creature pauses, shivers, then disintegrates into a puddle of brownish goop.

Sweet. Taking down a Tinea's one for the record books.

Adair sits nearby, her face colorless. "You killed it. Together."

Lincoln and I bump fists. "That's right." I wiggle my bottom. "We are a lean, mean demon killing machine."

Lincoln laughs; Adair doesn't. Surprisingly, she's acting more shocked than arrogant, which is a nice change of pace. Gripping her elbows, she speaks through chattering teeth. "How'd you know how to fight like that?"

Wow. A question that doesn't involve Scala Heir-related whining. Adair needs to almost die more often. I jog in place, cracking my neck from side to side. "Lincoln broke the baculum in two, so obviously he's going for the demon's arms. And if he's taking out the arms, then I need to get the legs. That's the only way to kill a Tinea."

The Prince wraps his hands about my waist. "Nicely done."

I kiss the tip of his nose. "Back at ya." Suddenly, I'm very aware that I'm wearing a skin-tight cat-suit and Lincoln looks yummy in his body armor. The air around us pulses with energy. If Adair weren't staring at me like I was another Tinea, I'd totally kiss Lincoln right now.

The Prince reads my mind. "Later, Myla."

I purse my lips, half frowning. "Got anything more specific for me on that?"

Lincoln frames my face with his fingertips. "There will be time for us. I swear it." He's talking about more than a kiss. Desire blasts through me. *Oh, yeah.* My eyes flare bright red.

The Prince leans in closer, his mouth outside my ear. "I think that's a record for fastest time from zero to sparkling."

My mouth curves into a semi-snarky grin. "You're such a competitive little creep." *And I wouldn't have it any other way.*

Stepping back, I exhale a long breath. We can't afford to stand around cracking jokes. "I need to find Walker. I'm late to the bunker as it is."

Lincoln's brows arch. "*I* need? Do you think you're going alone?"

I mock-frown. "I thought that was the plan." Lincoln's staying with me? Wow. A bright spot in an otherwise bleak day. My heart lightens.

"When Armageddon invaded Purgatory, the plans changed. I'm not going anywhere until I'm certain you're safe."

I kick the ground with my heel. "I'd tell you to join your people, but you won't listen to me anyway."

Lincoln shoots me a sly grin. "And secretly, you totally want me around."

My cheeks turn pink. *Am I that obvious?* "That too."

"Knew it." With a wink in my direction, Lincoln turns to Adair, offering his arm. "Can you walk?"

She keeps her hands to herself, for once. "I'm fine."

"Very good." The Prince tilts his head. "I'm afraid you must travel with us until we can get you home."

"That's okay." Adair's voice is barely above a whisper. I eye her for a long moment, my forehead creased in thought. Our fight with the Tinea demon changed her somehow, but I can't put my finger on it. I shrug. Whatever it is, she's certainly less irritating.

"Hello, there!" Walker limps toward us, his arm raised in welcome. I'm happy to see that his skin's a healthier shade of pale. Around him, the stadium looks pretty much deserted. "I can portal everyone to the bunker now, if you're ready."

My gaze shifts between Walker and Lincoln. With my two favorite guys along for the ride? *I'm more than ready.*

CHAPTER TWENTY-SIX

A.

Exiting the portal, I step into the dim light of the bunker's main chamber. Walker, Adair, and Lincoln follow behind me. The space is huge, square, and made of poured concrete. Industrial lanterns dangle from long ceiling cords, casting halos of light on the floor. Steel shelves line the walls, each one overflowing with supplies. Metal folding chairs lie unopened in stacks. Mom, Tim, Cissy, and Zeke wait along the opposite wall.

I wave to them. "Hey, guys."

No one speaks. That's odd. "Don't all say hello at once." I grin.

Still no reply. The hairs on my neck stand on end. Alarm rattles through my body. Twisting about, I glance at the communications console. The monitors are still dark. My forehead creases. Everything was supposed to be turned on by now.

I gesture to Cissy and Zeke. "What are you two still doing here?"

No one says a word. Tim and Cissy huddle closer, taking a few steps away from the others. Adair scuttles off to a corner and skulks, sitting with her arms wrapped about her knees. At least she isn't screaming.

My forehead creases a little more. Why is Cissy anywhere near Tim? This is off, way off. The alarm bells in my body ring louder, setting my teeth on edge.

Walker frowns, pointing his long arm toward Tim. "Why haven't you transported the young quasis?"

Tim's black eyes flare red, his mouth twists into an evil grin. "Why? You have to ask *why*?"

A bolt of chilly fear runs down my spine. I never liked that Tim.

Walker bares his teeth. "Answer my question, TIM-29."

"Because I know who this one *really is*." Tim points his bony finger toward Mom. "You'd never accept being a seamstress, Senator. You're plotting against the ghoul government, you and that witch you call a daughter. I chose to side against my people once, when I decided to work for you. I won't make that mistake twice." He tells a good story, but the tremor in his voice hints at a different tale. For Tim, this is about more than being a patriotic ghoul. He still cares for my Mom and he's pissed she doesn't *like him-like him*. He wants revenge.

Tim spins Cissy around. He holds a short spear against her spine. "This weapon's covered in poison. Make no mistake; one scratch will kill her. None of you move."

Oh, damn. And here I thought Tim was so adult for helping out even though Mom loved Xavier. My wrath demon spews fire into my veins. What a whiny little loser! I glare at his bony hand on Cissy's arm. So help me, if he hurts her, I'll rip his head off. And that's just for starters.

Lincoln speaks in a low and deliberate voice. "We came from the Arena. The demons attacked everyone, ghouls included. The Oligarchy barely escaped with their lives. We're on the same side, friend."

"The demons attacked, eh?" Tim scowls. "And whose fault is that? You forget, I worked with the Senator for years. She'd never give up on the republic. She's still scheming and fighting, mark my words."

Mom's voice is calm and soothing. "Please understand, Tim. I'm not the same–"

"Spare me." He turns to Mom, eyes blazing. "I'm not sure how you've angered Armageddon, but you'll pay for it. The Oligarchy are coming."

A new portal opens; through it steps the Oligarchy in their deep red robes. The Scala lies on a stretcher between them, the old thrax's eyes closed in deep sleep. The portal disappears.

Bands of anxiety bind my shoulders and neck. The Oligarchy are *here*? The whole reason for this little bunker excursion was so I could hide from power-freaks like them. Once they know who I am, they'll try to control me. Rage and frustration careen through my body, tension coils through every muscle. Damn, damn, damn!

I grit my teeth, forcing my breathing to slow. Stay calm, it's only the Oligarchy. These aren't the scariest monsters in town, by far. It's not like Armageddon's here.

Tim's sneer melts into a look of awe. "Mighty Oligarchy, I bring you a prisoner to appease our invaders." He gestures to Mom. "Senator Lewis." Next, he points directly at me. "And *that* one may pretend to have special powers. Don't be fooled."

The Oligarchy set down the Scala's stretcher. "Excellent work." Their heads swivel in unison as they survey the room. "And this place is safe from demons?"

"Yes, it's surrounded in angelfire." Tim nods his head so vigorously, I'm shocked he doesn't get whiplash. "It's the perfect place to conduct your negotiations."

The Oligarchy nod. "And you're certain this plan will work?"

Tim's huge black eyes beam with pride. "Yes, it's like I told you. Senator Lewis would never *really* become a seamstress. She's been planning to restore the old republic. Believe me, *this* is why Armageddon invaded. Get rid of the Senator, you'll get rid of him too."

I sigh. Tim doesn't know how Mom changed after she lost Xavier. He can't imagine Senator Lewis doing anything but fight. My mouth droops into a frown as I stare into the Oligarchy's open, gullible faces. They're grasping at any straw rather than face the truth about Armageddon.

The Oligarchy let out a low hiss, then speak in unison. "The King of Hell arrives any moment." Their heads turn in a single motion, scanning the room. "Let us hope that handing over the Senator is enough to appease him."

My jaw drops. Armageddon invades Purgatory and *this* is the master plan to drive him out: hand over my mother? Talk about living in a dream world. My insides twist with worry at the thought of Mom in the hands of that fiend. Who am I kidding? Any of us could be handed over to the King of Hell. It's across-the-boards terrifying.

"You told Armageddon where we're all hiding?" Mom rolls her eyes. "He'll come here all right, but not just for us."

The Oligarchy look around the room, their gaze pausing on the Scala and then Adair. "We see the Scala Heir is here as well."

Tim rushes to Adair's side, pulling her up from the floor. "Yes, mighty Oligarchy. She'll be useful to you. If the Senator isn't enough, you can negotiate with her as well."

The Oligarchy's eyes flare bright. "Yes, most suitable."

Adair struggles under Tim's grip. "I'm not the Scala Heir. It was all a fake." She points directly at me. "She's the one. She's the Heir."

My back teeth lock. *Now* she decides I'm the Scala Heir.

The Oligarchy let out a gurgle that I'm guessing is their laugh. "You're whatever Armageddon believes you to be, little girl."

Adair staggers backwards until her back hits the concrete wall. "But I'm not the Heir, really." All the color drains from her face.

"It won't come to that." The Oligarchy hiss in what I'm guessing is meant to be a comforting tone. "Armageddon will take the Senator and leave."

My stomach churns with an unpleasant realization. The Oligarchy may be grasping at straws in offering Mom to Armageddon, but they aren't all *that* stupid. They brought the Scala in here and are acting nicey-nice with Adair for one reason: they'll give Armageddon anything he wants in order to save themselves. And the King of Hell wants his son back. No doubt, he wants whoever succeeds the Scala too.

"Don't worry, Great Scala Heir." The Oligarchy bow slightly to Adair. "The plan is perfect. Handing over the Senator will work."

Walker's eyes blaze red. "Time to change the plan." He lowers his head and a portal starts to take shape by the far wall.

The Oligarchy's gaze snaps in Walker's direction. "Don't try to circumvent us, traitor." The portal vanishes.

Crud. The Oligarchy shut Walker down. We're running out of options.

An idea appears in my mind. Maybe I can distract the Oligarchy with an igni display. I don't need much time, just long enough for Walker to open a portal. I nod to myself; that's an awesome scheme. Raising my hand to shoulder-height, I close my eyes. Lincoln instantly grabs my wrist, pulling it down.

"Myla, please." His mouth barely moves as he whispers to me. "He'll know."

No question which 'him' Lincoln's talking about: Armageddon.

I catch the Prince's gaze, see the spark of desperation and fear in his eyes. "Hiding you, it's the reason we're all here."

My gaze shifts to Adair, who still huddles against the wall, pale and shivering. "What about Adair?"

A muscle twitches along Lincoln's jawline. "What about Armageddon getting both the Scala and the Scala Heir? With that kind of power, he could control all the five realms. This is bigger than any of us, Myla."

I nod, gripping my hands behind my back. I feel the weight of being the Scala Heir seep into my bones. This is the pits. Why didn't I back down when Mom said I shouldn't ask questions about my father?

Across the room, the Oligarchy gesture to the Scala. "Maxon." The old man half-opens his eyes. In Latin, the Oligarchy whisper the words for "Imprison them." The Scala raises his withered hand, a flurry of igni dance around his fingertips. He repeats the words of the Oligarchy, "Imprison them," and closes his eyes once more.

The igni break free from his hand and fly about the room, encircling everyone except the Oligarchy and Tim. The bolts quickly turn into electric cords that bind our hands and feet. Tim lowers his spear from Cissy's back; he no longer needs it.

I stare at the igni wrapped about my wrists, feeling their calming effect on my soul. Sensing my power, they reach out to me, little tendrils of thought that seep in through my skin. I want to set them free so badly, it's like a pain in my chest. Their music and laughter gently echo inside my head, dozens of spirit-children calling me to come out and play. *I can't, little ones. I have to hide.*

The Oligarchy's eyes blaze bright red. "Every Scala develops a special skill with igni beyond the soul column. Our Maxon creates ropes and cages." Their four mouths coil into satisfied grins. "Don't bother trying to escape. Nothing can break your bonds." They turn to Tim. "Go outside to Armageddon. Tell him we await his orders."

Nodding, Tim creates a portal and disappears.

The Oligarchy inspects our faces. "There's no need for all of you to suffer for the Senator's crimes." Their voices come out syrupy and low. "Help us. We'll keep you safe from Armageddon."

"And how will you manage that, exactly?" Mom lets out a sigh that says 'I can't believe I'm having this conversation again.' "You can't protect *yourselves* from him."

The portal reopens. Tim steps through, his chest slashed wide open, a mass of purple organs wriggling inside. "Lord Armageddon says thank you for the offer, but he's here to kill us all."

Tim crumbles to the floor, dead. The walls shake as something tries to break through the sands and into our bunker.

Armageddon is coming.

Unholy Hell. What a disaster. This bunker was supposed to hide me away from Armageddon and the Oligarchy. Instead, both baddies are yards away and everyone I love is imprisoned, myself included. Unless something changes soon, I'm calling on the igni. Maybe there's still a chance to open a portal and escape.

The Oligarchy quiver in their red robes. "Armageddon would destroy us all?"

Mom scowls. "Of course, he will." She snaps her fingers. "Like *that.*"

The Scala's eyes pop wide open. Clearly, he picked up enough English to understand when someone says 'Armageddon will kill you.'

The old thrax sits upright, his crinkled face trembling in terror. "Armageddon is here!"

Seeing his chance, Lincoln calls to the awakened Scala in Latin. "Thrax! Brother!"

Excitement rushes through my bloodstream. If there's one thing I've learned about the thrax, it's that they loooooove their traditions. And there's no bigger thrax tradition than to do whatever royalty tells you.

Hearing his native tongue, the Scala turns to Lincoln. He says two words in a reverent tone: "My Prince."

Ha! Knew it.

The electric bonds around Lincoln's hands and feet disappear. The Scala collapses back onto his stretcher. "Come here, my Prince."

The Oligarchy's stare snaps onto the Scala. "Maxon! Imprison him!" They point to Lincoln.

The old man's gaze flips back and forth between the Oligarchy and Lincoln. His lower lip twitches. Anxious silence fills the room. One thought runs through every mind: Will the Scala honor Lincoln or the ghouls?

The old man sighs. "I cannot harm my Prince." He reaches out a withered hand to Lincoln. "Come sit beside me, brother."

The Oligarchy bare their teeth. "How dare you?"

The Scala raises his hand. "You want imprisonment too?" A few igni swirl lazily about his palm. "I can oblige." He lets out a low cough. "Your people care for me and keep me safe, so I've been willing to follow your orders. But when it comes to my Prince, there can be no negotiation." His eyes narrow. "Don't rely too much that *I* rely on you."

The Oligarchy stare at the Scala, the gears of their collective mind churning through scenarios and Group Think, trying to brainstorm how to bend the Scala to their will. A long minute ticks by before the four ghouls slowly lower their heads. "As you wish, Great Scala."

My mouth rounds with a satisfied smile. Other than hand the old guy over to the King of Hell, they've got no other options here…And they won't do any handing-over until Armageddon guarantees their safety. Long story short, Lincoln bought us a little time. I roll my shoulders and stretch, feeling a sense of calm seep into my body, despite my bindings.

Lincoln kneels beside the Scala's stretcher. "I am Lincoln Vidar Osric Aquilus from the House of Rixa, High Prince of the Thrax. Release them all. Now."

The Scala stares at Lincoln for a moment, then he flicks his hand. "I obey my Prince." All our igni bindings disappear. I rub my wrists, feeling the blood flow once again into my fingertips. *Nice work, honey.*

The Scala grips Lincoln's arm. "They say Armageddon is coming. I must escape!"

The old man looks so wild-eyed and desperate, I can't help but feel sorry for him. Chances are, he'll end up with daddy Armageddon in a matter of hours. A shiver runs across my shoulders. Poor guy.

Lincoln gently pats the Scala's frail arm. "Yes, Armageddon attacks." He turns to the Oligarchy. "I wish him portaled to safety. What do you want in exchange?"

The Oligarchy lower their heads and close their eyes. "Group Think is a jumble. It isn't safe to portal anywhere."

Lincoln shoots them a knowing look. "So, you haven't thought of a suitable trade for his safety. Yet." The Prince returns his attention to the Scala. "We'll keep trying, brother. But we must stay here for now."

The Scala's papery hand grabs Lincoln's arm. "Ignite your baculum. Give me an honest death, my Prince."

I bite my lip, remembering the words of Armageddon in my vision: 'I'll drag you to hell to suffer.' Honestly, if daddy Armageddon were beating down MY door, I'd beg for death too.

Lincoln shakes his head from side to side. "No, brother." He turns away. The old man grabs a dagger from a holster on Lincoln's thigh. Fast as a heartbeat, the ancient thrax buries the blade into his own chest, stabbing himself through his heart. His white cloak blooms red with blood.

Holy crap.

I've seen my share of blood on the Arena floor. Matches don't always have a happy ending. A familiar set of emotions sweep through me: shock, pity, grief. But this time, those feelings are amplified by the tiny voices in my heart and mind. Igni mourn their friend's injury with a child-like intensity. I bite into my knuckle, trying to stifle the sobs that swell in my throat.

Cissy's the first to speak. "Lincoln! The Scala!"

Spinning about, Lincoln leans over the thrax, inspecting the wound. "No, brother!" The old man's chest heaves and falls silent. His wrinkled hand tumbles off the stretcher.

Lincoln sets his fingertips on the old man's neck. "He's gone."

The igni's weeping grows louder in my mind. My legs go wobbly beneath me. *He was all they knew for a thousand years.*

The Oligarchy's eyes blaze blood-red. "Traitors! Murderers! You've killed our—" The dead Scala moves. The Oligarchy shut their mouths.

One by one, the igni seep from the Scala's lifeless form and swirl around his body. He begins to breathe again. The dead man opens his eyes; both glow bright blue. Around him, the tiny igni multiply into a wide column of light. Inside my mind, their little voices turn silent. The quiet's unnerving; I gnaw my lower lip.

Something is coming. *Something big.*

The dead man points to me. His movements are jerky and odd. "I give my powers to the new Scala."

There's a millisecond that lasts a million years where I flat-out panic. Can't we get someone else to do this job? Maybe I can go back to being Myla Lewis, human paramecium and Arena fighter extraordinaire. Forget my father, forget my new powers, and forget the millions of souls that need transport to Heaven or Hell. I know who I am and want no part of it. *Let me go.*

Then, the igni burst into a song that only I can hear. There are no words this time, only gentle voices and sweet music, enveloping me in a blanket of calm. My heart rate slows to almost zero. My breath all but disappears. The world around me fades until there's only their lovely music. A column of ingi slowly swirls across the bunker floor, heading straight for me.

'It's alright,' they seem to say. 'It will be over quickly.' Their music's like a drug, drowning out all the terror I felt before. My brain floats in strange bliss as the igni-whirlwind slams into me.

That's when the fear comes barreling back. *What the Hell is happening?* I howl as a shock of energy zooms down my spine, igniting every nerve ending in my body. Thousands of tiny lightning bolts attach themselves to my flesh, burning as they slide inside my skin. It's excruciating.

I gasp for breath, and slap at my arms and legs, trying to knock off the igni. *I don't want this. I don't want any of this. Find someone else!* It doesn't do any good. The tiny bolts pass into me, unstoppable.

The dead thrax leans back on his stretcher. His eyes close. His breathing slows. "Esme. I come to you. At last. Esme." He smiles and falls silent. His chest ceases to move. This time, he really is gone.

A new sensation rushes over me, something beyond emotion or words. I am everyone and no one. I am all places and the void. I sense every emotion in the universe, yet am empty of feeling. My tail relaxes. My eyes roll back into my skull. Power floods my body.

I am changing.

Visions appear in my mind's eye: Manus demons tearing down the doors to my high school…Rows of mansions in Upper Purgatory burning in a long line of flame…Crini demons smashing the empty cottages of the thrax compound…And Armageddon leaning against a wall of black stone in the middle of the Gray Sea, his great mouth coiling with a satisfied smile.

More igni slip under my skin. The column of Scala power dims and thins. Every cell in my body vibrates with energy. A jolt of realization hits me. The demon invasion, Armageddon, and Purgatory; I know precisely what I need to do next.

If only I have the strength to do it.

I still don't want this power. Refuse to accept it as my future. But right now, at this moment, I know it's the only way to save those I love. I will have to try.

The last of the igni enter my body. The room becomes dead quiet. I scan the faces around me: Zeke and Cissy stand stock-still. Adair sits curled against the wall, immobile. I'm not even sure if they're breathing. Lincoln and Walker smile. Mom's brown eyes bulge in a look that hovers somewhere between terror and pride.

The Oligarchy are the only ones who speak. They turn to me, lick their lips and hiss: "The new Scala."

It takes all I have to force my shoulders back and my spine straight. *I have to try.* I meet the Oligarchy's gaze head-on. "Yes, I'm the new Scala. And now we'll discuss how to drive the demons from my homeland." I turn to Walker. "Bring me the angel Verus."

The Oligarchy bow. "We cannot allow unauthorized portals at this time, Great Scala. There's some kind of interference in Group Think. It's not safe."

"Really? How'd you like a quick trip to Hell?" I raise my hand, hundreds of igni encircle my palm. I watch the tiny lightning bolts whirl about my fingers.

The Oligarchy bow. "We can allow portals for you, Great Scala."

"That's more like it. Walker, go get Verus."

Walker nods. A portal opens. Its edges blur and waver. Gritting his teeth, Walker steps into the black emptiness and disappears.

I pull open a folding chair and point to the empty seat. "Grab a chair, boys. We've lots to talk about."

The Oligarchy gasp. I'm guessing they aren't used to a Scala with a backbone. "As you wish, Great Scala." The Oligarchy pick up metal folding chairs and drag them across the concrete floor with an ear-piercing series of squeaks. I'd probably laugh my head off if I weren't so freaked out about whatever-the-hell-it-is that just happened to me.

I try to keep a confident pose as I survey the scene. The Oligarchy still drag their chairs around while everyone else stands about, looking googly-eyed with shock. This is crazy. Why am I launching this plan again? Oh yeah, a bunch of *tiny lightning bolts* told me it was a good idea. I let out a long breath. We're so fucked.

Lincoln steps up behind me, setting his arms about my waist. His body feels warm and solid behind mine. "May I have a minute, Great Scala?"

"I'm *Myla*." *As in a person, for the record.*

"I see. Follow me, please." Lincoln slips his hand in mine, guiding me into the small antechamber off the main room. It's a snug space with dark walls lined pantry-style with food and water. Cots are stacked in one corner and there's a makeshift kitchen of sorts. The exit to the surface is one huge circular steel portal that looks very, very closed.

Lincoln shuts the door to the main chamber and drags out a cot. My brows arch. What exactly is he up to? The Prince sits down and pats the space beside him. "Let's talk."

I raise my hands to shoulder level, palms forward. Frustration twists in my belly. We are so not doing whatever-it-is-he-thinks-we're-doing right now. "This is no time for chit chat. Hell's about to break loose. For real."

Lincoln rests his elbows on his knees. "A few minutes ago, you sucked in enough supernatural electricity to power a universe. We're not doing anything until I'm sure you're okay." He cocks his head to one side, his mismatched eyes filled with concern.

Dammit. I was okay as long as there was something to be pissed about (or in the case of the Oligarchy, bossy to). Now that Lincoln's acting all sweet and lovey, I start to lose it. My bottom lip quivers. "I'm fine." My eyes sting. "Maybe."

Lincoln rises to his feet and wraps me in the mother of all hugs. His arms are warm and roped with muscle, his body firm and comforting. I cuddle my head into his shoulder and start spilling my guts. "This whole thing began because, like a dumbass, I wanted to know who my father really was. Now it turns out that my dad's an archangel who's in Hell, getting tortured for all eternity. So that sucks.

Then I meet you, get all lovey and—BOOM—I'm the Scala Heir. Which was weird, but hey, the old Scala could have lived another thousand years, so no big deal, right?" I poke Lincoln softly in the belly. "Am I right or am I right?"

He tries to hide a chuckle. "You're right."

"Well, he didn't last a week. Now I'm the Great Scala, which is a very sketchy job description that involves everyone trying to control me." I sniffle into his body armor. "If I'd just listened to Mom, I'd still be fighting Arena matches, skipping school, and living what now looks like a pretty sweet life before I mucked it up."

Lincoln rubs my hair in long strokes. It feels really-really soothing. "I'm so sorry this happened to you, Myla."

I loop my arms around his waist. "Maybe after this is all over, we can see if someone *else* can be the Scala? An Heir must be running around someplace." I rub my nose with my knuckle. "Oh, I've heard of some pretty amazing magic users. Maybe one of them can zap the igni into someone else." I groan. "I want to get today over with, kick Armageddon's ass out of Purgatory, and forget any of this ever happened." I nuzzle into his shoulder. "Except the *you* part, of course."

He kisses the top of my head. "Let's get through today. We can discuss everything else later."

I let out a long breath. "You're right."

He cups my face in his hands, guiding me to look in his mismatched eyes. "Are you ready to go back now?"

"Nope." I point to my lips and grin.

Lincoln kisses me once, gently. "And now?"

"Yup."

Smiling, he slips his hand in mine, then steps toward the door. "Oh, Lincoln?"

The Prince turns to me and pauses. "Yes, Myla?"

"Thank you." My chest fills with warmth. "No one else thought to ask me how I was after, you know." *Getting zapped with enough supernatural electricity to power a universe.*

Lincoln gives my hand a little squeeze. "We're a team, right?"

I nod. "Absolutely right."

CHAPTER TWENTY-SEVEN

$\mathcal{A}$

I sit on a metal chair in the bunker's main chamber, one of ten that have been dragged into a makeshift circle. Lincoln sits beside me; the Oligarchy ghouls sit in the four chairs after his. We wait for Verus, and no one even *pretends* to make small talk. Occasionally, a huge boom sounds as Armageddon tries to break in. Other times, we'll hear soft chatter from the antechamber as Mom, Cissy, and Zeke sift through the bunker's inventory, looking for useful stuff. Adair waits in the antechamber too, not making a sound. It's unclear if she's sulking or in shock, but as long as she's quiet, who cares?

The plan is simple. Inside the bunker, I'll bring together representatives from angels, thrax, quasis, and ghouls. Then, I'll force everyone to decide how to defeat Armageddon. Oh yes, and we'll also make a pact to free Purgatory after the defeating part is over. Lincoln will play thrax representative for the parlay. The Oligarchy represent the ghouls, and I'm covering the quasis. Once Verus shows up, we'll have a delegate from the angels and we can get started.

The room shakes again. The metal shelves rattle, cans and boxes tumble to the floor. I wince. Armageddon's getting busy.

A portal opens nearby, its edges blurry. Through it steps Walker, Verus, and Levi, one of the angels who trained my class at school. Was that only weeks ago? It feels like a million years. Walker's face looks pale again. His mouth creases in pain.

I rise to my feet. "Walker, are you okay?"

"I'm fine." He waves his hand. "Please continue."

My head tilts to one side. "Talk to me. What happened?"

Walker forces a smile. "The Oligarchy are right, there's some interference in Group Think. I got injured creating the portal, but it's nothing I can't self-heal if given some time."

"Thank you." My voice cracks when I speak. "Be well." I watch him step away, my face twisting with a frown.

Lincoln gives my hand a squeeze. "He'll be fine. We need to focus on the negotiations."

I nod my head once and retake my seat. "Right."

"Greetings, everyone." Verus slides into a chair on my opposite side, carefully straightening her white robes in the process. I feel a weight lift off my body, one I didn't know I was carrying. After the fight in the Arena, I wasn't sure Walker would even find Verus alive. I guess I've gotten attached, despite her sneakiness.

Levi takes a position behind Verus's chair, his silver armor gleaming in the dim light. Neither of them are showing their wings.

Verus looks at my eyes for a long time, her face positively beaming. "You've now taken your true form as the Great Scala." Every inch of her seems to scream 'and isn't that the greatest thing ever?'

I squirm in my seat. In *my* book, my Scala powers are bad news. "Yup. I'm the Great Scala." *For now.*

Verus nods. "Excellent." She gestures to the group. "I welcome this opportunity to parlay." She spots Lincoln and I holding hands. "You two have formed an attachment?"

"We have." I stare at her through narrowed eyes. "One of these days, I'd like to discuss your skills as matchmaker."

The lead angel's smile broadens. "I wasn't sure you'd noticed."

Lincoln arches his eyebrow. "Some of us didn't."

Another sonic boom shakes the walls as Armageddon tries breaking into the bunker. Time to get negotiating.

Leaning back in my chair, I take a long look around. Lincoln, Verus, the Oligarchy, and I all sit in a circle. Verus's guard Levi stands behind her. Walker has taken up position behind me. Mom, Cissy, and Zeke are in the antechamber, sorting through supplies. Adair's doing…Eh, who cares what she does?

I inhale a deep breath. Here's where the plan really begins. Straightening my shoulders, I try to ignore the little butterflies with big sledgehammers that have taken up residence in my stomach.

Remember, Myla: just get through today.

I clear my throat. "We're all here to represent the four peoples affected by Armageddon's attack on Purgatory: angels, ghouls, thrax, and quasis. Our goal's to come up with a plan to defeat Armageddon and change how Purgatory's run."

The Oligarchy snarl. "*Change* Purgatory?"

I bite my lips together. "I'm pretty sure *something* needs to change or we wouldn't be sitting in a bunker with Armageddon pounding over our heads. But first things first. Who knows what's happening outside?"

My gaze flips to the ceiling as I think about Armageddon and his demons roaming the lands above. Pangs of worry and anger strum through me. My home, under attack.

"I can make a report," says Verus. "The demons from the Arena have fanned out all over Purgatory, killing quasis and ghouls alike." Her eyes flare blue. "They've used their inspections to scope out exactly how and where to strike. It's a precision bloodbath."

Lincoln shakes his head. "Do we know how many are outside the bunker right now?"

Verus nods. "A few hundred. About five thousand in total roam Purgatory."

Lincoln gestures to the Oligarchy. "Can your ghouls transport those demons out of here?"

My head bobs up and down. That's a good idea. Millions of ghouls live in the Dark Lands. It'd take only a few hundred to portal outside the bunker, grab the demons and go.

The Oligarchy tilt their heads to one side. "We can open portals, but getting demons to step into them in another matter. With few exceptions, ghouls aren't warriors." The Oligarchy shoot a knowing look at Walker. I suck in a quick breath. *Of course.* Walker's a descendant of Aquila, and she kicks ass in a big way. Walker and the Aquilinea are probably the best fighters the ghouls have.

Behind my chair, I hear Walker shift his weight. "It's possible to call the Aquilinea, though that's only a few dozen warriors. Can the Dark Lands supply the rest?"

"Sadly, no." As they say this, the Oligarchy don't look sad in the slightest. *They're so full of it.* "We'd like to discuss other options for appeasing Armageddon. Perhaps if the new Scala were to journey to Hell, then Armageddon and his army would vacate–"

I grip the edges of my metal chair, my eyes flaring red with rage. It's one thing to think you can manipulate an old man on a stretcher. And Adair? If you promised her an adoring audience in Hell, she'd probably go willingly. But no way am I turning into their patsy. Crap like this is exactly why this job sucks and I don't want it. I open my yap, ready to tell them all that and more, when Lincoln takes to his feet.

The Prince sets a protective hand on my shoulder. "That's not going to happen."

The Oligarchy smile, showing four mouths of identical ragged teeth. "Why not? She has the old Scala's power. The igni can take her to Hell and back."

"Really?" My mouth arches into a snarl. "If I'm transporting anywhere, it's to Heaven." *Which isn't a bad idea at that.*

Verus guesses my thoughts. "The Gates of Heaven limit what igni may transport. Only the dead may pass through."

"But there are no such restrictions in Hell." The Oligarchy smile in unison, which is super-creepy to watch. "Surely you can transport there, defend yourself, and return at your leisure."

Rage courses through me. I grip the chair so tightly, the metal twists in my palms. "Yeah, me against *all of Hell*. That's a great idea." *Dicks*.

Verus's eyes flare blue. "The angels stand with the thrax. Sending the Scala into Hell is not an option."

Closing my eyes, I force myself to take a few deep breaths. Don't let them sidetrack you. Stay focused on the plan. "Thank you." I look from Verus to Lincoln. "Both of you."

Lincoln retakes his seat; his fingers weave with mine again.

"Now that sending me into certain death is off the table." I shoot an angry glance at the Oligarchy. "Let's hear some other ideas."

"I have an army of angels at the ready," says Verus. "Can you portal them in?"

The Oligarchy close their eyes. "We can't."

Verus groans. "Of course, you can. Even if every ghoul in Purgatory were dead, you've millions back in the Dark Lands who can pick up our troops."

Lincoln nods. "I can have thrax warriors ready as well."

Beads of black sweat drip down the Oligarchy's cheeks. "We did not say *won't*. We said *can't*. Group Think is blocked."

Twisting about, I search Walker's face. "Is this true?"

Walker lowers his head. His features crease in concentration. "Group Think is silent." A muscle twitches by his mouth. "No one can create portals without it." He frowns. "It was unstable before when I portaled in Verus and Levi. Now it's gone."

The Oligarchy's faces turn slack. "Even our people of the Dark Lands cannot portal to us now." They look downright mopey. *Good*. They were only hanging around because it was a safe place to negotiate. Plus, Tim had conveniently organized all their bargaining chips here in the form of my mother and Adair. I'm sure they never expected *they'd* become prisoners too. Now we're all in the same boat. Hope sparks in my chest. That can only help us work together.

Still facing Walker, I drum my fingers on the back of the chair, memories flashing through my mind. Images from the Arena iconigration flicker through my consciousness. *What happened that day—it must have been a test.* I snap my fingers, then point at Walker. "Do you remember the iconigration? The pig demon Clementine opened a briefcase for Armageddon."

"I remember," says Walker. "It stopped the Scala's carriers from opening a portal. I'd never seen anything like it before."

Then, I said 'Armageddon was up to something' and you told me not to worry, Mr Smarty Pants. Not that I'll point that out right now. Although I'm really-really-really tempted to.

I tap my knee with my pointer finger. "That was Armageddon's way of testing a system for blocking Group Think, I'm certain of it."

Verus wags her head from side to side. "That makes sense. Armageddon would need a way to stop ghouls from portaling in armies for a counter-attack. He'd never start this war without having thought that through. I'm afraid we're locked in for the duration."

I turn to Lincoln. I know this is a total long shot, but I have to ask. "How about the thrax back in Purgatory?"

The Prince frowns. "I had some top warriors here, but everyone was returning to Antrum today with transport ready to go. Once the fighting started, protocol requires an immediate evacuation. They're all long gone, I'm afraid."

That news shouldn't make me so sad—after all, I knew it was a long shot—but suddenly the all-aloneness of our situation seems all too clear. It's just the people in this bunker against Armageddon and his army.

Damn, this Scala job sucks.

Verus sighs. "Without ghoul transport, armies must cross no-man's land to reach the Gates of Purgatory. That takes months. At the rate the demon army's moving, this war will be over in hours." She rubs her forehead. "Which is as Armageddon planned."

The Oligarchy rise to their feet, their long crimson robes swaying. "We have one option remaining. Send the Scala to Hell. Draw Armageddon from our lands." Their bony hands all point in my direction.

Unholy Hell. *I cannot freaking believe we are back to this stupid idea again.* I'm about to lay into the Oligarchy with the mother of all 'screw you' speeches, when I hear it. Sweet music. A mix of tiny voices. The igni have returned.

Lincoln and Verus leap to their feet, yelling at the Oligarchy about their lame idea. The ghoul's eyes all glow red as they scream their response, which basically amounts to 'what else can we do?' I close my eyes, feeling the Scala power within me shift and grow. The many igni voices align until they speak as one. Suddenly, it's very clear what they want me to do. Although as options go, it sucks, big time.

I set my palms on my eyes, my internal debate raging with the igni. They keep pointing out a path to victory, I keep saying that this Scala job is the pits. I won't do their crazy idea. *No, no, no!* But after a while, I finally cave. They're right; this is the only choice we have left. Damn.

I rise to my feet. "I'll go."

Everyone falls silent.

Verus blinks her eyes in disbelief. "*What* did you say?"

Please don't make me repeat this a million times. I hate this idea enough already. "I said, I'll go outside and face Armageddon. Send him back to Hell with my Scala power." And so help me, if I live through this, I am chucking these igni out of my head, STAT.

"You can't." Lincoln's face twists with worry. "They'll kill you, and that's if you're lucky."

I let out a long breath. I tried this line of reasoning with the igni. It didn't work. "If I go outside and hide so they can't see me, I might have a chance." *Did I mention I hate this idea?*

Lincoln steps in front of me, taking both my hands in his. "You think you can send all the demons to Hell?"

No, I think I have a legion of insane lightning bolts inside my head. But I'm not telling him that. This plan is risky enough as it is; the only shot we have is if we all believe it's possible and work from there. I force myself to look stony and resolved, or something close to it. "Yes, Lincoln. That's exactly what I can do."

Lincoln nods. "Then you have my full support." I have a sinking feeling that he's lying through his teeth too, but I love that he has my back.

Walker turns to me, his face drawn with worry. "You saw the old Scala at the iconigration. He almost collapsed sending a few dozen icons to heaven. Even at his best, he could only move a few hundred at a time *in one place*. You're talking about five thousand demons across all of Purgatory."

Anger boils up my spine. "You're being a downer, Walker. I'm a first-generation archangel, whatever that is. Plus, I'm an Arena fighter, a Lewis, and someone with a lot to lose. I can do this." I slap on another super-confident face in spite of my insides, which positively writhe with nervous energy.

Verus retakes her seat. "Armageddon doesn't know there's a new Scala. He won't be expecting one to attack."

"Exactly." I turn to the Oligarchy. "And what if I'm able to do it? Will you agree to change how Purgatory is run?"

The Oligarchy's coal-black eyes flare red. "*How* would it change?"

"This land returns to quasi rule," says Verus. "And we set up a special force of ghouls, thrax, quasis, and angels to help patrol the borders."

My eyebrows pop up. *Clever Verus.* I nudge the angel with my elbow. "Nice idea." Her mouth rounds with a smile.

The Oligarchy fold their skeletal arms over their chests. "Never."

I huff out a breath. Patience is not my strong suit, and what little I had was wasted today on Adair. Now that little word pushed me over the edge. I flash Lincoln a red-eyed look of rage. I try to whisper my question, but maybe don't do the best job. "Can I kill just one?"

A smile gleams in Lincoln's eyes. "I got this, Myla." He turns to the Oligarchy, his face becoming stony and unreadable. "Think this through, mighty Oligarchy." His voice sounds so calm and confident, even though I know he's nervous inside. How does he do that? "You're trapped in a bunker. Any minute now,

Armageddon could break in. When he does, he'll keep his promise to kill you all."

The Oligarchy shift uncomfortably in their seats, exchanging nervous looks. *Yay, they finally accept the truth about Armageddon.*

Lincoln gestures to me. "Once Myla sends the demons to Hell—and I have every confidence that she will—you'll lose control of Purgatory, but you'll keep your lives and the Dark Lands. That's the offer on the table." He leans forward, bracing his arms against his knees. "If you don't agree, then once Myla wins, we'll offer you the same terms as Armageddon. Death." His voice lowers to a growl. "Do we understand each other?"

I love it when Lincoln's bossy. My lust demon comes up with the super idea to jump the Prince right here and now, but I have to overrule it. Shame, though.

Armageddon's army sends another volley of who-the-hell-knows at the ground around us. More cans and bottles tumble to the floor. Bits of concrete dust waft down from the ceiling.

Lincoln shakes his head. "Armageddon isn't far now. Every moment we delay makes it harder for Myla...And you."

Moving in unison, the four ghouls brush white dust from their blood-red robes. "The Oligarchy agrees."

Sheesh, finally.

"Excellent." Verus lets out a satisfied sigh. "I'll draft up binding documents for the treaty." She turns to me and Lincoln. "Great job."

"Thanks." I slump into my chair, the reality of this treaty washing over me. To save Purgatory, I agreed to send Armageddon and his army back to Hell. Anxiety and adrenaline fight their way through my system. Minutes tick by while everyone scurries around with last-minute preparations and I freak myself out by thinking of everything that can go wrong with this plan. Finally, I decide that I'll go crazy if I sit around here any longer.

I turn to Lincoln and exhale a long breath. "Time to face my demons."

Lincoln gives my hand a squeeze; there's no question he'll go with me. We share a sad smile. In a few minutes, we'll waltz out to Armageddon's army where I'll test my new Scala powers on all of Purgatory.

Not exactly a sure thing.

"Wait, Myla." Mom steps into the main chamber from the antechamber. She's now wearing her Senator's robes. She looks regal, lovely, and strong. Cissy stands beside her in white robes with purple trim, the gown of a junior senator. Zeke wears black body armor with the quasi seal on his shoulders: a circle on interlocking stars. Adair's nowhere to be seen, which is nice.

I gasp. It's like they stepped out of a history book from the Ryder library.

"What's this about, Mom?" She once said something about the bunkers holding Senate robes, but I can't imagine how dressing up could help now.

"Verus just told us about the treaty." Mom makes a regal gesture around the room. "I am still the Diplomatic Senator of the quasi people. I will request parlay with Armageddon, then go outside with my guard and junior senator. Hopefully, we can distract him for a time while you get started."

I frown. "Will he really respect a Senator's request for parlay?"

Cissy grins. "We have the Scala and Scala Heir in our bunker. He'll talk."

I glance about. "Where is Adair, anyway?"

Cissy fidgets in her robes. "Uh, she started getting hysterical." Cissy makes her 'eek' face. "So I maybe slipped her a sedative. There was a medicine kit on one the shelves."

Zeke chuckles. "My girl totally roofied her." He keeps shifting positions to show off his muscly self in his cool new armor. Lincoln and I exchange a look.

Mom taps Zeke on the shoulder. "Let's stay focused, Mister Ryder. We need to get ready to head outside."

If Mom's calling him Mister Ryder, that means he's driving her crazy. I curl my mouth into a Cheshire cat grin. Welcome to the end of her comments on how I should have dated Zeke.

The Oligarchy frown. "Your plan is flawed. Maxon Bane is dead."

I bite my lower lip, thinking. "Armageddon smells Scala power. As long as he doesn't see me, he'll think the Scala's nearby. It should work."

Lincoln smiles. "It's genius." He bows slightly to my mother. "Excellent addition to our little operation."

"Thank you." Mom's voice is level; she's in Senator mode now. "We'll say we knew of his plan and have prepared for a counter-attack." My stomach goes all goopy with pride. It's so freaking cool to see Senator Lewis live and in action.

Mom points to a spot along the back of the room. "There's a secret exit behind those shelves. It opens to the great dune behind the rock wall. We've checked the periscope. Armageddon's troops are deployed on the low sands in front of the wall. If you stay behind the dune, you'll be hidden."

I picture Mom, Cissy, and Zeke facing Armageddon. My mouth droops into a frown. "I don't know Mom, that's too dangerous for you guys."

Zeke shrugs. "It's a lot less dangerous than sending you out there alone."

Lincoln nods. "He's right."

I scratch my neck, trying to think of every contingency. This is all going so fast, we're bound to leave a stone or two unturned. My gaze lands on the four ghouls seated across from me. Those four blockheads certainly need some extra consideration. "And what about leaving the Oligarchy here. You know, by themselves?" I don't trust them alone for five seconds.

Verus takes to her feet. "Levi and I will remain in the bunker with WRD-7 to ensure the Oligarchy finalize the treaty and–" She takes a deep breath, choosing her words carefully. "Maintain their focus."

The Oligarchy turn to face Verus. "We shall never waver."

In a miracle of self-restraint, I stop my eye roll before it starts. *Sure, you guys would never waver.*

Lincoln gives my hand another squeeze. "What do you say? Do we have a plan?"

I scan the faces in the room, everyone appears set and focused. Closing my eyes, I take a quick internal inventory. I'm jacked up on nervous energy, but that's typical before a fight, comforting even. "Yeah, let's get rolling."

Mom heads to the bunker's exit with Cissy and Zeke behind her. Meanwhile, Lincoln and I explore the shelves along the back wall. It doesn't take us long to find the panel that Mom told us about. With a light shove, the shelves easily slide away, revealing a low and dark tunnel in the concrete wall.

Here we go.

Dropping onto my hands and knees, I crawl inside the darkened hole. Lincoln follows closely behind me. Sensing him nearby—feeling his movements in sync with mine—steadies my frayed nerves. Forever ekes by as we scramble inside the passageway, following a never-ending series of turns and straightaways. Finally, we reach a panel of sand at the tunnel's end. Dim light reflects through the granules. My heart jumps into my throat. We're close to the surface.

I set my fingertips inch-deep into the sand. It's warm and fine. An odd calm flows through me as my mind captures every aspect of this moment, taking a kind of picture that I may treasure (or be haunted by) for the rest of my life. I'm outside myself, knowing that I pause at the tunnel's end, about to test my new powers, and with so much at risk. After that, the moment's gone, collapsing into one great crush of nerve-jangling panic. My fingers tremble in the sand. The best thing I can do is move on. Fast.

Gritting my teeth, I press my body through the sand and emerge onto the Gray Sea beyond. A fierce wind howls through my ears and whips my hair about. Low gray clouds hang overhead. The stench of sulfur hangs in the air. I belly-crawl to the top of the dune with Lincoln close beside me. We lay side-by-side on the warm sand and peep over the lip of ridge.

My breath catches. The scene before us can't be real. About twenty yards below, hundreds of demons are arrayed in concentric circles on the desert floor. Armageddon stands off to one side, his tall body leaning against the black stone wall. At least he's far enough away that I don't feel his aura of terror. I swallow past the tightness in my throat.

I quickly catalog the body position of all our enemies. None see us in our hiding-spot. Instead, they're all focused on the massive Manus demon at the center of the crowd. This gorilla-like monster is the largest creature I've ever seen. Hoisting its long arms high above its head, the Manus slams its fists onto the desert floor, scooping up piles of sand and throwing them off to one side. With each throw, I feel my heart sink a little lower. He's almost uncovered the circular metal portal that marks the doorway to our bunker. Not good.

My eyes grow large with understanding. So that's what's been rattling over our heads. The Manus demon's trying to break in, or scare us into coming out. I scan its boulder-sized body and trunk-like limbs. Dang, that thing looks tough to kill. Who knows how hard it will be to move to Hell?

The circular door springs to life, igniting into a ring of white flame. The Manus demon leaps out of the fire's path. The muscles around my throat tighten. Those flames are Mom, Cissy, and Zeke, about to face a horde of demons. Hells bells.

Armageddon sneers. "At last." His three-knuckled fingers twitch at his sides, anxious to touch his victim's flesh and suck out their souls.

If he lays a finger on them, I'll lose it.

The great circular door lifts from the sands. It's a flat disc held up by four white pillars. On the floor between those columns stands my mother, Cissy, and Zeke, their bodies twitching as Armageddon's aura slams into them. Adrenaline rockets through me. Every fiber in me wants to leap down the rock face and start kicking ass. I dig my hands and feet deeper in the warm sand, trying to root myself to the spot.

Armageddon steps to the edge of the circular platform, his nasty grin stretching wide. "Greetings, Senator." He grins. "Come out to parlay?"

Straightening her shoulders, Mom speaks in a calm voice that echoes through the desert. "I come here today on behalf of angels, ghouls, thrax, and quasis." She's doing a really good job of fighting the terror of being close to a greater demon. "This unwarranted invasion of our—"

Lincoln gently sets his hand on my upper arm. "We're on."

I inhale a shaky breath. The distraction's working. Now it's all up to me. My body almost vibrates with fear. I've never felt this scared before.

I wiggle my body into the sand. The warm granules press comfortably against my belly. Closing my eyes, I raise my hand and call out to the igni. My heart thuds so hard, my pulse booms in my ears. *Please, let the igni hear me.*

Child-like laughter sounds in my head. A few tiny lightning bolts spin about my palm. My body tenses with excitement.

Lincoln's voice rings in my ears: "Great, Myla. You're doing it."

The laughter grows louder. Then, it's drowned out by Armageddon's voice. "I have a surprise for you, Camilla."

My eyes pop open. *What's he up to?*

Mom folds her arms over her chest. "What could you possibly do to surprise me?"

The King of Hell snaps his fingers once.

Although I'm aware of my mother and Armageddon, my consciousness stays fixed on the power dancing about my hand. The igni multiply, their thin bodies tickling my skin, their voices growing louder.

A dark spot appears in the Gray Sea sky. It grows larger, turning into a massive pair of flying demons with the eagle bodies, lizard heads, and bat wings. In their claws they carry a giant metal box. With a great thud, they drop their burden onto the gray sand.

I squint through the fierce wind. A rusted container about eight feet square sits on the desert floor. My attention's drawn to it; something important lies inside.

Fewer igni circle my palm. Their music fades from my mind.

Armageddon knocks on the metal container. "*This* is for you." The sides of the box fly open, killing a few demons in the process. Armageddon doesn't glance in their direction; instead his focus is riveted on the body chained to the box's floor.

I can't help but stare as well. A figure crouches along the bottom of the container, heavy chains wrapped about his hands and feet. He has matted hair, a grizzled beard, and cocoa skin that's covered in purple bruises and oozing wounds. Scraps of gray fabric hang about his broken body and dirty wings. He's an angel, or what's left of one.

Armageddon gestures to the broken figure. "Senator, may I present the archangel Xavier."

All breath leaves my body. This is my father, the one who traded an eternity in Hell for my mother's life.

Mom stares at the broken angel. Tears well in her eyes. She half-turns to my hiding place on the ridge, but catches herself before going too far. She stops, steels her shoulders and swings her attention back to Armageddon. "I fail to understand how your surprise relates to this hostile invasion, Armageddon."

A chill crawls over me. My body freezes with shock. More lightning bolts fade from my hand.

Armageddon grins, showing a mouth of pointed teeth. "Ah, but you haven't seen the best part yet." He snaps his fingers again. The pair of flying monsters take to the air. Their talons sink into my father's back and begin to heave.

Oh, my sweet evil. They're pulling off his wings.

My gaze flicks to my father's bearded face, contorted in pain. He grips his heavy chains, teeth gritted in agony. The lightning bolts around my hand die out.

Lincoln grips my shoulder. "What's going on, Myla? The igni are gone."

"That's my father."

The flying demons pull harder on my father's wings. My body's frozen with shock. My mind empties.

Armageddon rocks on his heels and laughs. His dark joy hits me like a punch to the gut. All breath leaves my body. My father's been tortured while Armageddon laughs. Somehow that's the most painful blow of all. A sob wells up in my throat.

Tears stream down Mom's face. Cissy holds her hand and whispers soothing words. Zeke stands silent and stunned. Mom speaks in a low and ragged voice. "Whatever you're trying to do, Armageddon, it won't work."

The desert echoes with my father's howls. Loud cracks sound as bones snap and his wings are pulled free. Armageddon turns to Mom, his face twisted in evil glee. "Still not working?"

Mom's face is colorless; her bottom lip quivers. She opens her mouth, but no sound comes out. I find my voice, though. Sob after sob break free from my throat.

My father's body arches in pain as new wings sprout from his back. Small buds appear on his shoulder blades, tearing at his flesh. He screams again as huge golden wings burst from his shoulders. The self-healing power of archangels, used to torture him through eternity. This is so wrong.

I stare at my father's broken body. Anger flows down my neck and shoulders, tightening every muscle. My wrath demon spews fire in my belly, filling me with white-hot rage. I turn to Lincoln, ready to explain what I'm about to do. Once I see the fury in *his* eyes, I know I won't have to.

I rise to my feet, my tail flicking behind me in a predatory rhythm. Lincoln stands at my side.

Armageddon's head snaps in my direction. "Look, who we have here. The little Arena girl and the thrax High Prince." His eyes sparkle. "You're King Connor's boy." His gaze flips back and forth between me and Mom. "And *that* girl's your daughter, isn't she, Camilla?"

Xavier slowly lifts his ragged head. His blue eyes glow with a soft light. He looks to Mom and rasps out one word: "Daughter?"

Mom offers him a gentle nod. Part of me knows I should see the love in her face and feel some kind of pain. But nothing can drown out the howls of rage inside me. *I am tearing those chains off my father if it's the last thing I ever do.*

He swallows. "Is she—"

"Yes, Xavier." Her eyes brim with tears. "She's yours."

The archangel strains to twist his head. He gaze rests on me. "She's lovely, Camilla." He forces his broken voice louder. "You're lovely."

They are soft words, and something inside me wishes I could feel their tenderness. But right now, all I know is fury. This ends, now. "That's not all I am, father." I raise my hand and call to the igni. Their voices chatter angrily in my brain as they whip around my palm. These are the dark children, the ones who send souls to Hell. They look the same as the good igni. Huh. I wasn't calling the right ones before.

I grin. *Well, I've got the hang of it now.*

Armageddon leans back on his heel, folding his arms over his lean chest. "So, you're the true Scala Heir. Interesting."

I summon more igni around my palm. Their voices take on a harsh edge, like razor blades scraping across metal. "You almost have that right." The igni multiply into a white column that's seven feet tall. "I'm not the Scala Heir. I'm the Great Scala." Beside me, Lincoln ignites his baculum.

Armageddon's eyes flare bright red. "What are you saying? Where's my son? WHERE IS MY SON?"

"Killed by his own hand," says Lincoln. "He died a true thrax warrior." He tosses his blade from hand to hand, sizing up Armageddon.

The demon leader throws back his head and howls. The sound rattles the desert. "My son is dead? MY SON IS DEAD?!" He crouches to Xavier's side, grips his hair and yanks up his skull. "I want to you watch your daughter closely now, because I'm going to break her bones and drag her to Hell. She will fulfill my vow to torture Maxon." He turns to me and offers a smug grin, certain he just scared the fight out of me.

Not even close, buddy.

Every cell in my body pulses with fury. "Try this on for size." I blast my column of white lightning straight into the sky, pumping the storm clouds with bright flashes. "How about you get your goddamn hands off my father?" The clouds roll with an ear-splitting peal of thunder. "NOW."

Growling, Armageddon leaps onto the ridge. Beside me, Lincoln flinches as the greater demon's aura slams into him. Nothing happens to me this time; igni must block the effect. Armageddon strides toward me, raising his hand to strike. Every instinct I have screams for me to move, but I can't control igni and dodge blows at the same time. And if I lose the igni, I lose this fight too.

The King of Hell swipes his fist toward my head. I wince, waiting for the blow. At the last moment, Lincoln jumps between me and Armageddon's fist. His baculum collide with the demon's stone-smooth skin, sending a shower of blood-red sparks through the air. The King of Hell pulls back his arm; his flesh is unharmed by the sword. The demon continues his onslaught, every volley coming faster. Time and again, Lincoln meets each blow before it connects with my—or his—exposed skin.

My regular self would be horrified at this moment: Lincoln in danger, my father in chains, everyone I love at risk, and all of Purgatory relying on me. But I lock those thoughts away, sealing them inside an internal vault. My mind snaps into the hyper-focus of battle mode. There is nothing but my task—moving demons to Hell—and the next step to accomplish it.

I size up Armageddon's blows and Lincoln's counter-strikes. The Prince can only give me a few more minutes; I need to move faster. To my right, the igni column glimmers with power as it pumps more white light into the dark clouds. I set my fingertips a few inches into the column's sparkling skin. Igni voices grow louder in my brain. Something new joins them as well: images of demons across Purgatory.

An idea forms. I know exactly how to speed things up. Excitement kicks inside my chest.

I pump more igni into the giant soul-column, then step inside myself. It's oddly peaceful within: no wind, no sounds, only a hallow column of bright white light. Visions flash through my brain. I picture every demon across Purgatory. Crini, Manus, Papilio… more than five thousand evil faces flicker through my mind's eye.

Turning my gaze upwards, I propel the soul-column higher until, like a geyser, the igni blast through the top of the clouds and rain down across Purgatory.

My mouth curls into a grin. It's working.

In my mind's eye, I see tiny lightning bolts descend around thousands of demons. The igni spin about the monster's bodies, holding them in place. For a moment, all my captives' misery, hatred, and cruelty crash through me, an avalanche of evil. I sense where each one stands, what each one is, and where each one belongs.

So I send them there.

The igni whirl and multiply around every demon. Thousands of soul-columns appear across Purgatory, a demon inside each one. Their lights flare brighter, then they all disappear, taking the monsters inside on a journey to Hell.

All of them, that is, except one. *Armageddon*.

My brain anxiously whirls through options and scenarios. How do I get this guy out of here? Somehow he blocked my last wave of soul-columns. I can't let that happen again.

Armageddon takes another swipe at Lincoln; the Prince blocks the onslaught. Turning toward the demon, I raise my arms to shoulder height, my palms up and flat. I call the igni to me, asking them to change their path so they no longer reach for the clouds. They obey, and the full force of the soul column careens up my body, across my arms and straight into Armageddon's side.

Take *that*.

Part of me knows this is an insanely risky move. I have no idea what it will do to create this kind of connection between me and the King of Hell. I lock those thoughts away and refocus on my task: getting Armageddon out of here.

As the igni smash into him, the King of Hell lets out a spine-crushing howl. He throws his arms wide, creating a column of red flame about his body. Lincoln is blasted out of the way, the force of the red fire as strong as a grenade explosion. Leaping back to his feet, the Prince races toward me, baculum blade in hand.

My igni column merges with Armageddon's hellfire, creating one great pillar that encases us both. I vaguely hear Lincoln scream for me outside the column of hellfire and angelic igni. He strikes at it with his baculum, but he can't break in.

The vault where I've locked away my emotions starts to splinter. Fear rattles through me, numbing my mind. I now stand on the Gray Sea, face to face with Armageddon. A circle of hellfire and angelic igni surrounds us, the column ending far above us in the clouds.

More fear rockets through me. My control over the igni slips. Around us, the column becomes more hellfire and less angelic igni.

Armageddon smiles greedily. He's winning and the bastard knows it.

The King of Hell snaps his fingers. Fiery bindings appear around my body. Panic courses through me. More igni disappear. The flames lick about my dragon-scale fighting suit, unable to break through and burn me.

Fast as lightning, Armageddon's consciousness travels through the igni, merging with my own. Fresh terror zooms through my every nerve ending. *This is bad. Very bad.* An assault on my mind begins. I can almost feel his three-knuckled fingers flipping through my memories and fears, finally settling on ones that suit his dark purpose.

Unwanted thoughts overwhelm me. I try to stop them, but it's no use. I want to run, but can't move. One after another, images appear in my mind's eye: the panic in Cissy's face as a poisoned spear nears her back…The Oligarchy's smirk as they suggest I be traded to Hell…Walker crumpling onto the floor of the Arena, his face writhing in pain after the Crini battle… Lincoln blown away by Armageddon's pillar of hellfire…Mom's despair in seeing Xavier's tortured body…The gut-wrenching cycle of terror, anxiety and rage that's coursed through me since I woke up one morning with blue eyes.

All of these horrors, all because I'm the Scala.

Despair seeps into my bones, sucking out the marrow of my fight. I never asked for this job, this burden. It's too much for me and those I love. Before my eyes, the column becomes made of even more hellfire, far less igni. I'm losing ground.

This is hopeless. *Whatever I do, I'm going to die here.*

Raising my gaze, I stare numbly at my captor. I'm imprisoned inside a pillar of fire with Armageddon. How did it come to this? I close my eyes, calling out to the igni. *Don't leave me here. Fight on.* They swirl and dive through the hellfire, refusing to disappear entirely.

My back teeth lock. What did I think would happen, taking on Armageddon with untested powers? I'm an eighteen-year old girl, he's immortal evil personified. I'm a fool.

Armageddon chuckles. "I have a surprise for you as well." A black pit opens in the sands between us. A spirit crawls up out of the darkness, her face bloated and covered in scars.

Unholy Hell. That's the woman I saw in the Arena, the one who sacrificed herself to the Limus demon because she didn't think she deserved Heaven. Now Armageddon will force me to watch as he consumes her soul. My throat chokes with silent sobs.

Armageddon paces before me, his small black eyes narrowing into slits. "I've been following you for some time. You stopped two of my evil souls from entering Heaven. No one gets in my way without paying a price." He glares at the miserable spirit. "I noticed you wanted to save her, so I did. For a special occasion." A grim smile tugs at the corner of his mouth. "Schemes within schemes. That's why I'm King."

Armageddon pauses before me, his body looming above mine. "You've archangel blood and the old Scala's power. You've moved every other demon to Hell. Yet you're too weak to touch me." He grins. "Want to know why?"

My voice comes out a low whisper. "No."

"I saw your mind. You wait for someone else to shoulder your burden. Someone smarter, stronger, better."

My eyes sting. "Yes." *Maybe if that person were here, things would be different.*

"I'll let you in on a little secret, something only the King of Hell would know. Anyone *seeking* to become the Great Scala is evil. It's more power than a good soul would want, or a bad soul should have. When the good take power, it's always a service, a burden. And *that* makes them weak. Like you."

Around me, the igni all but disappear. The fiery bindings on my body flare hotter. He's right. I am weak. I can't do this.

Armageddon snaps his fingers once more. The spirit crawls forward until she reaches the feet of the King of Hell. I see her face. Bloated. Red-eyed. Tear-streaked.

I choke back a wave of nausea. Armageddon set this soul aside so one day he could force me to watch her demise. With such evil in the realms, what can anyone really do?

Armageddon raises his pointer finger, smiles right at me, and then slowly lowers his hand toward the woman's shoulder. Tears roll down her scarred cheeks as he touches her exposed skin. She screams as her spirit-body begins to fray and fade.

Watching her shriek, something inside me finally snaps. A realization knocks into me with a wallop. There's no one smarter or better coming. It's me and this poor woman and, so help me, we aren't dying here. I don't care about the consequences. I don't mind the burden. I *am* fighting.

I raise my hand through a break in my bindings. Fresh igni swirl about my palm.

Armageddon arches his eyebrow. "You won't win."

"Then I'll go down fighting."

Armageddon's eyes sparkle. "It's your death, Myla." Beside him, the woman's body all but disappears.

"No, *Myla* is already gone." I call more igni to me. They arc and dive about my arm, loosening my bindings. "*I'm* the Great Scala."

Whatever I feel, whatever powers are within me, I throw it all at Armageddon. I save no corner of my soul for trips to magic users who may strip my igni powers, for becoming the old Arena fighter again, or for a future where I'm anything but the Great Scala. I *am* this fight.

I call to the igni, and they careen down from the clouds in a great flood, wiping away Armageddon's column of hellfire. My bindings disappear. The ghostly woman falls free to the ground. White lightning bolts envelop the King of Hell, pulling him down the very pit he created by my feet. Armageddon claws at the sand as his body is yanked away. His eyes glow bright red as he disappears into the darkness.

He's gone. I sent Armageddon to Hell. My body hums with excitement. I turn to the miserable spirit, ordering the igni to guide her soul. They swirl and dive in a great mass as they wrap about her, carrying her into the clouds and Heaven. Their child-like laughter rings in my ears. After that, everything turns silent.

I find myself back at the Gray Sea, standing on the top ridge above the bunker entrance. One thought ricochets through mind: Armageddon is gone.

I let out a long breath. My arms drop to my sides. The desert wind whips through my hair. Above me, harmless gray smog replaces the angry storm clouds. My legs turn boneless beneath me. I'm dimly aware that Cissy, Zeke, Mom, and Xavier stand nearby. I wobble in place. It's over. Lincoln's arms wrap about me as I collapse. All becomes darkness.

CHAPTER TWENTY-EIGHT

For what feels like an eternity, my dreams are empty and cold. Occasional sights and odd voices break through the void: Mom sponging sweat from my forehead…Cissy holding my hand… Lincoln gently kissing my closed eyes. Someone says "She's past the worst of it."

I wake up in my own bed. My brain is hazy. I stagger to my feet and peer out the window. Half the houses on our street are burned-out husks. The demons were here too.

The world whitens around the edges of my vision; I grip the windowsill.

"What are you doing?" The voice is familiar.

I squint but can't focus. "Mom?"

"Yes, it's me." She races to my side. Her arms grip my shoulders, guiding me back into bed. "What are you doing up?"

My head touches the pillow. I curl into a fetal position. "I didn't know where I was." I feel so cold, my teeth chatter. I try to open my eyes but can't.

Mom pulls the blanket up to my shoulders. "You're home, Myla."

Suddenly, my brain jolts back into focus, my eyes open wide. I grip Mom's hand. "What happened after I sent the demons back to Hell? Where are the ghouls?"

Mom gently brushes hair from my face. "The demons have stayed in Hell. The ghouls have kept their word to patrol our borders." She smiles. "You did it, Myla. Verus is preparing a summit in three weeks' time. Angels, ghouls, quasis, and thrax will all meet to discuss the terms of the new government."

"Where's Xavier?"

"Safe, thanks to you." She pats my hand. "Close your eyes, Myla-la. Everything's fine."

I roll onto my side and smile. "I did it." Something glitters on my dresser. I heave myself up onto my elbows. "What's that?"

Mom picks up the shiny whatever-it-is and hands it to me. "It's a gift from Lincoln." Two silver rods rest on my palms.

"These are Lincoln's baculum." My fingertips run over the intricately carved runes that cover the surface. "I can't believe he gave me them."

"He was with you day and night until the healers declared you were out of danger. Then he had to return to Antrum. He left the baculum and asked me to remind you of your promise to Nat. Do you know what that means?"

"Yes, I do." I told Lincoln's Master at Arms that I would practice with the sword for an hour a day. Now I can do it in style. Smiling, I slip the baculum under my pillow.

Mom rises to her feet. "You better get some sleep now, Myla."

"Yeah, that's a good idea." My eyes waver and close. I fall into a deep sleep and dream of the Gray Sea. I stand on a long stretch of rolling charcoal dunes under low silver sky. The wind whips the sand and my nightgown. Verus stands nearby, her robes and wings gleaming bright-white against the drab landscape. I'm torn between wanting to run up and hug her or kick her in the kneecaps. Tough call.

"Hello, Myla."

"Hi, Verus."

The lead angel looks to the horizon. Her long black hair cascades over her shoulders in a perfect arc. "I do love the Gray Sea." She turns to me, her almond-shaped eyes flaring blue.

"I noticed." My bare toes dig into the warm sand. "I'm not sure what to say."

"And why is that?"

"Part of me wants to thank you. Your dreamscapes helped my relationship with Mom and got me ready to become the Scala. But another part of me? I don't know. It's like I'm a pawn in some game of yours that I don't understand."

"You mean Lincoln."

"Yes."

"You two don't look unhappy. I should think you'd find each other irresistible."

I chuckle. "Oh, I don't know. There was plenty of resisting for a while." I eye Verus carefully. "Was that why you made the thrax stay longer in Purgatory?"

"Yes, but that's all I can tell you." Verus's mouth stretches into an all-knowing, other-worldly smile. It's a little irritating.

"Fine, keep your secrets. I've got healing to do and souls to zap around or whatever."

Verus bows slightly. "Until the summit, then."

"Yes, I'll see you there."

The world turns quiet and dark. More voices echo through my dreamless sleep. I open my eyes, blink and yawn. Cissy and Zeke stand near my bed. I drink in the sight of them and smile. They're safe, alive, and bickering up a storm. Everything feels a little more right with the universe.

Cissy stomps her foot. "I *know* it's been days since she's eaten." She wags her finger at Zeke. "But Senator Lewis said not to wake her up."

Zeke points to me. "Well, she's up."

Cissy's tail wags up a storm behind her. "You're awake! We brought you some broth." She sits at the end of my bed, bowl in hand.

I pull myself up onto my elbows. "How long have I been out of it?"

"Four days." She holds a spoon level with my mouth. "Open up."

"I got it, thanks." I take the bowl from her hands, raise it to my mouth and swallow. The liquid's warm and tasty.

"Guess what?" Cissy beams. "I'm going to Verus's summit too. I'll be your Mom's Junior Senator."

"That's great. You wanted diplomatic service."

Zeke sets his palm on Cissy's shoulder. "My parents are excited to keep her around." He kisses the top of her head. "And so am I."

Strange voices sound from the living room. My face crinkles. I'm not really up for meeting any strangers right now. "Who's that?"

Zeke and Cissy share a pointed look.

"We should get going." Cissy pulls the empty soup bowl from my hands. I must have been hungry; I don't remember finishing it.

My friends make their goodbyes and step out the door, careful to close it behind them. The voices grow louder.

I force myself onto my feet, stumble over to the door, and open it a crack. Mom stands in the living room in a red dress, talking to tall man in a gray suit. I can't see his face. My hazy head tries to place the outline of his body. It's familiar somehow.

Mom laughs, her chocolate eyes shimmer. An aura of confidence and power surrounds her. I can't remember the last time I saw her look so lovely and alive. Happiness makes me a little lightheaded. I lean against the doorframe for support.

The man wraps his arms around Mom's shoulders, pulling her into a long kiss.

Now I remember where I've seen that guy. It's Xavier.

Mom breaks the kiss, giggles, and rubs her knuckle against my father's belly. I'm totally grinning from ear to ear. Mom spies me in the doorway.

"Myla, what are you doing up?"

I reposition my weight against the doorframe. "I heard voices."

Xavier spins around to face me. "Hello, Myla." His turquoise eyes sparkle. He's now clean-shaven, so he looks more like the man from my dreamscapes: short brown hair, muscular frame, square jaw, and high cheekbones. Time with Armageddon left its mark: his cocoa-colored skin hangs as loose on his bones, as does his suit.

My father takes a few tentative steps toward me. "It's good to see you awake."

I smile. "It's good to see you, period."

He shakes his head. "I'm still not sure you're real." He takes another tiny step forward.

I scope out the space between us. At this rate, we'll be at it all day. I stagger over to him and wrap my arms about his neck. "I'm here, I'm real, and I love you."

Xavier folds his arms around my shoulders. "My girl. My beautiful girl."

My knees get gooey. Walking around wasn't my best idea.

"Let me get you back to bed." Xavier props me against his side, leading me past the couch and back into my room.

Mom follows us up to the doorway, and then she pauses. "I'll give you two some time." She closes my door with a soft click.

Xavier helps me onto the mattress and tucks the covers under my chin like I'm two years old. It's sweet. He drags a rusted chair beside the bed, sits down and adjusts the too-loose collar of his crisp white shirt. His voice cracks as he speaks. "Thank you for saving me."

"Any time." My heart thuds so hard, I'm almost surprised it doesn't break out of my rib cage. My father is here! My real, non-ghoul, totally awesome archangel father. I have so much to tell him, even more to ask him. Where do I start?

He reaches toward my face, freezes, and drops his hand.

I grin. "You're still having issues with the whole 'is she real' thing, am I right?"

He nods, tears welling in his blue eyes.

I take his palm and press it against my cheek. It's calloused but warm. Suddenly I know exactly where to start: the number one interest we share. "Name a demon, any demon."

"What?"

"You name the demon and I'll tell you how to defeat it." This is going to be so much fun, I can't stand it.

He inhales a shaky breath. "Limus."

I roll my eyes. "Please! Fire, end of story." I push his hand back at him and grin.

He laughs and cries a bit at the same time. "Okay, how about Papilio?"

"Now, that's a challenge." We launch into a long discussion of demon fighting, which is incredibly satisfying on multiple levels. Dad keeps his own set of demon notebooks, which he promises to show me. So. Cool.

The light in my window becomes darker. My eyelids grow heavy. I want to say goodbye, but can only manage a 'hmm' sound as I fall asleep. My dreams take me to a small clapboard house with an emerald-green yard. Above my head, the sky's a sheet of white light. I sit on the front porch in a rocking chair, smiling as I slowly sway to and fro. Everything is peaceful and lovely.

I awaken to the sound of whispers. Mom and Walker stand by my bed. By the light from my window, I figure it must be late in the day.

My face brightens. "Hey, cuz! Good to see you. Are you feeling okay?"

Walker bows slightly. "Fully recovered, thank you for asking. And you?"

"Better." I reach up and grab Mom's hand. "How long have I been out this time?"

"Six days in total." She wears jeans and a brown t-shirt. Rockin.

"Six days?" I make a barfy face. "That's disgusting. I'm going to shower and change."

"It's not that bad, Myla-la. We've been keeping you clean by–"

I raise my hand. "Let's stop right there. That stays a mystery." I haul myself out of bed and shuffle toward the bathroom. "I'll see you both in a bit."

I shower and scope out my closet. Mom did some shopping while I was out of it; all my sweats are gone. Bonus! I put on a pair of black jeans with a red top. I shuffle into the kitchen. Walker and Mom sit at the table, steaming mugs of coffee in their hands. Xavier leans against the counter, wearing a t-shirt and loose cotton pajama bottoms. Guess he's moved in. Nice.

I walk over and give my father a quick peck on the cheek. "Morning, Dad."

He positively beams. "Morning, uh, daughter."

I return the smile. "You can call me Myla or—if you must—Myla-la."

He nods. "I'll remember that, Myla-la."

I lean against a stretch of counter beside him, grab a Demon bar, and munch away. "Did anyone *else* visit me when I was asleep? You can always wake me up, you know."

Mom sips her coffee. "Myla, it's not like Lincoln can just phone or stop by."

Sometimes, I miss the old days when she had no freaking clue what I was thinking. "Why would I ask about him?"

"Weren't you?"

I chew and swallow another bite. "Okay, yeah. I totally was."

Mom sets down her mug. "You know how it is with Antrum and security. No phones, no television, no computers. He can't call ever. He can only write once a month. Ghouls can't portal in or out. It could be a year before you hear from him again."

My stomach twists. Maybe I shouldn't have inhaled that Demon Bar. "Thanks for being so encouraging. I thought you liked him."

"I do, just don't expect him to step through that door." She takes another long sip of coffee. "And this stuff about being angelbound. It doesn't mean you have to be with him. There are other men out there."

What the? This is the guy who stood by my side to fight the freaking King of Hell. I have blue eyes because we share this crazy energy together. Is she on meds now? I am not going to waltz out there and find anyone else like him, ever. My bottom lip puffs out. And besides, I don't want to anyway.

I crinkle the bar wrapper in my fist. "I just asked a question. I don't need a lecture on how my relationship with Lincoln is impossible. Walker covered that already, thanks."

Mom and Walker exchange a long look. I can imagine this was a big topic of conversation while I was out of it. Mom sighs. "Whether you like it or not, you two essentially rule very separate realms."

I turn to Dad. "What do you say?"

He frowns, considering. "I'd say I've never seen anyone take on a greater demon for more than a few seconds, except an archangel." He picks up a coffee mug from the counter, and then takes a long sip. "Your children would be unbelievable warriors."

Mom slaps her palms on the tabletop. "Not helping, Xavier."

He shoots her a smirky grin and winks. Mom blushes her face off. I bob my head approvingly. It's nice to have a dad around.

Mom smoothes back her hair with her palms. Blush response or not, she's not letting this one drop. "All I'm saying is that you should think about your options. Maybe we can find you a thrax who isn't the crowned Prince?"

"Sure. I'll go to the thrax store and pick out a new one."

She wags her head. "I know you don't want to hear this, but it's the truth."

Crap. Part of me knows she has a point. The Earl of Acca wants the High Prince to marry his daughter. Although Lincoln has a plan to defeat him, nothing is guaranteed. My eyelids feel heavy. All this reality is making my head spin. "Truth later. Sleep now." I step out of the kitchen with Mom close behind.

Walker waves to me over his coffee mug. "Goodbye, Myla." He offers me a sympathetic smile.

"Bye, Walker."

Xavier rushes toward the door. "Does she need any help?"

Mom shakes her head. "I've got her. Enjoy your coffee."

Mom walks me back to my room and helps me settle into bed, kissing me gently on the cheek as I fall asleep. My mind hovers between dreams and consciousness. It's a place that's dark, empty, and peaceful.

The sound of a portal awakens me. I open my eyelids a crack. The sky outside my window is pitch-black. Walker stands at my bedside.

"Hi, Walker." I peep at the alarm clock. 2 AM. "What are you doing here?" My brain's a sleepy jumble. "Am I called to serve?"

"No, Myla. That's all over with now."

"Okay." I curl under my blankets and shiver. This room's so freaking cold. "Night, Walker."

"I brought you something."

"That's nice." I try to open my eyes but can't. "You're the best."

Suddenly I feel warm and cozy for the first time in days. I fall into a deep sleep and dream I'm back in the thrax stables. I kneel on the soft hay as Lincoln gently rubs my back. My eyes flutter open. The world outside my window is still dark.

I awaken with a start and realize something: the High Prince lies behind me, his arms wrapped around my belly.

Unholy Moley. I fidget and scan the room. We're alone.

Lincoln's voice sounds low in my ear. "Hello, Myla." A lovely shiver runs down my spine.

I twist about to face him, sensing the warmth and firmness of his chest against mine, the cozy feeling of my head on his arm, and the comfort of heavy blankets encasing us. "Hi, Lincoln." I grin through a hazy brain. "How did this awesomeness happen?"

"Walker brought me here from earth. I'm playing hooky from demon patrol."

"Mmm." A sense of peace washes over my sleepy mind. I close my eyes and nestle my head into the crook of Lincoln's arm. "Walker brought you all the way here to cuddle?"

"No, this is my idea." I hear the smile in his voice; feel his warm breath circle the shell of my ear. "I decided it has therapeutic value."

"It does. Thanks for sneaking away."

He gently kisses my forehead. "I can't stay long. The Earl of Acca's threatening war."

"That family is hell on toast." I force myself to focus on his face. Acca is threatening war? I have a sinking suspicion what the Earl *really* wants. "Is he still pushing for you and Adair to get married?"

Lincoln nods. "But I'm recruiting more of the lesser Houses to the Alliance. I'll stop him, Myla." He exhales a long breath. "Actually, I'm supposed to be on demon patrol with the House of Gurith right now, convincing them to join up. I'm afraid I must leave in a few minutes."

A heavy pause hangs in the air. A few minutes. "I'll miss you, friend."

"This doesn't have to be goodbye. Walker told me your summit begins in a few weeks. If you're feeling up to it, perhaps you can visit Antrum before everything starts." His thumb strokes my upper arm. "Maybe we visit the House of Striga, find a way to remove the igni."

I pause, biting my lower lip. Not so sure I want my powers removed anymore. For the first time, I wonder if Lincoln's ever faced the same question. I scan his mismatched eyes. "Do you ever think about leaving Antrum?"

He glances around the room, considering. "Sure. I have my days." He leans in closer, offering me a shy grin. "I have a fantasy that you and I go to Earth and find a tropical island."

Hmm, this is rather specific. Color me interested. "What do we do there?"

He blushes and it's so cute, I can't stand it. "Fool around, fight demons." He runs two fingers up my arm like they're a pair of legs. "Have little thrax."

Wow. He wants to have a family with me someday. I can't decide if that's scary or sweet. Hmm…Sweet, definitely sweet.

I giggle. "And how do we do stuff like make money or find food?"

He rolls his eyes. "It's not that kind of thing. I put a lot more thought into what you're wearing and the demons we kill together." He bobs his eyebrows up and down.

Cheeky monkey. "So, you *have* thought about leaving." My smile fades. "Why don't you?"

"The same reason you're not interested getting rid of the igni anymore." He kisses the tip of my nose. "You aren't interested now, are you?"

It's my turn to blush. *How does he read me so well?* "No. Definitely not."

The Prince raises his brows in a look that says 'so, tell me.'

"I've complained about life in Purgatory for ages. But the problem's bigger than being told how to dress or serve. The way the ghouls ran things, a lot of good souls were destroyed. Now that I'm the Scala, I think I can change things. I need to stay here and prepare for the summit."

Lincoln nods. "I understand. You can make a difference, so you have to try. Not everyone gets that chance." He lets out another long breath. "I know the feeling well."

I run my finger along his jaw, and then over his lower lip. He's staying in Antrum for the same reason I'm staying in Purgatory, and somehow that means we'll be apart. Doing the right thing can be such a pain in the ass.

Lincoln's mismatched eyes search my face for a long minute. A smile tugs at the corner of his mouth. "As Scala, you'll have diplomatic duties to attend to, eventually." He slides a strand of hair behind my ear. The sensation sends a pleasant shiver through my belly.

I mock-frown. "None that I know of."

"Perhaps you'll be surprised by an invitation to Arx Hall."

"I don't know, unexpected invitations haven't worked out for me." In my mind's eye, I picture the embossed invite for Zeke's party that arrived six months and a million years ago.

Lincoln sets his knuckle beneath my chin, gently guiding my mouth toward his. Our lips brush; warmth blossoms though my chest.

On second thought, maybe unexpected invitations work out great in the long run. "But if the thrax High Prince asks me, I suppose I can't say no."

Lincoln slides his hand up my neck, pressing us into a deep kiss. "Come to me at Arx Hall." His voice is low and sweet.

"I really don't know when I'll–"

"Whenever you can. I'll be waiting." Tilting his head, he looks at me from his slate-blue eye. "Say yes."

Warmth and love radiate through me. "Yes."

$\mathcal{A}$.

The story continues in *Scala*, the second book in the
Angelbound Origins Series:
Available now at a retailer near you.

Titles by Christina Bauer

Angelbound Origins Series
1. *Angelbound*
2. *Scala*
3. *Acca*
4. *Armageddon*

Angelbound Offspring Series
1. *Maxon*
2. *Portia*

Beholder Series
1. *Cursed*
2. *Concealed*

Christina Bauer graduated from Syracuse University's Newhouse School with BA's in English along with Television, Radio, and Film Production. An avowed girl geek, Christina loves creating immersive fantasy worlds with action, adventure, romance, and kick-ass female protagonists.